I0666329

Too Old To Be A Hooker, Too Young To Be A Madam

Elissa Eaton

Too Old To Be A Hooker,
Too Young To Be A Madam

Elissa Eaton

Former Cosmopolitan Magazine Playgirl of the Year, Elissa Eaton has worked as a Hollywood stunt girl, travelled the globe as a syndicated Theater, Film and Society columnist, and was a resort and food critic for such publications as *The Beverly Hills Post, LA Restaurant Magazine, Hot Spots Magazine, Century City News, Spotlight Casting, The Movie Gazette*, and numerous others. Theater productions include Theater 40 in Beverly Hills, The Cast Theater, First Stage, The Santa Monica Playhouse, Group Repertory Theater, and other prestigious venues. Eaton has filmed with many famous directors, Ken Russell and Robert Altman among others. She has also produced her award winning plays throughout Los Angeles.

Too Old To Be A Hooker, To Young To Be A Madam was created at The Writer's Program at UCLA.

This book is dedicated to Tennessee Williams, my muse, on his 100th birthday.
March 20, 1911 - February 25, 1983

To my dear Mother, I'll miss you forever.

You never get over being a child as long as you have a mother to go to.
Sarah Orne Jewett

I hope you have some clout for me in heaven.

To Skylark, Shakespeare and Eclipse:
My most loyal friends are draped in fur. Three children wearing different colored coats.

Bravo to the miraculous Marieke. I never could have pulled it off without you.

Thanks to Victoria Larimore who had a hand in editing my book with expertise.

To my playful sidekicks bad boy Billy Peshel and the cerebral Jason Schafer - who never ceased to make be laugh while we brainstormed creating my novel.

To all my passionate playmates who shared the seasons of my flesh bringing crystal bubbles, long stemmed blue roses while shedding their thorns.

GENERAL REVIEW OF THE SEX SITUATION
Woman wants monogamy;
Man delights in novelty.
Love is woman's moon and sun;
Man has other forms of fun.
Woman lives but in her lord;
Count to ten, and man is bored.
With this the gist and sum of it,
What earthly good can come of it?
Dorothy Parker

The Soul selects her own Society –
Then – shuts the Door –
To her divine Majority –
Present no more –
Emily Dickinson

To be a playwright
you have to have the heart of a poet
and the skin of a rattlesnake
Tennessee Williams

Chapter One
The Third Floor, Bellevue

Résumé
Razors Pain you;
Rivers are damp;
Acids stain you;
And drugs cause cramp.
Guns aren't lawful;
Nooses give;
Gas smells awful;
You might as well live.
Dorothy Parker

I held the crystal goblet of Petite Rothschild vintage wine to my lips, lighting a Marlboro, the filmy smoke filling the air of my dingy one room flat. I sipped the silky smooth spirits, washing them down with candy red barbiturates as I held the Gillette razor blade to my wrist.

The foreboding sound of the ambulance came shrieking through the city, dodging horses and carriages trotting by the Plaza Hotel, that grand old watering hole on Central Park West, in the gloomy, gray autumn mist. The gaunt-faced, dark-skinned driver stopped abruptly in front of a brownstone walkup at 14 West 57th Street. It was high noon in Manhattan, and the riveting sounds of traffic cops blowing their whistles, relentless honking of horns and the hubbub and excitement of New York City could be heard on the horizon. The ambulance driver stared at the blinking blue neon sign that read *Readings by Madame Carla, $50.00 Sunday Siesta.* "Right, that swami's going to redeem my sorry ass soul. This must be the joint." He mumbled to himself.

The gypsy fortuneteller ran down the creaky wooden stairs to where I had fallen, her four bambinos following behind, clutching at her skirt strings, their round cocoa brown eyes wide with terror. Madame Carla's weather-beaten brow wrinkled in despair as she stared at my bruised naked body lying almost unconscious on the worn woven tapestry rug. Eyes and mouth open, crimson blood blending into the faded muted colors.

The bored European man threw a stark white sheet over me as I heard his gruff voice talking to the psychic. "What's her name? She's so young. Does she have a husband or any close relatives or friends here?" he asked.

"She from California. Been living here with broke actor for about six months. Her name April Moon," Madame answered in her broken Latino accent.

"Is there anyone I can contact?" he asked.

"I not know, Señor. She have rich mother in California and fancy friends come and go. Is she going to live?"

He slapped me across the face several times, taking my pulse, shaking me.

"She's still breathing. I'm rushing her to Bellevue Hospital. The doctors will give her a blood transfusion, and if she survives they'll put her in lockup."

"This so bad for children. They love her, sad girl has such big heart. She take care of babies for me and give them presents."

The man clumsily slipped me on the gurney, as the gypsy tried holding back her tears, reaching for my hand.

"I read cards for Miss April. I tell her dark-haired man with cold, gray eyes no good. I pray for her. I put curse on him, cabròn."

The man slid the gurney into the ambulance. Turned on a siren as he headed for the hospital. The blur of winter white trees capped with fallen snow were silhouetted by statuesque buildings creating a bleak eerie landscape.

Driving through the wrought-iron gate of the hospital was chilling. When we arrived, I was admitted and committed.

After signing me in, the male intern pumped my stomach, pressing down on my swollen body, groping my breasts lasciviously as I lapsed in and out of a twilight state seeing a shadowy figure floating above me.

"Are you my doctor?" I asked groggily staring up at him as he shook his head. "You're not God, are you?" I whispered.

"No darling, I'm your gay guardian angel." he answered. "I'm perfect for you. If I were straight you'd try to seduce me."

"Am I dead or alive, angel? I feel like I'm in purgatory." I mumbled.

"That's really up to you if you want to live. You're the one who chooses you're own destiny." Then with a flash of daylight streaming through the room he disappeared and an orderly appeared.

"We're going to run a pregnancy test, then the nurse will come and sew up your wrists." he said.

He dashed out of the room only to be replaced by a tacky looking, mean spirited African American nurse wearing a blond curly wig, wheeling in a cart full of sharp instruments.

"I'm gonna do you now" she informed me, grabbing my limp wrist, threading a long needle, carelessly poking at me.

"Aren't you going to put me out or give me a local?" I begged.

"No." she answered coldly.

"At least give me some painkillers!"

"You shoulda thought about that before you do yourself. It's cold turkey now, girl," she replied.

I started screaming, the throbbing pain was so unbearable. "Unfortunately I am alive," I thought.

"Please stop for just a minute," I begged, trying to catch my breath.

"Now girl, you stay still and hush up. I'm in a hurry and if you move it'll hurt more."

"Can I at least have some aspirin?" I asked.

"Where you're going next you'll be lucky if the head nurse gives you anything. The answer is 'no'."

"Where are they sending me?" I sobbed.

"You're going to 'The Third Floor,' psyche ward. You tried to kill yourself, now you're a ward of the state," she answered coldly.

"How long can they keep me here?" I asked.

"For at least ninety days if you're on good behavior," the nurse answered glancing down at my chart. "Silly girl, ain't you smart enough to know no man's worth all the fuss and pain. I'll bet he don't care for you. He's probably out having fun for himself with someone else." The next morning I awakened horrified as I looked down at my bandaged wrists clamped to the bed. There were metal bars on all of the windows of the room. The dim light faded and a flurry of snowflakes fell.

"Where am I?" I asked in a panic.

As an anorexic bleached-blond gay male nurse moved me to my destination, I realized that I was willing to die for misplaced love. I had physical strength, youth and beauty, giving me the option to turn my life around. That dark, dreary morning I realized that I'd never let anyone, especially a man, have enough power to destroy me. I was through being a victim. New York wasn't the first time I'd tried to end my life. At my sweet 16 party, at the Beverly Hills Hotel, no sooner than they'd cleared away the canapés and the Shirley Temple cocktails, I got drunk on beer. I lived with my mother at her duplex on Doheny Drive in Beverly Hills, she drove me over the edge with her sadism and rigid reign.

One afternoon I invited the most sought after, beefy, football player from Beverly High over to study. Mother waved goodbye, leaving for her beauty shop appointment. As soon as she left, he opened the door to her room, pinning me down on the bed, forcing his hard sweaty body into mine, ripping me apart with all of his fury.

Our housekeeper couldn't hear my screams over the sounds of the vacuum cleaner and the blaring of rock 'n' roll playing on the radio. I was a fourteen year old teenage virgin and always had fantasized that the first time I had sex it would be magic. That afternoon was a nightmare. I was disillusioned and totally devastated by life. The only satisfaction was that I had lost my virginity in my mother's bed. It was such sweet revenge as I quickly changed the blood-stained floral sheets so that she wouldn't suspect anything.

Later, as lightning lit up the night sky, I was soaking in the tub, trying to wash away his sickeningly sweet stench of cheap cologne and the blood that flowed between my legs. My mother entered the bathroom, perching herself on the edge of the tub.

"Mother," I asked, "if someone's never gotten their period can they still get pregnant?"

"April dear, did you let that young man that came to visit today violate you?"

"No." I answered without conviction, sinking deeper into the water, trying to hide my shame.

"I know you're lying. I suppose you let that diseased gentile bum use you. He comes from a trashy family. They're not of the privileged kind. They don't live in Beverly Hills, you know," she protested, raising her voice at me. "You're destroying your life!" she said wringing her hands.

"Leave me alone, you fucking snob. Get out of here!" I screamed.

"You stupid little nothing. You act like you were raised in the gutter!" she screamed.

"You're a sub-human bitch, get out of my life!" I lashed back at her.

"This is my house, you little drunk, I pay the bills around here. I sacrifice everything for you, you moron. I drive an old car and walk around in rags so I can send you to the best schools and treat you to argyle and cashmere sweaters from Saks Fifth Avenue."

"Go out and buy a life and stop living mine, you lonely old martyr," I cried as I started throwing up in the tub, sobbing. But my mother's rage was relentless. "I'm sick. Please just leave me alone," I pleaded.

"If you swallowed that boy's semen, your teeth will fall out of your mouth just like grandma's. That stuff is nasty. Now shape up, April," she said stuffing a soapy washcloth in my mouth.

"Stop, stop, have mercy on me," I sobbed.

"It's against your orthodox upbringing. All men are dirty. They're evil. And if you don't mind me and behave yourself, I'll let them lock you up in a mental institution and throw the key away." Little did I imagine that I'd end up in one some day.

"I'll be out of here before you can torture me anymore," I said, hoping that I'd never turn into psycho bitch. I had to get out of her iron clad reign.

"You better not be pregnant. I'll make you have an abortion before you disgrace the family with a bastard baby."

Often when I opposed my mother, she'd lock my phone in the closet, leaving it on the hook, letting me listen to it ring. She knew I was agonizing over some schoolboy's call. Once she even threw me in the closet, but my screams were so loud that the neighbors called the police and they came to my rescue.

That day so long ago, after I got raped, the phone was ringing off the hook and when my mother went to answer it, I barricaded the bathroom door, trying to end my unhappy life. I opened the beveled glass medicine cabinet removing a sharp razor blade and began cutting myself.

I grew up on the wrong side of the tracks in Beverly Hills. The land of pills, wills and unpaid bills. Although my roots are planted deeply in the heart of Laurel Canyon. Unfortunately my digs in Beverly Hills didn't have the renowned 90210 zip code. I just couldn't relate to the cliquish snobbery. I never got into a club and the boys were wusses. I felt like I just didn't belong coiffed with a jet black duck tail and over bleached yellow streaks I called hair. I was a toughie. A wild chick. Now don't you go looking for my picture in the high school yearbook, because the only place I ever graduated from was a trendy drug and alcohol rehab center. My friends said it was like going to college. Who would have ever thought that when I was dropping acid, in the '60s, "White Rabbit" by Jefferson Airplane blaring at my bizarre soirees that one day I'd end up in group therapy with an old rockstar, who by the way wasn't too slick. During my high school days my mother, my grandmother and I lived in a duplex on South Doheny Drive. When my beloved grandmother died, she left me half of a duplex and my controlling rigid mother gave me a complex.

In the alley on Maple Drive In Beverly Hills I first realized that life was cruel. It was the house my mother and I stayed in after my father abandoned us for scotch and soda, loose, boozy, floozy women and skid row. It was a hot humid muggy summer's day. My mother had made lemonade and deviled egg sandwiches. All the hungry, thirsty kids were laying with the Easter rabbits and baby ducks on the sweet smelling summer grass in our large backyard.

Suddenly I heard eerie screaming coming from the alley. One of the rabbits had wandered astray. I witnessed a sight that will haunt me forever. The sadistic little boy that lived next door was slaughtering my beloved little pet with a sledgehammer. Dark red blood was dripping from the rabbit's crushed skull, a once pure snow white coat. Then the sick little boy threw the lifeless creature down on the concrete pavement. I lay down on the ground sobbing uncontrollably.

"You're sick, how could you do that?" I screamed.

"Next time I'll get you." he laughed.

Months later that same demented sadist threw a rock at my head. Maybe that's why I'm a little spacey.

In some of Anna's loving moments she'd say, I've been having a love affair with you all of my life sweetheart. Come here and give me a kiss. I love you. You're my life. You're the most gorgeous girl in the world."

In one of her psycho dark moods Anna would scream, shattering my self esteem with accusations like, "You worthless little nothing. You dumb little tramp. I sacrificed my life for you, that's why I'm all alone." Talk about Jewish guilt. I can't remember much before I got raped. My therapist said that remembering would be much too painful so I cut myself because I could endure the physical pain more than the emotional anguish.

One time, the door was banged in by the family doctor. Before he had even finished putting tourniquets on my wrists, "Antiseptic Anna", spotting blood on the rug, lashed out at me at my most vulnerable moment. "April dear, don't bleed on the rug," she scorned. My father the charmer bore the resemblance of Clark Gable at the stable. At a very early age he treated me to pony rides plying me with sips of bourbon and ginger ale over long lunches at exclusive bars and restaurants. I was a runaway teen getting knocked up by a blond, blue eyed surfer boy from Venice. We drove to Vegas to get married. My drunken father punched him out, throwing him in jail, dragging me home to my scathing mother who drove the getaway car forcing me to have my first abortion. I was later dumped by my first love. That was the beginning and end of my youth.

Another black NURSE, definitely not of the Florence Nightingale world, wearing an orange Harpo Marx wig, whisked me off to the "Cuckoo-Cuckoo Bin" on the Third Floor. In an overcrowded ward they were out of beds, so they rolled in an extra cot. I lay there sleepless, spotlights shining over my throbbing head – till daybreak. Screams and the sounds of hysterical manic laughter filled the hallways. Hopeless, helpless prisoners held captive in the worst known "snake pit" in New York. We were treated like wounded animals trapped at a fox hunt. The next morning, they shuffled us into a tiny recreation room. Some patients held in restraints, muttering to themselves, drooling on their splattered gowns. Two young trailer trash lesbians were swapping saliva, groping each other in front of a small TV set. I was coming down hard from all the alcohol and drugs, pacing up and down the narrow corridors.

One of the butch-looking babes became very seductive with me.

"What's your name and what are you in for?" she asked. "You're a cool looking chick."

"Sorry, you just don't have the right equipment." I answered, walking away.

"Hey bitch," she snapped back, "you think you're hot shit. If you don't eat your beef stew at even one meal they can keep you in here longer."

A catatonic patient was led around the room by one of the attendants as a rather pretty, tragic looking girl approached me.

"How long have you been here?" I asked.

"I'm losing track of time," she answered listlessly, "no one even knows I'm in here. The head nurse is really mean. You better not mouth off to her. She watches our every move."

I'd been in this asylum for two days and I had to get out. No one was allowed to visit me and I couldn't even make one phone call.

A tired looking doctor walked into his office as I ran after him.

"Please doctor, I'm April. I beg you, please listen to me. If I stay in here for one more hour I know I'm going to go crazy."

The man in the white coat looked at me doubtfully, then gazed down at my wrists. "You're here for observation. Are you still suicidal?"

"No," I lied. "I learned my lesson. I didn't really mean to do it. I was just drunk. And I had a fight with my boyfriend. He threw me in a trash can on Park Avenue."

Doctor M smiled at me sympathetically, nodding his head. "I don't know, you're on suicide watch, April, looks like you were for real. Why don't we just wait and see how you do. I'll look at your chart every day."

"Thank you so much. Love's never been fair to me." I said. "I have a rich family in California, just name your price. If you get me out of here, I'll come and see you three times a week."

"Do you have a therapist who I can call?" he asked.

"My doctor's in New York staying at the Saint Regis Hotel. Please would you contact him?"

"I'll try to reach him, April. If he can see you, I'll try and pull some strings. Wait 'til you hear from me."

"His name is Doctor Seymour," I answered. "Please help me!"

"If you're released I'm going to suggest to him that you enter an extensive rehab treatment program immediately or you'll either succeed next time or end up in here again."

I heard my name announced over the loud speaker. The attendant took me upstairs to the administration building and I signed my release forms. Since I was admitted to the hospital with what I came into the world with, they gave me a rust colored itchy, woolen dress from a charity auction at Bloomingdales. I walked outside in the rain, barefooted hailing a cab. When I arrived home I climbed five flights up to my apartment opening the door. My actor was packing his suitcase ready to move in on his next prey.

"God you weren't kidding were you?" he said angrily grabbing at my wrists. "At least you could have gotten rid of the pot before you tried to do yourself in. If the cops found it that could have caused a scandal and ruined my career. We could have been arrested," he ranted on.

"What career, you ruthless bastard," I said softly.

"I tried to get you out of that place, but they wouldn't let me see you," he said defensively.

"I know you never loved me, but I thought you had some compassion and cared for me," I sighed.

"I have no guilt about you, April. You brought this on yourself. When we met at that party in Hollywood

I was hitting hard on your girlfriend Chelsea. I've always been attracted to beautiful Hollywood blondes." He said. "It was you who acted desperate and followed me to New York,"

"Okay, I finally get it. I've been used before. I'll survive your abusive behavior," I said sadly, looking away.

"You're too unstable for me. It was fun for awhile, but I'm not in love with you," he said condescendingly. "I never was or will be."

Suddenly it was all so crystal clear.

The bastard couldn't even look me straight in the eye as he grabbed his bags, heading for the door.

"I'm sorry for you April, try to get on with your life. You'd better dry out and go back to LA. and your sugar daddy producer if he'll still have you after finding out about me."

Then with the slam of a door, he was out of my life and I was alone again. Destination, self-destruction or survival, I wasn't sure.

I paid the taxi driver and slipped into the revolving door of the ritzy St. Regis Hotel, trying to escape the blizzard.

My shrink was waiting for me in the restaurant. He was a sophisticated, worldly gourmand with a sardonic sense of humor. Seymour and I had a great rapport, becoming fast friends. He had always been there for me, even after hours, but he had never crossed the line of professionalism yet. And bearing significant resemblance to a young Abe Lincoln he definitely wasn't my type.

Seymour greeted me with a concerned smile. "Sit down, April," he said, helping me slide off my London Fog trench coat. "You're drenched my dear, but you look amazingly pretty considering the circumstances."

As I slid into the cozy Italian leather banquet, I was dazzled by the, mysterious, European decadent turn of the century plush décor. Food aficionados, and a potpourri of international globetrotters and luminaries rendezvoused at the hotel's signature restaurant to enjoy eclectic Franco continental cuisine. The heady aromas of fresh garlic and herbs de Provence wafted throughout the spacious room and the buzz of lilting laughter and popping of corks was just what I needed.

"You look wounded," Seymour said as our hands touched briefly.

"I can't believe how lucky I am that you're here. You saved my life," I said.

"They wanted to keep you locked up in that institution for intense evaluation, but I knew one of the heads of staff and I convinced him that I'd be responsible for you. I've postponed my flight to LA indefinitely."

The white haired, waspy, well-seasoned waiter approached our table.

"Would you like to start out with cocktails while you study the menu, sir?"

"I'll have a glass of Louis Jadot Beaujolais, and a pot of herbal tea for the lady right now."

"My pleasure, sir," he said as he scurried over to the next table.

"April, tell me how this happened to you," Seymour asked, wearing a long face.

The waiter returned, pouring the amber colored liquid into the delicate Dresden china cup. My half frozen hand was shaking and my teeth were chattering as I lifted the cup to my parched lips. I really needed a drink.

"I know this isn't easy for you to relieve the horror, but I need to know the details so that I can treat you properly. Just relax," he coaxed.

I sipped the piping hot soothing ambrosia trying to piece the puzzle together. I had slight amnesia, but amazingly enough that fateful night flashed before me. I tried to evade the issue by studying the menu and wine list.

"Would you mind if I have some wine?" I asked.

"Okay, April, but just one glass. You're under my care now." He signaled over the server saying, "We'll have a glass of Pouilly Fuisse Macon Village and some Salmon and Chive Cream Tiraiche and Blinis with Caspian Ostra Caviar first, then we'll order."

Now I was back in my environment. I sipped the cold white full-bodied bouquet of French wine out of an imported Austrian Reidel and Saint Louis crystal long stemmed goblet nibbling on a willowy Parmesan dusted breadstick knowing I was going to survive. My appetite for food and life was coming back once again.

I started telling Seymour my story with clarity. "The night I had my breakdown. I had snuck away to meet my john for dinner at the Plaza. He had flown in for a business meeting and a confrontation with me. He was married with a family, but he was obsessed with me. I had drank too many Tanqueray

Martinis while he blatantly informed me that he'd put a private detective on my trail and had found out that I was supporting my lover with the allowance he sent me every month, threatening to cut me off if I didn't return home and end my affair. I was so upset that I ran out of the restaurant. When I arrived at my apartment, my gigolo was dressed to the nines, getting ready to leave for another all nighter. "Baby, where are you going?" I drunkenly slurred my words. "Are you off to meet that old Broadway star so you can get a part in her play? She's just playing you. You don't have to leave me, do you?"

"She's an important person. I'll get away as soon as I can. Don't wait up for me."

I poured myself a glass of wine and swallowed some pills, moving in closer to him, kissing his cold lips, pressing my breasts against his chest, trying to entice him, begging him to stay.

"You don't own me. I have to go now, I'm late." He said pushing me away mechanically.

"What time will you be home?" I asked.

"I don't owe you any explanation, April. The problem is that I don't have any passion for you anymore." he muttered under his breath.

"I'm so drunk and suicidal, I feel so alone tonight," I said, gulping down more pills with wine.

The bastard grabbed the sleeping pills out of my hand, spilling the bottle on the floor, slapping me around, throwing the seconals out the window into the snow. "You pathetic alcoholic! I'm sick of living with a neurotic drug addict! You need help and I need some space. I would have driven a cab rather than have my father and brother find your nude magazines at every newsstand on Time Square. Sleep it off," he screamed. "The only thing we had in common was a TV set and I'm bored with that," he yelled back at me. "I'm going to borrow some money so I can buy a round of drinks tonight," he said as he reached into my purse, stuffing a wad of bills in his wallet. "You won't need any money tonight, you're not going anywhere!" he yelled, slamming and locking the door behind him. "You're always flirting with death, get a grip on yourself."

That was when I had reached the breaking point, grabbing a razor blade, slashing my wrists, my throat, and my ankles.

The phony, heartless actor and I had one thing in common. We had both lost our dignity.

"Well, April honey, it seems to me that this was inevitable. You find a mutual attraction for certifiable bisexual gigolos and losers," Seymour said after listening to me for three hours at dinner.

"I just have that sensual look that all my male predators recognize. They take one look at me and know that I can make their night."

"You just want the passion without the commitment. You've never had a monogamous relationship," he said.

"I had a commitment and got committed," I answered.

"But let's analyze this situation," Seymour said. "You shared your body and your apartment with another emotionally unavailable vain person. What did you expect? What made him so special?"

"He was so much like me," I said. "Rebellious, reckless, adventuresome, handsome, oversexed. He lived for fun and he made me laugh, not to mention that he was great in bed." I said twisting a lock of hair around my finger.

"The men that you let into your life are like flash-lights in the dark. When you work at a studio in Hollywood, the set looks beautiful on the outside, then when you open the door it's empty inside. The dangerous men you choose have no substance. It seems to me that you never delve deeply or in-volve yourself in any real emotional investments, just superficial relationships. The only thing that mat-ters to you is how big his cock is and how hand-some he is. You're a thrill seeker living in a web of deception,""said Seymour.

"I can function in art not in life. I think I need an-other drink," I said.

"I have trepidations about you drinking too much. You might try to harm yourself if you become morose. You're plying yourself with alcohol and drugs to try and fill the dark hole. The stuff is just a band-aid to anesthetize your pain."

"I know," I said. "My life used to be so full when my boyfriend and I were happy at the beginning, that now my desperation makes the loneliness much more unbearable."

"April, you're a larger than life, charismatic character. You seem invulnerable. It's a barrier. You're intimidating to people you're such a strong personality. You don't allow them to come into your life that easily. You've had bad experiences with losers that are unreliable, uncaring, and abusive. Have you lost all faith in human nature?"

"Yes. Then tell me, how can I open up my heart when I feel so much fear? I'd give anything for the pain to go away."

"There comes a time when you must gracefully surrender or it'll drag you down to your knees, you'll feel so much more empowered." he preached.

"I just don't know if I can stop drinking and doing drugs. I get these panic attacks about ending up alone and I have to take the edge off the intensity of my life," I said as I gulped my wine.

"Maybe if you invent a different persona you might attract different kinds of people," Seymour suggested.

"The only problem is that bad girls like bad boys," I said.

"Deep down you're a very puritanical girl. A lot of your escapades are purely executed for shock value and to get even with your mother."

"But Seymour, I'm a narcissist, a major exhibition-ist. I'm comfortable with my sexuality. So why do I always end up with players?"

"You're just trying to replace your father. You have major abandonment issues. because he left you and your mother as a small child and your mother blamed you. You had very bad parenting."

"I'm paying a high price for passion. These men bring me such sadness."

"Your life is a dark dreamscape, very intriguing. It's all so Sylvia Plath, so Ann Sexton. When you go to Disneyland you pay, then you choose the ride you want to go on. In life you choose the ride and pay the price later." he said sipping his drink.

"And I'm paying a high price to go on that joy ride straight to hell," I answered. "I'll be right back. I have to go to the loo. Its that time of the month." I sighed.

When I came back to the table my dining companion was paying the check.

"Well, did the red velvet curtain come down," he smiled.

"No," I answered, "why do you ask?"

"April, I really feel attached to you and your stories turn me on. Did it ever enter your mind that you're getting nocturnal emissions sitting at the table next to me? I think that you should stay here at the hotel with me tonight. You can't be left alone in your state of mind. If you can't sleep I'll give you a barbiturate."

I was in shock, I'd been betrayed again I thought as I grabbed my purse running out into the night.

As I gazed out of my window on the TWA flight taking off at Kennedy Airport, heading for Hollywood, I looked down at The Statue of Liberty, dots before my eyes as the jet soared, streaking through the granite sky and billowy black cloud formations. Taking a sip of cheap wine the stewardess poured in my plastic cup, tears streamed down my face. I vowed to myself that day that my feet would never grace the sidewalks of New York again in my lifetime. My greatest humiliation was being unable to hide the bandages on my wrists. Years later the scars never healed.

Chapter Two

The Pink of Perfection
The Beverly Hills Hotel
The Polo Lounge

The legend of the Beverly Hills Hotel and my charmed lifestyle began when I sat in my cabana satisfying a ferocious appetite and quenching my great thirst for life with a club sandwich and thick chocolate shake, then dove into the sprawling Olympic-sized aqua swimming pool to work off all those sinful calories. It seems like every memorable occasion in my life was cause for a celebration at this grand old watering hole. My sweet sixteen party, my first wedding reception was held under the crystal chandeliers at the Crystal Ballroom and Sunset Room; of course so I could invite all my ex-boyfriends. The second marriage was toasted with friends over guacamole and Dom Perignon after sliding into the rich forest green leather booth at the Polo Lounge. I even frequently took up residence and held court in one of the bungalows to celebrate my divorces.

My bashes were like a scene from "California Suite" that would have made Neil Simon look like Simple Simon. I made many entrances climbing the oval-shaped staircase dressed to the nines in grand style, but never hung with the ladies who do lunch and the power dining. Although I regretfully admit that at some of my most romantic moments, while being courted at the Polo Lounge by some ardent admirers with Sterling Silver Roses, I had one of my girlfriends page me, just so I'd feel like I was in the mainstream, you know, cool. Such nostalgia.

Those long Sunday brunches beneath a sculptured 86-year-old Brazilian Pepper tree; surrounded by a paradise of tropical foliage, sipping freshly-squeezed orange juice, devouring Dutch Apple Pancakes serenaded by a roaming Mariachi band and roaming Spouses. Decades later, it seems like I never left.

The real history of the Beverly Hills Hotel cannot be found in my diary. Like an intricate mosaic, it must be assembled piece by piece, from faded registration cards, Hollywood gossip columns, and the memories of doormen, seasonal bellmen and Maitre D's.

Chapter Three

The Lure of Laurel Canyon
1969
(Lovers, Strangers, Truffles, Tarts
and Ex-Cons à La Carte)

*Yes I had many intimacies with strangers...
intimacies with strangers was all I seemed to be
able to fill my empty heart with. I think it was panic,
just panic, that drove me from one to another,
hunting for some protection - here and there. In
the most unlikely places.*
Tennessee Williams

69 was my favorite year, my favorite position and I was a great vintage. Man landed on the moon and I landed in Rome, throwing my garnet wedding ring into the Fontana Di Trevi. I just had to be free. I helped unfold and experienced the full flowering, hedonistic, reckless Rock n' Roll youth movement.

It was the night of the spoon, better known as cocaine. Growing up in the sexy, psychedelic '60s, the beat generation where Timothy Leary, the acid guru, ruled, we rocked. The beat went on with Sonny and Cher as we floated down the cosmic corridors of consciousness to nirvana. Being the original flower child, I was provocative, highly spirited, sensual and I believed in free love, thai sticks, tie dye and hallucinogenics. The '60s was my great awakening. A spiritual journey where I realized that I wasn't who I thought I was.

Life wasn't what I thought it was supposed to be. And being nothing I was everything just being. After dropping peyote, the truth serum, I had a metamorphosis. What a magical year. I was Cosmopolitan Playgirl of the Year, the article was titled "Do You Think It's Easy Being A Kook?" My boyfriend of the week was outraged when he read the ten page story and I was quoted as being decadent and hedonistic saying the only thing I knew how to do was chilling the champagne flutes on time. The groups Three Dog Night and Iron Butterfly called me "Flash The Earth Goddess," or "Crazyhorse" for I was a wild filly. My favorite pets were men. A Lessier Leopard named Mondo, a Tibetan sole dog named Hash, and a calico cat named Cokie. One night Mondo disappeared, and I was frantic. I combed the canyon, but he was nowhere to be seen. When I opened up the freezer, much to my astonishment, Mondo jumped out. It was a close call. I fed him his favorite treats, raw chicken backs and chicken wings then I slipped into my red crochet see-through mini dress, burned strawberry incense and scented candles, dimming the rosy red lights in anticipation of tantalizing my next one night stand in my Bohemian Boudoir. Sex with those dangerous men was intense and exciting, but part of the high was the risk. My pussy was catnip to my horny prey. It was the year of Sputnick and moon walking. We got dusted on Angel Dust, floated off to Woodstock, mellowed out at The Monterey Jazz Festival, did drugs and got a rush camping out and gazing at Joshua Tree. We all marched for peace shouting "Kill the pigs, stop the war, drop acid not bombs." Nesting in my ethereal tree-house in Laurel Canyon I was floating in and out of awareness hallucinating and tripping on people, life and nurtured by nature taking the "Magical Mystery Tour" of that decade, a sexy knockout living in the laid back hills in the countryside escaping reality surrounded by the majestic mountains.

Laurel Canyon and I were at the peak of our Folk Rock and artistic heyday. It was the civil rights generation. Hippies, groupies, flower children, Dennis Hopper, and exploitation films of violence where the prolific actor genius created immortal cinematic characters. There were draft card burners and brain washed chicks burning their bras, fighting for equality in the '60s, because of that bitch Gloria Steinem and the feminist movement. Being a nudist I almost never wore them. My perky fully rounded breasts were my trophies. I was just a babe but I wouldn't dream of burning my satin lacy, push up from "Trashy Lingerie" or Frederick"s of Hollywood. Who would have ever thought that I'd be sprouting no less than 38Ds investing in minimizers when I morphed into womanhood. And how many women have made love in a vault? My naked body was decorated by precious jewelry created by a famous sculptor.

One night I was wearing my see-through long dress made out of dishrags and a flame colored wig at one of my surprise birthday parties. My best friend, a famous film star who turned on the heat in "Beyond the Valley of the Dolls" put a banner on the wall of my house on Brier Drive in the canyon. It said "Kiss me again stranger." And of course I swapped tongues with every hot looking dude that was there, pleasuring all the lucky ones in the bushes. The next morning the phone was ringing off the hook and all the horny guys in Laurel Canyon were calling me in anticipation of a repeat performance not even knowing my name. I even received a call from Baghdad.

Being an aspiring starlet, I hung out at Heffner's with an avant garde crowd, loved dramatic experimental plays like *The Beard*. The pigs threw the cast in jail for using profanity and flaunting their skins on stage. One of the most exciting nights of my life was the dazzling opening of *Hair* at the Aquarius Theater and the post party held in the tents. I practiced the Primal Scream and EST, when I got bored with "The Vast Wasteland LA", I found myself longing for exotic far away lands. I've always felt such a passion for the seashore. We flew off to Maui, smoked "Maui Wowi" those fuzzy chronic lime green red haired buds, sipped Lancers rose wine in San Fillippi, Mexico, mesmerized by the golden harvest moon setting on a fire engine sky, then suddenly rising from a crystal emerald blue green sea. My lover, friends and I slept in tents on the beach. I had a cosmic moment making love under the stars.

We rode dirt bikes and galloped bareback over the ivory sand dunes on silver dappled stallions. Those cherished playmates are now either dead, in nuthouses or in rehab. Ironically my memory and I survived and now perhaps I can shed some light on your life. Then it would be worth the journey from the mind to the flesh. I think the reason was that I was always able to adjust to my circumstances, and if I couldn't deal with the painful truth I created an illusion that I could exist with, that becoming my reality until I turned it around. After having a taste of the real Hollywood, that colors our dreams at night realizing the unreality of living in my Barnum Bailey world, clouded by drugs and sex where I was the ring leader it became a futile lifestyle. And even with my devil may care attitude eventually I knew that something had to be wrong. At first it was fun, exciting, almost an aesthetic adventure but eventually I felt such despair and guilt about the hedonistic lifestyle filled with empty illusions, ex-cons and neo-nineteenth century types. Girls wearing long-stringy hair and pelvic hugging pajamas and Edwardian jackets or vanilla ice cream suits and love beads.

The promiscuous would be, has been celebrities, old artists who hang on the edge of night living alternative lifestyles, hiding in the shadows of show business at The Whiskey A Go-go, The Daisy, Pipps, The Factory, The Luau and The Candy Store wearing spandex, dog collars and platform boots, dullards who lived to collect unemployment. Narcissistic wax museum dummies who crashed the A list parties, their biggest fear was that their masks may shatter in the dwindling Hollywood twilight.

I make it all sound so great, so glamorous that you just know that something has to be wrong with the '60s besides green and purple spiky hair and Lawrence Welk. Big Brother was watching us in the form of Fascist Richard Nixon, when he was president, and one menacing maniac, his name was Charles Manson. From '69 to '70 there were riots and racial violence. We bombed the hell out of Cambodia, were blown away when we lost the Vietnam War and it all took away our innocence.

Chapter Four

Finishing School
Pebble Beach

Every time I walk my dogs in the hills of Laurel Canyon I can smell poison oak, the ominous scent reminds me of when I checked into Mrs. Douglas's Finishing School, an all girls camp where they taught me the social etiquette, how to pass the cream properly. I walked into the woods and I felt like the forest had put her arms around me welcoming me home. I was enchanted by nature falling in love with Pebble Beach and Carmel where we had our weekly outings over banana splits at the local ice cream parlor. The ocean was always my first love in life. I had my first orgasm galloping bareback over the sand dunes and jumping over ravines on my favorite horse Moss. Later becoming an equestrian, winning ribbons at horse shows for jumping and riding English and Western. The saddest day of my life, other than when my grandmother died, was when Moss broke his leg and the kids informed me that the Riding Academy was going to put him out to pasture, then send him to the glue factory. After such a great loss I was in a fragile state of mind. The next morning on a hike after a dinner girlie dance when I wouldn't let a lesbian insert a good humor stick covered with vaseline inside of my flapp she plotted out her revenge, ostracizing me from the wealthy, ferocious, bratty society set bitches. They were all aware of my fear of dead birds so they maliciously decided to play a little prank on me. Every night when I pulled down the starched white sheet in my bed, I was surrounded by a flock of black feathered crows bearing glassy blood stained skull caps resembling yarmulkes. The grotesque creatures were penetrating me intently with beady yolk colored eyes. It was my most intense nightmare. I felt like that summer would never end finally getting maimed falling to the ground from a bucking bronco, his angry hoofs nearly missing my head, gratefully returning home. Even today as I touch my thigh I can still feel the scars.

Chapter Five

The Whiskey, 1969

Silvery raindrops fell like jewels from a pastel sky, cloaked in a hazy blanket of fog; a patch of blue rose from the mountain greenery like a transparent granite veil. The canyon looked as eerie as an El Greco painting in the March morning mist. Flocks of baby sparrows flew over trees. I lounged in my feather bed, sipping a cup of piping hot Paradise Island tea.

Warmed by the blazing flames and the crackling of logs in the fireplace, reaching for my jewelry box on my vanity, I found the shark's tooth that Chelsea had picked up in San Felipe when we dropped mescaline on the beach.

"April, if you keep this shark's tooth with you forever, you'll be safe," she once warned me.

With Chelsea it was never why or how. Only where and when. I picked up the broken ivory symbol, becoming nostalgic. Seems like yesterday Chelsea and I were enrolled in golf class at Beverly Hills High. We were wild, beautiful, bratty teenagers.

"I'd love to shoot this golf ball up that old spinster bird's cunt."

Chelsea laughed mockingly about the teacher. I liked this girl's ballsy attitude. Chelsea had panache. She used to have fun at everyone else's expense and we became fast friends and room-mates for decades of decadence.

Chelsea and I went through adolescence and adult womanhood together, traveling abroad, sharing her flat in London, then to Paris and Rome frequenting five star trendy hotel rooms, living the La Dolce Vita lifestyle.

One sunny Sunday afternoon, we snuck into the Grauman's Chinese Theatre, having our first glimpse of Marilyn Monroe light up the screen with her plati-num blonde hair, shaking that well-rounded rump in *Gentlemen Prefer Blondes*.

We ended up at C.C. Brown's after the movie, devouring double hot fudge sundaes topped with whipped cream and almonds.

"Isn't this sundae almost better than sex?" I asked.

"But these cokes are fattening. Let's ask for a diet ones," she demanded from the old, worn out looking waitress.

Later on we walked down Hollywood Boulevard.

"Let's plant our ripe firm bums into the pavement on top of Marilyn's gold filigreed star on the Walk of Fame."

"But Chelsea, we could get arrested," I said in protest.

"Don't be a wimp," she laughed.

"Okay, you win."

The next morning we rushed to a drugstore and bought two bottles of peroxide.

"I want to be a famous movie star just like Mari-lyn, Chelsea. I'll do anything and anyone to make it," I said. "Then I'll marry a famous movie star and live in Malibu." I started thinking about star power very early in life.

Chelsea and I survived our failed marriages, horrible hangovers, Atkins diets, my career, my mother, bad hair days and my five abortions together. We sinned with our skins, sharing all of my boyfriends over bottles of French wine, brie, truffles and drugs.

We were emotionally invested in each other and through all of my manic mood swings and frequent suicide attempts, she was always there for me. Our laughter often cured my long struggle against loneliness and depression.

After a few cocktails, coke, and black beauties, she often revealed her plasticity. Chelsea's petite voluptuous sexiness suggested a sassy vamp bearing the uncanny resemblance of Bridgette Bardot from a long gone era, and Claudia Schiffer, the Guess/Victoria Secret model. Her narcissistic persona had all the trappings of a young Blanche from *A Streetcar Named Desire*.

Crickets chirped melodiously as Chelsea's cherry-red Stingray Corvette sped down the trail running high over the crest of the hilly wooded road of Sunset Plaza Drive. Shadows lengthened across a rich dark green background. Twinkling city lights and pine trees surrounded the countryside below in the hush of the night.

Approaching a stretch of the Sunset Strip a glaring neon lit billboard of the Marlboro Man, sparkling tree lined avenues, unique boutiques, and Euro French sidewalk café style bistros enhanced the ambiance of the boulevard. Chelsea stopped the car abruptly in front of the legendary Whiskey. Giving her keys to the valet, climbing out of the car. Her silky surfer girl sun streaked blonde hair streaming down her bare tanned back.

A flurry of whispering leaves swept across us as we approached the red velvet rope. Chelsea and I were ready to indulge our senses in some exotic, eclectic studs and the ultimate people watching scene of the hip edgy happening nightlife wearing our alterna girlie wardrobes. We were clad in clinging black leather mini skirts and vintage bare lacy lycra tops, adorned with peacock, boa-feathers and rhinestone earrings. Platform pumps and fishnet stockings accentuated our shapely legs. Our eyes were painted with a bright pinkish red sparkling shimmer. We were obsessed with the glittering rock' n' roll lifestyle. A parade of wannabes, pimps, hookers, rockers and club crashers clustered behind the coveted red velvet rope. A flashy desperate Hollywood blonde bimbo shoved her way to the front of the line. The girl gave her name to the beefy bouncer, wearing an earpiece, holding a clipboard in his hand.

"Sorry, your name's not on the list," he replied with attitude.

"Don't you know who I am?" she shrieked, "I'm a star!"

"Yes, I do. You're nobody. Do you know who you are? Now move it, lady, or I'll call security."

"Pond scum!" she yelled. "I'll have you fired, dickhead doorman."

"That girl's a low brow," Chelsea shared.

"April, I know that bloke at the door and tonight's after dark party is Chicago. I really fancy them."

"I hope we'll get in," I said.

"Don't worry, the bouncer's in love," she answered.

"Far out, Chels, I knew I could count on you. Did you ball the bouncer? Is he hung?"

I was inebriated, but I vaguely recall a little incident in the coat room," she answered, shivering from the cold. A gush of cold wind blew my skirt up in the air.

"I hope you brought your phony ID," she asked.

I went through my bag searching for our passport to drug addiction, alcohol and one-night stands.

My birth control pills fell out of my purse. A black gay straight man clad in Gucci sequins and colorful tacky glass jewelry picked up the plastic dial, handing it to me.

"Where have you been all my life, diva? You won't need these with me, I'm sterile," he said with a weak grin.

"Get lost, freak!" I screamed. "You're a real loser."

"I lost the IDs, but don't worry, as long as chicks are young and wearing black they let them in," I said.

"And big tits, small hips, and long legs are an aphrodisiac," Chelsea answered.

"Just so they don't think they're from Hicksville, Nebraska, or wearing flowered shirts," I added.

"How do I look?" Chelsea asked, studying her reflection in her metal keychain.

"Fab," I said.

As the line moved in closer, spotting Chelsea and I, the man in power promptly removed the rope, groping Chelsea's body lasciviously. "You chicks look real cool. Here are your tickets to paradise. The VIP Room. Come see me later."

"Thanks, honey," we said in unison.

The VIP Room was swarming with a powerhouse of celebrity clientele.

"Let's check out that well stocked bar," Chelsea said enthusiastically.

"Yeah, I'm in the mood to get ripped to the tits." And speaking of tits, the shocking purple bar was pretty eye popping. Adjoining it was a six-foot female nude ice sculpture with a wine dispensing nipple flowing freely for hundreds of guests.

"You little American birds are looking brilliant tonight. What's your bag? My name's Nigel." the guy said in a cockney accent.

"Way cool, " I answered to the bartender. "My name's April, and this is my roommate Chelsea."

"How much are the Tanqueray martinis love? And where are you from?" Chelsea asked.

"Drinks are on the house for you tonight, Chelsea, I remember you from one of the pubs on Kings Road, but I'm from the East end of London. I think it was Tweedle Dee Dee, where you hung out."

"Brilliant!" Chelsea answered, "That makes me crave roast beef and yorkshire pud."

"I hope you ladies won't take this the wrong way, but what are the odds of us getting pissed to the gills tonight and you girls letting me perform some dark devious deeds after I close down the bar. I've got some chronic Moroccan Hashish."

"Right, sorry dude, no can do, Chelsea's my old lady," I said, planting a lip glossed kiss on her lips. "We're in a monogamous relationship."

"That sounds lovely. I get blimey lonely shagging one bird at a time."

I took a sip of my dry gin martini, biting down on the bitter green pimento stuffed olive.

"Now don't get your knickers in a twist, you milk sop stupid wanker. Bug Off!" Chelsea screamed as we slinked away. "April, there's Luke the A-list party crasher. He's walking out the back door with a Dixie cup in his hand," Chelsea laughed.

"Oh my God, I love it," I said.

"The old mummy is wearing a tuxedo and bow tie like he'd been dug up from a shallow grave right out of Night of the Living Dead."

"April, look at that vulgar looking old woman with clown red hair in her gold lamé backless jump-suit."

"How old do you think she is?" Chelsea asked.

"Probably pushing thirty," I answered.

"She's crashed the party and she's eating the food at the buffet table like a pig in a trough, never coming up for air. "Chelsea commented.

"Check this out; she's filling her empty shopping bag, carrying her bounty. She won't have to buy groceries for a week, ya dig" I said.

"Her bags are so heavy she's waddling out the door sideways." Chelsea said judgmentally.

"That's because I put liquid amyl nitrate in her wine at the bar," I shared doubling over with laughter.

A server approached us with a tray of one hors d'oeuvre. I took a bite of the shrimp.

"This isn't shrimp scampi; it's shrimp skimpy," I said in disgust, making a face.

"Let's pop by The Roxy, then end up at The Rainbow for some sausage pizza if we don't score tonight," I proposed.

"That sounds lovely, but this party has a lot of flirting opportunities," Chelsea begged.

"I guess you're right Chels, there are a lot of Brits here tonight."

"I don't know what you see in them. Their teeth are rotten, they're uncircumcised and they're all pervs," Chelsea said wrinkling up her nose.

"That's why I like them," I answered.

"Oh look who just walked in. Raquel, Beverly Hills Realtor to the Stars," Chelsea remarked.

"Now I'm convinced that we're on the A-list," I smiled.

"That wench used to have multiple orgasms. Now she has multiple listings," Chelsea laughed.

The sounds of Joe Cocker's *Delta Lady* blared in my ear as muted colored flashing strobe lights swept the room. A brassy shagged, flame-haired, redhead wearing a rhinestone studded low-cut dress and glistening five-inch stilettos, pranced risquély through the bar, stopping at our table spilling her drink all over everybody.

"How the fuck are you, April?   You girls don't have dates tonight?" Raquel rudely said with her Chicago accent.

"Raquel, this is my roommate, Chelsea."   I answered coldly.

"You're beautiful Chelsea, what's up with you?" Raquel asked mockingly.

"I'm on my own because shopping on Rodeo Drive is more fun.   At least if I'm not satisfied I can exchange it for something I really like," Chelsea answered.

"Don't ruin my Tattinger moment, snatch."

"Really bitch," Raquel answered, screaming at the bartender.   "How the fuck do I get a glass of the good champagne around here?   I carry a lot of weight in my Frederick's of Hollywood push up bra."

"You blow me, love," he answered.

Raquel gave him the finger and drank a glass of cheap wine from the nipple dispenser.   "All the aliens are moving to Beverly Hills.   I just sold five million dollar houses to transplants this week."

"Don't you always date men that have transplants?" I asked.

"Be nice," Raquel answered sucking up to us, pulling a silver spoon and a small white vial out of her Chanel clutch bag, taking a snort, offering us some.   Chelsea jumped on the offer, inhaling the white powder ferociously.

"Here, try another toot," she said in her raspy voice holding the coke spoon to our nostrils after she'd snorted more herself.

"Later," she slurred as she staggered through the room, bumping into everyone.

"Raquel looks like she had another session with the 'Sultan of Silicon'," I remarked. "I know she has enough plastic inside of her to open up her own chemical factory," I said. "I hear one of her breast implants fell into a champagne glass at a party once."

It was the year of the leaves. The era of love and miracles "In a White Room" by Cream echoed throughout the club.

"That guy across the room keeps smiling at me," I said.

"Another broke gigolo actor on the circuit. Ego mania alert," Chelsea frowned.

"Just your type, April. You better stay away from him."

"Are you waving at that old rich looking dude he's with?" I asked.

The man approached us holding a glass in his hand.

"Hello, are you girls alone?"

"I'm April, and this is Chelsea."

"You both look very fetching tonight. You girls never miss out on anything that goes on in Hollywood, do you?"

Chelsea smiled handing him her card as we slinked through the room.

Raquel wandered through the bar, pouring herself another glass of wine from the spout.

"Rotgut, they ran out of the good champagne, cheap fucks."

"That lady really has a chemical imbalance, she's a nutter." Chelsea frowned.

"How dreadful."

"I know, they're saving her a seat at A.A.," I laughed.

Even the loud music couldn't drown out Raquel's gravel voice.

"This party really sucks. Fuck, I'm not going to stick around for the concert. Let's all go back to my pad and get fucked up."

No sooner did the words spout from her lips, then she tripped on her five-inch heels, falling into the wine spout, bumping her head.

"God Chelsea, we need to go on the wagon again," I said looking depressed. "Let's split."

Raquel was lying on the ground drenched in wine and ice. Chelsea and I broke into uncontrollable laughter, pushing our way through the dark, smoky din. Heading towards the parking lot we gave our phone numbers to every available cult follower that was guzzling cheap beer in plastic cups.

"April, can you find out who's doing the PR for Rockie's funeral if she dies?"

"I'll just cry if I'm not invited. It'll be the biggest social event of the year," I answered.

"I'll bet the soirée will be splendid and held by one of Rockie's rich friends in a mansion. I can probably meet a sugar daddy there, April. My mum won't wire me any more money from London," she whined.

"You're such a gold coast gold digger," I teased.

While waiting for the sports car we flashed on a yardage of exposed girl/boy flesh lined outside of the trendy club. Sunset Boulevard swarmed with drunks and shrieking sirens. Two ambulance drivers wheeled out Rockie's body.

"Poor old Rockie. 'The Snow Queen' just didn't know her maintenance level," I said sadly. Chelsea and I raised our half full glasses to the sky.

"Let's drink to being young and beautiful in the sexy '60s in Hollywood." Chelsea smiled.

"Ashes to Ashes, Lashes to Lashes. And to our friendship till drugs do us part." I chimed in.

We hugged each other then guzzled down our drinks and jumped into the car, heading for the Roxy.

Chapter Six
London, Paris, Rome, 1969

The moment may be temporary, but the memory is forever.
Bud Meyer

It was 1969, eight o'clock, on a barren winter-swept morning. I was lying in bed trying to recover from the night before at The Rainbow. A large leftover cardboard pizza box with two slices of cheese, sausage, pepper, reeking of onions, made my stomach churn. Two half-empty glasses on my nightstand filled with Merlot had the sweet smell of decadence. As I took a sip of the stale wine, my thoughts were interrupted by the shrill ring of the telephone jarring my nerves. When I heard Chelsea's voice, I quickly grabbed the receiver. She'd been out of the country, being a worldwide traveller at heart.

"Wake up, April," she said.

"Chelsea, it's eight o'clock in the morning in LA. Have a heart," I begged.

"Darling, I'd fancy chatting you up now. How bloody soon can you get your passport and fly here?" she said demandingly.

"I don't need a passport to drive on the lot at Universal for my ten o'clock call," I said.

"As you will, but I'm sitting at this trendy pub on a rainy afternoon partaking of some libations, warming the chill in me bones curing a beastly hangover."

"Who are you with?" I asked.

"I have an entourage of outrageous, jet-set Englishmen. You know, the hip society set with wine breath, while you're bearing the fertile burden of the artist in Hollywood, feeding those rotters."

"Thanks bitch, what time is it there?" I asked.

"It's only four o'clock in the afternoon and I'm getting swaggered, enjoying some cheeky chatter, anticipating glowing under the shining disco ball, monopolizing the club scene tonight."

I jumped out of bed, grabbing an outfit from the closet, the phone in my other hand.

"I'm still here," I said, sliding my black mesh stockings on my legs. "I had the obligatory sleepover last night. I wouldn't let this freak boing me so he started rocking the bed at five o'clock in the morning. The dude was too wasted to drive or I would have gotten rid of him sooner," I said.

"You sound so terribly American April but your life is about to change. Thanks to fabulous me. You can share my flat right on King's Road with me for three months, and it's free. Brilliant."

"What happened to your roommate?" I asked, taking a long gulp out of a Perrier bottle, slipping on a mini-skirt and halter top.

"Well you know Heather was always a little anorexic. She fell in love with a bisexual insurance salesman from Abbey Life, and went on an apple diet. That's the fad here ducky."

"And...?" I asked.

"She kept getting fatter and fatter. He dumped her for a tranny, then she fled back to LA and her cat after having paid the rent." Chelsea sounded amused. "Now I can party with you my love!"

"You're so callous," I quipped. "Oh my God! This is too cool! As of now, I'm on hiatus. I'll be there in three days."

"Perfect, just in time for the opening of Tramp, Jackie Collins' new disco. You remember Jackie. She's our Brit connection."

"I love it! We'll have a blast. We always do, but now we'll be continental cunts," I laughed.

"Oh, there's just one little flavor I have to ask you for pet," Chelsea said boldly.

"I knew there had to be a catch," I whined.

"This town's dry. Heathrow Airport's hot. Do you have any more of that chronic Humbolt?" she asked.

"Yeah, but isn't it dangerous to travel holding?" I asked.

"Just don't put it in your carrying case," she said.

"What did you have in mind?" I asked.

"You can stuff it inside your crotch," she laughed.

"What if they frisk me?" I asked.

"Just turn on the baggage checkers with one of your compulsory pussy thrusts and if they try, tell them that you're so embarrassed because you're wearing padded knickers cursed with the stigma of bearing a flat bum and if that doesn't work, flaunt it, slink, slap 'em to the ground," she laughed. "You'll fall in love with London."

"Do they have a Mary Quant salon nearby?" I asked.

"Yes, I'm wearing a red lip-liner called Slut. It makes my mouth seem fuller so I can look the part of pout," she answered. "Got to run darling! We're off to the Chelsea Antique Market. Call me when you book your flight, Cheerio" she said.

"And if I'm a no-show, you'll know I got booked. You're a bad blonde," I said.

"You'll thank me for the rest of your life after you've been devoured by those racy gay blades. They love long leggy American birds with big tits that are full of sass and pizzazz. Kisses lovie!"

"I love Champagne, French Brie, Camembert and men that don't get in my hair."

I just loved the excitement of the city. It was sunset, my favorite time of the day, New Year's Eve. I'd just flown into London from Paris where I'd almost gotten arrested by the garçons for taking a picture of the Mona Lisa with my brownie camera at the Louvre Museum. The lights glittered like diamond necklaces on the Rue de Madeleine. I'd frequented Tour D'Argent, that trendy French restaurant dining on escargot and duck a l'orange overlooking the Seine river. Europe was such an amazing adventure. I felt like I had finally grown into womanhood. I had the time of my life. No one abroad really could figure out who I was like in Hollywood so I was very deceptive while learning about the different cultures.

My flat in Chelsea at the Alexander Maisons on Kings Road was a simply marvelous location. Right around the corner from the Chelsea Antique Market. Think I'll partake in a sip of delicious full-bodied, golden French bubbles. This vintage is Cristal Brute champagne. I'll pop a molten chocolate truffle in my mouth and tell you about it.

I lived only a few cobblestones away from my favorite clubs and Tweedle Dee, the friendly neighborhood pub where I'd hold court entertaining everybody who was anybody that fluttered in and out of the mainstream. One of my mates while I was in England was Falcon. He was a notorious cat burglar. One morning I awakened in bed with a hangover. When I eavesdropped on him dissing me, I overheard him telling his room mate "I have to get rid of that dreadful, tacky American bird. Last night I took her to Tramp. She was ripped to the tits trying to shag every bird in the bar. then the peasant craved a cheeseburger at two o'clock in the morning, so we stopped at Wimpy's for a to go order."

"I heard your voices," he answered. "She was really loud and vulgar," he laughed.

"We were in my room and April devoured the junk food with fury. I'd bought some snacks and a crumpet for me self to take to bed. She grabbed the cheese, shoving it into her screech, her wig landing in the Camembert. Then her apple pie and ice cream floated into the burger."

"Sounds like a bit of a pig," the other englishman uttered, making fun of me.

"It was an epicurean nightmare. I'm going to dump her off when she wakes up, then I'll come fetch you and we'll go get pissed over brunch at The Ritz."

Falcon entered the room with a look of disgust on his face. I'd never felt so much humiliation and remorse as I climbed into his black Bentley heading for my digs hoping that Chelsea was home so that she could console me. We rode in silence, which added to the tension. Later that evening at one of the jet setter parties, as I brushed by Falcon at the bar he greeted me with a cold stare. What a loss of talent. His tool was a jewel.

Rome 1969

A week later after surviving my embarrassing experience with Falcon, Chelsea and I went to Heathrow Airport catching the red eye for Rome to visit some friends. I was in love with the U.K. and the racy English but I needed to reinvent myself for the Italians. Emulating the vampy latin goddess Rita Hayworth, I was a woven tapestry of so many different secret selves, that even I got confused about who I was after living such an erotic, charmed lifestyle. I tried not to let my expectations over-exceed the fantasies. Being an adventurer, taking chances jumping off of the cliff all the time, strengthening my wings on the way down and engaging in liaisons that spanned the globe. That's what kept life exciting. Did he know that I'd just made love to another one? Being a big flirt, my forte was teasing and pleasing men. I simply adored sex as long as it was strange stuff, suspense and intrigue.

My first night in Rome at a dinner party I met the phony American actor that was married to a Hollywood movie star. He was rich and hot looking until he opened his mouth. The man was very sexually attracted to me but was only after a one night stand. Chelsea was in love with a cowboy stunt man and the only sightseeing that interested her, was in his bedroom.

"I'd love to show you around Rome," the society set snob said over Kahlua and imported pastries.

"I'd really like to see the Vatican," I replied.

"You have two glasses you're drinking out of and one is mine," he answered, looking amused.

"Sorry, I lost track. I'm feeling a bit buzzed from the wine." I smiled as he popped another pastry into his mouth.

"It's not easy getting inside of the Vatican, you'll have to sleep with me," he said patting my arm, lasciviously staring down at my breasts.

"Ok, if you can pull that off then your wish will be granted," I answered.

"Where are you staying?" he asked.

"Hotel Parco Dei Principi right on the Villa Borghese."

"I'll have to leave now, I have another party to attend. Pick you up at noon tomorrow, wear comfortable shoes. Ciao." he said, kissing me goodbye indiscreetly on the lips.

The next morning he arrived in a taxi transporting me to the Fontana Di Trevi, the Spanish Steps, the Coliseum, then we sipped an aperitif over lunch at the Via Veneto.

"When are we going to the Vatican?" I asked impatiently as I moved his hand off my thigh politely.

"We were too late to get into the Sistine Chapel," I whined. My escort paid the check, leaving a tip, hailing a cab taking me to St. Peter's Cathedral and tried to convince me that it was the Vatican. When we arrived back at my hotel I jumped out of the cab.

"Liar, prick!" I screamed. "You should never try to manipulate a master mind manipulator. You're a bore," I laughed, slamming my door in his face.

Feeling safe now in my terrace view room, I ordered a snack. That would hold me over until dinner, I thought. A few minutes later there was a tap at my door.

"Who is it?" I inquired.

"Room service, Miss Moon."

As I opened the door in my negligée, being modest as always, my tour guide admirer barged into the hallway. He was stark raving naked with a man made tan, wearing long white gloves holding a silver tray balancing a bottle of vintage champagne.

"You're crazy, get out. You broke your promise!" I screamed.

Before he even popped the cork, the invader pushed me down onto the couch, jumping on top of me. Obviously this freak knew nothing about foreplay, as he jabbed his larger than life sized cock inside of me. I could feel the stubble of his shaved chest on mine.

"That was the worst sex on the continent. I have to meet Chelsea in half an hour," I explained, demanding that he leave immediately. "You destroyed my hair so I won't give you a tip," I smirked self consciously.

He was heading for L.A. the next morning and we never crossed paths again. Later on in the bar, Chelsea and I were having cocktails when two virile looking foreigners sent over a bottle of the Dom then joined us. Since I spoke very little Italian, Chelsea had to be the translator. After a few glasses of wine in frustration one of the boys that went crazy over me pulled out a Berlitzger dictionary and pointed to 'I love you'. Soon after that I hopped the next plane for London, leaving Chelsea behind with her Mr. Right Now.

I rang up all my Brit connections, camping out at their flats, driving around in limos, dining out at the hot spots, letting the gay guys wear my wigs doing the disco scene to the hilt. My favorite high was smoking hash rolled in tobacco leaves. It was unforgettable, until I got spot checked at the airport leaving for L.A.. I was a little more than paranoid for one morning as I climbed down the spiral staircase I realized that one of the men I had been living with was a drug lord.

"Come with me," the gruff English voice demanded as he escorted me into a holding room. Forcing me to suffer the indignity of a body search and opening all of my luggage. Inside of my carrying case, a magazine spread with my hot, nude photos fell out and suddenly a Latino guard appeared out of nowhere grabbing them.

"You're free to go señorita, we'll keep these."

"She big famous celebrity," he informed that surprised customs official.

That was a close call as I was transporting six ounces of Hashish, illegal youth pills, a few ounces of grass and two hundred seconals without a prescription. Now as I sit high on a hill the realization of my reckless escapades and the consequences that could have cost me my life, my youth and a long prison term is chilling. I'll never be sure, but it seems as if the bearded man that I was saved by must have been Angel just toying with me. I only have a vague recollection of him lingering in the room when I was at Bellevue, but my memory was clouded. I'll never know if I was dreaming it was so surreal.

"Adios," he said, offering me a quick wave good-bye. But his thick accent sounded very familiar on that ominous day.

Chapter Seven

The Artists and Models Ball, 1969

I doubt very much that I have any vice that I'd
need to introduce to you.
Tennessee Williams

It was Halloween night in Laurel Canyon, an escape haven between heaven and earth. The year was 1969. My friends and I were hanging out in the woods at the Artists and Models Ball celebrating the night of ghosts, goblins and fantasy. I could be whoever I wanted to be for one night of intrigue. I'd come as one of my secret selves. What a great excuse to go on a chocolate binge and meet some hot handsome stranger. There's intrigue, adventure, mystery and danger on Halloween night, something I thrived on so I came as myself. Since already I was living the La Dolce Vita lifestyle, I personified it at the masquerade party as Decadence. We gathered beneath the boughs and waterfalls as fuzzy squirrels scampered through the trees. The grass was high and so was I. The backdrop that chilly October night was very theatrical. Balloons bobbing in the wind were silhouetted beneath a full golden orange harvest moon and emerald muted green landscape. I was young, the epitome of sensuality and seduction in a black lace see-through nightgown and bikini panties, garters and silk stockings. Garlands and peacock feathers were strewn in my tousled flaming tresses. A necklace of crystal love beads, joints and amyl-nitrates, all hung beneath my bobbing breasts. I was a floating chemical factory. My wrists were adorned with bracelets made out of (reds) Seconals and (Ludes) Quaaludes. Vamp red lip gloss enhanced my full mouthed pouty look and I was ready for some action as I held a long stick of burning strawberry incense in my graceful hand, the sweet scent filling the air. Flower children, musicians, actresses, rock stars, phony Hollywood actor types and quasi hippies were sipping sangria from frothy goblets, smoking pot, hash, snorting coke and holding hands, walking through the hills, wearing vacant smiles on their faces, dancing to the earth-shattering sounds of The Zombies, haunting rock song "The Year of the Seasons." I danced past the drummer, climbing the platform as the entrepreneur who was throwing the bash was in the middle of making a speech and stuffed a popper up his nose. Everyone at the party was stoned and laughing deliriously.

As the harvest moon rose from an electric blue sky, a guy dressed as the devil bumped into me, spilling sangria all over my ostrich feathered coat, drenching my nightgown.

"Hey man," he said, "I'm sorry but I'm seriously fucked up. My people and I dropped a tab of Orange Sunshine in Big Sur and drove our van down here 'cause we was told we could score some cool looking chicks."

This dude was definitely a physical turn-on.   A loincloth was wrapped around his well-built bod as he flaunted his bare torso and well-toned abs. His long jet black hair hung loosely, over his tattooed shoulders,   eyes at half mast framing his gaunt cheekbones.

"My name's Satan, I'm a roadie," he said, his eye focusing on my nakedness.

"Well it would have been really uncool if you hadn't showed up for your own holiday." I laughed, seductively.

"You bet your sweet bippy baby, my ex ole lady's an artist. She did all the body paint on my chest. Do you dig it? So what are you into girl, you look bitchin'."

"My name's April and I feel very mischievous, I'm the Goddess of vice and fertility. I work in the movies just so I can make some money, but it's all about art and nature and creativity."

Satan softly stroked my arm,

"You're real pretty, and you have great tits. I ain't seen you around before, where you been hanging out?" He asked edging in closer, casting half an aroused smile, his hot breath warming me.

"I'm a gypsy at heart, I just had a spiritual awakening." I answered, giving him a tentative embrace.

"Far out. Tell me all about it," he said. "I feel the energy flowing between us baby."

There was a moment of awkwardness, then a pensive stare.

"I hang out at The Whiskey, and The Rainbow, and some guys in a group turned me onto peyote.

Now I live in the spirit world. I believe in magic not reality. It's the opposite of fantasy. We're all just infinite spiritual beings having a temporary experience." I smiled, taking a hit of hemp.

Crimson rustic leaves were falling on the ground. "So what sign are you and do you have a gig?" I asked.

He flipped a long lock of hair away from his face squinting his brown eyes. "Aries, hey baby, you want to check out my ragweed?"

I inhaled the sweet smelling ambrosia, failing to pass it back to him. Macho man grabbed the joint out of my hand, "Don't bogart that shit. It's San Simeon, $300.00 an ounce."

"Don't panic, so did you have any heavy realization on any acid trip?" I asked.

"Yeah man, it was euphoria. I believe in karma, love, death and recapitulation. I'm collecting unemployment and spending all my checks on psychedelics. It's a whole new consciousness."

"I agree, life is so transitory I might as well drop out, its all so futile." I shared.

We were swilling down the cheap wine as he clung to my curves becoming sexually carnivorous. "Try one of these awesome brownies, and let's take a walk on the lake." he coaxed.

"I'd love to jump in the water, it looks so enticing, but it's bone-chilling cold out." I said, shivering.

Satan put a blanket around my shoulders. "I'll keep you warm, baby. No wonder you're freezing. You're half naked."

I was light headed as strobe-lights shone brightly on the scenery and our hot moist mouths kissed passionately. 'Satan' was breathing heavily.

"I got a great big heart and big dick and I'm going outta my head getting a hard on, tripping on you baby. Hey man, can you dig that, it's far out."

Our two bodies collided together like a volcanic explosion. Two souls bathed in white light and moonbeams.

As we approached the lake, leaving the crowd behind, the sounds of the music diminished wafting over the lake as the night darkened his hands, wandered lingering on my breasts, then slid down my bare belly pulling down my panties in the dark, damp bushes as night turned into daylight, the leaves rustling beneath our naked flesh.

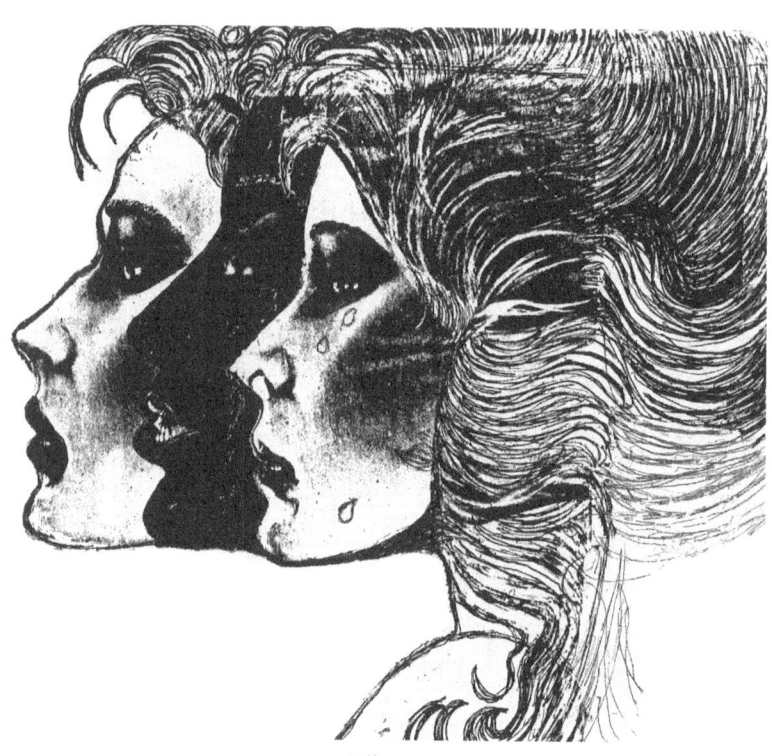

Elissa

Chapter Eight
Jet-Set Extras, 1979

If fame belonged to me, I couldn't escape her. If she didn't, the longest day would pass me on the chase.
Emily Dickinson

The raspy, steel pipes of Aretha Franklin belting out respect blared from my ghetto-blaster. Chelsea Flowers, Yolanda Washington and I danced around the stage lip-synching to the song. A carnival atmosphere and neon lights, glamour and glitz was a fun way to start the day.

On an empty soundstage at Sunset Lark Studios we jet-set extras were on an interview for a rock musical film about vampire priests, pimps and hookers. Blue and silver spotlights streaked across the stage. The location was Hollywood and sprinkled on the ground were gold stars and glitter. On stage left was a poster of a fire engine sunrise sky, street lanterns and strobe lights.

It was an early autumn afternoon. In the background the assistant director, Gimp the Pimp was limping, chewing an apple, flirting while passing out vouchers.

I was wearing a lavender, silk corset from Trashy Lingerie trimmed in lace clinging to my voluptuous breasts. Thigh high mesh stockings under black leather stiletto boots to the knee looked very enticing. Boa feathers hung over my shoulder and fuchsia roses were woven into my wild, blonde hair. My eyelids were covered with iridescent shocking pink shadow and black eyeliner. I walked out onto the set proudly pouting my vividly painted lips.

Chelsea wore an elastic tube top and tight, spandex pants. Big Iron and Antonio were dressed as pimps. Other atmosphere actors were milling around in the background.

The movie star look-a-likes sipped coffee and ate Danishes. Chelsea, Yolanda and I sat on box crates, laughing, drinking Cold Duck and gossiping. Yolanda had white makeup on her face and wore a platinum Harlow wig with rollers in it, four inch heels and a silver transparent plastic pantsuit, so tight that she could hardly sit down.

Chelsea Flowers dangled a long rhinestone cigarette holder from the side of her mouth. Flame and smoke ignited, singeing my hair.

"Chelsea, my afro's on fire," I screamed pulling a hand mirror out of my purse, checking out the damage.

"I'd kill to have your big hair dolly. I don't know how you get into your car. So sorry, love."

That bitch did that deliberately so she'd get the line today, I thought.

"You think you have problems, April," she said. "I have a five a.m. call tomorrow in Bell. Weather permitting I'm going to carry toilet paper in and out of Pic 'n' Save. I wonder if I need my green card?" she said sarcastically.

"Dig this, did ya see that guy that's dressed as a pimp? His name's Big Iron. He's a babe, check out those cowboy boots wit' them Playboy bunnies on them," Yolanda laughed.

"He looks like another dangerous man," Chelsea said. "How ghastly."

"I don't mind as long as he's dangerously armed with a big dick," I answered, shaking my hips from side to side.

"He'll most likely become aroused and want to lick off the tattoos I'm pasting on your nips. Hold still, Miss American Pie." said Chelsea.

A Brit from the streets of Soho with a passport and a hooker mentality, Chelsea had all the glamour of old Hollywood, youth and the bitchiness of Bette Davis on a bad day. Her platinum hair shone brightly on the well-lit soundstage.

Yolanda Washington approached us giving me a Hollywood hug.

"Hey girls, I hope they don't keep us waiting too long before they decide who gets the gig," she said looking concerned, walking stiffly. "I can hardly breathe. I'd better make this interview today or I'll be Broke City."

"You look like a common-looking wench. Some girls have no shame," Chelsea said mockingly.

"Get outta my business. You're an X-rated b-movie, Miss Flowers," Yolanda said arrogantly.

"Yo Yo, I can see your nipples right through the costume, but it's cool. Cher made it okay for girls like us to feel free about our bodies," I said.

"You mean tacky Cher gave you a license to be a highly evolved slut," Chelsea laughed.

Yolanda Washington was the baby in our group. She was a beautiful, illiterate, back-stabbing, Black barbarian from New Orleans with sidewalk gray eyes straight out of rehab.

"You shoulda seen Miss April at Frederick's of Hollywood yesterday. The sales girl told her that if she opened a credit card she'd score some points."

"I told her that the only points I need are right here," I said pinching one of my tits.

"Shake it, sista. Shake it, yo ho!" Yolanda laughed.

"Is anyone booked for tomorrow?" Chelsea asked.

"I'm appearing in a body suit at the Cucamonga Health Spa. I'm supposed to drown in a hot tub," I answered.

"Sounds a bit menacing, darling. I hope you have your infamous body insured by Lloyds of London," Chelsea said.

"Wow, no wonder casting asked me how long I could hold my breath under water," I said having an anxiety attack.

"Oh well, if you're afraid to risk, you're living with one foot in the grave. The Buddhists believe that we have only one minute anyway," I said mockingly.

"We get the message, Miss pseudo-metaphysical one," Chelsea said.

"Hey you guys, wanna join the Erection Connection? There's this two for one special this month," Yolanda asked.

"Certainly not, love. April and I received two day comps. The men were the weirdest sorts and there weren't any women there over twenty. One bird might have been thirty-five judging by her nasalovial fold," Chelsea said. "April, did you observe that every car in the parking lot was a Honda?" she said in disgust. "But I forgot, you gravitate to them."

"I had a blind date last night, girlfriends. Can you picture this? I drove all the way to Crenshaw Avenue to a beer bar and there was this total loser geek at the bar." Yolanda said sadly.

"Tell me more," I pleaded.

"Well April, when he opened his mouth he had no teeth. Ya dig what I'm sayin' sugar, I didn't even know how to get rid of him."

"You've got to be kidding. You should have just told him you were bipolar and about to have another incident," I laughed. "What happened to Jerome the janitor?"

"What's up wit' ya sister. He's a brother. I go mow mow over his high tight little ass, but he don't do me right an' I ain't nobody's hoochie coochie mamma. The dude's trying to run a game on me," she said angrily.

"Yolanda, sometimes batteries are better than brawn." I shared reassuringly.

"Check out the Jack Rabbit. You'll have a friend for life," Chelsea shared.

"That's 'til the batteries or the electricity goes out in the apartment," Yolanda laughed.

"That doesn't bother April. I rang her up one evening in the middle of a power outage and heard a buzzing noise in the background. That mad bird was using her electric toothbrush," Chelsea teased.

"What kinda goddess are you anyway, Miss Thing!" Yolanda snarled.

"I had Jack last night. He was so sensational that I made connections with ghosts from the past," I sighed.

"Must have been some of your old boyfriends, I presume," Chelsea said. "I much prefer a sexually well educated man with a manicure."

"Hot tip, Chels. The Pleasure Chest just launched their three inch executive model for women like you who only date professional men," I said throwing her an air kiss. "And Jack Rabbit would give your ex-boyfriends some stiff competition, Yo Yo," I said trying to keep a straight face. "Wake up girls, since the turn of the century, vibrators were used to calm down hysterical unfulfilled women just like us."

Yolanda looked up from reading her Essence Magazine.

"Check out this babe."

My gay boyfriend, Brian, interrupted our conversation.

"You look bitchin', bitch. April, I love your big hair today. It has a life of its own. I have to share this experience with you," he whispered in my ear. "I had a dream about Dennis Hopper last night. He was wearing boxer shorts. He told me that he'd let me see it if I didn't tell. I just fell in love when I saw *Easy Rider*."

"Ya'll got a little sugar in your tank," Yolanda teased.

All I could think of was Big Iron. He winked at me from across the soundstage with all of his male physical animal intensity.

"I've got the munchies. Need anything from the Roach Coach, girls? I've got some Acapulco Gold killer weed. I think we should walk outside the soundstage and smoke a joint," Brian said indiscreetly.

"Splendid!" Chelsea smiled coyly.

"You blow my mind, that's what I was just thinkin'," Yolanda said. "I could dig it, but if we get caught again we can get kicked off the set."

"Unless someone's hard up for some smoke, later," I said knowingly.

"I blame all this on our lovely president. Trick The Dickhead. That asshole's really on a war to stop drugs," Brian said in mock distress.

"Pot makes me happy, hungry, horny and creative," I frowned.

"I'd really adore it if Nixon would stop preaching to the nation that 'Pot Kills and Satan and The Goddess of Sodomites will get you if you smoke marijuana'," Chelsea quipped.

"I could live with the Sodomites and I wonder if it's really true what the president says about men growing breasts if they smoke pot," Brian asked in a whiny voice.

"Gloria Steinem, that bitch, would have had a Maidenform bonfire if she got wind of that. It's so sick. Dick Nixon's such a weirdo," I laughed.

"Alright girls, time to make a career move. Let's call casting and pick up some jobs, I like to get booked in advance," Chelsea said.

We lined up with all the other extras at the pay phone on the wall, calling *Cattle Call Casting*, a Chinese voice picked up.

"Wong Dong Hung here."

"Three names please. April Moon, Chelsea Flowers and Yolanda Washington. Not even an interview, sugarpie?" Yo Yo begged.

"Here April, ya'll got lucky," Yolanda pouted handing me the phone.

"Hi doll, it's April. You made another good choice," I said sweetly.

"April, you be butch dyke, I mean transvestdyke, on a new pilot tomorrow. Overcoat, tie, hat, mustache, 8:00, weather permitting. The stretch limo will meet you in the alley behind liquor store. That's past Fedco in Culver City, Page 487 in your Thomas map." Everyone who wanted to work in the movies came prepared with a Thomas Guide map.

"Thanks," I said.

"Put Yolanda on. I need someone who looks good in a string bikini," he said.

"But baby, I look fabulous in one," I answered.

"Sorry April, I need an extra who looks 18."

I handed the phone to Yolanda.

"Chelsea, what do you think casting thinks of me? I'm dying. I thought I was a glam queen, I'll have to call my date tonight and ask him if I can borrow his suit and tie," I said. "This is so sick."

Chelsea handed me the phone.

"Thai wants to talk to you about a job for next week," she said.

"Hello gorgeous, how much do you weigh? What color's your hair this week? And how old are you today?" he asked.

"I forget," I replied.

"Let's face it, April, I know you're on the wrong side of twenty-one. The only thing about you that might be twenty-one is your waist. Do you have a nice navel?"

"I was born with a diamond in my navel," I answered proudly.

"Are you an inny or an outie?" he asked.

"I'm an inny," I answered proudly.

"I have a belly button insert for you. I don't know the date yet. Call me back on the hot line in twenty minutes," he demanded, hanging up the phone in my face.

Yolanda was all excited that she'd just picked up a job.

"I have to report to Raulie Hills Ranch in the morning, I'm going to be at a pot marathon."

"I think casting's got your number," I said. "You'd better bring them some more buds."

"You won't believe what that bitch at Ratrace Registry just asked me, 'Yolanda are you still black and five feet eight?' She treats me like a ghetto princess!"

"Perhaps that's what you get for appearing like this and specking a caucasian call," Chelsea said mockingly.

"Oh fuck off, Chelsea! Anyway, I tells her I'm still black, an' she asks me what shade I am. I tell her I'm a mulatto. She hangs up in my face, an' tells me I'm too light for the call. I calls her back an' says I'm Duane Washington's sister and she says now she thinks I'm too black. An' now casting won't work me," she whined.

One of the short extras hung up the phone almost in tears.

"I can't even beg a gig. Last week I got a two day job on a circus film. I thought I was a sex symbol and when I got to Disney Ranch the A.D. screamed, 'Will all the little people come with me?' It said pregnant dwarf on my voucher," she said.

A flock of wardrobe people, and a director approached us.

"Okay, extras, line up on the stage, we're going to pick some of you for a bit in our film," the A.D. screamed through his megaphone.

Although they were whispering I could hear them laughing at me. It was humiliating.

The director pointed at me shaking his head as I popped my bubble gum in his face, posing. I really needed to get this job today, I was desperate.

"She's too old for this, but she's got raw sex appeal. The part calls for a girl about twenty," he sighed.

"She's worked the show before. I don't know how she ever got picked for this interview," one bored looking girl frowned.

I wish that bitch would stop giving me the evil eye, I thought, feeling very self conscious and less than.

"She's a sleaze bag. Very hard looking. And very difficult to work with. She thinks she's a star," the wardrobe man whispered to the director.

The director smiled lasciviously at me.

"That's exactly what I'm looking for. A sleaze bag hooker that thinks I can make her a star. Honey, come over here and show me those tits. Let's see if you have any talent," he said.

Gimp the Pimp pointed to Chelsea.

"How about her?" he said to the director. "She's the look we need and she's younger."

The costume designer sighed. "Have mercy on my Bob Mackie creation, she's much too over-weight." She glanced at another extra in the lineup.

"How about that black bimbo? She's a wonderful dancer. Lean and mean. Feisty. I like 'em feisty." Gimp the Pimp asked with authority.

The director frowned.

"No, too young. We'll take her for background. I'll use that tall cheap-looking redhead over there. She's a good type. A little too old, but she's the best of the worst we have today. I hope she can handle a few lines." He answered, snapping his fingers.

"Men, they're lizards, lizards." Yolanda shrieked.

"The baby mogul's treating me like a damn plantation owner. I wanna little respect, doesn't he know a funny thing happened in the '60s, the whole world turned black," Yolanda said.

Gimp the Pimp screamed through the megaphone,

"Okay, background artists of the street, nuns, vampire priests, bimbos, space queens, and my Ladies of the Royal Blue Galaxy, you can relax for now. Will the a, b and c hookers and pimps come with me? This job works today."

Chelsea ran up to Gimp.

"Excuse me, sir. I haven't had me coffee. I'm famished, and might I pop off to the loo?" she begged.

"Sorry, no time now," he answered.

I followed the A.D. to the lineup thinking *I just know, I feel it coming. I'm going to get discovered soon. I've been up since three this morning putting on my body makeup. And I got picked out of hundreds of girls to be Hooker Number One. I'm so excited I could die,* I thought. *I'm on the money today.*

"Hey, you with the frizzy hair, hurry up and line up on the street. No talking. Lose the dark glasses, and Yolanda, get rid of the rollers or I'll kick you right off this set and tear up your voucher. I'll report you to casting, and you'll never work with me again. Okay, Class A Hooker. I'm just waiting for my boss to come and give you your lines."

I threw out my chest and started posing. All the extras were lined up on the street whispering, shaking from the cold.

"Okay atmosphere, take a thirty minute break. We're waiting for the principals," the A.D. screamed. "Don't leave the set."

I called casting quickly before they started the scene. I was on a roll.

"Hi, it's April Moon. I hear that you have a hooker call at Universal next week. Can I get on it, honey please?"

"April, you're too old for the hooker and too young for the madam. I want someone fifteen. Try later."

Then the empty dial tone in my ear.

Oh my God, what a bummer, I'm washed up in Hollywood. I pulled a mirror out of my purse, studying the etchings on my distraught-looking face. Although I was still young, I realized that day that my face was looking older than I was ready to admit to. It's the flame colored hair, I thought, trying to convince myself, walking up to where Chelsea was sitting

"Chelsea, do I look like an older woman?" I asked. "I don't look as ancient as Saggy Sally, do I?"

"Poor wench with those tired tits," she answered.

"Sally thinks she's the bomb," I moaned.

"That's because she's half blind and has no mirrors in her apartment. Now mind your wicked horn. I see her walking on the set," she said. "And age is only important if you're a cheese, darling."

"What kind of cheese? Camembert or Brie," I asked, trying to be funny.

"It's okay, honey, a little nip and tuck will ease the pain," Chelsea said. "You got picked on a bit today for an over-the-hill hooker. Be grateful."

Yolanda pulled out some more cheap vino from a brown bag inside of her purse.

"A little sip and you'll feel brand new," she said.

"If I'd known we were going to get drunk on the set, I would have brought some vintage French champagne," I said with apprehension.

"Don't do me like that, girlfriend. Stop acting so superior," Yolanda said dryly.

"Let's get drunk and have fun 'til they start the shoot," I said.

Yolanda popped the cork. There was an explosion. She passed it around and we drank from the bottleneck.

Chelsea and I started gliding around the set seductively, vulgarly, dancing, moving our bodies with bumps and grinds. Clapping our hands and moving them toward our breasts as though floating through space. Clap, clap, snapping our fingers to the beat. My electric rock 'n' roll hair spilling over my shoulders like raging storms of wild wind.

Yolanda and Gimp the Pimp started dancing.

"Ya'll I feel trashy today. I jes' wanna drink wine from the nipple and party! Let's make a toast to sorority sisters. The jet-set gypsies. We're the babes," Yolanda moaned licking the bottleneck.

Gimp the Pimp pinched Yolanda's rear end as she danced up to Chelsea and I bumped into Big Iron. Then Yolanda did her Aretha impersonation to the music.

Chelsea and I put on our dark glasses, pushed out our bumps, posing and lip synching as *Respect* blared in the background.

Chapter Nine

Stunt Girls, A Flair for Dare, the '70s

The sort of panic that chooses to rush directly into the center of danger rather than fly away from it.
Tennessee Williams

"Ready, action!" screamed the director just as the sound of an atomic bomb exploded throughout the soundstage. Ten thousand pounds of popcorn flakes rained from the sky at "Sunset Lark Studios" on stage 30.

"Cut!" the director screamed through his megaphone. "Let's have a body count."

I opened my mouth to scream but no sound escaped my lips as I laid buried beneath mounds of synthetic snow. Suddenly my muffled cries came from under the avalanche, "Help! I can't breathe, I'm suffocating."

"Don't inhale the chemicals or you'll die!" the assistant director shrieked in an apathetic voice. "Hurry up, one of you grips get a shovel and dig her up. It's April Moon."

The flimsy movie set was constructed to match the interior of a church in Switzerland. Years ago the site was the location of many Esther Williams swimming sequences. Like art imitating life, the runaway cosmic film was portraying a giant meteor bearing chunks of moving matter that would strike suddenly, flattening the city, ironically blasting the World Trade Center, and The Twin Towers as it streaked across a painted sky, creating a mind-boggling array of special effects.

I lay there trapped. As the fog lifted in my head, I vaguely remembered walking on the set just as the fire department and paramedics were wheeling a stunt man out on a stretcher. I was relieved that it wasn't Roger my movie connection whom I'd done some very erotic stunts with in my bedroom.

"Great to see you April," Roger said as he greeted me with a big bear hug.

"Hon, are you sure that this is a safe gig? Why is that guy being wheeled out on a stretcher?" I asked.

Roger smiled apprehensively, his ham and cheese sandwich on Wonder bread dripping with mayonnaise still lodged between his brown, tobacco-stained teeth.

"April honey, it's safer than driving on the freeway with road rage. You have nothing to worry about. It's just a little scene that we're shooting today. A little snow will fall on your luscious bod."

"Well," I laughed, "my body was born for sin and I have a flair for dare. I might have to call the flesh fund if I don't survive this shoot."

He gripped my arm.

"Please, April, I'm counting on you. Don't bail on me. I promised the production company you'd work for three grand a day."

"I don't know, Roger, you made a deal with the devil."

"There's a one liner coming up in the brothel I can hook you up with if you do the stunt today."

"Okay," I said. "I'll go for it if you tell me about the other job."

"You're a raunchy hooker pulling tricks on a pig farm in Saugus, California. James Woods is playing your pimp. He turns you out and you get raped, and sodomized by thirty escaped Chicano prison inmates. Central Casting drops them off by the truckloads. The director and I thought you were the perfect type."

"Thanks a lot," I sniveled.

"This will be a great stunt credit for you. Sixteen mil is being spent on this baby. It's Hollywood's ultimate disaster epic."

"Show me where my trailer is," I said.

"Today you're going to get the star treatment, kid."

My spacious trailer was stocked with all of my favorite sinful treats. A bottle of chilled champagne, a joint and a king-sized Hershey bar with almonds. The mentally impaired cowboy looked almost hot in his tight-fitting denims, bulging out of his tie-dye GAP T-shirt. His greasy, gray, wild, unruly hair hanging over his stained suede fringed jacket.

"You know April, you really turn me on. You're an exciting lady. Do you think we can have a quickie before we start shooting?" he said moving in closer.

Well, I thought, relieved that there was no time for foreplay. I took a quick sip of the cheap Pierre

Andre Brute champagne, puffed on the grass as I plotted out the whole situation in my head. This man had sexual stamina. He'd taught me some great maneuvers.

Roger was a famous stunt man and I was a bit of an opportunist when it concerned men who were great in bed and had clout in Hollywood. But I preferred beautiful broke dicks that told me what I wanted to hear while they were pumping me. I took another gulp of the rot gut thinking that this Redneck Hollywood cowboy certainly had no taste in the finer culinary offerings of life. But what the hell, this was just about sex and furthering my career, certainly not the proper time for dick discipline. I started throwing out all the sexual signals, arousing his passion by unhooking my black satin lacy bra, flinging it in his face.

Roger ran towards me.

"You're certainly submissive today, honey," he said, climbing on top of me, pushing me down on the cot, his manly sweat dripping all over my naked body. His hot, foul breath reeked of stale beer. He rubbed his hard, throbbing cock against my thighs. "You're really hot today," he whispered as he pulled my tight-fitting shirt off me, throwing it on the ground. "I've been thinking about you all week. I love it, you're not wearing any panties. Let's have reckless, hard, raw sex."

I wish he'd stop talking and start performing, I thought, trying to fantasize that I was with one of the actors on the set, putting my hand over his mouth.

Roger threw my long legs over his neck. We were startled when a loud knock on my dressing room door interrupted his afternoon delight.

"Come on, Roger, April, honey we need you two on the set. We're ready to shoot," the assistant director pleaded.

After Roger had had his way with me, he zipped up his fly, pecking me coldly. "Hurry up and put something on, kid," as he ran out of my trailer, slamming the door behind him.

I threw on some clothes, returning to stage 30, lining up with the rest of the actors.

"Okay, stunt people! Take your positions in the center, and extras you stand to the side," the director yelled through a megaphone.

A bitchy wardrobe lady approached us. "Last call for cotton balls so the noise won't rupture your eardrums."

"Don't forget to use your rubber life tubes or you won't be able to breath underground," the director reminded us.

I looked pleadingly at Roger. "I'm paranoid, is it too late to bail?"

"April Moon, just pretend you're heading for the moon. Hold your breath, you'll be swept away, spacey lady," Roger assured me.

"People and extras, if you get this stunt right the first time I'll get you home before lunch." The director informed the cast and crew.

"Just think we'll be together underground with nothing but a rubber tube serving as a lifeline between our larger than life and death relationship.

Just close your eyes and suck like only you can do so well," Roger said groping me.

The director screamed, "Let's take one! The first thing you'll hear is a loud crackling explosion, then you'll all be submerged until you hear me call 'cut' to the cameraman. Okay, everyone in a crouching position. Are you all practicing holding your breath? Everything works in this shot. Ready, action."

The winter white snow fell on our parkas like a tornado covering us, sounds reverberated throughout the set as we dove underground. Everyone else managed to free themselves, although I panicked failing to use my rubber tube, fearing that it might strangle me.

"Help!" I gasped. "I'm trapped! Please don't let me die like this!"

I couldn't believe that this nightmare was my reality. It seemed more like a scene from a Stephen King TV spectacular, and I was an unwilling victim. I had to breathe in the toxins or my heart would stop beating. *Would they rescue me in time*, I wondered. What a frightening way to return to my maker, especially in a parka. I had always fantasized being buried in a trashy lacy see-through negligée.

Then a gruff voice said, "For God's sake, man, get someone to dig her up now."

Seemed like moments later a shovel pushed up against my body, I knew I was being saved as two brown hands reached down dragging me out from my temporary grave.

"Mi-ja, mi-ja" (my love), a voice said as I saw angels face, my eyes covered in snow yet knowing that my guardian angel had come to my rescue once again. "You risk life I watch over you," he promised.

"Bless you," I whispered.

"No more tricks, girlfriend. You write book now about adventure." He said, squeezing my arm. Then the church bench fell on my knee, knocking me down hard as my kneecap split in half. An excruciating pain shot through my leg. I was devastated, realizing that I might never walk again, then losing consciousness, I dropped to the hard cement floor.

The wardrobe lady hovered over as the grips shook me unmercifully.

"April, stop faking it. You have to do the stunt again after lunch. It's too late to replace you now." The crew tried awakening me, but I couldn't move, I was in shock.

"I think she's dead. Call the nurse and get her a shot of adrenalin. If you can't revive her, call casting and get someone else at once. Now get her out of here, and everyone else take an hour break for lunch. Be back on the set and ready to work in an hour."

Chapter Ten

Saint Patrick's Day Massacre

Being hatched on St. Patrick's Day, I made my grand entrance, lying in a bed of four leafed clover. Although being born on the day of a Saint I never made my ascent to Sainthood, but I had the luck of the Irish. Life was one continuous celebration since my birthday landed on the day of the green. Well, I played the game 'he loves me, he loves me not' with shamrocks, not daisies. But you could never catch me wearing 'Kiss me, I'm Irish' buttons or kissing the Blarney Stone, on the day of bag ladies and bagpipes.

I opted for Irish Coffee and the Dom.

I turned green the next morning after one of the birthday bashes at 'Ma Maison'. Renowned chef Wolfgang Puck always greeted me with a long stemmed green carnation as I drank champagne, feasting on oysters. I remember the orgasmic dishes he created, till my friends and I closed down the trendy eatery when they ran out of Beluga Caviar.

The next morning after partaking of too many libations, never knowing my limitations, at the nearest pub I gulped down bloody marys and nibbled on shepard's pie and all the men thought I was a great snake charmer.

St. Patrick sent me the love of my life, Patrick, the blonde, the bronze, the dumb and the beautiful

who I lived with for years and finally ended up marrying.

The jock with the golden lock. At least in my
lifetime I experienced that great passion and love.
We breathed poetry in the storm, yet it smelled
like spring. Our sweet summer sweat on cool crisp
sheets. I'll never forget sleeping in his arms at night.
Our long symbiotic legs wrapped around each other's bodies. That was the last time that I ever felt
whole. I had always been alone until Patrick and
I celebrated each other. I loved our long lunches
in bed, drinking champagne in the rain. The morning that he was destined to leave, I couldn't sleep,
awakening at dawn, adoringly watching him sleep.
Patrick's curly, blond ringlets strewn on my pillow, so
very long ago.

My emptiness ended when love began. The
emptiness began when love ended. How could
we come home after all those mindless bodies had
climbed us. I just made the mistake of believing
that I could find all things in one man and he let me
down. So I retaliated by bedding down with young
lovers, ex-cons and a porno star, while he was frequenting his favorite bar.

Chapter Eleven

Harmonies of the Human Heart
And The Climates of Our Minds
The '70s

The meeting of two personalities is like the contact
to two chemical substances. If there is any
reaction both are transformed.
C.J. Jung

I entered the elegant, old world, charming lobby of The Regent Beverly Wilshire Hotel and pushed the elevator button to the mezzanine. A fragile, wiry looking, gray haired woman was awaiting my arrival. Helena Davis, psychic reader to the stars, was smiling at me, holding out her magical hand.

"You must be April, I'm Helen. Chelsea told me you were coming to see me. Sit down, honey. What do you want to know?"

I smiled shyly, "I want to know if I'm going to ever find my soulmate?"

Helen handed me a taro deck. "Oh honey, you have such charisma and a great aura. My little screwball, if you'll just be quiet and listen to the voices in your own head I will tell you your fate. Throw the cards on the table, pick ten face down the fourth card in the middle is your future."

I threw the cards as she smiled, "Oh dear, you picked the Knight of Wands, The Lovers, and The World. You will meet the love of your life before christmas and you'll be with him forever."

He smiled and then the spell began. As soon as I looked at Patrick I knew that this handsomely rugged looking Irishman was my destiny. We stared at each other across a crowded smoke-filled room that cold winter November night. My best gal pal Chelsea had thrown a bash at one of her rich boyfriend's houses in the Colony. I was standing at the bar, flirting with all the guys, drinking Cordon Rouge Champagne at her seaside rolling hills estate when he came into my life. I was immediately drawn to this stranger when he asked my name. I'd felt those sensations many times before, but this was real; although I tried blaming it on the buds and the French champagne. He looked so hot in his western shirt and Frye boots.

"My name's April," I said, looking at him provocatively. "I feel a bit drunk. Too much bubbly. My partner in crime is trying to corrupt me. She keeps filling my flute glass with champagne. I never should have told her that I felt like being bad tonight. She's trying to get me drunk so I won't be able to drive home and I'll party with her and her new squeeze. He's gross," I said turning up my nose.

Patrick put his hands around my waist, "How could I let someone as wickedly sexy as you be bad without me. I'm going to have to rescue you. You shouldn't drive in your present condition."

"I could stay here in the guest cottage tonight, but I have to get home. There's a big storm brewing. Pacific Coast Highway may be closed down tomorrow."

"Let's get out of here, they're running out of hors d'oeuvres and you've had enough to drink," Patrick said tugging on my arm, flashing me an infectious smile.

"Okay," I said. "Let me go find my coat and purse."

Patrick and I slipped out the door without saying our good-byes, he tipped the valet and soon we were speeding down PCH, racing with the clouds in his convertible. The mellow sounds of Stevie Wonder "You Are The Sunshine of My Life" blaring on the radio.

"I'm really glad that we met. This is too cool, I've had my fill of all the Hollywood guys and their Hollywood lies for one night. Where are we going, Mr. Man?"

"It's a surprise. I'm going to take you to my favorite haunt at the beach. It has sawdust on the floor and a great view. You'll love it," Patrick replied.

When we arrived at Gladstone's a young blonde hostess seated us outside on the catwalk. The full moon shone brightly on the dark midnight blue sea and mystical shadows of pelicans diving into the waves for fish set the stage for romance. We feasted on oysters and other delicate crustaceans throwing French bread to the seagulls.

"I really like you a lot. I've never been with anyone like you before. You're so uninhibited and down to earth. I'm flipping out over you." Patrick whispered as he nibbled on my ear.

Oh my god, I thought. *I wonder what he means about me being uninhibited.   I hope that this enchantingly wonderful man doesn't know that I slept with his best friend with Chelsea and one of her friends watching. And even worse, I hope he doesn't notice that my hair has the frizzles in this moist ocean air. But at least I'm really blonde. If I only live for one lifetime I'd prefer being blonde.* We clung to each other, kissing passionately as silver waves crashed against the shore. I felt safe and sane at last with this warm-hearted affectionate person.

"April, who taught you to kiss and touch a man like that. You're driving me crazy."

He was stiff and gentle all at the same time, and no doubt a lot of bitches were chasing this studly jock.

"You look like magic tonight, April," he was blown away by me and I loved it.

"Patrick, you make me feel so happy," I said, giving him a big hug.

"I knew the minute I saw you that we'd be great together." he said.

I dared to drive off the cliff and swim the far shores of deep emotion, for the first time in my life I was unafraid to experience the ritual of true romance. We had touched upon something miraculous. I was a carnivorous butterfly and falling in love was never so much fun. We shared the most intimate sacred secrets that night. With the morning glare I awoke in his arms blessed by a miracle. A gusty wind howled through the canyon and wind chimes were music to my ears. Heavy rain was pouring down, splashing my bedroom window.

Late last night when we left the restaurant we had driven up the steep dirt road to my primitive knotty pine cabin on Brier Drive in the canyon. It was Sunday morning and we were warmed by the blazing amber blue crackling fireplace in my cozy rustic bedroom and the fusion of our bodies. Patrick had the lingering look of adoration in his eyes as we snuggled up together beneath the feathered comforter, his hands exploring my body, legs intertwined beneath the flannel sheets

"Good morning, baby. How'd you sleep?"

"I slept great with you. I usually have a hard time sleeping with someone. My head feels a little fuzzy this morning. I must have passed out last night."

Patrick held me tighter. "We're a good fit, April, I love looking at you without any make-up on. You look so free. You don't need it."

"I have no inhibitions with you. I'm totally comfortable like I've known you all my life."

"I don't want to leave you now, but I sort of have a girlfriend I made plans to have brunch with today, but if it's okay with you I'd rather stay here. Are you seeing someone?"

"I have lots of men friends, nothing serious, and I'd love it if you stayed for brunch." I started obsessing over this man. He has a girlfriend, that's depressing. I wish I hadn't had that one night stand with Darren, and that fucker dared to dump me just because I provided an audience for his fantasies, two bombshell blondes. Then he called me a loose woman as he zipped up his fly and slammed the front door behind him. Patrick can't blame me for who I was and was with before we met, can he? It was just a short interlude in my big wild life. Will he still be so sweet to me when he finds out that I have a big jock cock following? I want to come clean and tell him, but then I'll have to reveal myself. I should wait, just wait until he falls hard.

It was as if he was looking right through me. He became very intense.

"Is there something you need to tell me about yourself? I sense a sudden sadness in you, I feel like you're a lost child, it's that little girl quality you have. It makes me want to protect you from yourself and the wild crowd you run with. Do you have a lot of secrets?"

I pressed my body to his, hanging on tightly.

He pulled me closer. "This isn't just about sex. You have a beautiful body. I'll bet all the boys are in love with you but I'm crazy about you because you're real. I'll never get bored with you. I want you to believe me. My greatest thrill is giving you pleasure, April."

I put my arms around Patrick's neck as he kissed the tip of my nose.

"My heart is too delicate an instrument to be toyed with. Do you really mean it?"

"I'm here, aren't I? Don't be so insecure, April. I won't throw you away. I think there's a chance for us. What do we have to lose?""

He said 'us' didn't he? "Oh Patrick, I'm just afraid of getting too close. Love can make me fall apart, and sometimes when it feels too good I just run off and hide or sabotage the relationship. It's like I have this second sense that it's just never going to work out. Is that crazy? And you're a lot younger than I am."

He smiled as if he totally understood. "One of the reasons I'm so attracted to you is our chemistry and your spirituality, age is just a number. Your wildness and craziness are part of your charm. Let me put some love into your life."

"We drink too much and party too hard, I'm afraid that we'll destroy each other. But I'll never be like anyone else."

He kissed me for a long time, then his body folded into mine. The sheet had fallen from our bodies, we were lying in bed totally stripped, raw and bare, only the rhythm of our souls and our sexual healing. Love with him was ecstasy, wholeness, timeless, complete fulfillment. I was truly enjoying this fleeting moment in time. I felt this high, an uncontrollable surge of lightness running through me. I was blessed with a large capacity for love and even if this didn't last, being adored and worshipped in return would remain in my head forever.

I knew that day the lesson I would learn from Patrick was unconditional love as I experienced total intimacy. Patrick and I smiled at each other.

"Lying in your arms is such a safe warm place," I said with a soulful stare.

"When I crawl inside of you I forget about the rest of the world and all of my problems for awhile. Let's just stay in bed all day." He unplugged my phones as we listened to the thunder and the rain wash away the world around us.

We must have dozed off for awhile. Suddenly I saw a silhouette in the arched doorway. Chelsea was drunk, standing inside of my bedroom in all of her bold, blonde nakedness.

"I can see you're up to your usual hanky panky, looks like you got banged more than I did this weekend."

I was in a panic, in shock. "Chelsea, what are you doing here, I thought you were in Malibu?"

"My date was a beastly bore," she said in a raspy voice with an evil look on her face. "I decided to drive into town because I was afraid that you might be having more fun that I was with this piss poor bugger you twat."

Chelsea was hell-bent on destroying me. She popped open a bottle of my expensive champagne, holding three glasses and a joint in her hand.

"Are you going to share this big, beautiful, blonde boy with me like you do with all the others?" she demanded in a jealous rage. "I hope he doesn't have a little willy."

Chapter Twelve

The Movies, The Biltmore Hotel

Another one of my ludicrous jobs in Hollywood was filmed at the stuffy, world famous, 'old money' Biltmore Hotel downtown. It doesn't get more classic or more noir than inside this legendary lounge. It was a punk rock disco spectacular film. When we broke for lunch, Chelsea, Yolanda, Brian and I hung out at the bar, having 'Black Dahlia Martinis' named after Elizabeth Short.

Chelsea and Yolanda were dressed in short tight skirts, fishnet stockings and corsets showing lots of cleavage. I had a transvestite call and was wearing long baggy trousers, a Calvin Klein man's jacket, my hair parted in the middle slicked back with gel and a black mustache glued to my face, talking in a low gravely voice.

"Can you believe that day the hotel was hosting 'The Priests National Convention' and the 'Evangelists Ball' on the same floor?"

The segment the girls and I were working on was an annual New Year's Eve party for pimps and hookers.

When we finally wrapped at midnight, Brian and I walked through the lobby, turning a lot of heads. He was dressed as a pimp in his tacky gray and white pinstriped, three-piece suit and tie.

"April, can we be lesbians together" he asked as he escorted me through the lobby.

A stout, balding man was sitting on a couch drinking a scotch on the rocks and reading the *New York Times*. He glanced at us as we walked by.

"Are you gay?" he asked, directing the question to me.

"I just have latent impulses," I laughed as the automatic doors opened and we walked out onto the street, hearing the hums of traffic on Fifth and Grand Avenue. It was a grand job.

Chapter Thirteen

The Regal Regent
Beverly Wilshire Hotel
The Lobby Lounge
Mother's Day

It was Mother's Day. Patrick and I had been living together in bliss for more than a year and had enjoyed many "le grande classe" dinners at my Mother's expense. Being a true elitist, she had an anxiety attack when we dined anywhere south of Olympic and Beverly Drive. So, for the big fête that was Mother's Day, we decided to pamper her like royalty in the Lobby Lounge at the Regent Beverly Wilshire Hotel. Since this was the perfect spot to see and be seen, I often popped in to chat it up and unwind with a chilled glass of vintage champagne after a hectic day of shopping on Rodeo Drive or a great night of theatre at the Cannon.

The three of us were greeted warmly by the charming manager. "Good to see you, April," he said, kissing my hand, leading us through the salon to our Louis XVI round table. "We have a special menu today. Enjoy your dinner."

A server appeared as Patrick handed Mother a bouquet of yellow mums. "I'm David and I will be your server tonight. May I suggest the delicate scallops infused with red roasted pepper sauce? They are simply delicious. And while you're looking over the menu, may I bring some cocktails?"

"I'll have a glass of Chardonnay, please," I answered.

"Didn't I just see you in a movie?" he inquired.

"Yes, I'm an actress and a poet," I said in my phony Hollywood voice.

"And you, sir?"

"I'll just have a beer," Patrick smiled.

"And Madame?"

"A glass of water with lemon. And bring her a ginger ale, young man," she said sternly.

"Oh Mother, lighten up and have a glass of wine with me. The water in Beverly Hills is like drinking out of the sewer. I wouldn't give it to my animals," I argued.

"All right, April, dear, but just one glass for you."

"I'll be back for your orders," he said, putting rolls and balls of butter on the table.

"This is lovely, isn't it, Patrick darling? But I can't believe the waiter recognized April with her clothes on," she said, clinging to his arm. "What do you feel like eating tonight? It's my treat," she said in her saccharin sweet voice, smiling at him.

"I'm going to eat dangerously," I interrupted rudely. "I'm ordering two jumbo chilled shrimp cocktails, baby greens with grapes, feta cheese and sun dried tomato vinaigrette, and rare lamb chops."

"Do you think that will be enough for you?" Mother said, brushing the hair out of my eyes. "And pull up your top, dear."

As we sipped our drinks, the busboys catered to our every whim. "I feel very at home and relaxed here. This tea room has such a refined and European ambience," Mother remarked.

"You just love it because it's in the heart of Beverly Hills," I laughed. "It's la crème de la crème."

"Is that Warren Beatty and Annette Benning at that table across the room?" Anna asked.

"Yes, and that's Cybill Shepherd," Patrick added as we were lulled by the contemporary sounds of a piano. Patrick and Mother were always impressed with celebrities, socialites, and the famed and fortuned.

"You look beautiful tonight, Anna. Happy Mother's Day. I'm glad we can spend it together," he said, giving her a kiss on her pale white powdered face.

"And I love those long strands of pearls with the floral print dress," I said, touching her shoulder. "Can I borrow the necklace sometime?" I begged, inhaling the sweet scent of garlic wafting through the dining room.

"I'll take you to Saks and buy you a high-class outfit if you throw away that purple tie-dye dress. It's cut to your navel," came Mother's reply. "Patrick looks so handsome in his black suit and you look like a freak, dear."

I tried to ignore her as I grazed on the crimson and lime-green fluffy leaves of my salad. I was used to it by now. She was always embarrassing me at the opportune moment, putting me down. I never could please her, but today was her day, so I'd leave it alone.

"Have you found another job yet, Patrick?" Anna inquired.

"I have to go out to Orange County tomorrow for another interview," he replied with a shy smile holding my hand as we devoured tarts from the engaging pastry tray over rich chocolate ice cream and cappuccinos.

My Mother reached for the check after deciding she disliked the Chanel Number 5 perfume I had bought her. "This was very noteworthy cuisine," Anna shared. "Thank you for joining me. April, you'll call the minute you get home. And don't turn off your phone dear."   Mother said, kissing my hand, giving Patrick a long, lingering hug.

Chapter Fourteen

James Woods
In the Woods
Blame It on My Breasts

Some women my age, or younger, 've got breasts that look like a couple of mules hangin' their heads over the top rail of a fence.
Tennessee Williams

It was a hot, muggy morning. The last day of summer. Soon autumn would paint her pallet with earthen hues of burnt amber and scarlet star-shaped leaves. Patrick and I had taken a drive to the end of the world, a barren wilderness called Saugus. Although I'd studied the Stanislavski method, I was a free-spirited, reckless, big city girl who loved to escape from conformity and with each job in the movies ended up wearing less and less.

After all I was a player in Hollywood, the heart of corruption, vulgarity and ridiculousness. Being a sexual radical, I loved bearing my robust breasts and terrorizing my conservative elitist family and future conquests along the way, but this was an exception. I was cast in an X-rated film as James Woods' floozy, boozy girlfriend Honey whom he pimps out to a truckload of wetbacks at a flophouse.

The set was designed with harsh lighting, and my bare body scorched the screen.

Woods had a dark hidden raw sexuality and enough animal magnetism to match his star power. It was distasteful nudity and raunchy dialogue. My pimp was running the joint. One scene was shot in the woods. The actor was laughing, smoking a joint, while hosing me down.

"I'm gonna clean you up and you're going to make some money for daddy today. We are pitching in together on a ranch in Oregon. We're gonna make enough money to have a communal just like the hippies. I'll make all the money, and I'll marry all of you girls," he said, his bare bronzed chest and muscles gleaming of sweat in the sun.

"I just want to make sure you can handle all of the trade." he said mockingly. In the next scene, the Mexicans were plowing his weeds.

"Hey amigos, I have a ten spot for you to get these guys off for a minute." he screamed to the foreman. "Now don't waste any time. Do your business and get back in the truck. No sodomy please. No anal abuse and one to a girl. This is a class operation, muchachos," he said, as I lay back on a flee infested cot in a cubicle they called 'The Chickie Coop'. I was making over a thousand on a daily rate for handing the movie icon my black lace panties and bra.

"Nice lingerie," he smiled. "Those wetbacks can get awfully rough. They haven't been laid in a couple of years," he said, standing nearby, wearing a tight torn dusty pair of jeans.

"Thank you, my darlin'." he smiled.

"You look like a Honey with the light shining on your golden hair," Woods said off camera. "Is that guy that hangs around the shoot your boyfriend?"

Unfortunately, Patrick was standing in the wings, and I missed out on most probably a lusty location fling. Suddenly all of the laborers piled out of the truck.

"Bueno," they yelled making tread-marks in the dirt.

Beads of perspiration were dripping down my naked body under the terrycloth robe while waiting for the cameraman. The lights on the set were so hot. I just hoped no one that I knew would ever see this shoot, especially after so many warnings from my mother that if I didn't stop disgracing them that my family would cut off my trust-fund. This time I had really crossed the line. Ironically the payback came when I became a coveted playwright at a well known respectable theater. One evening I approached the conservative artistic director asking if he liked my rewrites for his upcoming production.

"I liked your performance with James Woods on cable much better," he answered playfully. "I wonder if this work is really fiction if you will?"

Chapter Fifteen

Independence Day
At The Rosarita Beach Hotel
The '70s

A prayer for the wild at heart kept in cages.
Tennessee Williams

A rickety worn cab wound along the dusty road to our destination: The Rosarita Beach Hotel in the mist of the early morning. A Mexican cab driver, wearing the face of a wilting flower with round, sad brown eyes and long dark braided hair, drove down a narrow, bumpy road through barren wastelands twenty-four miles south of the border.

The foggy, bleak landscape was cluttered with terra cotta colored wooden shacks. Children swung lazily in straw hammocks, surrounded by clothes-lines that were part of the scenery of the primitive little Mexican village.

After checking into the hotel, the manager escorted us to a dingy cubicle that he dared call "The Honeymoon Suite." The next morning when we headed for the surf, I went into a depression, seeing flocks of pelicans lying lifeless on the beach. I loved watching them soar through the sky, then swoop down into the water diving for fish with their giant distinguishable bills storing food for survival.

"Patrick, look away. Those carcasses are really freaking me out," I stammered. "They're grotesque."

"They just add to the gloom of the day," he answered.

"It's really strange for July weather," I mused.

"How unfortunate that the Del can't book us 'til late this afternoon, but at least we'll spend the Fourth of July night in Coronado. This day reminds me of an Ingmar Bergman film," I added.

"I'd be happy sleeping anywhere with you, baby. A tent would be better than the hard wooden bed we slept in last night," he said. "My feet were hanging over on the tile floor."

"After all those drinks, I thought we were in France," I answered. "Let's take a swim," I coaxed.

We jumped into the fertile blue waters where the Gulf meets the Pacific, crashing onto the shore.

I tasted his salty lips, feeling so carefree until I spotted a pelican bearing a lengthy wingspan, white and silvery feathers dripping in blood, floating on top of fluorescent foam. Its neck was broken, brown webbed feet sticking together covered with tar. I screamed, untangling myself from the kelp, running toward a patch in the sand.

"I need a stiff drink after seeing that," Patrick said as we fell down on our blanket.

"I'm totally bummed out," I answered, my voice cracking, hands shaking, pulling out a joint from my purse. Puffing away as sparklers exploded in the sky.

"Take a toke and hold that down. The young Latino boy over there with the purple shades keeps checking you out," Patrick said.

"I think I found my next connection. I'm running out of grass." I answered. "I'm starting to trip."

As the Mexican boy approached us, I became very flirty and feisty.

"Hola papa chita culo, you're the bomb, baby. You got any pot? I have mucho dinero."

"Muy bonita, chica. I go see my friend," the boy answered. "How much you need? How long you be here?"

"I need an ounce. We'll be here for the day." I smiled, checking out all of his body parts.

"Hasta luego," he said as he ran down the beach.

"April, you're so outrageous," Patrick scolded.

"That's how I get what I want," I laughed.

"You mean that's how you manipulate everyone," Patrick teased, pulling me closer to him.

A dark skinned waiter appeared, holding a bamboo tray in his hand.

"Como estas? Como se llama?" he said.

"Hola, I'm April, we'd like a margarita and a 'Sex On The Beach', muchacho. Light on the punch, heavy on the tequila and Bacardi."

"Senorita, you charge drink to room?"

"Si, amigo," I answered, showing him my key.

"Pronto," he said, dashing over to a young couple's umbrella.

"I'm chilling out," Patrick said contentedly.

Our waiter appeared carrying a tray with two frothy drinks in long stemmed tulip-shaped glasses. We sipped our exotic ambrosias from long plastic straws.

"The libations are getting me buzzed. It really kicks off the buds. Honey will you rub some cocoa butter on my back?" I asked seductively as the noonday sun burned off the morning haze.

I could feel the soothing rays penetrating my body. A guitar trio plucked at their strings, playing the music of the people.

"I'm getting seduced by the soul of this country," I sighed softly.

"Let's order another round," Patrick smiled contentedly.

Promptly the waiter appeared. Bartenders lit torches as firecrackers went off from afar. Patrick rubbed oil all over my stomach, separating my thighs, drizzling some between my legs.

A snow white seagull resembling a powder puff flew by, proudly carrying a gold starfish in his mouth.

I pulled on the string of my crimson crocheted bikini top, knowing that I looked so much better in the buff, trying to entice Patrick. My top fell onto the sand.

"April, this isn't a nude beach and there's a mother with her kids watching us across the way. I wish you hadn't brought the smoke. I'm getting paranoid," he said.

Paying no heed to his warning, I slid off my bikini bottoms.

It seemed like only seconds later two Policia in jet black uniforms jumped us, grabbing the baggie out of my hands. While Patrick argued with them, I fished in my purse for the loose joints, stuffing them into the palm of my hand.

"Gringo, you under arrest. You think you rich Americans can get away with anything. Not in our country."

"What are you arresting us for? Patrick shouted.

"Marijuana and nude sunbathing. Come with us or we'll shoot you."

After I threw my bathing suit back on they slipped the handcuffs around my wrists. I managed to get away from them long enough to duck my head into a broom closet and swallow the four joints, trying to hide my stash.

The urine-stained cement floor in the jail was straight out of Sartre's *Last Exit*. The stench was so terrible that I was afraid to lie down, and I was dizzy from the weed. The cubical was so small that I could hardly move no less breathe. I held onto the bars so I wouldn't pass out.

We begged the Federale to let us share the same cell, but we were thrown into separate cages next to a 14 year old Mexican boy.

"Help me, por favor," I screamed to the guards, my erect nipples sticking out of the now torn string bikini. Their demonic laughter echoed throughout the jail. It was chilling.

"What do you think they are going to do with us? Kill us? Or let us rot our guts out? They rape girls in places like this and I'm half nude."

"I overheard the detective talking to someone. They're sending us to the Tijuana jail tomorrow. The Federales get money every day from the government just to keep us there," Patrick reluctantly told me.

"Can you believe, over one lid of grass and a nude body?" I sobbed.

"I tried to warn you, baby."

I'm so scared," I cried out. "I know it's all my fault. I should have known better. Can you ever forgive me?" I pleaded. "You don't even smoke pot."

"I might have to try in my next lifetime," he answered.

"This dungeon is like a Bastille in Eighteenth Century France, except Mexicans don't use guillotines, do they?" I asked.

"They just chop off heads with machetes or hang them from trees and shoot tourists down in the woods, leaving them prey for the buzzards," Patrick answered.

"I'm praying to God that he'll get us out of this. Patrick, do you love me? You're the only man I could ever really be with."

"Just remember, whatever happens, I'd risk my life for you," Patrick said with sincerity.

But could I really believe him? I'd never been with anyone that said that to me before. Today surely would put our relationship to the test.

"We've got to get out of here. I'm going crazy," I said, almost fainting.

"If we could just make love once more and I could be in your arms before they decide our fate," Patrick answered.

"We can't give up!" I cried out.

Suddenly, I had an epiphany.

"We have nothing to lose. Tell them that I'm related to President Reagan and that there'll be a scandal if I stay in here. I'm starting to throw up. When they come, tell them that I have a heart murmur."

Patrick cried out for the jailer, "Chica is sick. Please let her go and take me, I beg you. She's dying."

Knowing that Patrick was willing to risk his life for mine gave me strength. About ten minutes later a detective with an eye dangling into his hollow cheekbone opened my lover's cell, poking a gun at him. He unlocked Patrick's handcuffs from the bars and dragged him down the dank, dark corridor.

Now I was all alone, having a panic attack, heart palpitations, temporarily losing my breath. It was so stiflingly hot, the perspiration was rolling down my face. I heard a young boy's agonizing screams. Then-

"Please don't hit me again. I can't move my arm," he begged.

"If you cry I'll tie you up with this rope," came the harsh voice.

Where were they taking Patrick? The more I thought about it, the more frightened I became.

Were they going to beat and interrogate him? Kill him? I was shaking uncontrollably.

From the other end of the hallway, a janitor mopping the floors came swabbing toward me. I caught a glimpse of his face. Was that Angel? As he came closer, his back still turned, I grabbed at his shirt through the space in the bars.

"Angel, is that you? You've got to help me!" but he pulled away.

"I wasn't sure if I was hallucinating from all the pot I swallowed but the laborer in the uniform looked a lot like my guardian angel. How could he abandon me now, when I needed him the most?

A chill went through my body. I knew at that moment I might never get out of there alive.

I don't know how much time had passed, but it felt like hours when I heard heavy footsteps coming down the hallway toward me. The same detective that took Patrick away appeared, unlocked the cell, limping towards me, grabbing me by the shoulder.

"Get out. You come with me."

"Where is the man you took from the jail?" I begged.

"I no tell you," he taunted.

Then he and his sidekick drove me back to the hotel. Marching me through the dimly lit lobby at gunpoint, I felt humiliated wearing only a scanty red-knit bikini. I tried fighting off my fear as they got a refund of our deposit, then took me back to my room in search of the money and grass.

Still sobbing, I reached for my compact to dry my eyes. In the reflection, a pale ghost stared back at me. Walking slowly to the bathroom, I flushed the plastic baggie down the toilet, pretending to pee, trying to get rid of any more evidence.

The angry cop wore the expression of a serial killer as he knocked me off the toilet seat onto the floor, screaming,

"Mala, bitch, you cross me!" as he stuck his withered hand down the throne, retrieving the wet buds. "You want to see your boyfriend again?" he demanded.

"He's my brother! Where is he?" I asked again frantically. There was no answer from the sadistic man, only his eyes roaming my body.

"Caliente," he muttered under his breath. Limping towards me, his feet thumping on the floor. I shook my hips at him.

His gun was his weapon; mine was my body. Flaunting it got me into this mess and now it would have to get me - and Patrick - out.

I slid my hand up his leg, caressing his crotch. His anger evaporated as his dull eyes widened.

"Sexy hombre. Me and you, tonight. But you must let my brother go." I pulled down my top seductively, revealing my tanned breasts to tantalize him, but the other cop walked in, so I quickly covered myself, knowing our pact was sealed when he took off my handcuffs and patted my ass on the way to the car.

As we drove back to the jail, I kept wondering if my predator would keep his part of the bargain and set us free. When we arrived, he went limping inside and brought out Patrick and that poor boy, handcuffed with a .357 Magnum pointed at their heads.

For the next hour we were driven through the hills with no idea where he was taking us.

"Take my money and leave us in the woods," I begged. I held the boy's hand in mind, drying his tears with my fingers.

The '70s Chevy finally came to a halt in the middle of the wilderness. The lowlife with the hangdog eyes took all of my money, handing me three ten-dollar bills and a card with the name and address of the hotel where he expected me to show up. "You come tonight or I track you down, puta."

Patrick and I jumped out quickly.

"If you let the boy go, I'll make it up to you," I begged.

"No, he has to be punished," came the reply.

After running through the muggy blazing inferno, we finally reached a small town where we crossed to the American side of the border. Finally free.

Stopping at the nearest beer bar, Patrick and I downed three straight shots of Tequila, licking the salt and lemon, while I called the Del.

Seconds later a black stretch limousine arrived. As we slid into the plush leather seats, the driver turned around and winked at me. It was Angel. Was I hallucinating again? Like divine intervention the radio was blaring that Beatles song *One Sweet Dream*, "wipe your tears, soon we'll be out of here. Pick up the bags and slip into the limousine. 1234567. All good children go to heaven...."

We pulled into the dazzling, majestic driveway of Hotel Del Coronado, a Victorian classic heritage landmark, for a century perched on twenty-six lush acres. The Del has long been a scene-setter for famous celebrities and filmmakers since 1888, the bright lights of Hollywood often taking center-stage.

Angel stepped out, grabbing our suitcases, with a big smile on his face.

"Bravo April, I knew you were a survivor. You smart cookie, girlfriend. I wanted to stick around and see you get out. Don't you know better not to do drugs and take off clothes in a Catholic country?"

"What does a Jewish girl know about that?" I answered humbly. I thought you'd come through and bail me out, hombre."

"You did it yourself, April. That was me, the janitor in the jail you see."

"How could you leave me in purgatory for all those hours?" I asked in dismay.

"I want to see you learn some lessons. You loco. Too reckless. You pay price. If I help you, you never know boyfriend risk life for you. And you save him. I meet you in lobby now. You fantastico! Hasta la vista," he said vanishing through the trees.

"That was so surreal," I thought, blown away by all the opulence of this landscape and my new found freedom.

As Patrick and I walked through the well-manicured lawns, gardens, and walkways, we stopped, mesmerized by the reflection of the salmon-colored, enchanting, castles in the tranquil, crystal, clear waters. This was like a fairytale in a rags to riches fantasy.

At the front desk I invented a bizarre fable to tell the warm, gracious hotel manager, as we had no credit cards and only thirty dollars in cash.

Still clad in my scanty, sand-encrusted suit, drunk and barefooted, Patrick in his briefs, I convinced the manager that we had gotten ripped off at The Rosarita Beach Hotel. It was my lucky day that he remembered me from previous weekends, not too long ago when I had checked in as husband and wife with an infamous actor, our stay billed to Universal Studios. This was before Patrick had moved in with me in the canyon.

A bellboy led us to a large luxurious suite in the seven-story, ocean towers overlooking the bay.

"Are you in the movies?" he asked incredulously, opening the door. "This place has been sold out for months. They gave you the penthouse and it's a full food and beverage comp. Enjoy your stay."

"Thank you," I said handing him a tip as he scurried out of the room.

That magical, fateful day, I felt the power of my street smarts, and the indestructible force of my guardian angel.

When we entered our suite, there was a bountiful fruit basket filled with camembert, brie, and a bottle of chilled French champagne with a note from the Manager welcoming me back.

"Did you know the man very well? I can't believe how you pulled this off so smoothly?" Patrick asked.

"Far be it to question the powers of a young blond girl with big tits scantily dressed," I answered coyly.

"Did you have to fuck that freak to get us out of jail?" Patrick asked, suspiciously. "Tell me the truth. I'll forgive you."

"It's polite to wait until you're asked. He thought that I was a puta and I'd show up at some dump tonight, stupid bastardo. Yeah, that fucker had class, I've never heard of anyone getting a refund from a Mexican jail, have you?" I said, cynically.

But would I ever be the same carefree creature or was I permanently scarred from the experience? That night we celebrated the Fourth or July from our sky-lit terrace, sipping Cordon Rouge Brut, munching on Beluga Caviar. We feasted away on Duck a l'orange, crustaceans and fluffy chocolate soufflés.

Patrick poured a glass of bubbly, approaching me with his well-toned, tanned body in his cut-off, tie-died denims. Clusters of multi colored firecrackers danced over our moonlight terrace. The setting was a backdrop for romance. Light and shadows shaded the magnificent hypnotic waters and as the sky darkened, we spoke only of matters of the heart, but I still felt afraid.

"I'll never forget how you saved my life today, April."

"Then you forgive me?"

"I love you, baby," he replied, hugging me tightly.

"Patrick, when you begged the guards to take your life and spare mine, that gave me the power to save us. My mother's the only one that has ever loved me so fiercely, even if we do have a sick relationship."

"Let's make toast to - forever," Patrick whispered as we kissed.

"The Buddhists believe that forever is only one minute. If you look the other way, the rainbow will disappear."

"I'll never look away, April. We should just go for it and make it legal."

I was going to marry the rugged Midwestern boy with the aquiline nose.

We clung to each other. He was my sanity and insanity. The moon rose from the roar of a midnight blue sea, floating in a fire engine sky, reflecting footsteps in the sand.

"See that old couple walking on the beach?" he asked.

"Yes, that's so sweet, he has his arm around her." I answered.

"I can just see us twenty years from now, honey, still making love, toasting each other on this same terrace," Patrick said as a shooting star appeared in the sky.

Chapter Sixteen

Devil's Disciples
Drugs, Demons & Derelicts
Anonymous
The Loser's Handbook

I think the worst thing about love between a very young and a somewhat older person is the terrifying loss of dignity that it seems to call for.
Tennessee Williams

Seems like only yesterday that the pastel pink peach blossoms had fallen off the tree and laid on the rich fertile soil like a blanket of dust welcoming in the spring, wearing all of her seduction. The grass was high and soft, sensual breezes were perfumed by sweet scents of trellises hanging on the vine woven of lilac lace. In the heat of the night I started thinking about why we attract certain people into our lives. Are we forever destined to be attracted to a certain type? Could it be that we souls wild at heart mirror certain facets of ourselves and some that we're lacking in and we desire. Maybe they're reflections of the secret selves we've tried to abandon. Perhaps we have some chemistry and karma to work out in this lifetime. Why was I always meeting fixer upper men with a list of resentments?

If I changed my consciousness could I change my life, or is there a blueprint that seals our fate?

Meanwhile, my phone was ringing off the hook and Yolanda's voice came piping through the hotline.

"Hello there, Miss April. I'm sick of isolating. Let's go out and play, girl."

I grabbed the phone. "Hi honey. I've got cabin fever. Meet me at the Gucci 13 step meeting on Rodeo Drive in an hour?"

"Oh yeah, what's up with the 13 steps? I gotta get my groove back."

"Oh you will at that meeting all the guys that have been sober forever try to get it on with the newcomers and celebrities. It amuses me," I shared.

"Hmmm," Yolanda said softly.

"Seems like the losers are really needy." I said. "There's a lot of hope, hopelessness and psychological revelations."

"Guess what Miss Moon, I ran into this hottie at the Sundowners meeting last Sunday and he was asking all about you, he's so fine. He's an extra, we worked on a film with him." she said. "Can you believe, his name is Big Iron. He's perfect for you, just your type. A bisexual Midwestern boy. Another dumb, broke dick."

"I know there's a lot of humanity, madness and redemption in the smoke filled rooms, but I'm glad you have such a high opinion of me."

"You earned it, girl, you know you just love your blue collar workers." she answered.

"Look who's talking," I teased. "Your last boy-friend's credit was only good after he was dead for two years. Then a letter came in the mail from Discovery Card and they offered him a $50,000 loan."

"Stop fuckin' with me," Yolanda answered arro-gantly.

"Well, I don't know if Big Iron's such a cool idea. When I asked my Jungian shrink for advice he said, 'Just remember April, love tortures and purifies the soul. Just don't ever go out with anyone that's your type.' See you at the meeting, hon."

My indigo blue Z sped down Sunset Boulevard heading for Beverly Hills. The wickedly sexy beauty wearing a sweet smile was waiting for me at the church. My drinking partner and I had polished off three bottles of Cordon Rouge Brute champagne over lunch last week, becoming falling down drunks. Was it any wonder that we were on the wagon.

Yolanda was wearing platform heels and was poured into a low necked, flowered, slinky, sun-dress. As we walked through the crowded church all heads were turned in our direction. When we were seated and after the reading of the 12 Steps, I glanced around the room as I locked eyes with Big Iron. The speaker had begun but I couldn't focus, I was getting so aroused checking out his six pack abs and long lanky legs in a crotch-tight pair of faded jeans and suede cowboy boots, looking like he held life's secret in his groin. I hardly heard a word of the share. Another perk, he looked like Jeff Bridges in his prime. At the coffee break I was licking the chocolate off the tops of the donuts while a lot of cuckoo birds were checking us out. This hot looking guy wanted me to beep him.

"How long have you been sober?" I asked.

"About forty-five minutes. You rock. Are you going towards Hollywood? My car's broke."

He was history and no sooner than I fled from him I could feel Big Iron sweeping my body amorously with his eyes. Two minutes later he was hitting on me hard, grimacing.

"Howdy. I haven't seen you here before," he said excitedly. "Are you a newcomer?"

"I've been on the fringe of the program for awhile now." I answered.

"You wanna leave and go to the Cheesecake Factory, and grab a bite?" he asked.

AA was famous for bad coffee and I accepted the invitation.

After a lot of sexual tension and a casual dinner, I realized that Big Iron wasn't the one. I asked him about his background one night over cappuccinos.

"Where's your family?"

"My folks are all low bred, trailer trash where I come from. Last time I gone home to visit, my older sister climbed out of the sack half naked trying to tantalize me. Bare ass brazen bitch. She used to rape me when I was a kid at the shack after she'd had a quart of whiskey. It would've been easier being with a boy. So I spit at the sleazy slut and I was outta there."

"Sounds like you have a lot of anger towards women."

"When I get mad I try and sweat it out at this bathhouse on Santa Monica Boulevard. Now I want you to know, I ain't gay or nothin'. The bath house gets me burnt out, steamy saunas, guys kissin' and getting' it on in there. Disgustin'. I get rejected in there sometimes too."

"Have you ever been married?" I asked.

"Not to a woman. But maybe it's cause I don't like spending the night with 'em. Sleepin' is a very personal thing." He answered rubbing knees with me under the table then said, "You drip with sexuality, but I get this weird feeling yer too much into the flesh and you'll try and manipulate me."

Oh help, another case of confused chromosomes. I contemplated intently, then I decided to overlook his shortcomings. He knew how to use his hands under the table indiscreetly and I fantasized him pounding me hard with his long hammer. After all I was a size queen. That night I dragged him home up on the hill. I awakened the next morning, wearing a short black flimsy nightie with black thigh high stockings and red garters on underneath. I started kissing the nape of his neck, nuzzling up next to him, massaging his back as he started to rise.

"Good morning, does that feel good, honey. Are you waking up?" I asked.

Big Iron rubbed the sheet. "Can't you see, I am up baby, and I need some more comfortin'. Lie down next to me and hold me."

I sat up in bed and started brushing my hair looking at myself admiringly in my Betty Boop hand mirror.

"What are you doin'? You don't need no makeup, you wildcat. Stop teasin' me. Every time I look at them long firm legs and flat stomach I get hard, baby. But ah don't want you to feel this is just about sex."

By now I was almost doubled over with laughter. He pulled me down on the bed, his hands roaming my body, easing them down between my thighs, pulling on my lace panties.

"I know you want it as much as I do."

I smiled seductively. "Honey, how about a chocolate kiss?"

Jumping on top of me, his hands sliding around my backside in a state of rapture, he sighed. "I don't think I was ever with a woman like I was with you last night. I mean really been there. Not just performing, trying to convince myself."

"You really made me feel good last night too, honey."

"Did you know you've got the greatest tits in town and I jus' love older women."

We kissed, clinging to each other.

"Oh Big Iron, you're so romantic. Do I satisfy your needs, honey?"

"April baby, I've never slept with a woman like that before last night. You give me back my manhood." He answered bewildered.

I asked him, "Why is it different with me?"

"I think it's because I know I'm satisfying you too, you nympho. The next morning I always wanna run, get out quick. Today I wanna stay in bed with you all day long."

I wasn't so sure I could hang out with this brain dead dick all day but over coffee and sweet buns it would be fun.

"That sounds great, honey. but I have to leave later because I have a wardrobe fitting and an appointment with Philippe for my sculpture nails. Think I'll paint them slut red."

"Do you love me? I've told all my friends at the Amber Connection that you're my girl. Let's live together. I love you. I want ya to have my babies."

Was this guy for real? It must have been my well educated tongue, I thought giving him an apathetic look.

"Hollywood is really in my blood, honey. I'm chasing after fame. I'm going to be the next Jean Harlow, a famous sex goddess you'll see."

"Is that why?" he asked with haunted blue eyes.

"You're scaring me away talking like that. Baby, don't make me hurt you." I answered coldly.

"Why are you running from me? Is it our age difference? How old are you anyway? You never would tell me." He asked with intensity.

"That's for me to know and you to figure out," I laughed. "I don't deal in years, just spirit." I quipped, pushing him away.

"You're so Hollywood." He said with a tone of hostility in his voice.

"That's what I love most about me. I can laugh at myself and cry at the same time and never be tamed. I'm just an irreverent butterfly,"

"What're ya laughin' at. Have you been smokin' that wackie tabackie? Better not be drinkin' either. I'm gonna strip ya down an' if you try an' slip out the evasive back door on me, I'll hunt ya down and throw ya right back in the sack where ya belong. Jus' with me. I never kin' figure out you women."

Big Iron jumped out of bed putting a cassette in his ghetto blaster, strutting his wares around the bedroom. Looking at himself admiringly in the mirror, lifting up his T-shirt, grunting and patting his well-tanned stomach.

Putting on a tape of YMCA by The Village People, he danced to the beat of the music.

"Do you do that all the time? Get that loose with all the guys? Or am I that special?" He asked, sounding like a whining ignoramus.

"I just love your blue-collar mentality. It makes me feel so superior." I started doing exercises with dumbbells on a slant board, stretching seductively, laughing, breathing as if I were in labor, my breasts bouncing up and down. "God, I can't believe you. You're so conceited. Get over yourself." I smirked at him.

He looked angry. "Are you jus' playing me? Am I just another Boy-toy? I'm gonna screw you properly again after I put on my cow punk metal and rockabilly tapes and drink my protein."

Oh my God, I started laughing convulsively. Big Iron grabbed a bottle of protein powder from his bag and started gulping it down.

"Would you still love me if I told you I killed a man?" He asked urgently.

"Depending on what you used to kill him with." I answered, gasping for breath. He started prancing around the room camping it up.

"My name is Big Iron. We get it up for U.S. Steel. On a scale from one to ten, I'm an 18. I'm low and firm and full of sperm." He laughed crazily. "I'm a heavy hitter, but I got too old for the tightrope. Gotta lose a little weight, I gotta get back in shape. Pump more iron." Big Iron ran into the bathroom and came out wearing a G-string, hard hat, tinted blue/black sunglasses, arm pad, knee pads, and a leather belt strapped around his waist with blunt instruments dangling down between his tool.

I know that I'm a weird chick attracting whacks but God help me, is this the end? Is he going to kill me? This is so eerie, what a calamity. He'll need a crash helmet for an encounter with me, I thought in a panic.

"Are you in an excited state, honey? I must admit baby, I'm gettin' back in shape. I want you to want it, beg for it. God, I love the feel of a woman's warm body next to mine. Is your body thirsty for mine yet? Is your mind ready to obey me cunt?" He demanded with a savage stare. The evil degenerate groped me fiercely, trying to pin my arms back to the bed. Evoking my constant swing of fear to fury I escaped a near death experience running out the door buck naked rather than becoming another statistic wrapped in a body bag, headlining the local news. I should have paid heed to my mother's warnings, I thought regretfully that day.

Chapter Seventeen

Jerusalem West
Nate N' Al
(Beverly Hills Deli)

*You never get over being a child as long as you
have a mother to go to.*
Sarah Orne Jewett

It was a lazy sunday. I was walking down North
Beverly Drive entering the exclusive deli "Jerusalem
West", in the morning glare where mother and I
were meeting for brunch. I was dressed in a micro-
mini skirt and a long Chiffon see-through top. My
frizzy hank of hair was braided and adorned with
a headband. Mother bore the resemblance of a
20's or 30's vampy movie star. Her Vidal Sassoon
bobbed chestnut hair and soft hazel eyes flecked
with gold framed her gaunt cheekbones.

"You didn't call me when you got home last
night. You know that I can't sleep when I don't
hear from you. With the diseased bums you meet
at the studios no wonder I'm always worried sick,"
she said sternly.

"I went out with this guy after we wrapped last
night. I got in late," I answered. "He flipped over me."

"There's no future with an actor. You should
know that by now. April dear, you've had enough

bad experiences with those ne'er-do-wells. I won't always be here to take care of you."

That thought had never occurred to me. I was an irresponsible whacked-out woman with a seriously responsible lunatic mother.

"Yes you will," I answered sadly, studying the menu.

"You have no self esteem April. I suppose he's another country bumpkin. Did he ply you with liquor? It's poison. You know Jews can't drink, don't you? And I suppose you paid for his dinner," she said, raising her shrill voice and frowning at me.

"Yes, I did. He didn't have any money, but you're so material. I'm hanging out with some artists also." I said, glaring at her.

"They could be murderers. I saw one on TV today that was your type. You'd probably go out with him if you met him on the streets." she preached.

"Oh fuck, why do you say those things? You're so negative and overbearing." I sighed, looking at her with annoyance. She used to ruin my day. Now I had learned to switch the channel.

"Those bums have all the qualifications. Let's face it, dear, with your history of men with criminal records, they could even be dope dealers. What do you know? Or junkies. I hope you're not smoking any of that Hash. They're all idiots in India, you know," she said with disapproval.

The lines that came out of her mouth were so insane. She was such a bitch. "Stop it, you're driving me crazy. I'm having enough trouble and struggle.

Have you seen the news. There might be a Screen Extras Guild strike."

"Don't worry, you won't starve, I'll help." She promised reassuringly. "April dear, haven't you been watching the news? They spray the pot plants with formaldehyde. People are dropping dead like flies these days."

"No kidding. That's embalming fluid. No wonder pot's not legal. And with Tricky Dicky as President that's also a factor," I frowned.

"It will never be legal. The government doesn't want retards. They need bright, intelligent citizens. Marijuana alters the mind and makes zombies out of people. And speaking of zombies, how's your girl-friend, Yolanda? She's a very pretty girl. But is she on drugs, dear? If she ever spends the night, April, you should lock up your money and jewelry. Those studio girls are trash. They come from trashy backgrounds."

I could no longer control my laughter. This woman was so bizarre, and I'd smoked a roach in anticipation of a food orgy at Jerusalem West.

"You're acting very silly, dear. Don't be so smart. You'd better behave yourself, young lady, or you'll get bupkus from me. Now, shape up, April. What would you like for lunch?" she asked.

"I'm starving. Everything on this menu looks del-ish," I answered, my mouth watering.

"This deli's high classed. Whatever you like when you're with your mother. The Goose That Laid the Golden Egg."

She's always throwing in my face whatever she does for me. Talk about laying on the Jewish guilt.

She's the queen of that. I'm going to pig out, I thought.

"I'll have a knockwurst, a potato knish, kishka, a side of chopped liver, stuffed derma, then I think a three decker skyscraper with corned beef, pastrami, brisket, rare roast beef, salami and slaw. Russian dressing on the side. And raw onions. No bread, just lettuce. My diet, you know."

"You're not on pot are you, April? You look like you're anesthetized dear."

"Of course not," I said, self mockingly sipping my coke looking around the room in a daze.

My mother started waving at the server. "Waiter, waiter, young man," she called out to the gay blade with spiked hair style like a porcupine. "Don't get too friendly with the waiter. Well at least he's not blonde and he looks Jewish. You'd never start up with him," she said disapprovingly.

"Mother, he's a homo. I was putting him on. I really dig your new haircut. You look beautiful," I said in a loving way, sucking up to her.

"April, pull your hair off your face. You come to me looking like a lunatic with a skirt that's so short it should be worn by a teenager. Your hair looks like a wild animal's. You're a beauty if I could only see your face. I'll send you to the best beauty shop on North Canon Drive and maybe if you're well groomed you might attract a decent Jewish man. Your breasts look matronly and your speaking with a lisp. Have you seen your cousin the plastic surgeon lately? He must have pumped you up pretty good," she scolded, putting the napkin over her lap.

My cousin was famous. I called him the Leonardo Da Vinci of Beverly Hills. My good fortune was every west side insecure bitch's dream.

"Your lips look like Donald Duck. Oy. I'm fritzing," she said.

"Well you always told me to hook up with a professional man, and he's Jewish," I said.

"Cousins don't marry cousins. They make crazy babies. Talk that way, and his wife might throw him out like a dog and send him to you," she said.

"I'll never forget when I came out of the anesthetic in the operating room and the radio was playing *Mrs. Robinson*. I wonder was I hallucinating, or was the universe laughing at me. Just for the record, mother, the only things that are real about me are my breasts," I said.

"You just have no mazel to hook up with that drunken Irishman," she said.

"His name is Patrick, Mother."

"He learned from his father to bum around in the bars all night long and cheat on a woman. At least Patrick's father worked and supported his family. You've been paying all the bills for years," she said.

"No one is ever right for me, unless they live in Homlby Hills like you do, are they?" I asked.

"April, dear, you're a girl with a dollar in your pocket. A woman of means, and for a Jew you were born with a beautiful nose. You'll do the best you can. You always do! At my expense. Even at your party Patrick's mother asked me why you were kissing all the men, but not your husband. Gottinu."

"What do you expect? You can only take Orange County so far. Next," I answered.

The waiter arrived with lunch. I scarfed down most of the skyscraper, the mustard dripping down my chin. Groaning. Moments later I felt so drained emotionally and guilty for eating such fattening food.

"I feel nauseous. Can we send the sandwich back?" I pleaded.

"April, your hair's in the food and you've already eaten most of it. Finish your lunch. I devote my whole life to you, just so you can throw it away for Patrick, that nothing. At least if you ever do meet someone decent, don't let him know you're all used up. I'm surprised you still have a tooth in your mouth, dear, after all of your one night stands." She said with evil intent.

Well, obviously I didn't follow her advice. And I don't even have a single cavity. But in the gist and sum of things, Patrick was the only man that ever mattered to me. One day in my den in Laurel Canyon I found an old faded photograph of us standing under a waterfall in Maui. At that moment I realized that I'd never love anyone like that again. I wish she'd stop nagging me. Doesn't she know how much pain I'm in? I thought, looking down at the table.

"April, you can do better than Patrick. What's there to miss? You were his slave and scrubwoman. You ran a flophouse for him and his boyfriends for years and threw your youth away without any regard for your mother. And how about the wear and tear on your body?" she said.

"But mother, I really love him, and I'm still young, you're so negative!" I protested.

"April, dear, you never had anything with him. You could have had lots of respectable nice rich men that wanted you, but you'll probably go running back to him, you always do." she said.

I had had it. This cold woman sitting across the table from me would never understand. I had to bail.

"All right, mother. Let's get the check. I have to go. I have an early hooker call tomorrow. And I have to stop at Ball Beauty Supply and pick up some phony eyelashes. Please watch the news for me and tell me what's going on with the Industry. Thanks for lunch," I said giving her a hug.

"Chicken little, you always think the sky is going to fall on you. You'll never starve. Young man, young man. Just remember, April, the struggle is the most fun in life," she said waving at the waiter. "I'm an optimist and you're so pessimistic, dear." she said with a saccharine smile.

The boy approached us with a check.

Oh sure, I thought, being broke is not my comfort zone. Maybe I could hit her up for some money on the way out and walk off all those sinful calories at the mall. In spite of it all, I loved her because she was the only mother I'd ever have. Thank God. Only one to customer, please.

Dipping her fingers in the water glass she asked, "Do you take visa, waiter?" He nodded and she handed him her card while looking at me. "You know you're my life, April. You can thank me by calling your Aunt and apologizing for getting drunk and making a fool out of yourself at the Seder. My sister is burned up at you. I hear that you got a five year old child drunk," she scolded.

"I'm on the wagon again, and it's no hayride. Manischevitz wine tasted rich after not drinking for three days. And the child got me drunk!" I answered.

As we walked out of the dimly lit din into the blinding California sun, a Brinks truck drove by and the driver jumped out.

"Now remember dear, don't ever stand in front of an armed man, and don't let that alley cat sleep in your bed. Love you. Call me the minute you get home." she smiled sweetly, kissing me on the cheek.

Every time I pass by that deli I peer through the window staring at our favorite booth, now occupied by strangers. I'm regretful, and in denial that she and I would never spend another Yom Kippur or Rosh Hashana together again in my lifetime. Now I recall her ghost. How naïve was I to believe that she was infallible.

Chapter Eighteen
Lance Lust

Sigh no more ladies, sigh no more, men were deceivers ever.
Shakespeare

Sometimes his streaked yellow hair reminded me of mom's own lemon meringue pie. Not bad coming straight out of a Clairol bottle No. 24: Born Blond. Lance was a six foot one scarecrow, arms and legs like tentacles, teeth as white and even as a picket fence. When he looked at me with his piercing blue eyes, I felt like I was being seduced by the Pacific Ocean. This loser went straight from West Point to hard core in a single bound. Call it talent or was it his scent of madness that lured me into his entrapment.

The only talent Lance had was in the bedroom. Like a cardinal bird he was hatched in a plywood shack in Humboldt, Tennessee. The nocturnal creature prowled the hard lands, seeding the world.

"Baby cakes, let me get another Lucky Lite beer and my Saratoga Golds," he asked.

After he'd gulped down a few beers he became melancholy, hung over from the night before, experiencing another mood swing. Then he'd go on a crying jag.

"You know I try to do good, honey, don't you? I read the Bible every day," he whined as one of his religious programs blared from the radio. "You know that I don't mean to ever hurt you, honey," he said sheepishly.

I don't think he tried to hurt women intentionally, but his over inflated ego ruled his ever ready dick. Even as far back as Bayou Territory women had been too easy for him. Sex was like a dress rehearsal wearing duller climaxes after he'd tired of his prey.

Lance was born a movie star. He was seduced by the Hollywood hype with easy money and the promise of success, never really liking to work. Before landing in L.A., the ex-con climbed the somber concrete walls of the Terminal Island Federal Correctional Facility after painting his face with black shoe polish, then robbing the Bank of Hawaii.

And can you believe that when they sprung him loose for being an ideal prisoner, he ran an orphanage for emotionally disturbed monks. Although he was probably more emotionally disturbed than any of them.

His favorite career was as an X-rated skin flick idol.

"I can make love to all these pretty little chicks and get paid for it at the same time," he bragged. "Well someone has to do it, it might as well be me. I never met a woman that I couldn't satisfy," he reminded me when he was in a drunken stupor.

"So I go with the flow, flesh was just another lesson I had to learn. My life has always been a fight and a wound which I dream of being healed."

Chapter Nineteen
A Sexual Tragedy
Lust
The '80s

Since earliest manhood the center of his life has been pleasure with women, the giving and taking of it, not with weak indulgence, dependently, but with the power and pride of a richly feathered male bird among the hens.
Tennessee Williams

Thanksgiving Day in the Canyon was a primitive festival of nature. Through my stained glass windows, rosy red-breasted sparrows and bluebirds chirped and splashed in their birdbath. I was sitting on my sky terrace at noon when Ginger's voice came shrieking through the service:

"Pick up! Pick up! I know you're hiding in there! I hope you're planning to show for my traditional Thanksgiving dinner. I have your present," Ginger continued. "Remember when you were in London shopping at the Chelsea Antique Market and Lust, the actor bumped into you? He wants to meet you. He just broke up with his girlfriend. He got pissed off just because she was working at Whip City. He's in a blue mood."

"I'll cheer him up," I said, knowing that my sexual fantasies were about to be fulfilled, choosing not to remember that I was living with someone.

"I tried to do that last night," Ginger said, "he was so hard I nearly got shoved through my wrought iron headboard into the next door neighbor's apartment. I can hardly walk today. He's all yours," she continued, "He'll pick you up about four."

Ginger's digs were at the Marina Del Rey. She was one of those Heidi Fleiss characters. They called her 'Madame Marina'.

"See you later, Ging. I'll bring some Piper from Greenblatt's," I answered.

Lust was born a superstar; I was well bred. From 1969 to 1981 he had been one of the top international porno stars. When I lived in New York, I was a top model for Playboy Magazine and could be found on almost every cover at the newsstands on 42nd Street. When he was a cadet at West Point, I'd been sipping Mouton Cadet and eating Beluga caviar at '21'.

Lust had flown into Rome to do a film. I was sitting on the Via Veneto, fanning myself with the menu, staring at cobblestones and out of work actors; the actors had named it the 'Via Vomital'. A soft breeze through the overhanging trees kept the sun from being too hot on my back. Suddenly one of the cowboys started shrieking:

"That's Lance Lust, the infamous movie star."

"I hear he has the biggest cock on the continent," exclaimed one of the envious actors.

"I worked on one film where they flew him in especially just to fuck three chicks,"said another.

"I watched him get it up on cue all day long."

The sun was forming a muted colored rainbow, melting into the Cinzano umbrellas. I watched him from afar, telling myself that one day I'd have a liaison with the great decadent Lust. I was sure that fate would intervene.

Chimes from the Swiss doorbell clanged at four o'clock. The big white 1955 Bentley had climbed to the top reaching Wonderland. When I came to the door I looked like a mixture of a '40s diva retro-romantic gypsy and a silent screen star. I was wearing a low black backless, silky, peasant dress, bare legs, spike heeled strappy sandals, and hoop earrings. My lips glowed with Siren Red shimmer gloss, and I reeked of Chanel No. 5. That's what Marilyn would have worn, wouldn't she? I was ready to explore my wilder side with this fine looking mysterious new man.

When first we met I knew that I'd found the wild sex I'd been looking for.

"Come on in," I said, flashing him a self conscious smile. "Would you like a glass of wine? My housemate's out of town."

"I brought my Lucky Light beer," Lust smiled popping open a bottle.

Nothing existed but the two of us and the harvest moon against a wick colored sky in this liquid spill of night.

"I have an affinity for platinum blondes. You certainly are beautiful," he said taking a long, lingering look at me. He couldn't even begin to imagine what I'd been through to come this far. That night he asked no questions.

I was anticipating that this would be the best Thanksgiving Day present that I'd ever gotten. I picked up a bottle of wine and a corkscrew, handing them to Lust, unconsciously flipping my long, wavy hair.

"No thank you, honey," he said. "Could you get me a beer first, please. I brought five cases with me, but if I run out we can take the shortcut to my house on Sunset Plaza Drive." He'd felt immediately at ease with me, but then again what woman hadn't he felt that way about. I came back with his beer in a frozen tulip-stemmed flute glass.

He took a vile out of his pocket filled with a white powdery substance, dipping a spoon into it, then holding it carefully to my nostril. The cocaine exploded in my head like a sunburst floating in the sky. My pupils grew larger and my cheeks were flushed as the bitter taste trickled down my numb throat. I stared at his eyes mesmerized, then handed the spoon back to him. My head was floating into the chandelier.

"I've really been looking forward to our meeting. Let's go downstairs and have a drink." I said taking his arm.

I showed him down the spiral staircase that led to the knotty pine wine cellar. Blue and purple embers were glowing from the stone fireplace. A café table was set with long-stemmed Waterford crystal glasses. A bottle of Louis Roederer Cristal

Brut champagne was chilling in a sterling silver ice bucket.

"April, Ginger told me that you were very sexy but you exceed my wildest expectations. I love your big hair. You look like a dandelion ready to pollinate," Lust said looking amused. I adored his charming persona.

"You're a wildly appealing man," I found myself saying.

He pulled me closer to his well toned, tanned body,

"Baby cakes, let's take a passionate journey into the unknown together. I like you a lot. You're an intriguing woman."

I thought about my boyfriend, Patrick. Poor Patrick. I felt a twinge of guilt. My emotions were so confused. I thought about Patrick but not for too long. We kissed, he started stroking my hair, kissing my eyelids.

"I can't believe your boyfriend would leave town and trust you here alone. You look so intriguing with the candlelight silhouetting your face." I couldn't help wondering how many other women this flamboyant man had fed the same line to.

Lust started kissing my bare shoulders. I opened my lips, feeling the warmth of his tongue in my mouth as he ran his hands all over my body. I knew right then that my life would never be the same.

"I hear that you just broke up with your girlfriend," I asked coyly.

"I haven't had tremendous success with relationships, but there are many women in my life that
I'm still friends with."

I smiled, "Well, it's always nice to have friends."

Drinking the foam off of his beer, he paused, "I'd
be really happy if I could just stick with one woman.
Would you ever want to get married again?" he
asked looking intensely at me.

"I've ruled out marriage. It destroys the romance,
not to mention the sex life!"

Lust pulled me over to the chaise lounge, pushing me back into it then climbing on top of me. He
pulled up my dress with his eager hands, nuzzling his
head between my legs licking me, the stubble of his
beard and tongue tickling the spot.

Everything was so glamorous and romantic that
evening. The night was enhanced by sensual soft
lighting. Slowly I wrapped my thighs around his
shoulders. I never got to Ginger's house. We celebrated each other, filling the dusk with our desire.

After my first orgasm galloping bareback over
the sand dunes in Carmel, now sharing the pleasures
of the flesh with Lance was just as intense as when I
was a young, innocent girl.

"I'm afraid to close my eyes that I might lose
consciousness. What if I wake up and you're gone
and this was just a lucid dream." he said sheepishly.

We fell asleep listening to the crickets bathed by
the full moon. That night was the beginning of my
downfall.

Lust had starred in over two hundred porno flicks
and loops, but his most pleasurable role in a film

was *Lipps and McCain*. He portrayed Lipps and in one scene did a loop with three Girl Scouts. By the end of the scene, I can assure you that everyone got their cookies off.

He was resurrected on Easter Day. The nocturnal creature prowled the night where maidens were born to flower for an hour perfumed with silicone cleavage and gingerbread brains.

He alone held the key to this ludicrous side show while trying to seed the world, reeling them in with his long thick worm, rolling up the sun with the pagan princesses of the night.

That was before I held him captive in my English Tudor hillside retreat, and my life became out of control.

The year was 1981. A few nights after the July 30th murders on Wonderland Avenue, where four of John Holmes coke cohorts were bludgeoned to death.

I was alarmed by the sound of a gunshot echoing across my house. Lust was crouched on the floor, bare-chested, hair disheveled, a towel draped around his body. He held a .357 Magnum in his shaky hand, his finger on the trigger, screaming, "Bitch!"

I ran into my den, then was frozen, unable to move. Trying to speak, the words were mute in my mouth.

"You cunt, you're making me crazy, you beautiful bitch! I'm suicidal and I want to share the grave with you."

"Put that gun down, we can talk this is lunacy." I said in a stern manner.

"I wanna fuck, you wanna talk," he said guzzling his beer, flinging the gun down, chipping my glass table, then lighting a cigarette, swilling down an alka seltzer.

"I didn't mean to cause you pain," I answered, obsessing on the hole in the wall.

"The only dependable distraction I have to forget my problems is making love to you," he said, pausing for a moment. "That was just a potshot. I thought it might get your attention," he said, smoke filtering out of his flared nostrils. "Let's comfort each other a little," he begged with an insincere smile.

"You freaked me out," I scolded.

"It isn't just you, April. I'm getting a lot of pressure from the feds about Johnny Holmes and the murders. They might drag me in at any moment for questioning."

"Tell me more," I begged.

"I can't reveal all my secrets to you," he said pacing the floor in a chain-smoking frenzy.

"Please you can confide in me,"

"I can trust myself inside of you. I know every little part of your body, but I never could figure out your mind," he answered continually wrinkling his brow.

"I'll try not to judge you, but you're so self-absorbed with your substantially sized cock, that you can't relate to me on any other level than sex," I said picking up a roach, lighting it and holding it up to my mouth, pulling my plush velvet robe tighter around my body. Then pouring myself another glass of wine.

"You always made me feel like I was worthless," he answered his voice cracking.

"It's all about your huge ego. I need a deep connection of the spirit and flesh. You're passive aggressive," I answered leaning back on the couch as he continued pacing the floor in his bare feet.

"Aren't you the noble one attempting to keep time and destiny from crumbling around you," he answered.

"You're either miserably drunk and gloomy or elated most of the time. You need to check yourself into rehab and see a psychiatrist. Maybe they better bump up your medication. You need someone who specializes in mood disorders," I said.

"I drug and drink myself into oblivion just to escape the chatter in my head," he answered.

"When you get hyper and hostile, your behavior is unpredictable," I said angrily. I've given you enough last chances.

"I'd rather have any physical illness than being diagnosed as bipolar. It's a biological based illness. It's not my fault," he said panic in his eyes.

"Welcome all dysfunctional compulsive alcoholics, drag queens, and drug addicts to my hillside halfway house," I said with disgust. "I feel like I'm living in an asylum."

"You're so cynical and analytical, April, your greatest enemy is your brilliance," he said touching my cheek with his clammy cold hands, his left eye twitching then staring up at the ceiling.

I opened up my heart-shaped pillbox, swallowing a Seconal down with another glass of wine. It tasted refreshing sliding down my parched throat. Soon I hoped the pill would kick in and hopefully nothing would matter, even surviving this crazy-maker.

"Let's face it, we're both cursed with the timeless struggles of being artists," he said moving in closer, flashing his crooked smile at me.

"In my heart I'm mainly a poet. You're a bizarre skin flick actor addicted to your own drama and you call that art?" I asked coldly.

"Blah, blah, blah," he muttered under his demented breath.

"I know you've been partying with that scum-bag slasher crowd again," I said impatiently.

"Okay, I'd been wasted for three days straight on Wonderland with Holmes before the murders. I just needed a place to crash when you kicked me out again."

Lust wore the dissipated face of a man that had given up.

"You're a fucking drunk and a speed freak hooked on China white blow. You promised me that you'd get clean if I let you come back," I said with a look of exasperation.

"How about your pill popping, and pot and wine?" he asked trying to rationalize his addiction.

"At least I don't use hard drugs. Jesus Christ turned water into red wine at a wedding, and he also ate pot bread. The pills wipe out my anxiety attacks from living with you," I answered knowing that was a poor excuse riddled with guilt.

"Tell it to those freaks at AA. Let's face it, we're both flawed and we're not going to get fixed," he shouted.

"Well, at least I'm trying to straighten out my life and I don't want to get dragged into your vortex. You slip in and out in moments when your shadow self takes over," I said pouring myself another glass.

"I might end up in jail doing hard time being framed as an accomplice of these hit crimes. You don't think that I'd commit murder, do you? You don't even care."

"You've betrayed me. I'm just a convenient situation. I want you out."

Just then the voice of a detective came piping through his answering service. "I'm looking for Lust. Call Detective Brown immediately at Hollywood precinct, homicide. It's about John Holmes. We have him in here for questioning."

"I'm really paranoid about being grilled by the pigs," he said resting his head on his sweaty palms. "I try to convince myself that I must go on and kick my habit but I'm not really here," he sobbed. "I'm broken."

"Calm down and try to get some sleep. You'll need it when the man interrogates you," I coaxed.

"My problem is that I never really knew how to live without ignoring the consequences of damnation. I wonder if I'll know how to die gracefully. For me life has lost its magic." He reached out to me with pleading eyes as I ran out of the room.

I awakened puffing on the sweet grass, staring up into the sky. The sun looked like a buttermilk pancake and I wondered if anyone else in Laurel Canyon was as stoned and thinking as dark thoughts as I was. A hundred years from today nothing would matter. Certainly not Lust, I realized that I was in grave danger. What if I was involved in an interrogation?

With a sudden burst of energy, I slid out of bed, kicked off my sandals creeping into the living room. I realized that he might be a murderer, I had to leave him, and get rid of the remains from last night.

The coffee table was littered with empty beer cans, ashtrays filled with cigarette butts, roaches, a half full, stained wineglass and an empty bottle of Merlot. The smell of stale camembert cheese melting into the table made my stomach turn. I wondered how many glasses I had drank last night. I had amnesia. I needed some caffeine.

Today I felt that aching sinking feeling grinding into the pit of my stomach. Black reality sped in with the first sip of my morning coffee. *But I was in control, wasn't I? How painful to love someone that you know it could never work with* I mused. What had I lost? How could I lose something that I never had.

Suddenly alarmed, I heard Lust try to fit his key into the massive wooden wrought iron Spanish door. He pushed it open, staggering in, flicking on the stereo, then pulling a bottle of beer out of the refrigerator. Coming towards me,

"Do you want a drink?" he asked.

Somehow he felt no need to explain about last night. There was no guilt. I lit a joint and handed it to him. Lust hadn't shaved for a week and he was wearing a white torn T-shirt and faded jeans, reeking of stale beer, cigarettes and Savage cologne. His skin was sallow and there were dark circles under his eyes. He stared at me intensely. "What's wrong, honey?" he gulped.

"Reality. There are too many stone walls surrounding us, like your habit. One day I woke up and realized that the size of a man's cock isn't the barometer for love. I'm cutting you loose. No sooner than the blood had dried on Wonderland Avenue, you stay out all night again?" I said, walking away. When I reached the bedroom, some of my anger had evaporated.

As nightfall approached I lay in my king-size bed, frightened and edgy. A stream of light crept in under the door. Jumping up quickly, I switched on the Tiffany lamp on my nightstand. That night he went on a wild drunk, entering my bedroom through the veranda.

"You'll never get rid of me. You can't give it all to me, then take it away. You're gonna get me off any time I want you to, you lousy bitch! You're the most oversexed woman that I've ever been with. Don't play games with me!" he screamed. "You cunt from hell, I'm not just some boy-toy that you can throw away when you get bored," he ranted on. "I'll make you feel good. You're still in love with me. You're no different than any of the other whores! I'm famous."

"You confuse sex for love, intensity for intimacy and drama for passion." I said, my long tresses bouncing behind me as I walked away from him. "Your career is so over with your nine inch dick, you asshole, You're so insecure. You were fun to play with for a while. I'm done. I've never heard so many Hollywood lies."

"Miss rich bitch, user of all men. When you get bored and it doesn't go your way, you disappear in a puff of smoke. I loved you more than any woman alive. I entered the body of my wildest dream. Now you want to treat me like one of your tricks."

"I have too much self esteem to let you use me anymore," I said.

"I still have a neurotic need for you," he begged. "Though the last time we got it on it was just like fucking a beautiful body without any emotion."

"I just got tired of your trophy girls," I said reaching for a robe.

"Just give me one honest answer. Do you still have any feelings for me?"

"I can't love. Life is just an experience. Get out!"

He grabbed me, slapping me across the face so hard it almost knocked me unconscious, throwing me down on the bed, then trying to pull me close to him. I was silent, afraid to say anything that might make him throw another tantrum. I felt like the end was near. The man was a maniac, especially when he was drunk.

"Baby cakes, tonight I want to make you happy. I love you. I'll make love to you all night long."

"Please let me go," I begged.

"You're pure sensual womanhood. Can you blame me?" he asked.

"I can't live with you or fuck you anymore." I said sadly.

Lust was into me on a love-hate level. Mostly hate, for he despised women. And now he realized that he'd met his match.

He moved closer trying to tantalize me so that he could be in control, knowing that his only weapon was sex.

"I'm just sorry that you don't love me anymore. I tried to satisfy you. Tell me that you want it. I'm not angry with you anymore. You can expect me to flip out every now and then. At least I care enough for you to let you know the score." He suddenly went through another mood swing, trying to win me over again. "Honey, I love you. Is it about the murders?" he asked.

I was aware that I was involved in a sadomasochistic relationship, each partner frequently changing roles.

Months later my relationship with Lust had all the intimacy of a one-night stand. I felt the power. Time to get out alive from the demonic forces.

"I'm sick of living with a burnt out porno star. I'll give you about one hour to get your clothes out of here!" I screamed.

"But first I'm going to give you my coming home present and it won't cost you a dime, bitch!" he shouted grabbing my filigreed gold choker, pulling it tighter around my neck. "Down on your knees, do it the way I taught you to. I can use you any time I want!"

I spit in his face sobbing loudly, trying to free myself, but he grabbed me by my loose hair, breaking an expensive wine goblet and throwing it at the beveled mirror, screaming, "Suck my cock!" as he unzipped his fly, pulling it out of his pants, gagging me with his urgency.

I tried getting away but he held my head with one hand, pushing my mouth down harder and harder, ripping off my scarlet lace nightgown and bikini panties, slapping me so hard I winced. I jumped up out of bed, running towards the spiral staircase. Before I could get away, he leaped in front of me, throwing me down on the hardwood floor. I felt his bare chest against my breasts.

I tried sitting up, but he pulled me back. I kicked him wildly, my long sculptured nails clawing at his face. A trickle of blood ran down his jagged scar, forming a pool on the tapestry rug. He grabbed me again, I tried to be calm, but there was panic in my eyes. He started making love to me, running his tongue over my face, licking the tears away. In spite of myself I felt that wonderful ache throbbing in my groin for his hot male flesh. Suddenly I felt that all the blood had been pumped back into my body. When he was gone it seemed that all the oxygen had left the room.

"It may be over between us, but it's not finished," he said.

I started sobbing silently. Now I wanted him as badly as he wanted me. I could no longer escape his entrapment.

After many hours of raw hard core sex, he whispered, "Stay with me, I'm ready to come again."

Then an animal-like cry escaped his lips. "I feel like I could stay inside of you for the rest of my life." he moaned. He was at peace for only a few moments, then Lust threw the comforter off of the bed, lighting another cigarette.

The toxic fumes formed a cloud of smoke throughout the room.

"I'm going to make a quick run to the Canyon Country Store. I'm out of beer," he said harshly pecking me on the nose.

"You're just going to score some drugs. If you leave you can sleep in the gutter where you belong."

He paid no heed to my threats, slamming the door behind him. I'd danced to the beat of death and desire. I'll never regret the sexual experience. It was the most volatile battlefield I've ever made love on. He gave a performance in the bedroom that will last a lifetime in my memories.

Later that night he returned, banging on my windows until dawn. Even the cotton that I'd stuffed into my ears couldn't drown out his frantic pleas of remorse. The coyotes howled their mournful cries in the wilderness, then the silence.

I fell back into a restless sleep. The next morning when I opened the shutters I found him lying lifeless on my doorstep. A shattered glass bottle of beer, and an empty vial in his hand, his bloodshot blue eyes staring into mine. I crouched down on my knees, grabbing his cold limp wrist, but he had no pulse.

Pushing up his sweaty blood soaked Gap T, I reached for his chest, but there was no heartbeat. For seconds I tried resuscitating him, pressing down hard with the palm of my hand, praying that his heart would start pumping.

Unfortunately he wasn't responding to all of my attempted rescue breaths. As I brushed a clump of streaked, matted hair over his face, I held his hand until I heard the sirens.

The police and paramedics arrived, swooping his corpse into a body bag. He'd overdosed, hitting his head, falling onto the scorching black concrete pavement. His dream unfulfilled, enshrouded by the smoggy skyline of Hollywood and its glamor, guns, drugs, booze and madness.

Chapter Twenty
Seasons of the Flesh

There are things that happen between a man and woman in the dark that sort of make everything else seem unimportant.
Tennessee Williams

It was Fall. The leaves were changing colors, falling off of the trees, blowing in the wind. One early morning I was in my kitchen preparing for a lavish dinner party that night finding an old long stemmed flute glass with *Bitch* engraved on it in red letters that Lust had given me, on Valentine's Day. Suddenly I flashed back on that disastrous night before his tragic demise sad and guilt ridden by the memory. Patrick had come over to rescue me from Lust, throwing him out of my house in a fury.

The skin flick star was becoming abusive, threatening me, refusing to leave on his own.

"Pack up your stuff and split," Patrick shouted. "April wants you out of here!"

Lust loaded up his car, a beer in his hand, as I threw his answering service over the cliff. Ripping all of the coveted posters from movies that he'd starred in with John Holmes off the walls, "And take your beer keg with you, man," Patrick shouted.

The last time I'd thrown Lust out I loaded all of his clothes on top of his car. The next morning when he came home it looked like I was having a garage sale in Laurel Canyon.

Does that sound cold?

After Lust was supposedly out of my life Patrick spent the night with me. The next morning when we awakened, Lust was passed out, his white antique 1955 Bentley shining in the sun parked in the driveway of a little old lady's house. Patrick professed great love for me and wanted to get remarried until that fateful night two weeks later.

Patrick, Yolanda, Chelsea and I were hanging out at my house, drinking wine on the terrace. Chelsea and I heard the phone ringing off the hook. Floating into my bedroom, Lust's voice came echoing through my answering service.

"I really miss you honey, pick up if you're there."

Grabbing the phone, I temporarily lost all sense of reason. I was irresponsibly high, blinded by desire. Unfortunately, I had to pay the bitter consequences for the rest of my life.

"Come on by," I said.

A half an hour later Chelsea was hanging my drapes in the bedroom. I was leaning back on the bed, swirling a swizzle stick around in a glass of Veuve Clicquot champagne, smoking a joint when the porn star appeared. My transparent long white Grecian gown showing the outline of my high breasts, titian hair piled on top of my head.

I handed Lust a joint and some matches. He lit it, blowing smoke rings onto the ceiling, kicking off his worn distressed brown work boots. He continued, pulling his gray thermal sweatshirt and faded jeans off, clumsily throwing them on the floor, reacquainting me with his fantastic build.

He then poured himself a beer, tumbling onto the Ralph Lauren floral comforter, leaping upon me. At first I writhed in his grasp.

"Do you want it, baby cakes?" he coaxed. "I'm no good without you. I'm living the torment of sleepless nights," he sighed, pinning my shoulders to the mattress. I struggled, pushing him away, but couldn't stop myself with his mouth so dangerously near. His breath was warm and my head was whirling from the effects of the wine and marijuana. I had lost myself to him again. Nothing in the world existed for me but passion. I was his.

I felt his skin against mine as he tasted my breasts, worshipping my nipples, sensuality raced through my entire body the more aroused he became. Pulling off my rhinestone barrette, my long, thick hair fell over my bare shoulders. The fear of being caught by Patrick melted away as I committed the greatest of sexual crimes.

"This is not right," I moaned trying to move as he teased me with his finger, then running his hand between my thighs, nudging me to spread my legs. There was a short silent struggle, then I surrendered.

For Lust it was just a game. He didn't care how much he destroyed other people's lives. To me it was blind intoxication and that familiar tingling.

"Relax, baby and enjoy the ride," he whispered. I was out maneuvered again.

Climbing me all body parts in motion at once, his smooth rounded bottom bobbing up and down, the strong young cock moving in and out of me.

Chelsea was mesmerized. She continued hanging around, munching on a box of English truffles.

"I hope I'm not in the way," she purred flirtatiously, watching us intently.

"You're welcome to join us in a menage," Lust glanced up briefly at her.

"You naughty, boy, are you trying to corrupt me?" she asked as she was about to offer herself to us, when Patrick and Yolanda blew into the room from the French doors. He went berserk when he saw Lust, grinding away on me.

"What a ghastly evening. I bloody well need a pissing drink," Chelsea whined, sweeping out of the room, her eyes wide with terror. She was followed closely by Yolanda, as I heard the hum and clunking of their cars racing down my driveway.

Lust jumped off of me while Patrick, looking stunned, stared me in the face.

"What the fuck is going on in here?" he shouted, his eyes narrowing as he picked up the vase of red sweetheart rose buds that he had bought for me, throwing them through my oval stained glass picture window.

"Shame on you April." He said with a cold stare. "You sleazy son of a bitch, that's my girlfriend you were fucking," he paused for a moment, glaring at Lust. Then he lunged at him, grabbing his arm roughly. My stomach was fluttering, my mouth was dry, and I was close to tears. Trembling I threw my naked body over Lust, fearing Patrick's Irish temper.

Patrick pushed me away, grabbing him, his rough knuckles pummeling him. Lust was over powered by the muscular jock. Patrick's anger mounted as he kicked his enemy in the stomach with the spikes of his gym shoes. I was coming down abruptly from my high. My head was aching and throbbing. I felt like I was going to be sick as I took a downer from my pillbox, swallowing it down with champagne.

"Leave him alone," I begged.

"I'd like to knock his eyes out," Patrick ranted on as he continued terrorizing his victim.

"He's not worth going to prison for," I said convincingly, biting my lip.

Patrick reluctantly loosened his grip on Lust's neck, shoving him into the wall. Slowly standing up, blood trickling out of his nose, Lust grabbed his clothes, disappearing from sight.

"I'm sorry, I'm stoned. I didn't know what I was doing. I love you, I didn't mean to hurt you. He was just a lust fuck," I cried, trying to put my arms around Patrick, moving in closer, but his body or mind wasn't responding to mine.

He leered at me slapping me across the face. I winced from the pain, falling back on the chaise lounge.

"You trashy bitch. You're a sickie, get a grip. I'm afraid for you. Check yourself into a rehab clinic. You're dirty, I never ever want to touch you again. I don't need your mercy fucks."

He stormed out of my house, slamming the door behind him.

Swallowing some more pills, I surveyed life through my tinted tainted blue lenses. Soon everything started to sway, including the palms outside of my broken window. The first hint of light filtered through the darkness, then shadows came through the trees. The sky turned gray as sunlight was beginning to creep over the canyon. I was broken, living a nightmare. I wanted the night to end and morning never to begin.

How could I be so self destructive and unstable? I thought. Now I belonged to no one and had to take responsibility for myself and deal with my life and the guilt.

Chapter Twenty One
Recurring Nightmare
Soul Mates
Patrick

Eternity was in our lips and eyes.
Shakespeare

I wake up screaming, clutching my wedding band. The garnet ring is still a constant companion on my finger. But what happened to the marriage?

All my life I'd been an elusive butterfly until Patrick and I celebrated each other. In my dreams we had exchanged glances. Our eyes lingered although we never spoke a word in one of our last reincarnations across the crowded corridors. We had a link between death and life. Then one magical mystical, hot, Indian summer day destiny and passion spun the plot. Our mortal flesh melted into one at sundown as we lay on sand kissed sea dove shore. Never before had I felt that intense, raw, sexual, spiritual chemistry. Patrick was my summer playmate, my winter rain. In my dream we were making love on a sun-dappled, deserted beach, sipping raspberry ambrosias in frothy golden goblets served by silver sea monkeys. He touched my hand with an absolute convincing show of affection.

"Have you chosen to pass by here between lifetimes? I'm really attracted to you, I feel like I've lived with you all of my lives. Were we lovers in the 17th Century? You greet me as if we were old acquaintances!"

"I've known you for all of eternity, although I haven't slept in your arms for many sunsets. I've missed the warmth of your smile." I answered mysteriously.

"I'm enchanted by your aura, you're a beautiful, sensual mermaid with kelp in your hair and hazel green eyes."

"A mystic read in the tea leaves that if I drove alone to this deserted sand castle today my soul mate would be waiting for me." I shared.

"What did the woman tell you that he would look like? I hope I'm the right one."

"I know that you came from the high heavens. My psychic said that you'd be dressed with a crown of curly golden ringlets like daffodils spun of winter wheat."

"What else did she say?"

"That you'd look like a Greek God, a mirage appearing in your chariot with an aquiline nose and a sculptured body that Rodin or Michelangelo could have carved out of stone."

"Well I drove up here in my Harley dune buggy." He laughed.

"I've brought a picnic basket filled with delicacies," I said excitedly popping open a bottle of champagne. We had a candlelight dinner lit by a full orange moon. Waves crashed symphonically against jagged rocks as we fed each other aphrodisiacs, bittersweet chocolate strawberries and purple grapes off the vine. I jumped into the high ivory blue sea naked. Patrick followed chasing me to the top of a sandy dune. We clutched our arms around each other as the moon continued to rise. Passionately kissing, he sipped sweet nectar from my nipples as we rolled downward, swallowed up by the great gush of a wave drenched in our own desire. If I could only freeze that moment in time. But seasons change and lost love has gone astray. The world has become a strange and lonely place. My lovers and playmates hold no importance in my life. The soul wants what the soul wants, or the soul wants nothing at all. Why were we fated together, stars in life's play, only to be spliced apart in this soundtrack. The ghost of infatuation and broken dreams lie like dust in the sand, but his memory lingers on. My fleshless lover you and I will not drink up yesterdays senseless syllables until we toast each other in our next reincarnation. I wake up screaming, clutching my wedding band. The garnet ring is still a constant companion on my finger. But what happened to the marriage?

Chapter Twenty Two
Patrick

Well sooner or later at some point in your life, the thing you lived for is lost or abandoned and then you die or you find something else.
Tennessee Williams

In the late night wilderness, on my terrace, Patrick and I said our last good-byes.

"Are you still seeing that coke whore?" I demanded.

"We would have been together forever if you hadn't moved that sleeze bag porno star into your house, telling me he was your gay roommate, and we needed time away," he said, rage in his eyes.

"I got tired of staying up all night waiting for you to come home from The Whiskey. The illiterate groupies named you 'The Hamburger Fuck'," I answered in exasperation.

"I was just out with the boys getting drunk," he said "No biggie."

"Right, Patrick."

"You might have pulled off all your lies and deception if I hadn't been Lust's makeup artist when he fucked three chicks in a soft-core film, and you had the balls to tell me he was your gay roommate." he stared coldly at me.

"I thought you forgave me. You asked me to re-marry you," I asked.

"Come on, can't I love two women? You're the one who wanted an open marriage. It's just puppy love," he said flaunting it in my face. "And how about all your blow boys."

The pale golden moon rose from the mountain, hanging her robust head over a cliff, then disappearing behind a cloud. I knew that I was going to get dumped. I was devastated.

"You'll have to make a choice. I won't share you with another bitch," I said, trying to hold back the tears, hoping that he didn't hear the crack in my voice.

"You're older and wiser than I am. You've seen so much of life. Traveled all over the world. I want to find out what people and customs are like in other countries. Set me free," he said sternly. "You know that I'll always come back to you," he promised giving me a tentative hug.

"We have so much history I can't imagine being without you. I'll be good. Forgive me," I pleaded. "Let's at least try it one more time."

"Once we were one, you broke the trust," he said, lifting a chilled bottle of Cristal Champagne out of a cut glass ice bucket, pouring it into our flute glasses. Then the sky turned from lavender to purple framing the snowcapped mountains. That was why we named our scenic spot 'Purple Mountain Majesty.'

We'd split up and reunited so many times like that old Dolly Parton song 'Here He Comes Again'.

It was hard to believe that thirteen years later we were over after a torrid whirlwind of fusion, passion, and emotion. Fog fell on the hillside rolling in like a smoky veil, clouding Patrick's face framed by wild unruly blond hair blending into the misty landscape.

In the blistering cold December chills ran through my body. Kissing me goodbye, running his fingers through my hair, his face became transparent, fading out of my life. When he was gone, my sea of playmates were of no importance. I was afraid of hurting anymore, but I had to be introspective, step back and access. There had to be a time that I could surrender to the diminishing shadow of my youth and let the future unfold, but I'd never felt so frightened and alone. The sky never turned purple on my terrace again.

Chapter Twenty Three
Chelsea and April

There was no sound. Everybody had left. There was nothing to do but drift about the emptiness of the rooms.
Tennessee Williams

The shrill chimes of the doorbell rang. I looked through the peephole of my front door at my cliff-side bungalow in Laurel Canyon. Chelsea was standing there with two mocha lattes and a basket of crumpets in her hands. I opened the door leading her into the kitchen. We sat at a little round table and started chatting.

"Lovie, You look upset," Chelsea said.

"Patrick just dumped me and I can't even get a job in the movies. I'm just trying to get through life in one piece, Chels."

"That's brilliant," she said.

"It's a lot of work," I sighed.

"What a load of rot, even I was too old for a high school call today. I hope the fellows in casting aren't buggering you also," she said handing me a cup of piping hot coffee. The Starbucks sipping female was always trying to make me feel better.

"Before Patrick and I were together I was just tired of being taken advantage of by drifters. I cringed over their imperfections and predictability," I said.

"We women go to bed with a man for a little validation and still end up alone at the MAC counter at Barney's getting a makeover. All the chaps in LA are rotters, April."

My shrink thinks we're like sorority sisters, wearing loneliness like our second skins, I thought.

"Today it's tearing my guts out that feeling in the pit of your stomach, that grinding feeling, that strange realization that you're all alone and even all the money or success on this planet can't cure that."

"With so many people on the planet to spend time with a beautiful bird with such charisma shouldn't give up hope. There are lots of fellows out there. Go have yourself a fling." she said, touching up her makeup.

"I am having a fling. I spent an afternoon with a theatre critic. He's going to review my play at Theatre 40 in Beverly Hills," I said, sipping my coffee, too depressed to eat anything.

"Most men are threatened by your independence," she said with conviction. "But I'm sure that if he's shagging you properly you'll get a good review."

"He's already dropped enticing blurbs about me in his column. I'm just afraid of ending up alone."

"You're not going to end up alone. You are alone, you just take it more seriously than I do, but you must face reality, pet. He's not coming home," she said sadly, sipping her coffee, munching on her guilty pleasure, covering it with strawberry jelly and cream cheese.

"I hate my reality. One is just not enough. With-out someone to touch me and love me. I'll always be lonely. Even animals can't live without love. They just crawl into the ground and die."

Chelsea glanced at her rhinestone rimmed watch, giving me a quick peck on the cheek. "I'm so sorry love."

"It's all just a hallucination, the opposite of what it seems to be. But a hundred years from today, who will know?" I cried.

Chelsea put her arms around me, wiping my eyes with a kleenex.

"Don't slink into your greyness, darling, act like you're on a battlefield at all times. That's survival," she said.

"The darkness that haunts me is what I have to pay not to compromise. So it's all alone," I said.

"I was vaccinated against committing those petty crimes," she said in a harsh tone, studying her image in her hand mirror.

"To me, compromise is when you change the answer to fit the questions," I said.

"That sounds quite odd," she frowned, her brow wrinkling.

"It's the link between death and life, I'm ready to settle down, not settle. I guess you just have to move on and remember, laughter rides in the same carriage as sorrow," I answered.

"I still have my dream. love. I can't quit this busi-ness. It's exciting to me still, April. I guess it's all the glamour that keeps us going everyday a new set, being someone else, the hope of becoming a movie star and marrying a rich fellow. You wouldn't try to top yourself, would you now?" she asked with apprehension.

"Sometimes I wonder if I stuck my head in the oven if I'd be the next Sylvia Plath. I'm in a very Virginia Woolf mood today," I said. "You never know."

"You're a hot-blooded bird. It's not the blimey way, ducky. Toodaloo, love. I have a lunch date at Morton's in twenty minutes with the Donald. I'll ring you up later. Don't fret. It will cause laugh lines," she said rushing out the door in abandonment.

Chapter Twenty Four
The Vagabond Ghost
Déjà Vu

It is in our own idleness, in our dreams that submerged truth sometimes comes to the top.
Virginia Woolf

I wake up screaming, clutching my wedding band. The garnet ring is still a constant companion on my finger. But what happened to the marriage? You drifted in and out of my life for over a decade of decadence. We shared the mystery of heaven and hell. Now you haunt my dreams like a dark ominous shadow, a vagabond ghost that prowls in my heart. I dream, in a waking sleep, lucid images of fantasy driven by reality, calling out your name. You appear for fleeting moments, quickly vanishing from sight. I gaze at the key lying on top of my antique oak vanity and study my reflection in the mirror. The key and I are both tarnished and faded with time, reflecting memories of sweet sex, romance and far away places where we'd roamed, countries that I can never return to without you. A misty pallet of grey gloom painted an eerie landscape. Pine cones silver as the winter snow and a blanket of soft raindrops fell from a bruised blue sky. In my dream I hopped on a plane heading for magical Maui, the land of swaying sugar cane and wave-crested golden sanded beaches setting the Sunset for steamy romance and frothy tropical ambrosias.

In the heat and passion of a tropical morning I stood on a sun-lit beach, wearing a long scarlet flowing gown, the scent of the jungle strewn in my hair. I had to escape, I had lost my way in jaded LA and the waterfront was a cool place to seek refuge. Like magic, slowly a handsomely rugged-looking stranger from the hotel approached me. He rose from the sand with his seductive swagger. Here I was in this exotic far away land with a mysterious man I knew that I'd known before.

"You're a vision. Would you like me to show you a picture of the house we're going to live in?" His sparkling sunny smile and turquoise green eyes lit up the sky. I tried to act flirty, but I was almost speechless. I smiled awkwardly after looking at pictures of the structure of my dream house. He looked amused and I could tell that he was immediately taken by my female prowess as adoring eyes roamed my body.

"I'm Patrick, what's your name and where's your home, wildflower? Are you traveling alone?" he asked.

"My name is April and I'm on my own. I'm a mountain lady. I sleep under the Hollywood sign."

"Which canyon do you live in?" he asked.

"In a tree-house high on a hillside in the middle of an enchanted forest." I was so swept away by this young pup who was wearing almost nothing, showing off his well tanned body.

"Would you like to have a drink with me? I'll take you to this lagoon right on the island. The pond is full of all kinds of rare wild birds and ducks. They even have flamingos."

"It sounds very enticing."

The waves crashed against jagged rocks, bathing the sand with ivory foam.

Patrick took me by the hand leading me to a sea of feathered winter white swans bearing proud, long, graceful raven-haired necks and plumage. Leggy powder puff pink Chilean flamingos lounged lazily in their lagoon.

I heard the sounds of shrieking shrill shore birds, then the ominous wail of the Lahaina trolley in the distant horizon.

I awakened from my dream to the purr of Eclipse, my calico cat and Sky, my shitzu, washing my morning face with kisses. I was a lady living on the edge of the cliff in wild abandonment, fighting off my panic attacks and deepest, darkest demons. I long to return to the land of swaying sugarcane, recapturing the enchantment. I'll never forget him because he took me to all the places I wanted to be without ever leaving myself. Now I lie in my sky meadow hillock high, alone without him and the darkness that comes with the sunset. But the vagabond ghost still prowls in my heart. I wake up screaming, clutching my wedding band. The garnet ring is still a constant companion on my finger. But what happened to the marriage?

Chapter Twenty Five

Christopher
Equity Waiver
Part One

He sizes women up with a glance, with sexual classifications, crude images flashing into his mind and determining the way he smiles at them.
Tennessee Williams

It was the 80's and my greatest passion and obsession was the theatre. I was a struggling, broke, resident playwright at Theater 40 in Beverly Hills and Group Repertory in the San Fernando Valley, having productions of my plays produced all over the country. It was the most inspirational, exciting chapter of my life.

I thrived on the process and the standing ovations. Even hosting openings and sweeping the stage with my peers from the repertory groups were a labor of love.

One night after one of my productions, at a cast party held in the green room, I met Christopher, a flamboyant sculptor, playwright/actor, artistic director. After having too many bubbles, I ended up at his loft located in the heart of the theatre district in Hollywood.

As the night unfolded I was so drunk that his chauffeur drove me home early the next morning. Chelsea and Yolanda had dropped by for breakfast at my house in the canyon. As we were drinking coffee, chatting and munching on Zen Bakery Blueberry Raspberry muffins, the voice of Christopher came piping out of my answering service. A baroque concerto was playing in the background.

"I painted the most erotic water color that has ever been done on a woman with my tool. It's the best of all my masterpieces. You're unbelievable, simply exquisite. I named it 'Whore'. I want to share it with you tonight," he rambled on. "I love your Mound of Venus. I'd like to romp through your strawberry fields forever with my long brush strokes, my love."

Suddenly he started playing choir music, then we heard a loud crash.

"Oh darling, I just tripped over my fifteen thousand dollar drum from Istanbul," he slurred.

"Who is that whack?" Chelsea asked.

"He's an avant-garde artist, a bit bizarre."

"Pick up, love. My French chef is cooking couscous for supper. Chow, chow, love."

"Oh dear, I wonder what he meant by 'he loved my Mound of Venus'? Do you think I slept with him last night?"

"Don't get your knickers in a twist. You probably didn't shag him or he wouldn't be so enamored with you and ringing you up before noon, you couscous," Chelsea laughed.

"You got that down right," Yolanda said.

"Well this playboy is way over the top. He's 50, a little older than what I usually go for, but he might produce my plays. He owns the block on Santa Monica Blvd and Highland."

I tried recalling the evening, but all I could remember was polishing off that second bottle of Macon Village and feeling his hand groping my leg at his bar, then waking up in my bed with my clothes and makeup still on. It was like I'd lost my mind again. I wondered what those poor Alzheimer's victims felt like. I knew I had to stop drinking. I wasn't using my addiction. My addiction was using me. But I just couldn't stop. Maybe I'd better not try to quit cold turkey. I'd just go to some AA meetings and cool it a little. Smoke a few bongs and monitor my maintenance level. Only half a bottle and a few valiums. But not until after my dinner with Christopher, I thought.

"I'm gonna save a seat for that guy on the phone at AA," Yolanda laughed.

"I think you and April are due to attend a meeting also," Chelsea said sternly.

"I always meet cute brothers at those meetings," Yolanda chimed in.

I knew that I couldn't go on like that for much longer. The blackouts were devastating. My shrink repeatedly warned me that one moment being drunk and unconscious I could either get raped, kill someone driving my car, or die alone in the gutter somewhere. I was running scared, but not scared enough.

"What's with that guy you met at Gay Pavilion?" Yolanda asked.

"He's probably not straight, but he's a real hottie Latin. I invited him to my party for broke dicks this weekend," I said.

"Every girl has to bring one."

"You're a stalker magnet," Chelsea said.

"But he was very polite," I answered.

"I'm sure the Hillside Strangler was very polite also until he lured his victims into the bushes,""Chelsea answered.

"Let's see if he calls first," Yolanda said.

"Some guys just get girls' phone numbers to see if they can score, then lose them."

It was summer and Chelsea and Yolanda were dressed in Nike black and white striped stretch pants with tight midriff tops and denim baseball caps. I was still wearing my purple tie died slip-dress, turquoise beaded earrings and sandals. My hair was wild, tangled and dark circles under my bloodshot, puffy eyes showed off too much dissipation.

I walked into the kitchen splashing cold water on my face, gazing at my reflection in the antique mirror above the potbellied stove and smoked some pot. I didn't feel safe. My mouth was dry, throat tight as a tourniquet. As I sat down next to my girlfriends in the cozy parlor, I looked at Chelsea's freshly scrubbed face illuminated by summer's rosy rouged cheeks and clear sky blue eyes. She was the picture of health and fitness. *Although she could lose a little weight*, I mused.

"Can you tell I dropped off five pounds?" Chelsea posed for me. "I was feeling rather beefy," she beamed.

"You're beautiful, diva," I said, trying to lift my coffee cup to my lips, but my hand was shaking as I popped the pale blue number ten valium into my mouth, spilling some of the piping hot mocha java on the hardwood floor.

"Get a grip, girlfriend. April, squeeze into yer' workout clothes, we need to go the gym," Yolanda begged.

"I jus' done a Q and a black beauty but I haven't had a drink in forty-five minutes. Let's go, girl."

I had barely slept and I was praying that the pill would kick in and make my hangover and that sinking feeling in the pit of my stomach disappear with the depression. I was just hanging on, and surely not ready to do a treadmill after swallowing a downer. They'd have to call the paramedics.

Christopher was still babbling. "I'd like to see you tonight, April. Last night awakened my endorphins. I might have a slot on Saturday and Sunday nights at one of my theaters for the play you gave me last night. Let me turn down my choir music." There was a slight pause, then, "See you tonight at seven."

"Seems like your bizarre Southern gentleman has consumed too many Planters Punches," Chelsea laughed. "What a twit."

"I think he's a sophisticated psychopath," I said with a forced smile.

"Well lots of luck with the perv, Miss American Pie. We're shockingly late for our high maintenance yoga class. Since you're not going to join us, Chee-rio," Chelsea said as she and Yolanda rushed out the door.

"Now don't you be doin' the evil," Yolanda said, stuffing the remaining muffins into her bubble gum pink Betty Boop purse.

Chapter Twenty Six

The Movies, Whore

You can lead a whore to culture, but you can't make her think.
Dorothy Parker

Today I heard Brian's laughing voice on my service.

"You won't believe who I saw stripping on the Sundance Channel. You can't dance, April, you just did your own thing, but your nipples looked great, doll. And you always dreamed of being in an indy film." He laughed.

Being graceful had never been my forté. When my agent informed me that I had to dance on the interview, I tried ducking out of it, but to no avail. The casting directors loved me, "Just wing it," they begged.

When I arrived at the terra-cotta bricked Spanish courtyard in my red lace crotchless panties under my black Frederick's of Hollywood laced slit-up skirt, my breasts were riding high in my black satin bustier, red fingernails sticking out of long fishnet gloves. Other sexy young actresses were auditioning that night. When the director called my name I strutted towards him, following him into the house.

"Did you bring your own music?" he asked.

"No," I answered nervously.

"It's all right, ducky dear, I'll put on some rock Bossa Nova," he said in an English accent.

I was hardly shy, having confidence, knowing that I had the most amazing body. I twirled around the wooden framed spacious room, my curly flame-red hair flying in the air.

"Thank you, April, now would you do a strip and take your clothes off?"

"Only for Ken Russell, the great director of the decade," I purred pursing my rosy red glossed lips. I stripped provocatively, throwing my bustier in his face. Within minutes, I was wearing nothing but a vacant stare. Well, needless to say, I knocked out all of the competition with my knockers.

When casting gave me the call, the girl said, "Park at the church and go inside and strip. You'll be Lonely 'Stripper'."

I was hardly too lonely bedecked and bejew-eled dressed topless in a festive costume made out of bamboo shoots, rainbow feathers and a beaded thong from Trashy Lingerie. A fetchingly sexy star screamed at the horny cameraman and A.D.'s who were gawking at me, hovering around.

"Okay guys, give the lady a little respect."

He then checked out his crotch, laughing, "Yikes, I think I'm getting a hard on," as I danced and slid down the gold brass pole in the dark, smoky bar.

Chapter Twenty Seven

Christopher
The '80s
Part Two

So it happened. It had been lost, all dignity, and now she was frantically digging a hand kerchief and a compact out of her bag while her breath came in sobs.
Tennessee Williams

The doorbell rang loudly. On a blue sky sunday, I opened the door escorting Christopher into my house.

"Hello, love," he said kissing my hand, holding a bouquet of Sterling Silver roses and an opened bottle of vintage Rothschild in the other hand. "Here put these in water before they wilt."

I put the delicate bouquet in a crystal vase handing him two glasses.

"I've missed you," he said pouring the ruby red wine, offering me a glass.

"Last night was all sort of a blur. Did you ravage me?" I asked. "I vaguely remember your driver taking me home."

"I wouldn't doubt it, I had to carry you to the car. Let's take a drive out to my beach house in Santa

Barbara and I'll refresh your memory, darlin'. Don't forget your overnight bag."

I slid into the plush cream colored limo. We hardly spoke as the driver wound down the scenic coastline. Christopher put a glass of champagne in my hand, sipping on his Martini. His ash brown hair tipped with gray and pasty white skin paled in the moonlight. I was feeling on edge. The not knowing, daring to ask more. This smooth operator came with a well stocked bar and condoms I hoped.

I needed to stay alert so that I would be in control and have my play produced without spending any money. When I got applause and raves from the critics I felt higher than any drug that I'd ever consumed. And lower than the lowest when the over-inflated egos called the shots. But this was a powerful man who was well respected in the world of theatre. My world. Obviously last night I had charmed him. Now I was determined to manipulate him in all of his manhood. I'd take what was mine. Center stage. That enormous eye the audience merely an eyeball. I had to control my destiny.

We pulled into the terra-cotta bricked driveway as the black wrought iron gate swung open.

"Welcome to my dynasty," he said taking my arm, helping me out of the car. "I hope you like my palatial digs."

"Sure, this is really cool," I answered.

In Laurel Canyon, I didn't have the ocean and a chauffeur, I thought.

"Tonight we'll take a midnight swim and walk on the beach. The water's luke warm," he said nonchalantly.

"Oh Christopher, I'm passionate about the ocean," I smiled self consciously.

"Sugar, I'm delighted, this Indian Summer reminds me of those warm southern nights. It was like poetry lounging on the veranda, drinking mint juleps. The fireflies swarming in the swamps."

Christopher was becoming drunk and maudlin as we perched in the trellised gazebo, mirrored by the ocean. The sky darkened as a silver moon shone on rippling waves. It was a splendid star-studded night. I breathed in the salty sea as I felt soft breezes caress my skin. Rolling hills capped the landscape like a plush green blanket framed by majestic oak trees. The butler appeared with a bottle of the Dom and a pitcher with floating green olives.

"The champagne is for you, April. I'm having martinis. My family tree was soaked in gin."

"I prefer champagne. I rarely touch the hard stuff. How do you spend your time when you're here?" I asked.

"I'm a decadent dilettante. I hope I'm not too eccentric for you. I own thoroughbred horses and play polo while playing with life. I have enough money to buy your world, April." He bragged.

This setting was the perfect backdrop for romance. I started fantasizing about Antonio, the lonely lost looking Latin I'd just met with the amazing body. My thoughts were interrupted by the butler's presence and my ardent admirer bearing a halfhearted cold smile across his lips, speaking in a whiny Southern drawl.

"I put my money where my Maserati's are. Now let's talk about you," he said.

I'll bet he's always too drunk to drive. Those poor pedestrians. This man overrates his own magnetism by the status of his sports cars as a symbol of his sexuality, I mused, as we feasted on blackened barbecued duck, mustard greens, corn muffins and sweet potato pie. Accompanied by peach cobbler toped with freshly whipped cream. All we needed now was Glen Campbell singing 'Southern Nights', for an encore.

Christopher lacked the soul of the South, having been swept away in the whirlwind of Hollywood. Sade's 'Smooth Operator' came blaring through swaying trees. Every time I hear that song I think of him and that ethereal landscape of seascaped paradise.

I looked out at a rock blending in with the whimsical purple sunset. The whales were frolicking. The silence between us was only broken by a birdsong, an occasional wave and the pounding of the surf. Then Christopher looked at me pensively.

"Dear, the moment I first saw you I knew we'd be great together. I fell madly in love with you," he said swirling the olive around with a glass swizzle stick, reaching for my hand.

"I thought we came over here to discuss my plays" I said lighting a joint from my sterling silver cigarette case. "Would you like some?"

"No thanks. Do you come from an orthodox background? God, you're so gorgeous, I can't even concentrate when I look at you," he said. "I love Jewish women. They're all so balsy and bitchy," he laughed. "But you're so exciting. You shine."

"I don't appreciate being put in a box with all the others." I answered, challenging him.

"April, you're not like anyone I've ever met before. Now, about your play. First of all, you have to flesh out your characters. They're more like pop art. A character has no history. He never dies, he's not a human being. I die, you die, but take for instance Hamlet - he lives forever. I love the local color, but not for 50 pages. Your plots leave a little to be desired. And why did you turn Betsy Ross into a bull dyke? I knew it was a device, but I just never figured out where it was going. Or that chorus line. What was your vision?"

"You mean the nymphettes? Everyone thought they were very Brechtian," I answered defensively.

"You're all over the place. First, let me say, dar-lin', that since world drama began with the Greeks, and Aristotle, there have been certain rules or guidelines laid down for the construction of a well-written play. Of course they have all been broken. Do you hang out with Drag Queens, dear?" he asked.

"Only now and then, why?"

"If you're going to write about them at least hang out with them, or do some research. You don't know the difference between a pre-op and a transsexual. But you could make a fortune writing porn," he said sipping his drink.

"I just got a rejection letter from this famous producer. He said that my play was like reading James Joyce. I know that I'm making a statement. I'm going to rock the world with my pen. Don't you think that I should pursue my artistic dreams? Isn't there anything you like about my work? They say I'm like Beckett, Shakespeare, Dorothy Parker, and Tennessee."

"Too bad dear, you and James Joyce are both dead in Hollywood. *The Silken Silent Sisters Of The Silver Screen*, it's a really exciting piece. Fresh and original. Not to my aesthetic taste. You must do the work before I can take the risk of a full production. Do you think you can? The scene with your porno star reads like the X-rated version of Saturday Night Live. Although I must admit that it will bring the house down," he laughed. "But even in porn, there has to be a beginning, a middle, and an end. The beginning is the foreplay, and the end, the climax," he said patting my thigh lasciviously.

"It's the chopping block. What is your suggestion?" I asked twisting a strand of my long blond ringlet in my fingers.

"It needs a through line, a spine, if you will. Your writing is abstract, bizarre, very avant-garde. Highly stylized. It's hysterical, right from the gut. The language is gorgeous. You've created greatness in your characters. They're way out of control. The prose is lovely. Poetically dazzling and very theatrical. But, I just don't know if you can write a play.

Nevertheless, I'll try and deal with it in terms of what I think you want. The play's a bit of insanity and comedy but whose truism is it anyway? Where do you want these women to end up? There are the eaters and the eaten." He poured himself another drink. "See, I'm giving you a compliment and an insult."

"I think the core of the play is the internals of the women staying alive together against all of the forces. Take Tennessee Williams' women, they're always eaten up alive by men," I said. "These women really need each other."

"The play has a style like nothing I've ever read before. It's a germ, a little seed worth working on. A little gem. You're like a goldmine, ready to be tapped," he said waving over his butler. "More martinis, please, and champagne for the lady."

"Sometimes I feel like poor Blanche. I don't know why I put myself in the position in life of trying to be in the limelight. My plays only matter to me anyway. My great regret is that I never met Tennessee Williams in this lifetime. I'm so like many of the women in his plays."

"Be thrilled, you're unique. You have a great career ahead of you. With a little more control, I predict you'll be the hottest new woman playwright on the continent writing erotica. I love it when your bizarre metaphors and energy clash. You're doing what all other writers are trying to do. They'd die for your talent. But there has to be a beginning, a middle, and an end, or the critics will kill you. Would you like some cocoa and chocolate bonbons, dear?" he asked, handing me the box.

"I'd adore some, do you think you can help me?" I asked wondering if this situation was a safe place for my fragile artist.

After a lavish gourmet dinner in the gazebo, Christopher convinced me to spend the night at his guest cottage. Later that night, there was a knock on the door. He staggered into my bedroom before I could even open it, wearing a bathrobe, holding a half finished martini in one hand, a bottle of brandy and more bittersweet chocolates on a tray with the other.

"You were magnificent. A wild animal. Shaking your long strawberry blonde hair all over my body," he said handing me a crystal decanter of Remy Martin Extra cognac. "It's four hundred dollars a bottle," be bragged.

I almost had an orgasm biting into the sweet confections.

"I'm glad it was good for you. I can't remember!" I said taking a sip from the brandy snifter. I knew I shouldn't have spent the night here! This was very awkward.

"I can't believe you don't remember. You're the most passionate woman I've ever been with and you were very much awake. I hope you're not embarrassed being so aggressive. I can make love to you and still be your friend." he said slurring his words.

I was so overwhelmed and speechless, clad in my sheer black nightgown and slippers. I slipped into my terrycloth robe. "Let's take it slow," I pleaded, trying to change the subject.

"I'm swallowed up by you. We have nothing to lose as long as we're both faithful to each other. Why are you so nervous?"

I felt like I was ready to flip out. "You're talking crazy, faithful?" I laughed. "I'm just an irreverent butterfly. You'll never pin me down," I said, clutching at my robe nervously. It was like his eyes were piercing through my flesh.

"You're a swan, I want to sleep with you all night, I sense there's a tragic tone to your life. You need me, be my house pet."

"You're cultured and I find you very attractive, but please I want you to go. I need some sleep." This man turned my stomach . I didn't know what to do. I knew I shouldn't have had that fourth glass of wine, I thought to myself, feeling weak and dizzy.

"You're turning on me. You've made yourself responsible for my sexual pleasures," he said grabbing me. "Let me see your mound of Venus. Please let me see your mound of Venus," he pleaded redundantly, starting to remove his bathrobe, moving in closer.

"No, I'm a victim of amnesia, and you expect me to feel responsible," I said angrily pushing him away.

"Have you ever been hospitalized? Last night you perform, and you can't even remember. You didn't seem drunk, you didn't even stagger or slur. Like an animal you attacked me. Honey, let me keep you," he begged.

"I won't take your money. I just want you to produce my plays. I'm in pain over my career."

"Everyone is in pain, they just can't relate to the suffering in one another. I feel for your humanity. Come play with your warrior. You're very sexual, so am I. I wasn't like this before you, my girlfriend's a lesbian, and I've kept it all repressed so I can't minimize the moment as easily as you can."

"Can't we talk about this tomorrow?" I pleaded.

"No woman has ever walked away after making love to me before!" he shouted.

"That's because they probably remembered. Leave, now!" I screamed. "I don't need any sexual pressure. Stop it, let go of my arm," I said sternly as he grabbed me.

"I just need to be with a woman, I need some compassion. I got ripped apart today, I lost a million dollars, and you're leaving me, ignoring my sexual pleasures," he ranted on, now standing before me in his Ralph Lauren briefs, looking out of shape compared to what I usually went for.

He's the one that needed to be put in the nut house, I thought to myself. I have to get out of here. I'm trapped. I don't even have my car, not that I could drive in this condition.

"You performed, and today, you can't even remember. Don't I mean anything to you? Don't you love me?"

"Put your robe on. You're making me angry." He just didn't get it, his ego was so inflated.

"Just think of all the sensual kinetic energy yet to come. Are you afraid of my little mindless creature? You're supposed to be a woman of the world. I feel like a wounded warrior."

"You're fantasizing an intimacy that doesn't exist," I said mockingly.

"My body folded into yours. I'm wild, and I'm real. You slide in and out of reality."

"That's because I live in a world of fantasy."

"Take Dali, for instance, if he'd seen the world through reality's realm, the textures of his work wouldn't have raw jagged edges of surrealistic genius." He protested in an angry tone.

This lunatic was a tormented artist. I needed his help, but it wasn't worth the drama. "Some Southern gentleman. You're drunk. Leave me alone. You're redundant as a Pinter play on a slow opening night."

I spit at him, clawing his chest as he dragged me in front of a mirror, shaking me sliding his clammy fingers up and down my breasts. My flesh cringed at his touch.

"You aging starlet, playwright. Struggling to hang onto your youth. You're faded. A burnt out over the hill extra. Your face shows the dissipation of a woman that's seen too much of life. You're a joke and you don't want me, you lowly bitch. You're not of my class. Go back to your cowboy racist rednecks from Hicksville. You have a lot more in common with them. The only way you know how to entice men is flaunting your tits. If you don't remember that night let me refresh your memory," he said pulling down his briefs.

"Let go of me. You've threaded yourself into every actress and playwright in Hollywood," I screamed as he threw me down on the chaise lounge. I started hallucinating thinking that this couldn't be from the wine as I lay there unable to move. Christopher removed some rope he'd been hiding in his pocket.

"I'm going to read you a monologue from my play *The Marquis De Sade*, thus you'll succumb to this ill fated experience. 'Lift your veil, soon the chocolate shall drive you to nymphomania. You'll be begging me for sexual satisfaction. The aphrodisiac thus preparing you for your sexual duties. Eat heartily, I've ordered you the finest bitter sweet swiss chocolate wafers and bonbons abroad. Do you like it hot and whipped? Soon you shall understand that I am the connoisseur of discipline. I am a dom.' He screamed pacing around the room a script in his hand. 'Oh sweet sodomy is the first law of nature and has led me down a path of sexual tyranny,' he recited laughing like a maniac. 'Lovely lady, make my sexual ambitions reality. Have you ever been buttonholed?'

"You're a gawdy carnival of display, you've poisoned me, you swine!" I cried out. "Please stop, why are you doing this to me?"

"Because I can," he gloatingly said. "I'm glad that you enjoyed the chocolate aphrodisiac, dear, out of sight and earshot, you're a victim of my passion and will endure all that I choose to inflict on you. Every man is a tyrant when he fornicates. You have tasted the consecrated wafers, now we will partake in unnatural intercourse. I'd like to explore your dramatic talents by flogging you in my private theatre, while I give you a sound thrashing an orthodox type of sexual orgy. I'll be your dramatist for tonight while I enter you from the back passage!"

Chapter Twenty Eight

Jaded But Not Faded
Naked in
Sylvester Stallone's Coffin

The cinema has no boundary. It is a ribbon of dreams.
Orson Welles

The rumor was out in Hollywood that Sylvester Stallone was filming an avant garde mortuary scene in a movie at Universal Studios called Paradise Alley. The voice of Rush Fix the horny casting director from the studio came frantically screaming through my answering machine.

"Hi honey," I said, grabbing the phone. "Do you have the plumb job for me?"

"April, how old are you today?"

"I forget."

"Do you still have those long racehorse legs, honey how much do you weigh, and is your hair blonde, black or orange this week?"

"I'm five pounds over, but it all went to the right places," I answered proudly.

"Good," Rush said. "Sylvester Stallone is looking for a zoftig over the hill, floozy looking redheaded, leggy actress with big tits and big hair to play a dead, nude hooker in a film he wrote. Sly's staring and directing also. He saw your pictures from that bikini shoot."

"When's the interview?" I asked.

"It was yesterday. Why didn't you call me back?"

"I was staying at Rod Steiger's house in the colony. Rod thinks I have an autonomic personality and I should do more dramatic roles," I said.

"You should always be prepared for the unexpected," he scolded.

"Sorry," I said apologetically. "Any dialogue in the script?"

"The only lines you'll have are on your face. Now tell me what you're wearing?"

"The same thing I was wearing last time I saw you. I'm stark raving naked." I answered.

"Well push up those luscious bumps into your corset, Redhead Galore, and get to Universal in a half hour. I'll leave you a drive on pass, it's Stage 30. And don't be a stranger. Stop by my office after the interview and let me know if you got the job." Rush groaned.

"How much does it pay?" I enquired excitedly.

"It's a week's work and it pays three thousand dollars with overtime," the man replied.

Hanging the phone up, I frantically laced up my bustier, threw a long fire engine red wig on my head and raced recklessly over Mullholland in my black Corvette convertible. The mystical mountains were carved into a pale velvet blue sky like a roller coaster ride at Magic Mountain. As I walked on the set two guards escorted me to Stallone. When we met he shook my hand and, with his tough guy attitude, "Nice to meet you," he said. "Yous can use the dressing room over there to put on this robe, then come back here."

I put on the faded blue terrycloth robe and walked into Sly's dressing room.

"Lose the wig and the robe, kid." He demanded gruffly. I slipped out of the robe. as it fell to my ankles standing in front of the icon, in all of my bold, bronzed nakedness. I was really glad that I'd gotten an awesome suntan at the beach, but I was shaking and I needed to go somewhere after for a glass of wine to kill my hangover. Maybe I'd pop into Musso and Franks. I shouldn't have drank so much at the beach but I was having so much fun, it was worth it.

Sly grinned at me approvingly. "You're great," he said as his eyes swept my body. Now I felt the power. "You'll be Moaning Mary, she's a dead, crackhead hooker. She tripped on a marble and broke her neck. Before we embalm her, we're going to pack her in dry ice and sell her to the winos in Hell's Kitchen for five dollars a pop. They'll just think she's a heavy sleeper. We start shooting tomorrow. It's a four day shoot, don't wash your hair until we finish your scene. See you on the set."

The next morning I was in make-up and hair at 6:00 a.m. sharp.

"Good morning, Doll," the gay hairdresser said. "Would you like some breakfast while I'm transforming you to look like LaLa Lady of the Living Dead?"

"No thanks, honey, I'm in the buff for a week on this set. I have to starve, but I'll have some coffee." I answered.

"Well you look pretty good. Now don't pay any attention to me, I'm just going to put some talcum powder and KY Jelly in your frizzy hair to make it stand out more for the effect."

"Okay," I said. "I'm all yours."

"After I'm through with you, you'll go to make-up and they'll put white foundation all over your face and body. Now don't you be taking a bath until we're finished with your sequence and you know there won't be any wardrobe, don't you?" he laughingly shared.

I was horrified. "Oh my God. I have to show up for a premiere tonight, I can't go looking like this. Sweetheart, be reasonable," I moaned. "I'll look like an escapee from Camarillo after electric shock treatments." I just knew this job would make me famous. This was it. It's worth it, wasn't it? I thought. The Italian Stallion's the hottest property right now, and I'll be on the big money. I can buy some killer weed, I thought.

The baby mogul, better known as the A.D. screamed through his megaphone, "Okay, quiet on the set! They're bringing Sly in and no smoking."

I was lying on a steel table in the refrigerator room of the mortuary, shivering from the cold.

"Okay Moaning Mary, when I say action, rise up from the coffin, let the sheet drop from your body, jerk and freeze until I say cut."

We didn't get it the first shot and when we took a ten minute break, I ran to the 'Roach Coach' for a Diet Pepsi. I hid behind the set loosening my robe, rubbing ice cubes from the dixie cup on my pink nipples so that they'd stand erect. A camera man walked by, spotting my act.

"Would you mind doing that again when we roll?" He asked politely looking at me intensely as I flashed him a saccharine smile. Being an exhibitionist, I was getting a kick out of this little incident. I just loved shocking people, but not on film.

Sly wanted to get a surprised and frightened reaction from a heavyweight boxer who had never done any acting before, so he had me sit up when the boxer came over to look at the body. It didn't work. The scene began, the actor went over to the coffin. I sat up straight, nipples erect, rolling my eyes around in my head, mouth opened wide as if I were catching flies and the actor cracked up laughing. Sly just turned to me, pushed me down, and continued the scene.

"Let's face it you guys, acting is fun, and if it isn't, it's not worth it, so let's just have a good time," he said with underlying gentleness.

By the end of the shoot I discovered more of the man with a wicked sense of humor than the tough guys he's so known to portray in Hollywood. I bragged about my big movie scene to anyone who would listen. It would show my talent as a great comedic actress. When my playmate of the week and I attended the screening and they showed my footage, I was humiliated and horrified to see that I had been replaced by a dead tattooed wino. Another disappointing incident of being spliced away, lying in dust on the cutting room floor, because I was too nude for the silver screen!

Chapter Twenty Nine

Anna's Last Days
Part One

Anything at all, except nothing: nothing could not be allowed to go on and on like this.
Tennessee Williams

It seems like its been forever since my mother died. It wasn't a dream. I watched her slowly fade away for years. One summer day when I was visiting Anna at Cedar's, holding her small, bruised, wrinkled hand her eyes were moist as she kissed me on the cheek.

"You're a pessimist, 'Chicken Little,' but I'm an optimist and I hope to get better. Come here, sweetheart, give me a kiss."

I kissed her cheek. Her sallow skin had yellowed like parchment with age.

"I'm weak as a fly, but I'm afraid to die and leave you all alone. You have no one. I wish you'd meet someone nice. I can't protect you from the grave," she sighed softly. Her bones had become so brittle the nurses had to lift her from the bed in an electric machine. It destroyed my spirit seeing the agony she endured every waking moment.

"I'll take care of you, darling. Don't be afraid, you'll be fine," I said knowing that she was doomed as she nearly choked on her chicken soup. One day I tried to get some compassion out of my aunt who was once like a sister to me. She deserted us while Anna was failing in health.

"I feel like she's slipping through my fingers," I cried.

"Shape up, babe," she answered. "You're such a drama queen."

Next time I visited her in the emergency room, the moment she saw me she pulled the breathing tube out of her mouth.

"These nurses are torturing me. They keep poking my arm with all of those needles. If I'm never going to get well, I don't want to live this way anymore," she said in a weak voice of desperation.

I knew when she stopped asking me about our finances that she'd finally given up.

A month later, at the six thousand dollar a month pricey home, some bitch had chopped off her thick, wavy, luxurious, silver hair. The blank hopeless stare on her face made me crazy and sad that she had experienced so little pleasure in all of her years.

The poor woman's age-spotted flesh was grotesquely saggy. The bluish veins on her hands had almost collapsed on her transparent, powdery-white skin.

After an orderly had given her another shot, the cotton fell onto my lap. I picked up the soft squishy ball, wiping off the blood that was trickling down her arm.

"I brought you your favorite from the deli, chicken matzo ball soup and chopped liver. Here mother, try to drink a little soup," I coaxed, handing her a cup and spoon. "It's from Nate n' Al."

She lifted the spoon to her lips with shaky hands as the rich hot broth trickled down her chin.

"May I take the tray?" the condescending nurse asked with a broken German accent.

The final visit to purgatory was at a snake pit that they called a rehab center, where time stands still for all the forgotten ones. It was a dingy, dark, scary place. My worst fear and nightmare came into being when I entered her room, witnessing a screaming bedridden gray-haired obese old woman.

"Get out of my room!" she yelled as I sat down on a chair that I pulled up next to my mother's bed-side.

She was the original crazy maker.

I watched Anna slip in and out of a coma, then for seconds semi-consciousness. She was so far gone I'd had to call in the hospices.

"You can't sit in my chair, I'll call the police," her roommate ranted on.

Suddenly my mother opened her eyes, looking up at me expressionless.

"April, will you help me out of here," she said sternly. "I want to go home."

"Do you know what year it is and what the president's name is?" the hospice lady asked.

"No," she answered, looking confused.

"You're old and your legs have given out on you. We can't take you with us," she answered mockingly.

"You monster, insensitive fucking cunt. You're fired. You're so dead!" I screamed.

"I don't care. You're mother's dying. I'd be surprised if she lives to see another day," the bitch said, grabbing her sweater and purse, running out of the room without feeling any compassion or remorse.

Then as if in a trance, Anna started rambling on articulately in the same controlling voice, "I have to go to a movie with auntie. Would you like to come with us?" I never had the heart to tell her that the only person that she'd been inseparable with all her life had disappeared. I felt such empathy for the poor, helpless soul who'd never failed putting me in touch with my love and anger.

"I have to run some errands, but I'll be back, and maybe I'll join you," I lied convincingly as she reached out, putting her arms around me.

"You're my life, sweetheart," she said as I walked out of the room. I was so sad and guilt-ridden that I could never please her or live up to her expectations. Then her life passed on.

After visiting my mother I went back to her house into the bedroom, my eyes wandering towards the dresser. There were two pictures. One of a young aesthetic looking beauty, the other was a dark dimpled lovable looking little girl with silken black corkscrew curls. *How could the universe do this to us,* I thought. We both had been scarred by life.

I drove away in the dark that comes with the foreboding feeling of disaster. I'd never been taught to see things in perspective. It was all drama. Later on I'd learned to nurture my inner child, becoming introspective about our relationship.

Early in life, I was exposed to the social graces and the finery and sophistication, but she never gave me the human resources. If I had been more venerable to my mother I could have been destroyed. My family were the Beverly Hills elitists, but I was an artist with an unfettered spirit who couldn't be reigned in by bribery.

I took the shortcut home, speeding over Coldwater Canyon to Mulholland, focusing on the energy from clusters of blinking lights trying to quiet the chatter in my head for a minute, but I was dreading the foreboding inevitable phone call that my gut instinct told me was awaiting my arrival. When I opened the door of my den, the red light on my answering service was flashing. I had twelve messages. My hand was shaking as I reached for a glass of Perrier and my pill box, swallowing two 350 milligram Somas, medicating myself, hoping that the pills would ease some of the pain. Waves of anxiety subsided as they kicked in, giving me the courage to press the button and listen to my messages as I started emerging into the numbness.

"Your mother just passed away about an hour ago," the gruff voice of an apathetic male nurse said. 'We need you to call the mortuary and make arrangements to have her body removed immediately. We can't keep her here."

I was totally overwhelmed and in shock as I dialed the number. Years of pain were choked up inside of me, yet I was unable to cry and release my tension and grief.

I called my jealous aunt and when she heard the news all she could say was, "Do you know if she left everything to you?" She asked in a saccharin sweet voice hoping to sabotage me leaving me penniless.

"Yes," I gloated.

"Well just don't let some kook take it away from you."

No one in my cold hearted Jewish family even called, no less sent flowers or cards. I was in it all alone, but I realized that grief was inevitable. Knowing that there was no money for them and being aware of my ferocious nature that they'd never win in court I was abandoned once again.

Then that tape started playing in my head. I knew that I'd always be afraid. All of my life I'd believed that she was indestructible. I had to pick up the pieces and go on with my life and learn how to live, love and function normally. But for now I could think of nothing else. My only ally was really gone and I was an only, lonely child who felt totally disconnected from life.

My only consolation were my animals. The soft purr of my calico cat, Eclipse, and the bark and wag of Sky's tail. I realized that it took a long time to heal after a loved one dies. I wondered if I'd ever feel sane and have any peace of mind again.

The next morning I dragged myself out of bed, throwing on some sweats and a torn t-shirt. I didn't care about anything not bothering to put on make-up or comb my matted hair. There was no room in my heart for trivia. My stomach ached from emptiness. I tried eating a piece of toast, but I just couldn't keep anything down in the middle of an anxiety attack.

At noon, the long black hearse finally arrived in front of my door. A short older Latin man with a handlebar mustache rang the doorbell, handing me a small carved wooden box in exchange for a check.

I closed the door, putting my mother's ashes inside. Some day I would sprinkle them into the sea. She never would have wanted to have her remains in Laurel Canyon. She was so Beverly Hills. For now I had to have her close to me in spirit. I'd gained newfound freedom. Now I was rich and independent. The great creator had protected me from evil.

I started pacing the floor, trying to clean my house as if that small gesture would change my life. I erased all the menacing messages off of my answering service , in shock, not in denial. Suddenly realizing that no one would ever love me so deeply again, I searched my house for traces of her, finding lipstick, a jeweled pill box and a copy of 'The Rubaiyat' of Omar Khayyam with an inscription inside of the book "Anna, A Book of Verses Underneath The Bough, A Jug of Wine, a Loaf of Bread and Thou Beside Me Singing in the Wilderness. Oh, Wilderness Were Paradise Now. Love Your Ardent Admirer". I placed the poetry book back into my Gothic Mediterranean cage-like bookcase. In my den I found her evening attire. She once painted her lips crimson red, carried a vintage beaded, embroidered bag with a now tarnished gold mirror inside. The compact reflected a glimpse of Anna as a young, beautiful, frightened, romantic girl. Once she had experienced love, desire and hope. As time elapsed she lived vicariously through me.

Chapter Thirty

Ovulating Oysters
The Beverly Hills Hotel
The Polo Lounge Reunion
Part One

Wit ought to be a glorious treat like caviar. Never spread it about like marmalade.
Noel Coward

Driving west on sexy star studded Sunset Boulevard, my car climbed the mysterious decadent driveway of 'The Pink of Perfection,' that grand old watering hole, The Beverly Hills Hotel. Since the early 20th Century, the regal oasis perched on top of glittering Rodeo Drive has remained the quintessential spot for people watching, to see and be seen.

A striped awning blended into the majestic California Mediterranean landscape swamped in a tangle of gangly fan palms among twelve acres of tropical foliage and gardens perfumed by bright multi-colored rose bushes and aromatic blossoms of fruited citrus trees.

I breathed in the sweet scents squeezing through the Paparazzi pigs, as my Manolos sunk into the plush crimson red carpet at the Porte Cochère. Coconut palms swayed in the balmy breezes as a bellboy opened the door to paradise.

"Nice to see you again, Miss Moon," he said with sincerity.

My Central Casting Sorority sisters, Diva Boy Brian and I were meeting for one of our long lunches. Mingling among antique white lace curtains and hunter green walls were age resisting geriatric ex beauty queens there to indulge themselves in 'The Power Lunch' after a quickie visit to their Beverly Hills plastic surgeons for a power peel.

As I entered the bar, a well-seasoned Maitre D' was guiding guests to indoor and outdoor seating.

"We've been saving your favorite booth. Welcome home, Miss Moon," the sophisticated, weathered, silver haired man said. His face was flushed and beaming as he led me through the dimly lit room. "One of your lady friends is waiting for you," he said pulling out the large forest green upholstered booth where all the hubbub was happening.

I slid in next to an anxiously awaiting Yolanda. The elegant ambiance had all the clamor, glamour and glitz of pretend people who had to be there, but weren't really present. I reveled in the false gaiety. The popping of corks, lilting laughter and delicate pink flowered baskets were scattered about a clubby bar adorned with beveled mirrors.

Our waiter approached our table wearing a frozen condescending smile. "You have a call, Miss Moon. Didn't you hear the page?"

"Thank you," I said as I picked up the black receiver at our booth. "Yes Raquel," I answered. It was Racy Rockie 'Famous Realtor To The Stars.' "Shush," I whispered to Yolanda. "I didn't invite the wicked shallow bitch."

"What's up?" I said into the phone in a cold flat voice. "Are you at the office, honey?"

"Yes, I'm on the floor. I do everyone big and small. I've had sixty offers today," she bragged on as I covered my ear.

"I hope you didn't take your sunglasses off," I answered.

"I'm so excited," she screamed into her defective cellphone.

"I'm just thrilled for you." Talking to her was phone jail. She didn't have any boundaries and continued on with her idle banter.

"I haven't had anyone decent call me from Bel Air or Beverly Hills. The NOC (not of our class) clients I'm working with are all tacky transplants. But I can so live with that. I made three figures last year," she whined. "Your property is a Beverly Hills charmer. Will you put in your will that I have the exclusive listing in case you die before I do?"

"Suck my dick, sick bitch!" I answered in a rage, placing the receiver back in the cradle. I loathed the vapid, classless social climber. *She'd kill for a listing*, I thought.

Chelsea made a grand splash reminiscent of a spastic runway model. She was a vortex of twisted cellulose humanity. Her flowing sheer flesh-colored Versace chiffon dress accentuated every traffic stopping curve. Coiffed hair was swept up in a french twist, with a jet black beaded velvet bow. She was all pretense and designer labels.

"Sorry I'm late, girls, but my dermabrasion lady was running over. I had to wait a month to get an appointment. I just saw a Silver Cloud Rolls Royce that has my name on it, I wonder who the owner is?" she mused.

"You is so shameless," the cantankerous Yolanda blurted out.

"There's a VW Rabbit parked outside that would be perfect for you, Yolanda," Chelsea teased, throwing her platinum blonde head back full throttle.

"You're looking very retro chic in your black oval rimmed Jackie O Chanel glasses, Chelsea," I said, planting a kiss on her moist, glossed lips. For years, I'd had a girl crush on the English bird.

Chelsea lit a Viceroy cigarette with her sterling silver lighter, flaring her nostrils, blowing a trail of smoke in he air.

"Chelsea's a role model for you, YoYo, of how to make a fashion statement," I chimed in.

Yolanda was clad in so-not-now, tightly-fitted, stone-washed, low ride jeans, revealing a pierced navel and butt cleavage, and an aqua Tee, exposing her breasts. Her hair was woven into gawky corn rows braided tightly into her scalp. Our waiter graced the booth carrying a tray of tri-colored chips, chunky lime green guacamole, homemade salsa and salmon dip.

"Would you ladies like to see a wine list and lunch menus while waiting for your other guests to arrive?" he asked.

"Yes that would be delightful," I answered as he handed me a manila envelope.

"The PR staff sent you this press kit. Everything's complimentary," he added.

"Thanks," I smiled.

"Ya got any Lays barbecue chips, Mista?" Yolanda asked impatiently.

"Sorry Miss, we don't carry that in our kitchen, but we can order out for you," he said in an affected European accent.

"Cool. April, you eat like them rich people," she shrieked in her monotone voice.

YoYo never ceased to embarrass me. And now when I was reviewing this fabled hotel surrounded by top gun independent producers, high profile financiers, impeccable service and legends and luminaries she brought her 'Ghetto Princess' presence and scary hair to the table. The Maitre D' was standing as stiff as a mongoose proudly at his prestigious post with a frozen grin on his face, appalled by her presence.

As Brian approached our table, Chelsea waved him over, puffing on her long cigarette holder.

"It's the glamazons," Brian said, greeting us with a big smile as he slid into the booth next to me.

"Hello sweetheart," I said, giving him a big hug.

"I'm really impressed, April. This is the coveted booth number three. It's only reserved for important unconventional VIPs."

"You's doin' great, girl," Yolanda said. "I'm sure glad you's a food critic."

"Opulence is just a way of life for our April now." Brian beamed, squeezing my hand.

"She knows what she wants and she's the love of her own life," Chelsea teased.

"And she's still my favorite hooker. You're a literate illiterate with chutzpah," Brian teased. "We simply adore you, April, even with your free floating amorphous Hollywood condition."

"I gave up my appointment with José Eber for you, that's devotion dahling." Chelsea purred.

The waiter stopped at our table, with more hors d'oeuvres and a chilly smile. "Have you decided what kind of wine you'd like to order today?"

"What would you suggest?" I asked.

"We have a new signature addition. It's dry and bubbly. The luscious grapes are grown in the hilly vineyards of Champagne France. Or if you'd prefer a Rothschild we have several special vintages in our cellar."

"I'd like to start out with a bottle of the Veuve."

"Would you prefer the Veuve Clicquot and the Grande Dame, miss?" he asked.

"That will be fine, and some Perrier," I added.

"Very well," he answered.

"And we'll need a few minutes to study the menu." I smiled as he scurried away.

"I'm so pleased to see you again, Brian," Chelsea said.

"Tell me what's going on in the life of my Koda-chrome blond," He asked. "Are you still obviously on a constant manhunt?"

Chelsea smiled mysteriously, lifting her dainty French manicured hand, showing off a Cartier diamond ring.

"I'm dating a simply high achieving professional man. Brilliant," she bragged on.

"How old is he?" Brian asked.

"He's ancient, old money, darling," Chelsea laughed.

"You can only take the Geritol set for so long," Brian commented. "What happened to your last boyfriend. I need information."

"He had irritable male syndrome," she said impetuously.

"What's up with that, girl?" Yolanda asked.

"The chap had zero sex drive. Banging someone for minutes always puts a relationship onto a down-hill spiral," she smirked in disgust. Chelsea had an icy edge about her. A sort of Machiavellian quality as she smiled at all her prospective suitors throwing air kisses throughout the room. *She was sweet and tough at the same time*, I thought to myself.

"When my doctor divorces his prissy Rodeo Drive wife he's promised to marry me. Until then, I'm free for the highest bidder," she quipped. "Simply brilliant, darling."

"What's your man gonna do with you after he runs out of body parts to fix, honey," Yolanda said, her left eye twitching.

"Despite Hymie's erectile dysfunction he got a hard on when he saw my gold thong sticking out from my surgical gown. But when he shags me on Viagra it's like having a broomstick up me pussy."

"Let's face it, for Chelsea it's finance before romance," Brian laughed.

"The last time I went under the knife I just had a little adjustment," Chelsea said defensively. "I was always envious that April has the best tits on the planet, so Hymie made me a pair and they were free."

"I'm flattered, but you're so self obsessed and invested in yourself." I commented.

"And Yolanda looks so young, despite all of her drama, what's going on with The Queen of Chaos these days," Brian asked.

"Black don't crack," Yolanda answered defensively.

"Only in your pipe," Chelsea sneered at her.

Diva boy was looking hot in his red and black "All American Boy" T-shirt and newly colored streaked blond hair.

"I'm wearing the dominant colors. Do you like my new image?" Brian asked in a falsetto voice.

"It's certainly different but you should have left the blonde hair to Madonna," Chelsea teased.

"I agree," I shared.

"I so love your flaming techno colored hair, April. Usually when one gets a little older it doesn't mesh well, but for you it adds a whole new level of bitchiness," Brian said, giving me the evil eye.

Yolanda was getting trashed fast, after stealing everyone's drinks, dropping her cell phone into her glass.

"Okay, Yo Yo, I'm the designated libation pourer today," I said slipping her more Perrier.

"This glass tastes even better than the last one," she slurred.

Yolanda had that blank stare with no recognition in her eyes. I couldn't help cracking up. The girl was drinking designer water thinking it was alcohol.

"Yolanda dear, how's the Rehabilitation Center?" Chelsea inquired.

"Hey man, it's awesome. The place is right on the water at Point Dume," she bragged.

"I'll have to come round and fetch you for an outing sometime," Chelsea offered. "Its nice they let you join us today."

"Ya guys, I met this shrink. His name is Dr. Gland, and he's a white boy. He wears them Porsche glasses an drives a black Harley," Yolanda slurred.

"Where'd you meet him?" I asked.

"We was staring at each other all through a lecture on opiates at a Chemical Co-Dependency lecture. The janitor wants me back but he's on hold," she shared.

"Darling, I tried calling you at the halfway house, but they informed me that they kicked you out because of your fallacious behavior," Chelsea said sternly.

"He got me back in. Now when y'all meet him don't you go sayin' I got trashed today," Yolanda added with a worried glance. "He says booze don't mix well with my Prozac. If I don't take my medication, I can say mean things, so he upped my dosage and we do the wild thing, girlfriend. I got my own private room with this cool view and he gives me booty calls late at night," she said guzzling her Perrier, her head drooping to the side like a wilted lily, her hair blending into the avocado dip.

"She'll never sit in the front row with the elite on fashion week in New York," Brian laughed. "Yolanda would drive the social sisters to take their valium. I'm off....I have an important meeting at Sony in ten minutes," he said, rushing off.

"Please sign this check, Miss Moon. Everything is complimentary, including the tip and parking," said the accommodating vacuous waiter.

"Thanks April," Yolanda said staggering out of the banana leafed corridors.

"Love you," Chelsea smiled giving me a Hollywood hug, the scent of her Christian Dior Poison perfume lingering in the air as she slipped into her peach Armani cashmere shrug, a total fashionista. We were all carefree on that fun filled afternoon but Yolanda was still grappling with life, Chelsea was obsessed with money, and Brian and I were artists chasing fame, haunted by our darkest demons.

Chapter Thirty One
Antonio, The '80s
Part One

The first time I laid eyes on him I thought to myself, that man is my executioner! That man will destroy me.
Tennessee Williams

Antonio was a cross between a stallion and a pitbull. I was enamored by the thirty-something macho Mambo King. He was the epitome of Don Juan from hell, a gigolo type number.

One twilight evening a patch of sun set high above the Hollywood Hills lighting up the Hollywood Sign, bathing it with golden hues in the enchanting land of the lost. My retreat was reminiscent of a cottage in the countryside. As the pale blue sky darkened, Antonio darkened my mood. He was holding an embroidered royal blue box, two bottles of Marqués de Riscal wine, and a long stemmed crimson rose in his hands.

"Como esta, my little chiquita," he said in his thick spanish tongue. "I hope you're not angry at Antonio for stopping by, but you disconnect phone again."

"I've been very busy. Ignore my mint green face mask. Welcome to my humble hacienda, Chico,"

I said. His hair was slicked back in a ponytail. An Adidas bag slung over his arm. His demeanor breathed the air of decadence.

"Te amo, my beautiful princess. I'm your Knight of Pentacles, your Prince of Darkness. I've brought you my cajones for your well being," he said proudly.

I opened the box laughing hysterically as chines echoed through the spacious house.

"What sweet temptations you bring me. Let's hang out in the bedroom," I said invitingly, grabbing the wine, some glasses and a corkscrew. I couldn't resist temptation, the moment I laid eyes on him again.

Antonio followed me into the bedroom popping a cork. "This aged Spanish wine is from my native country. Here, I hope you enjoy it," he said sniffing the cork. "Let's make a toast to getting back together, si?"

"This wine is divine, Antonio," I said, sipping the spirits.

"I've missed you so much, my darling," he said moving in closer, licking the nape of my neck.

I was wearing a sexy lavender Euro-chic lace slip dress and he was in the attack mode.

"You try to set me on fire, no?" he said.

"I always succeed don't I, you big bronze hunk."

"You make fun of Antonio. I'm a man of greatness, aristocracy. The only people who know you read your column within a five block radius of Beverly Hills. Come to Spain with me. You need me. You can't speak the language. I'll be your tutor," he said.

"I'm not making any promises," I answered.

"I know why you run from me, because I'm just a wanderer that has fallen out of grace. I'm weak, April."

"My shrink thinks that weakness and strength are linked together," I said reassuringly, patting him on the arm.

He took a quick sip of wine, looking puzzled.

"Boom, life is so harsh. I need another drink. It really makes me sad when you hide from me."

"It's not all about you. I just won't tolerate the mood swings."

"Your Latin boy-toy feel love for you," he said putting his arms around my waist.

I felt the hardness of Antonio's body, his manhood bulging beneath the zipper.

"It's still here, can't you feel it?" he pleaded. "You're so sexy. You have such a high class trashy look."

"I just can't handle your jealousy. I have fun with you, and we've shared all of our deep dark secrets, but I'm not ready for a live-in lover." I said with conviction.

"You hurt me when you say I'm much more involved with you than you are with me," he said holding me tightly. "You make it hard all the time. My cock no lie." he said pressing my hand between his thighs.

I tried pushing him away, but to no avail. Giving way to temptation, my hand sliding down his leg.

"Feel it, it belongs to you, my darling."

Pulling away from him, I poured us another glass of wine.

"I want we should be together. I really communicate with you. You're the only woman I know that's smart enough to deal with me," he begged.

"Commitments usually get me committed," I said firmly. "Let's keep it light."

"You're just like my mother in Madrid. Both wild, loco, unpredictable redheads. That intrigues me," he said leaning back on my bed, puffing a cigarette and sipping his drink. "Is it because I'm so much younger than you?" he asked.

"I've always been with men that were younger than I was. Cher and I have a lot in common. She was quoted as saying on David Letterman "If I waited for a man my age to ask me out I would have never had a date.""

"She's a cow," Antonio said.

Through my stained glass windows a kaleidoscope of colors turned the night into mysterious intrigue. I had been over the edge with depression lately. Cedars Sinai Hospital had called earlier, informing me that my mother was back in the intensive care unit again. Seems like it was a ritual with her. She used to preach to me that any age was sweet, and it was tearing my guts out. I couldn't be alone tonight. "Can you stay over tonight?" I asked him.

"Si, you make me so happy. I love it with you. When you're not with me, I dream with your big chichis and red pusita."

"Are you high, Antonio?" I asked.

"I feel like a wild toro. I just came from the boys."

"Did you score me some grass?" I asked hopefully.

"You're such a pot whore, April. I know that the only reason you put up with me is because I'm your connection," he said. "Here. Are you happy now?" he asked.

I grabbed the long stemmed amber buds lighting up a bong. Antonio pulled a white envelope out of the pocket of his jacket, pouring a vial of white powder onto the mirror on my vanity. He cut the crystals with a razor blade, took a quick snort with a straw, then rolled it up in his cigarette.

"Here, smoke some of this. It will make you brilliant," he said passing it to me.

"I think I'll pass on that stuff," I said in protest.

"Come on, darling, try some. I'm a wine and coke aficionado and this stuff has only been cut once. It's pure Peruvian rock cocaine."

"Okay, just one puff," I answered. I smoked the coke and my heart started racing.

"Bueno, now we'll be more simpatico and you won't get drunk and make a fool out of yourself. I'll teach you how to drink," he said.

"This is definitely not my drug of choice. I'll be awake and hung-over for two days and I won't be able to eat. I'm sticking with the wine and pot," I said feeling paranoid as I lay on my bed, gulping down the smooth libations.

Antonio moved closer, holding a paperback copy of *Les Liaisons Dangereuses* in his hands. "I want to have this kind of arrangement with you, dearest," he said, reading me the most decadent dialogue in the book, then smiling lasciviously. "Tell me, how do you feel when you please a man with your lips and your well-educated tongue?"

"I feel powerful, in control. That's how I've kept you around for so long."

"But I have a problem putting down roots. You know that I'm a drifter," he said.

"Don't you miss Madrid?" I asked.

"It's too hard to live there now, with so much violence," he answered.

"Then where will you go?" I asked.

"Let's go to Costa Rica and buy a farm. Are you still fertile? If you're not, in Costa Rica men can have five wives. I'll even marry you. Pronto. I used to think that if every woman in the world had my baby, I could rule the planet. Just like that, boom," he said excitedly, running his fingers lightly over my breasts.

Antonio just didn't fit into my life plan. Vanity was the only thing he ever invested in.

"Look at me, April. No one has a body like this, no?" he said lifting up his sweatshirt, patting his ripped abs. "I want we should just go, my princess."

"But Antonio, let's get real. You've acquired a taste for the finery of life. You, live on a farm? I don't think so."

"Let's not talk about it anymore. I'm in the mood for a club tonight. There's a bar on the strip that has live salsa, hip-hop and great Latin bands," he said.

"Okay let's get all glitzy and glammed to the nines and go dancing," I perked up a little, running over to my vanity, painting my face with rosy cream blush..

"It will be an evening of sensual, sinful treasures. It's the trashiest, flashiest club in LA," he smiled.

Brushing my hair, studying myself in a full length mirror in front of my closet door, I asked, "What should I wear tonight?"

"I wonder what would look good on me, April," he said rummaging through my cluttered closet while polishing off his wine, pulling out my Dolce and Gabbana gown. "Darling, I just love your red sequined dress. Is it vintage? I hope you won't take this the wrong way, but I think it would look better on Antonio than you. And by the way, I was Dietrich in a cabaret act in Madrid. And I look better blond, but I'm not gay," he said unconvincingly.

"Oh, I see that," I laughed, trying not to act shocked.

Antonio pulled a long blonde wig out of his gym bag dancing around the room to the sounds of *The Gypsy Kings*, wearing my dress dabbing his face with make-up, preparing for the nightlife.

"I much prefer Versace, but do I not look like The Siren of Sequins?" he asked.

"You look like the devil in drag diva," I laughed. "But I like a man that's full of surprises."

Much to my amazement, Antonio was just another case of confused chromosomes. But he was my only answer to Antonio Banderas, and definitely more available. I just hoped that he wouldn't stretch out my dress.

Chapter Thirty Two

A Rendezvous With Death
On Psychedelics
Eternally Hollywood Mortuary

I can choose anything except temptation.
Oscar Wilde

It was the summer solstice, the longest day of the year. I awakened that grey morning in a twilight sleep. The voice in my head was saying, *'we're not safe'*. I didn't feel sane, being involved with a loser like Antonio. He was always leading me into a dark ditch.

I was desperately trying to crawl out, get sober and stay away from my lower companions. I'd been going to AA Meetings and hadn't had any wine or substances for two weeks, a veritable miracle.

At dusk, I was startled by a loud bang on my door knocker. I looked through the peephole and saw Antonio's darkly decadent face.

"Hola," he said in his calculating way.

"It's my ruthless lover," I answered without opening the door. Chelsea had come by and we were going to see an Indie film at Laemmle Sunset 5.

"Open up, April. Do you feel like being corrupted today?" he asked seductively.

Chelsea broke the silence, letting him in.

"I have a wild idea. I brought a basket filled with aphrodisiacs, acid and bottles of champagne. It's a beautiful night for a picnic."

"But Chelsea was going to read the 12 Steps with me. I'm not drinking anymore," I said firmly.

"I want to go to the cinema," Chelsea begged "and not on my own as well."

"Come on, girls. I'm driving," he said, grabbing my arm. "Bring the AA book with you and get your purses. We can read over a bottle of Moet," he said.

"April, you've been so good, you deserve to have a little buzz. I feel like a wild burrito." Antonio said playfully. I had cravings and couldn't resist being reckless. Besides I was outnumbered wasn't I.

We jumped into the manipulative, chemically fueled Latin's black Mustang convertible, the wind whipping my sun bleached hair.

"Where are you taking us?" I asked as he popped a bottle, the bubbles squirting all over my face tickling my nostrils.

"It's a surprise, my princess. You'll just *looove* it," he answered.

Antonio pulled up in back of a mortuary somewhere in the heart of Hollywood. "We've arrived, Chicas. I have an embalmer friend who works here. He says it's easy to get in at night. Chelsea, you take the wine, April, here's the blanket, and I'll carry the rest."

With a little persuasion, we hopped over the fence and invaded the privacy of the tombs of the lonely strangers of the night. Our host poured the ambrosia in plastic designer cups. Chelsea and I stretched out on the ground as Antonio paced nervously around the plots, then laid down next to us.

"You ladies are mucho muy bonita. I brought my Sony camcorder. I'd like to take pictures of you naked, dropping acid, kissing on top of the tombstone, drinking while reading the 12 Steps. The experience will last for eternity. The name of the cemetery is 'Eternally Hollywood'."

"That's brilliant, darling. And you might join us," Chelsea said mischievously. "This is skin crawlingly real."

"Si, si," he answered, smiling as he lit up a glass bowl of cocaine and we passed around a joint, swallowing the mood altering psychedelics.

"I wonder if this is bad karma invading their slumber. It's so peaceful and serene here," I said self justifyingly. "It's a little spooky."

"Si. I love it with you girls. This place makes me feel so at home," he said moving in closer.

"I fret over what outfit to wear to the soirées, but I always rock the room. If we were dead we'd never have to worry about clothes again," Chelsea laughed.

"And you'd still rock the grave. Let's shake up this place," Antonio smiled. "Pick a tombstone to pose on," Antonio coaxed, pulling us up from the grass.

"Beloved father and son," I wonder if those poor chaps had small willies?" Chelsea mused, mesmerized.

"Let's pose on this one," I said. "It's freaking awesome. 'Dead Mother and Daughter'. I'm going to pretend that I'm deceased all day then I won't have to worry bout my out of control life," I said sadly, trying to blur the pain, feeling guilty while drinking more and dropping a downer. *This is a little creepy*, I thought as a gust of wind blew the cup out of my hand.

"I love crashing a party with the elite. It's a class funeral parlor. My friend told me there are a lot of movie icons buried here," Antonio bragged. "Your beauty and nudity will be protected by me and my camera. I *loove* both of you," he said, planting passionate kisses on our mouths. "I'll be your graveyard *loover* tonight."

"Cool, I'm forever pondering the meaning of my whole existence. Maybe that's all I ever needed," I said, flinging my arms around his broad shoulders. *I've always loved seclusion and hated crowded streets*, I thought as the acid kicked in I started hallucinating, reflecting on rolling hills, greenery and a kaleidoscopic of constantly changing colorful stained glass luminescence and symmetrical patterns.

I never envisioned being stuck in a mausoleum or wall crypt. I wanted my ashes sprinkled by the sea. I was wearing shorts, flip-flops, and a spandex top, bra-less with no panties as always.

Antonio was clad in Guess designer cut-offs, bare-chested. Chelsea lifted her short flimsy dress over her head, flaunting full nudity. Her creamy alabaster firm, high breasts and heart-shaped shaved bird looked enticing in the moonlight.

Antonio grabbed my hair, throwing me down on a grave, pulling off my top. I slid off my shorts as Chelsea lay next to us, putting her arms around me, her hands roaming my body staring into my soul with her large glassy eyes sending me into oblivion. I was feeling totally enraptured by the touch of her skin.

"I'm tripping on you," I whispered softly in her ear.

"I adore you sweet. Your nipples look like pink rosebuds. You're shockingly naughty," she said, nibbling on them. "I've always had a little crush on April," Chelsea moaned as she swapped tongues with our oversexed Latin lover.

"I welcome a little competition and If I had only one lifetime I'd want to be with both of you. Would you girls consider my balls?" he said as Chelsea mischievously, slowly pulled the zipper down on his denim jeans and we lay drunk and stoned, clutching each other's bodies heating up the starry night 'til the red glare of sunrise.

Chapter Thirty Three
Antonio, The '80s
Part Two

(She) had known in her profession a fair quantity of young men with languid grace and a measure of beauty who only looked at mirrors.
Tennessee Williams

Antonio sped up Mulholland on his Harley, his hair dark as his mood, rippling in the wind. Parking his bike on the edge of the cliff he did a line watching the silver dots sparkling, lighting up the city. Then hopped on his bike. He had an agenda. He took the shortcut to Laurel Canyon, driving up the private driveway through the wrought iron gate.

When he arrived at his destination high above the Hollywood sign it was twilight. There was a mist on the mountain.

The faded blue and white shuttered cottage was perched serenely on the hill surrounded by greenery. Peach trees and lemon trees were blossoming wild in the wilderness, framing the white picket fence. He walked through the lattice worked arch laced with morning glories. The aroma of sweet basil and rosemary lingered in the air.

I peeked through the peephole of my front door. Antonio was tapping on my window pane, beckoning me to let him in.

"Go away," I said with conviction.

"You changed your phone number again. Will you at least give me the new one?" he asked pleadingly.

"I don't give my phone number to the devil," I said flatly.

He was holding a bunch of yellow and orange sunflowers in his hand, clutching a bottle of red wine in the other.

"Ok. Just let me give you these flowers and share one glass of Louis Jadot Beaujolais with you, then I'll leave pronto, my darling," he said.

I was out of wine, feeling tense and temptation ruled over logic.

"Why wouldn't you let me in?" he asked as he followed me into the living room. "Get me a vase and I'll arrange the flowers for you," he said with his thick Spanish tongue.

I handed him a mosaic hand carved vase and a corkscrew. Antonio was looking fine in his gray and white chic-pimp style punk pin-striped tux jacket and gray shirt with narrow tie and suspenders. A flip of slick long black hair was hanging over one eye. His demeanor breathed of confidence. Faded denims hugged his long spindly body from every boyish angle.

"I love it. Your hair looks like Veronica Lake."

"Stop making a joke out of me. I wish that you'd stop pushing me away," he said putting his arms around me.

"It's because you're a dangerous man. A big risk," I said curling up on my white wicker Pier 1 love seat in my skin-tight torn low-rise jeans and T cropped to my chest.

He was stroking my bare multi-colored toes. "You look like you climbed out of a dumpster, April."

"Its European hippy chick" I said.

"I'm just playing with you, my precious. For me it only happens when you're around," he said his hands cupping my face.

"But you're trying to possess me. I'm afraid that our journey together will lead to a disastrous destination," I said moving his hands away.

"What if I'm a good boy. I try to please you, chica," he said while studying himself admiringly in the full length antique mirror. "We're attracted to each other. No? Is that a bad thing?" he asked spreading some creamy brie on a piece of hard sourdough bread accompanying it with his glass of wine.

"Yes, it is because of your objectionable behavior."

"My baby, we don't need anyone else. Let's just do our own thing. Si?"

"Why are you so obsessed with me, Antonio?" I asked with apprehension.

"I know how to survive and exist, I just don't know how to live or love. You no love me the way I make you cum?" he frowned "I'm your looooover, no? It's still there. We can't hide it. I loooove it when I taste you," he said.

"I call that lust" I said, moving away from him.

"Say something. I love it the way you cum. I get hard watching your body heaving under mine. Here. Have another glass of wine," he said passionately, lifting the bottle and sniffing the cork. "I brought you a little surprise from the boys," he came closer, putting plump buds in my hand.

His vision of life was so different than mine, but when it came to marijuana I'd make an exception. And unfortunately I was still wildly attracted to his mysterious dark aura. He was my escape from reality and responsibility. "I was afraid you'd be angry with Antonio for showing up like this. I just couldn't get you off my mind, so I decided to take a spin up the hill and visit you and piggy," he laughed.

Piggy was my Shih Tzu who he was jealous of because the pup had priority in my bed. As I overlooked the city below, bluish granite clouds framed a multi-colored rainbow on the mountain. A moon popped up in all of its radiance as we watched the star filled sky. Then the night turned to black.

Antonio pulled out a little red book from his pocket and read me a quote from Jung: "This is so us, my princess. The meeting of two personalities is like the contact of two chemical substances. If there is any reaction, both are transformed."

"I love that quote, Carl Jung believed that in one's lifetime we have more than one soul mate," I said.

"Please do not fear me, chica."

"You're still in the meridian of your youth. But when you start to fade the world will become your enemy. Don't throw it all away just for a vice." I said.

His eyes were dead as he flashed his well practiced wicked smile at me grinding his teeth.

"I have to get high," he said with desperation in his voice as he pulled out a vile of white powder, pouring it into the bowl, inhaling it, filling the room with puffy white smoke. "I just want to forget, I'm so lost, I'm washed up. Would you care to join me?" he asked.

"I'm going to pass." I answered coldly feeling overwhelmed by his presence.

"I do a few runs for the boys every now and then. I get my drugs for free. Plus I make some dinero," he said smoke filtering out of his nose. "I want we should be together. I really communicate with you," he said with a wild crazy look in his eyes. His bitter tongue touched my lips. "My greatest pleasure is giving you my sex," he said running his finger up the zipper of my jeans.

He got excited so fast I panicked, soothed only by the amber flames of the wood burning fireplace throwing him off the couch. He laid on the hardwood floor propping his head up on a pillow.

"I think as you women age you stop trying to understand what makes relationships work," he said with the expression of a wide eyed animal.

"We women get burned out with bad boys like you."

"I loath all the cannibals and condescending mummies I meet in America. The desperation repulses me," he said lighting his pipe as I smoked a joint.

"No one really wants to reveal themselves," I said.

"Darling they won't reveal themselves because they're trying to hide their deep, darkest secrets," he said.

"I know. So they share their pretend lives with faux friends," I mused.

"The young and beautiful ones clad in Gucci and Calvin Klein. The older matrons wearing Dior sunglasses, driving BMW's, hiding what's left of their youth," he said stretching out on the floor, sipping his wine.

"Do I fit into any of those categories?" I asked.

"Your persona is queen of the big, bad hair day with your larger than life locks. I think you have a loose corkscrew you hyper headed twisted sister. But I'll always love you," he laughed. "I even get turned on by you in your look alike thrift shop find getup," he said.

"I know how you feel about me and I'm very taken by your flattery, but I have to get sober and you're a terrible influence," I said sadly. "I'm thinking of checking into a rehab center in Malibu."

"You don't need to be around those puppets. They can't even make a simple decision without calling their sponsors."

"I think you should go with me for support," I begged.

"No, that's not my style to hang out with those losers and drink bad coffee and smoke cigarettes. I have a better idea. Let's go to Trader Joe's and pick up some Ariel champagne. It only has less than one half of one percent of alcohol in it. It'll take the edge off. We're out of wine."

"No. I can't afford to be with you anymore. It doesn't work. You're physically, emotionally, socially and professionally destroying my life."

"You give me guilt. I feel like I've put on my sunglasses in the middle of the night, fallen asleep, then woken up pulling them off and its still dark."

I was hyperventilating, but he coaxed me into going to Trader Joe's with him. I jumped on the back of his cycle and we roared off into the cold steamy night.

Chapter Thirty Four

The Blues On Hill Street Blues
Antonio
Part Three

It is a hustler's smile, the smile of a professional stud. Now aging a bit but still with considerable memorabilia of his young charm.
Tennessee Williams

I do desire we may be better strangers.
Shakespeare

It was the '80s. I had landed a stunt job and hooker call on a TV show called *Hill Street Blues* and had talked the director into giving Chelsea an extra call that day. I was standing at the coffee machine when the radiant blonde arrived.

"I'm ever indebted to you for getting me this job. How simply lovely. Thanks. I'll have a go at sucking up to the director and pop off and have a fag," she said in her clipped English accent.

"Chelsea, I've got to talk to you. I'm scared. Last night Antonio called me from jail. He got busted again," I admitted, keeping my voice low so no one could eavesdrop on our conversation. "He said the cops confiscated his little black book. My address and phone number are in there," I continued.

"Where is he now?" she answered, suddenly interested. I had gained her full attention and set schmoozing was forgotten at least for the moment.

"He's out on bail, but thinking of running from the law."

"You'll be worried about more than that when those helicopters circle over your blimey paradise and break out the guns. You might get your head blown off with the barrel of a twelve gauge one day, April. The chap's a big time dealer, ducky, and he's a bit off also," she said.

"I know that now. But what am I to do? I'm terrified," I admitted, my voice cracking. I was shaky, beads of perspiration were running down my body.

"That bastard finally was honest with you. The technology of the Los Angeles Malicia is unpredictable. Do you really need that kind of aggravation?" she asked. "I thought you were a smart bird. You have to finish it with him."

"He's not easy to get rid of," I admitted, even though I knew that I hadn't tried hard enough to break my bond with him. While I had known Antonio was a drug user, I was in denial about his nefarious business dealings.

"Just lovely, it's possible that they have your flat under surveillance," she warned me in a detached tone, adding fuel to my anxiety.

"Do you really think so?" I asked, gasping for breath.

"If they think he's going to jump bail," she threw in nonchalantly disapproval creeping into her voice as she lit her cigarette.

"They couldn't know that."

"You do, he told you over the phone, didn't he?"

"Yes," I reminded myself.

"Darling how stupid of him, they monitor all those calls." Chelsea added.

I was instantly hit with a wave of nausea, my throat went dry, and my knees were about to give out. I sank into a chair, realizing what she was saying was true.

I looked up at Chelsea. She was dragging on her cigarette, going on,

"You'll always be worried and one day you might never know what happened to him. He'll drag you down with him. You're such a winner, April. I hate to see you get burnt by that loser. If he really cared about you and wasn't just using you for a roof over his head, the scum bum wouldn't try to hide out at your house," she said.

"He didn't have to pay for a private cell when he was in the joint," I answered.

"I know what'll make you feel better." Chelsea pantomimed toking on a joint, "I have some chronic. We must be careful, I mustn't get nicked for getting stoned."

"Let's go to my trailer," I said, glancing around. The last thing I needed at this point was to get fired, or get caught with drugs myself. But I couldn't help it. This was a dire situation and it called for drastic measures.

"And we'll wash it all down with this," she discretely pulled out a bottle of champagne from her Louis Vuitton bag, smiling. "I'll grab some paper cups, and meet you there in a few."

"Don't be long," I begged. "I'm having an anxiety attack."

It was almost seven o'clock before we wrapped that night. I had somehow pulled off my stunt, as Chelsea breezed through the background.

I spent the entire commute home thinking about what Chelsea and I had talked about that morning. Were the cops watching my house? Did they think I was an accomplice? Wasn't the girlfriend always the one at the top of the list of suspects? I tried to block it all out of my mind. I was looking forward to a long steam bath, and a night of uninterrupted sleep. I had just the pill to make that happen.

I spent my evenings paranoid that someone was going to break down my door at any minute. I needed to get away. I spent Saturday at the beach, writing and getting a suntan.

As I approached my sanctuary, his whistle stopped me cold.

"Senorita. You take my breath away."

He stepped out of the shadows, running his hand nervously through his hair, waiting for my reaction.

I was speechless, my heart racing. In the first moment, I had thought that they were finally raiding my house, and the handcuffs would be slapped on at any moment. But then I saw his face, blending into the darkness.

His dreamy brown eyes stared at me, waiting.

"What're you doing here?" I finally broke the silence.

"I had to see you. Don't worry. I don't want anything from you, my princess."

"Antonio, you shouldn't be here. We're probably being watched as we speak," I shot back with fury.

I knew if I let him in, it would be my downfall. And I was right. That night, my Latin lover came back again. One flash of his worldly grin and I surrendered to his charms. Although I felt no passion for him, only empathy. There was a mist on the morning, then the sun came up and we drank coffee on my terrace as Antonio started muttering his dime store physiology.

"Most people walk around in the emergency state tryin' to chase success. I think my luck ran out. Life is cheap. It's a real deal just so you don't get caught, or you can get snuffed out at any time by the long arm of the law. They burn your passport, burn your dream. I sold it to a cop last time," Antonio rambled on.

"Oh no," I said, throwing my pot over the cliff.

"Those lousy pigs. Don't worry your pretty little head. I'll have fun beating this one. I leave the country pronto. Hasta la vista, bye-bye," he said gulping down his java. "When they pull me over they found ounces of crystal meth. Last week I made ten grand just dealin' drugs, or I could never have paid the rent. The last time I got popped, I had to show in court, my mouthpiece turned out to be a muy bonita chica. We sunbathed nude, smoked a joint on our lunch break behind courthouse. She got me off, boom," he boasted.

"Where are you staying now?" I asked nervously twisting my hair.

"I stay with the boys. It's good for business. They have a maid, a valet, and cook," he said.

"Do you have another girlfriend?" I asked.

"I did. But I shaved her head so that I'd be more in control. She got mad at me and ran off with her eighteen year old girlfriend she met at some poetry group called Lesbians in Literature. She threw all my drugs down my motorcycle tank. I love it when the dumb coke whores try to challenge Antonio. I have too much street smarts for that. They're all transitory bitches anyway, si?"

"You're getting boring," I said, trying not to show my hurt. It hadn't taken long for him to find his next victim. This tidbit of information turned me back onto my pathway of resolve. And the reality that this was a sick damaged soul standing before me.

"Los Angeles has lead me to a downhill spiral of abandonment and despair." He said, a tone of anger in his voice.

"I need to find that one person. Some people travel through eternity's sunrise never finding their soul mate, ending up pawning their souls. I'm just afraid of waking up one cold morning, looking at the clock ticking and realizing that it's too late to get what I need in life," I said. "I found someone once but I let him slip away."

"I'm the one." he answered.

"What do you want from me, Antonio? I won't get involved in your sordid lifestyle again. That's why I broke up with you."

"I just needed a friend last night, si?"

"I think you should be going."

"Will you let me crash at your house for a couple of days in case the policia come looking for me?" he begged.

"I don't know about that. I could get into a lot of trouble."

"I'm a fugitive running from what they call justice. I'm afraid that somebody's friend that the boys killed will try to come after me. You could go down, too. I love you so much, I had to warn you."

"I'm afraid of those hawks flying around out there. They look like vultures... spooky. And you're afraid of the Federal Bureau of Investigation and the mafia. It would be a job for them to track you down here on top at my hideaway," I softened. I couldn't believe those words had come out of my mouth. "But you can't stay here," I corrected myself.

"Please don't turn on me. You don't know how they treat us ex-cons. I spent five years in prison in Spain. That place nearly killed me. My heart's broken. I'm tired of running. I'm just a horny, angry, young boy who needs some love. I haven't slept in a week. I could flee to Madrid but they might find me and bring me back to LA and fry me," he said.

"Are you sure you're not being just a bit paranoid?"

"It's easy for you to say that, I think I'm psychotic by now," he said sobbing loudly, drinking more coffee, pouring a generous shot of brandy into it.

"Try to eat something, we can deal with this better tomorrow. I'll talk to Blue, maybe he can help us – he's my underground connection," I said as he gave me a desperate hug.

"God bless you, April. I don't know what I'd do without you. No one else in my life ever knew how to be with me. Before I came to this country, it was three squares a day, and a steel bunk with a mattress when I got arrested in Spain," he said. "I never want to tell before."

"I'm so sorry," I said. "What was it like?"

"Just like it sound – D block. At least I could read and be left alone, much better than the labor camp farm they made me work in," he said.

"Sounds really depressing. How about those poor young boys that get thrown in and aren't gay. How do they handle it?" I asked.

"They usually can't, the first day they come in, the black guys gang up on them, they too intimidated to stick up for themselves. Even in isolation I hear the screams from the fresh new fish getting harpooned in the upper tiers."

"Did that ever happen to you?" I asked.

"Some beaner hit me over the head with a steel pipe because I wouldn't give in. They threw me in solitary." he said with intensity.

"Did you play ball with them after solitary?"

"You mean the screws? You always play ball with the hacks, if you're working a scam for whisky, or drugs," he answered. "I needed to medicate myself."

"Did a lot of people kill themselves or try to break out?" I asked.

"It's not that easy to break out, sometimes they kill someone over two packs of cigarettes. A carton represent money. I can still hear that reverb from cell doors slamming shut in unison when man pulls handle of that electric slammer."

Chapter Thirty Five
Bottoming out at the Ritz

All that is lost with my youth that sweet bird that suddenly, some day flies away from your heart and leaves you with someone like me, and me with someone like you.
Tennessee Williams

It was dusk as we approached the private winding driveway. A valet greeted us, taking the keys to my car. We entered the hotel set on scenic acres rising above the glistening waterfront, stepping into a world of opulence, warmth and elegance, reminiscent of a grand home.

We walked through the French doors to a nearby sandy beach, overlooking thousands of yachts as pleasure boats glided by. "The swanky soirée was being held in the English Gardens," I lead Antonio by the arm to where I was reviewing the charity event that was starting to buzz.

That evening in May hundreds of guests strolled the grounds of the Ritz-Carlton Marina Del Rey, sampling a potpourri blend of scrumptious delicacies from sixty five-star premiere restaurants, and rare vintages from international vineyards, created only for the most discriminating palettes. Star chefs spanning the globe were on hand signing their best selling cookbooks as premium champagnes and spirits flowed. The sun was fading away, then another burst of sunlight as shadows shaded the trees. Now darkness was falling upon the night as scented candles and tiki torches lit up the sky.

The hotel's service is renowned for uncompromising standards at this escapist haven. Hip looking servers passed around sterling silver platters.

"Would you like to try a soft shelled crab?" one asked, flirting with Antonio.

"Me gusta," the Latin replied, his eyes rolling around in his head as he bit into the delicate morsel with delight. "I'm a food, wine and opiate aficionado. This party rocks."

"It's my pleasure," the boy answered, brushing by him seductively.

Antonio squeezed his hand, then gave me a big hug. We were dressed to the nines. Antonio wore a black Armani suit and steel blue silk tie. I was wearing a long shabby chic lacy skirt and camisole, Victorian style, a big floppy straw hat adorned with a crushed powder blue rose and bold hues of purple and crimson eye shadow lent a mysterious aura and seduction to my persona.

"Let's try a glass of wine from that vineyard from Barcelona," he said as we walked over to the booth. "This might be my last sip of fine wine, I have to go back to court again on my drug charges, I might go back to prison."

"I have Latin based wines from Spain, Chile, and Argentina," the vintner said, pouring us two glasses of Merlot.

"Muchas gracias, sir," Antonio said. "This is smooth and full bodied. Bueno."

"I want to taste the Piper over there and top it off with the Caspian Osetra caviar garnished with Blinis," I said dragging him by the arm to the next station.

"Oh my god. This caviar is orgasmic," I squealed, guzzling the bubbly.

"Amigo, will you pours us more and please fill the cups to the brim this time?" he demanded.

After a few more glasses the Mambo King spotted a sultry svelte auburn haired model type wearing Prada that I'd seen on the cover of Sports Illustrated magazine, sipping a martini.

Strutting his wares, Antonio approached her, "Como estas, chica. You are the epitome of casual California sophistication. You look like an angel," he said slightly touching her bare shoulder.

"This is the coolest Epicurean tour de force of tastings. I so adore dining al fresco," she said in a throaty voice, walking away, leaving us standing there.

"Malo (bad) bitch," he said.

"My favorite wine is Marques De Caceres, the Red Reserve. Let's drink some, my darling."

As we were getting drunk and grazing on rosy pink curls of shrimp, the blond spiked headed waiter appeared again. "Would you like to try some hot Seared Sesame Crusted Hawaiian Tuna Japonaise cradled in Wasabi Mashed Potatoes?" he asked Antonio completely ignoring my existence.

"Si. Caliente (hot)!" Antonio screamed as he devoured the Pacific Rim cuisine, burning the roof of his mouth.

"It's my pleasure," the boy stammered, handing my date his card with a wink, approaching the guests.

"Isn't the fem boy a little young for you? He's under twenty, I'll bet." I teased.

"He looks like an ultra cool hot hung man with a bubble butt," he added. "he'd make a great appetizer." Antonio laughed.

"This cuisine is sex on a spoon," I moaned.

A muscle ripped stud was gyrating erotically to the pulsating music as the plumb upscale crowd mingled.

An aristocratic looking couple passed by. "You two look so glamorous. Are you a couple?"

"Not exactly," Antonio answered.

"You look like movie stars," the woman gushed over us.

A cluster of chic young ingenues nearby were savoring their cocktails. One wacky type blonde was poured into her dress, flaunting teeny weenie hips, balancing herself on way too high heels.

"Guapa (I like that)," Antonio said. "May I get you a drink?" he asked, deserting me.

"The only buzz I get is from a vibrator or a faucet. This drink is a virgin," she laughed, chain smoking, licking her shiny bronze Cupi doll lips, tossing back a head of thick bleached, streaked hair José Eber Rodeo Drive style.

At the next booth, bright blue and green hypnotic cocktails flowed non-stop. "I need another drink." I said demandingly.

"They have spicy Sangrita Tequila Gold oyster shooters over there," Antonio said, joining me again.

"Would you care for ceviche with some shooters?" a Latin caterer asked.

"Si, make mine a double please," Antonio said, kissing the girl's hand.

After a few rounds of mojitos, I was gone. Drunk wasn't even the word for it. My head was swimming and I was starting to weave and slur my speech.

"Como se llama? (What's your name?) I'm Antonio. I need more tequila," he said to the pretty exotic girl munching on his hors d'oeuvre.

I blindly looked across the horizon. My blurry vision spotted the French celebrity chef standing high on a bluff, blending into the dazzling panoramic view, lifting his glass, blowing kisses at me.

I wandered by the glam divas, clutching their Veuve Clicquot with six-inch nails, finally locating the chef's booth. He was savoring the night with celebrity wine masters passing out his signature dish, a stylish blend of provincial cuisine. Caramelized tomato, onion, basil tarts, signing his best selling cookbook. At the next display an Italian chef was drawing a big crowd.

"We frequent complimentary hors d'oeuvres and wines from Italy, Australia and the hills of Tuscany; ports, grappas, and Bordeaux's." He boasted. Intoxicatingly romantic jazz was piped in through the trees. I must have looked like a tragic sexpot clumsily swaying to the mellow sounds of 'The Girl From Ipanema,' and the dreamy pipes of Antonio Carlos Jobim.

My cream colored hat fell to the ground, revealing wild ringlets kinky from the humidity. I was seduced by soft breezes, air scented by the sea, and chefs lilting laughter as corks popped, exploding into the sky.

"I'd like to taste your dish," I said evocatively to the French chef handing him my card. "I heard a rumor about you. Are you really noteworthy by the length of your appendix?" I laughed, spilling red wine all over his starched white tablecloth. "I'd love it if you'd cater an affair in my bedroom some night," I said staggering into a bush. "I'll give you a good review," I slurred.

"Cherie, you will make an amazing dessert, but for now you must have an espresso and you need to eat. Oui?" the man said coldly, helping me up.

"Let's make a toast. Cognac please," I protested, rubbing my body into his.

"I'll have my sous chef call you a taxi. You need to lie down and sleep it off," he said, firmly handing me a cup and plate. "You must try my bittersweet Tilow Rless Chocolate Cake. It will sober you up, April," he said grabbing me by the waist, putting me into a chair.

Finally Beverly Hills Cab arrived and I was escorted by fantasy man past the auction, legendary luminaries, and losers who dwindled into the night of privilege.

I made my grand exit tripping on my floor length hem as he helped me into the cab. At least that's the way the story was told to me by one of my food critic friends who I called in a panic at six o'clock the next morning. Some of it was a blackout with snippets of recall and humiliation.

Chapter Thirty Six
Date Rape Hollywood Style

The whispering shadows seethed about her like demons of some dim inferno and now was the time to go on again.
Tennessee Williams

Reaching my home in the Canyon and the safety of my own bed I passed out cold with my party clothes on, clinging to my body.

I was rudely awakened by a Latin, bearing a shameless dick, wearing no conscience. Antonio pulled the sheet off of the bed, lying down next to me, massaging my feet, leaning over, resting his hand on my warm breast.

"I wanna see you. Let's make love," he pleaded.

"No, let me sleep. I'm wasted. Take your blow and blow out of here." I mumbled, fearing that my nakedness excited him.

"Antonio has a great affection for you. You so muy guapo (very beautiful)," he said dumping white powder on a deco mirror. It glistened under the amber light of my Shonbeck crystal chandelier.

He stuck his finger in, licking up the substance. "This tastes right. It's primo uncut Peruvian," he said in a cold standoffish demeanor, primping in the mirror nonstop, grinding his teeth as he took a couple of long snorts. "I'm a connoisseur," he said with quiet intensity. His pupils had a permanent glaze, he was so stoned he had a wild look in his eyes half mast in junkie ecstasy, sucking the smoke, holding it down. His life was a dark dreamscape, my obsession for him was gone. The hot fleshed beautiful Latin preyed on people that had psychological problems, aware of his amazing physical attributes, finding it easy to manipulate them, coveting their talents, claiming them for his own, refusing to take an active part in his own life.

"You say you don't want to fuck me anymore, but you tease Antonio with your titas."

"You're a great arm-piece, let that be enough," I answered, my eyes half closed.

He shook me and I awakened, starting to sober up.

"I've been searching all my life for someone like myself who's been looking for the answer in all the wrong places," he said unfastening his Givenchy black belt, unzipping his pants, throwing the clothes on my chaise lounge, then leaping back onto the bed, naked, stretching out his legs, lighting a candle.

I was feeling uneasy now, very much awake. I had to figure out how to get this dangerous man out of my house. Sometimes we make the wrong choices at the crossroads of our lives. He was one of them.

"I want you to go and leave me alone," I demanded, pushing him off of the bed.

He jumped back, his eyes heavy-lidded, snorting more cocaine. "This is the perfect chemical combination. Try some."

"No. You're strung out and my head's throbbing." I said shaking with fury.

"Why did you leave me at the tasting? I had to take a cab all the way here."

"I was drunk and didn't want my magazine publishers to see me in that condition."

"You were all over that chef. I resent that."

"I gave you free reign. You hooked up with a tranny and an aging potential sugar momma," I said taking a gulp of flat Perrier from the nightstand.

"You think you're above it all," he said, his eyes mocking me, pushing his tongue into my mouth, then hiking up my skirt and sliding his hand between my legs. I tightened my thighs but he worked his mouth up my body, breathing hard and rhythmically, when he reached his destination, burying his head beneath my skirt, pulling my legs apart.

I felt a spasm at the slightest tickle as he licked me, but I knew that I had to deny myself his sexual favors, as he didn't believe in using condoms. Also he'd been with too many boys and girls together. Antonio loved no one and was attached to nothing. He was an adventurer, a collector of people.

Candlelight made eerie shadows on the wall.

"I'm going to grace you with my most valuable asset. It's mucho grande," he boldly said, placing my hand on his erect cock, then pressing his belly against mine.

I removed my hand, pushing him away.

"I feel like I'm going to throw up, you have to leave now," I said with conviction.

His eyes grew fierce. "I'm going to capture you and dominate your body," he said, pinning my arms behind my back, pushing me into the mattress with sexual fury. He slipped his hand underneath my camisole, ripping it off. The embroidery and lace falling all over the leopard velvet comforter.

"What are you doing? Stop!" I pleaded.

"Shut up, I'm calling the shots from now on. You're my prisoner of fantasy," he said, cursing me.

I tried fighting him off in order to defend myself, but of no avail, screaming as he held his hand over my mouth to restrain my frenzy. I could barely breath. I lay frozen. My glowing pale body, rich with unmarred skin, quivered.

"Please don't hurt me," I whined as I felt the sting of his hand streak across my face.

He was crouching over me like a demon whipping me into submission, biting my flesh. I lay stiff, knowing that I was entrapped. No one would hear the cry of a woman alone with her predator on top of a deserted mountaintop.

Antonio went wild with desire to cause me pain. His hatred fierce and cruel. He forced his way into me, penetrating his sex with sick desire and violence, pressing his large body against my taut curves. Then callously he spared me no tricks of his trade. Aroused, he fucked me on the bed, my head thrown back, wild hair spilling to the floor. Pounding me, palpitating, moving his tool slowly in and out, contracting his firm round buttocks, reaching a violent climax.

Chapter Thirty Seven
Selective Amnesia

But I have been foolish, casting my pearls upon swine.
Tennessee Williams

After the food tasting, I awakened in a fog early the next morning that gloomy gray May day riddled with amnesia, shame and remorse. I glanced around the room, my aching head spinning, grabbing my purse, spilling out all the contents, frantically searching for the keys to my vault. Heathcliff, the Shih Tzu was bouncing a Trojan upside down in his mouth, and a sticky wad of Kleenex was crumpled up on the sheets. The smell of burning embers in my fireplace accentuated by the sickly sweet fragrance of Purple Passion scented oil turned my stomach.

I tried piecing the puzzle together as clouds started forming in the sky. Jumping out of bed, I ran to the garage, sadly to discover that the faded Indigo blue 280Z was not there.

Collapsing on my bed, I reached for a leftover glass of Louis Jadot Chardonnay from the nightstand, swallowing the stale, bitter, pale gold wine, lighting a roach, feeling even more paranoid.

Rummaging around inside of a drawer, I searched frantically for my bell jar, a permanent home for the valiums I'd hidden from Antonio. Maybe I'd locked them in my desk. Panicking and sobbing when I couldn't find the key, pacing the floor in a catatonic stupor, grabbing a hammer, pounding the lock, finding the vial, my eyes over-flowing with tears.

My shaking hands dropped the pills on the floor. Retrieving them, I swallowed three ten-milligram blues, one sticking to my coated tongue washing it down with the warm wine. Leaning back on the plush down pillows, reaching for my cordless phone, I dialed Antonio's number.

"Hola," he answered in a sleepy Spanish accent.

"You heartless macho fucking bastard! How could you stoop so low as to rape me! I was passed out cold in a drunken stupor, unable to defend myself!" I screamed urgently.

"You know you wanted it as badly as I did, you little bitch. You're always teasing me," he answered in a flat dispassionate tone.

I had a vague recollection of the incident, but there was no stopping the Latin all fired up from cocaine and alcohol.

"You didn't use a condom, did you? AIDS doesn't go away," I sobbed.

"That's all hype from your country for you vulgar Americans to believe," he answered.

"Did you take my car, you user?"

"No. It's probably still at the hotel. You treat me like a peasant because I have no assets. I took a cab to your house to get my Harley. You left me there and took the keys."

"Do you know if anyone from my magazines saw me in that condition?"

"All your important editors, publishers and restaurateur mummies thought you were pathetic. They were dissing you. Are you afraid that you'll lose your title in Beverly Hills?" he laughed sadistically. "You lose control when you drink. One day I was at Trader Joe's and I saw an old bag lady wheeling her shopping cart in front of the store and I thought of you. She was dipping into the garbage. That could be you if you don't get a grip on yourself."

"You're the one that keeps pushing the drugs and alcohol in my face, you loser. You're only asset just didn't measure up or you'd be in my bed," I cried.

"You sound drunk, darling. Call me back at a more civilized hour. It's the crack of dawn. I have to get my beauty sleep if I want to be a diva," he mockingly said as I heard the hollow click of the phone in my ear.

The sick self-obsessed drifter had taken away my willfulness and cursed my womanhood. I'd lost another part of myself, I wondered how much more I could tolerate in this lifetime. I was so broken it was as if my body no longer belonged to me.

I still have nightmares of his fiery eyes burning with hate as he laid on me without mercy. That day, I went on a binge, then disconnected my phone, and a week later checked myself into rehab, suffering the consequences of misplaced affection.

When the nurse gave me a blood test, the cold hypodermic needle plunged into my skin, a reminder of the hard brown cock that penetrated me in the night.

Chapter Thirty Eight

Hollywood Forever Cemetary
Anna

Mother's dying almost stunned my spirit. She slipped from our fingers like a flake gathered by the wind and now is part of the drift called "the infinite".
Emily Dickinson

I drove along the long stretch of nondescript seedy streets of East Hollywood. The familiar sight of hookers walking in short skirts and fishnet stockings, exposing their breasts, and motels inhabited by low-lives was outside of my comfort zone. That day I had to bury my mother. It was all about darkness towards the end, the monsters in her bed. Then death made an appearance, landing her frail body into the grave. I'd always thought that the only way she wouldn't go totally crazy was to keep a distance from her own life and try to live mine. I had a rendezvous with death, saying goodbye to Anna at 'Hollywood Forever'. I call it 'Heavenly Horizons'. I needed to honor her spirit. After all, she was my flesh and blood even in eternity. As I entered the cemetery, a retro-vintage hearse equipped with a driver and antique lace cream-colored curtains was awaiting new celebrity arrivals.

I walked along the pathway, amongst perfumed gardens. Silhouettes of past lives were buried in the shadows of the lake. Then came an unearthly, muffled cry of an owl that had fallen out of the nest and broken his wing. It was like a metaphor of her doomed existence.

As I placed a long stemmed blue red rose on her grave, I questioned my own mortality once again pondering over the answer. What if my whole life had been all wrong, a lie?

She will be protected here, buried under the stars, surrounded by the charisma of Rudolf Valentino and infamous movie icons. Anna will be more famous in death than in life.

And she's still a property owner that isn't required to pay taxes. Her lakeside plot is located on Highland and Santa Monica Boulevard, a far cry from Beverly Hills, but it's all so very old Hollywood. I passed an ethereal pond with dark rippling waters. Now a lost, lonely, wasted life lies dust sprinkled under a grand old oak tree at the Hollywood Forever Cemetery. Often, my reflection bears a frightening, chilling resemblance of her face. I blinked my eyes in anguish as I bid farewell to Graves the mortician. My silver cloud 280-Z sped through the swinging black wrought iron gate. I felt emptier and more alone than I'd ever been in my lifetime, more determined than ever to follow my destiny, the theater. But wasn't it only human to feel so sad on that mournful day.

I have finally arrived after walking along that dark path and also I've gained a lot of strength. I'd learned that giving up the pain wasn't giving up the love that I would always have for her. I'd become a more compassionate and accepting person, prioritizing my values, and had come to a deeper understanding of myself, of God and the universe. I was less selfless and I began noticing slow and subtle changes in my perceptions.

Years later I hadn't totally recovered. I probably never will from the trauma of seeing that strong, dominant woman become helpless, living at the hands of the ruthless thieves of the medical profession. But I'm finally able to laugh without the guilt and faking it.

Enthusiasm has returned to my life through art and creativity. I now focus not only on the loss, but I'm grateful for the torrid love, hate, life-long relationship we once had. I've moved forward with my career. Summer looks green and bright and the dread of winter coming this year no longer scares me. Seemingly trivial things can be enjoyed once again, like that chocolate latte at Starbucks. As the days and dates of my mother's demise pass by, I've begun to start living instead of dying.

Chapter Thirty Nine
The Reckless Years

Whenever I have to choose between two evils,
I always like to try the one I haven't tried before.
Mae West

How would I describe my life? It was a tapestry/potpourri woven out of my darkest dreams and fantasies, an adventure as theatrical as a Fellini film. Exploited sexual orgies and seduction, never knowing what I was going to experience next. We were like "The Big Chill" on acid. Another thrill. Nothing lasted. Between the decadence and desperation, I was still searching for the traces of my life. I drifted with the drifters. Beautiful men without ambition or souls. Starving out-of-work actors and poets, losing the will to commit.

I was distanced from the terror of my own feelings and the realization of the purity that I had long lost forever. Then I met Patrick, my soul-mate, and I still couldn't commit, my mood swings shifting often in lustful longing or regret. The new becoming more important than the why and then. I was always redefining the dynamics of what I wanted with detachment for what I could be caught in. A trap, wanting to escape from my own self-inflicted reality, exploring and embracing my darker self. My parties in the Canyon made me a Hollywood legend. It certainly wasn't my acting, although I had a good act. We dug the zombies, becoming zombies; mesmerized by the Beatles higher than "Lucy in the Sky with Diamonds."

I looked like a slinky dream, living the lush life. The smooth mellow sounds of The Mammas and the Papas 'California Dreaming', blaring throughout my sky cliff mountain meadowlark retreat, best describes that erotic era.

My young actress girlfriends and I dropped Quaaludes and booze to cure our anxiety attacks when we didn't get the parts. We sipped Piper Brut with a lot of brutes, paying the piper the next morning after sharing our skins till the birds chirped in another day.

Years later, I ended up in boy-toy detox, no longer intrigued with Hollywood and the hopes and dreams of fame and fortune. Rehabilitation was my bedrock of reality. The resolution was that I just had to keep going. The joy and need to create art was so overpowering it filed that empty hole. My greatest heartache and terror was experiencing life and sobriety on its own terms.

Chapter Forty
Recovery and Discovery

What doesn't kill me makes me stronger.
Albert Camus

The plump, cinnamon skinned, dark eyed, Latino nurse lead me into the lab at the rehab center. No sooner had she checked my vital statistics, then she jammed a hypodermic needle into my vein. "Welcome to the other side," she said.

I felt like a Trekkie being indoctrinated into a 'Star Trek' episode. Segment: 'The Hall of Shame'.

"Let me try your other vein, honey."

"Oh my God," I winced.

"You'll get used to it, they test you randomly, so you'd better stay clean and not fall into the black hole of chemical fueled behavior." She warned me.

"I'm done, the only slip I'm going to have, is under my dress," I said. "And I don't even wear slips."

"Hey, you! My name's Bianca. What's yours?" she said.

"I'm April."

"I hope you don't mind, April, I have to check your purse. It's just standard procedure," she said.

"Cool," I said dumping my studded, fringed, black leather purse out on her desk. The bag was stuffed with make-up, condoms, Snickers Bars, Poison perfume, and my usual paraphernalia. "Check it out. I threw six ounces of Moroccan buds down the garbage disposal and flushed all my ten milligram valiums and sleeping pills down the toilet. I feel like I gave away my power. I'm freaking out, Bianca."

"Your life has become unmanageable," she said sweeping her long hair away from her eye. "You got here in time!" Bianca replied.

"I'm through experimenting."

"You're very pretty and a lot of famous actors will try and hit on you. Don't let temptation take you down again. You're fragile, in a very vulnerable state. Using is not a solution for a spiritual problem," she frowned at me.

"Are there any fun patients here?" I asked.

"April these people are very depressed. Do you think that if they were going to marry Donald Trump and take a trip to the South of France they'd be coming here?" she scolded.

"I've hit bottom or I wouldn't have dragged myself into this clinic. I'm a dead woman," I said with reassurance.

"You're not supposed to have sex, no less a relationship for the first year," she said.

"I'm pretty burnt out with men. But what if the guy's not an alcoholic?" I asked.

"After a year if you ever go out with a normie, never tell him you're an alcoholic until the third date at a coffeehouse. And never do the unthinkable until the fifth date. And even then you might get dumped, honey. Those guys are weird."

"Why?" I asked.

"That's been my experience," she answered. "I'm a recovering alcoholic/addict also."

"What happens if someone fucks up and goes out? I asked.

"If you use more than once they'll throw you out of here," she answered. "You're just using to medicate your pain. Surrender to God and your higher power and you'll have a life you never dreamed that you'd have."

"I'm hung-over. I've hardly slept in days."

Bianca squeezed my hand. "You're shaking," she said wiping the beads of perspiration off of my brow with a Kleenex. "What brought you to rehab?" she asked.

"Unfortunately I gravitate to the younger breed," I answered.

"You have to have a 90 minute session with the addictionologist to find out what group therapy and counselor we're going to assign you to. We're doing a study on Naltrexone."

"What's that?" I asked.

"It's an alcohol and opiate blocker and if you qualify your therapy will be free. If not, it could be quite pricey, but I have to do an intake before I can sign you in."

I could no longer hold back the tears that were welling up in my eyes.

"Go ahead, that's good, get it out," she coaxed. "We have some time before you see your next appointment."

"My Latin lover from Madrid called me a pot whore and raped me when I told him that we were over," I cried.

"Bad boy, that muchacho. Was the bastardo high?" she asked.

"Yes, he was strung out on coke and drunk on wine," I answered. "He was trying to get me hooked on crystal meth."

"Malo." What did you see in this abusive, controlling man?" she asked.

"I couldn't help remembering the purr of Antonio's Harley roaring up the mountain and the sheer excitement and entrapment of it all. Now holding his hand would be like engaging with a corpse. My fatal addiction and uncontrollable attraction with the Eurotrash actor had ruined my life.

"My destruction has always been being attracted to dangerous men. Let's get real. Bad girls like bad boys. It's that wild whirlwind chase. Being caught between ecstasy and an air conditioned nightmare," I said sadly.

"Sounds like you're a drama queen and catastrophizer, maybe you're just into the whole death ride for the excitement. That's the deal. You've made some bad choices, but this clinic's known for its amazing recovery rates." Bianca said.

"Then you think there's hope for me?" I asked.

"If you do the work, there's always hope. It's not what happens to us, it's what we do with it. Sometimes our greatest enemies pull us out of the ditch. What's your drug of choice?" she asked.

"Pot. But I'm a wino also. I love Cristal champagne not Crystal Meth, Pouilly Fuisse, somas and 10 milligram valium to curb my anxiety attacks. I often couldn't remember anything the next morning," I said.

"You were a very expensive wino, but you were no less addicted to drugs and alcohol than the bag lady drinking Ripple wine out of a brown bag on Skid Row," she said. "Blackout drunks are the most dangerous kinds," she frowned.

"I was on assignment for a big culinary magazine and Antonio was such a beautiful arm-piece. We got drunk at a trendy hotel at a big food and wine festival. A chef put me into a cab and I left him, then he came back to my house and raped me. I begged him to stop. The used condoms offered mute testimony of the night before. I had almost no recall," I said.

"I'll have to leave you now. I have another patient. Just remember, don't drink or use nothing from the neck up. One moment unconscious and you've reached the finishing line," she said. "Don't be strong, be smart and stay away from slippery places. And just remember no sex or relationships for a year. Even if he's a normie, April."

"I know," I answered.

"If someone offered you a drug now would you take it?" she asked.

"No," was my reply.

"That guy is like a bad drug. Good luck. I'm here for you if you need to talk." She waved a fast goodbye.

As I walked down the dark corridor of the rehab center, I was in a blue mood, feeling very suicidal and alone, blending into the shadowy landscape. I was ready to surrender to the perils of evil drugs and alcohol.

I had the biggest challenge of my life ahead of me.

I knew that I had to reveal myself in group therapy and in private sessions with my shrink or I would never walk away from rehab with the cure. I tried to believe that I could hurdle this obstacle as a new and challenging experience, although there is no cure for alcoholism and drug addiction.

Chapter Forty One

Lament to a Lovely Lonely Lady Named Anna
Epitaph

*And so as kingsmen met a night we talked
between the rooms until the moss had reached
our lips and covered up our names.*
Emily Dickinson

　　To the memory of my beautiful, ethereal looking mother, Anna, who passed away. The day she died I entered the room and noticed that the dozen red roses I had brought for her were withered. Their drooping crimson petals were symbolic of impending doom. I kissed her graceful, cold, ashen hand and said goodbye for the last time. All her angst, pain and suffering was ended on that hot steamy summer's day fading into the darkness that comes with the sunset. I now question my own mortality but I've learned a lot about death and acceptance losing my dearest Shih Tzu, Heathcliff, and now my mother. I'll always cherish those fabulous fleeting moments we shared dining at the finest restaurants in Beverly Hills, her hometown. Anna loved the Peninsula, The Four Seasons, Ruth's Chris Steakhouse and many others, but the highlight of her life was that we no longer had to stand in line at Lawry's

Prime Rib as I was now a food critic. Thank God my mother lived long enough to hear the standing ovations I received for a production of *The Silken Silent Sisters of The Silver Screen* at Theater 40 in Beverly Hills. The mother and daughter scene at *Jerusalem West* (a takeoff on our days at Nate N' Al) brought the house down, later also produced at "The Cast" made theatre history. And I still have that dream, finding a home to pursue my artistic desires, my plays! The rest I leave in the hands of God.

I thank him for what I have been, who I am, my magical creative powers, and what I shall become. Dearest mother, I'll never forget that Thanksgiving dinner we shared at Scandia and the magical evening we sipped Crystal champagne amongst the stars devouring moist chocolate soufflés and cherries jubilee at Lescoffier Room as you joyously said

"Dear, I love you for bringing me here but there are so many waiters and sommeliers dancing around us I don't know who to tip."

Well, I hope she's smiling down at me now from a fancy restaurant in the sky dining with the great creator, I need some clout in heaven!

Chapter Forty Two

Rehab, a Luxury Getaway & Sonny Who Didn't Make My Days So Sunny

But honey, you know as well as I do that a single girl alone in the world, has got to keep a firm hold on the emotions or she'll be lost.
Tennessee Williams

It was an Indian summer heat wave. Blistering sun and soft sensual breezes warmed my flesh. I was Ms. Beverly Hills Food Critic, the Lean Restaurant Queen of Fine Cuisine. My biggest perks were being treated like royalty at five-star hotels.

I didn't have group therapy and a session with my substance abuse counselor until Monday at the out patient pricey, trendy Malibu rehab center. I'd just gotten an assignment from a prestigious Beverly Hills magazine and my gracious PR friends were going to pamper me in the penthouse suite at Loew's Santa Monica Beach Hotel, my castle in the sand.

A gracious staff always rolled out the red carpet on my arrival. Loew's dazzling sensual shoreline was Neptune's lusty playground for a sea of stars, millionaires, and trendsetters. I walked into the lobby looking like an ultra chic typical Angeleno clad in tight cut-offs, bare torso and a sheer chiffon halter top. My painted red tanned toes peeking out of my ankle strap shoes.

I took the elevator to the top. When I entered my skyscraper paradise, there was a bottle of French Chardonnay cooling in their VIP ice bucket. Also there were doggie treats, a vintage water bowl, strewn with rhinestones and a note from the General Manager welcoming us back. Enclosed in an envelope were comps to their signature restaurant.

I rang up room service politely exchanging my wine for a fruit basket. Plugging Eli into the socket. Much to my horror and dismay flames were shooting out of the wall and it wasn't the Fourth of July.

I picked up the phone and called housekeeping.

"Hi," I said, "I'm a guest staying in the VIP Suite. Room number 862 on the 8th floor. Could you please send me some of the Hershey Kisses you leave when you turn down the beds at night, and I need an electrician. How long will it be? Thanks, Chica, muchas gracias. Chow baby.

I often feel abandoned by people, places and things but the one thing that never lets me down is my best friend, my vibrator. Unless of course there's a power outage. After years of usage, I literally tried returning Eli to the Pleasure Chest without any success. The gay guy behind the counter looked at me and laughed.

"Where did you plug this in, at your trailer park and you look like your dye job was done at Earl Scheib. Sorry, but it was a nice try girlfriend."

Minutes later a tired-looking corporate type electrician arrived and checked out my sex toy.

"I'm so sorry but its burnt out."

"Well, I'm staying here for three nights. I'm a resort and food critic. I'll give you a good reward," I begged. "Could you just make it work 'till I check out. Sweetheart, be reasonable." I finally got a rise out of him.

"Okay, lady, the best I can do for you is fix it so it'll work one more time. Just hold the wire like this when your using it."

When Heathcliff, my shih tzu and I reached the pool, I noticed a fine looking man with Pilates toned arms, holding a cell phone to his ear. Sonny had a European air about him. He looked like he'd just stepped out of a James Bond promo trailer, emulating a 20's Valentino-esque film noir star.

I ordered a cappuccino from the bar while checking out the territory. A lot of busty, well tanned, barefooted beach babes were flaunting their wares in string bikinis. Broke dick fixer upper men swarmed the Olympic sized pool, basking in the hazy Santa Monica sun after their fitness trainers had pumped them up to perfection, swooping down over their prey.

I was lounging in the whirlpool, gazing at the panoramic view of the sparkling silver blue coastline. My body massaged by luke warm bubbling water, gazing at cascading waterfalls. I was enthralled by nature in all of its magnificence and tranquility. I thought of Antonio, remembering all the fun filled weekends we'd shared at this hotel, trying to rationalize why I ever became involved in the destructive deadly affair that led me to rehab.

Suddenly my serenity was interrupted by the exotic looking man I'd seen in the lobby. He brazenly jumped into the hot tub holding his hand outstretched to me.

"Are you an actress? I think I've seen you in some films. You have a wicked smile."

"Hi, I'm April," I glanced seductively at him.

"I'm Sonny," he politely said. "How do you keep in such good shape?"

"I eat dangerously, enjoying the sweet spices of life. I'm a food critic/society columnist," I answered, glad that I'd just bought a black latex swimsuit with the plunging mesh V neckline that I was wearing.

Sonny flashed his sinfully decadent smile, wearing the air of superficial phony sophistication. His died blue black hair was slicked back with gel, glowing in the rays of the California sunshine.

"Are you staying at the hotel?" he asked.

"Yeah, I'm covering the film festival and reviewing the hotel," I answered.

This man possessed magnetism and intrigue behind oversized Armani shades. I wasn't on a hunk hunt but I just couldn't resist the temptation of a perspective coffee date.

"Are you in the business?" I asked.

"Yes, I'm acting and producing films."

"Cool," I said, with a wide smile.

"I'm half Cherokee Indian. I play a lot of ethnic roles."

"That's great," I said, reaching for my comb, trying to untangle my hair.

"Can I buy you a drink tonight?" he asked, taking my hand as I quickly pulled it away.

"I'll be pretty busy this weekend, but you can call me at home next week," I answered reaching for my sterling silver card holder in my beach bag, giving him a passport into my world.

Just then a member of the spa approached us.

"Is Sonny behaving himself with you?" he asked with a knowing grin.

"I don't go for men that behave themselves," I answered in a flirty tone.

"Maybe we can hang out by the pool tomorrow?" Sonny said, touching my bronze flecked shoulder.

"Maybe," I smiled.

"Does that mean yes?" he asked with confidence.

"See ya," I said jumping out of the tub, fleeing to my oceanside room, preparing myself for a long dinner with friends at Ocean Avenue, my favorite restaurant.

No sooner than I had arrived home in the canyon, I heard his sexy Southern drawl calling on my service.

"Hi, it's Sonny, remember me from Loew's?"

"Hey," I said.

"Can I buy you a drink tonight?" he asked.

"I don't drink anymore. I'm in rehab," I answered.

"No kidding, I don't mean that kind of drink, I'm on the program too."

"You're a friend of Bill W., an AA connection, how cool?" I said excitedly.

"We were both very out of control and we lost our privileges." Sonny said sadly.

"By the way, you interrupted my orgasm in the hot tub, you bad boy."

"I'll make it up to you tonight. I owe you, baby."

"There's an open group therapy meeting at the clinic tonight and the members can bring a friend."

"Sounds great. And we can go out after?" He asked.

"Meet me there at seven. I'll leave the address on your service. Till then, for now." I said, jumping into my steam bath. This man turns me on, I must prepare myself and look fetching when I see him, I thought as I shampooed my hair, grabbing the conditioner, fantasizing about the alluring stranger all day and into the night.

Welcome to the land of self-absorbed dysfunctional alcoholics. We all sat around in a circle in the sparse white room, confessing our deepest darkest secrets.

The rehab center was a safe environment to be nurtured and challenged. I could be flirty and not threatened by intimacy and commitment. That was my greatest fear with members of the opposite sex after my experience with Antonio.

"Would anyone like to share tonight?" the speaker asked.

A short, moronic, robust Latin girl raised her hand.

"My name is Rosa, and I got a new vacuum cleaner," she beamed.

"Thank you for sharing."

Then a man raised his hand.

"My name is Dead." The anorexic heavy metal rock hellion was a cross between Marilyn Manson and Kiss with shades of Ichabod Crane. "I'm hooked on crystal meth." he blurted out. His long stringy dread locks woven with crimson and blue streaks hung loosely over his chalk white face, mascara dripping from sad lifeless eyes. I couldn't hear a word he was saying, his speech was muffled, as he had a bad habit of holding his fingers in front of his dark purple lips when he spoke. "I don't feel safe," he said wringing his hands. "My antidepressants are giving me insomnia, and I'm sick to my stomach. I would go off them, but I already paid for them."

The counselor looked my way as I raised my hand.

"Would you like to process?"

"My name is April. I'm a drug addict and alcoholic. For me there was no other option than sobriety. I went to a crazy shrink and told her that I got drunk, had a blackout, and had just given some stranger a blow job. She then asked me what I drank. 'Pouilly Fuisse and Cristal champagne,' I answered. 'You're a class act. You don't drink Ripple like the winos on skid row,' she answered. I was in denial and tried to believe her, but soon afterwards I bottomed out."

"Well I'm glad you're here," she said.

"Can I say one more thing? Once I saw a hypnotist. I went under immediately. 'Every time you take a drink, think of the wine turning into moths fluttering their wings or cobwebs in your stomach,' he said Well after a few sips my stomach started turning, but a few weeks later I drank again. I'm really glad to be here. This is the real deal."

"Thank you for sharing. This meeting has only a few minutes left, but if you have a burning desire, please feel free to share."

Sonny raised his hand.

"What's your name?

"My name is Sonny and I'm an alcoholic. I have two years of sobriety. My life was way out of control. It just wasn't worth the trip. After the first drink there was no other way turning back. Then the progression of the drugs and my disease took over. One day I guzzled a quart of Jack and held the barrel of a shotgun into my mouth. I was rescued by a twenty-three year old bisexual stripper who took me to an AA meeting at the Log Cabin and dragged me home, then I partied with her and her girlfriend. I met my sponsor at a meeting the next day. He checked me into Saint John's Hospital in Santa Monica and I detoxed and stayed sober," he shouted, pounding his weather-beaten fist on the table.

"You have a lot of rage, Sonny," the therapist exclaimed. "But we don't have time to deal with that now. Keep coming back."

"An any motherfucker who tries to tempt me with booze is like dangling meat in front of a hungry dog," he screamed, banging his head on the chair.

I was so embarrassed I wanted to die. I got the toxic, out of control person out of there so he couldn't have any conversations with my peers, the elite of the mentally ill. Sickly enough, I was weirdly attracted to psycho man.

"You hungry, April?" Sonny asked.

"Not really," I answered.

"I hope I didn't embarrass you in there. I was diagnosed as manic/depressive. Sometimes I turn into a loose cannon."

"I see that," I smirked at him, biting my lip.

"Am I forgiven? We can't go out for a drink. But maybe you'll be hungry later. Let's stop by my place for a few minutes, then we'll decide."

I was barely sober. I'd gone through many sleepless nights, the shakes, facial tics and harsh withdrawals. I wasn't going to throw it all away and for some pretentious, cocksure, out of work actor, was I? I was so proud of myself when the anonymous movie star stud gave me my three-month chip.

We arrived at his shabby garage apartment, a dump on the westside. He led me into a cubical which consisted of a bed, TV, computer and telephone.

"This guy's just letting me stay here until my movie sells, or an acting job blows in," he informed me.

Sure, I thought. *Loser.*

"Sit down on the bed. Make yourself comfortable. Would you like something non-alcoholic to drink?"

"I'd love a Diet Coke please."

He sat down next to me. Our hands touched as he handed me the glass. I knew who he was, but I was so attracted to him I didn't care. My self-destructive side was full circle. Sonny was a carbon copy of all the men that had orbited in and out of my life. Perhaps a little more culture trash than most.

"I'm real proud a' you for gettin' sober," he said, squeezing my hand.

"It's been quite a challenge, but I have a great support system." I smiled warmly.

"The person that has to struggle the hardest becomes the greatest in life," Sonny philosophized.

"It's the steeper and higher the climb," I answered, trying not to focus my gaze on the musty stained carpet.

"Then the butterfly landing," he smiled.

"I get really depressed when I fuck things up that I have control over, but I can't take responsibility for those that aren't like floods, earthquakes, torna-does and tailgaters. So it takes the edge out of my life," I smiled pensively.

"You heard a lot about my bottom. What was yours like?" he asked.

"Round and firm," I answered, trying to be facti-tious.

"Tell me, was it a man or a woman?"

"It still hurts too much to talk about it," I answered.

"I'll honor that. What was your drug of choice?" he asked.

"Grass. After my therapist gave me a random breathalyzer test I threw six ounces of chronic buds and downers down the garbage disposal."

"I'll bet you had to buy a new one," he laughed looking amused.

"You got that right. I finally surrendered and gave away my power. I realized that I was powerless."

"What was your revelation?" he asked.

"The play "Sunset Boulevard" made a great impact on me. It was that line when Glenn Close who rocked the stage as Norma Desmond said, "Just like me, he didn't know the meaning of surrender." Then her male obsession fell lifeless, floating in the swimming pool," I said sipping my drink. "I'm just a tormented artist using my pain to create and breath provocative theatrical life into my plays."

"You're bright, perceptive, and funny. When we first met I thought that you were clueless. You look very Hollywood, but you have a lot of depth," he said, stroking my hair.

"I love the plasticity in me, it balances out the dark side," I opened up to him, taking his hand.

"You're so pretty, I feel like I'm falling for you." He said impetuously.

"Sometimes I can't tell the difference between fantasy, art and life," I answered, trying to avoid the subject. "Remember that fifties lewd, brilliant comic Lenny Bruce?"

"Yes, I do, the shock jock before Howard Stern," he said.

"He was quoted on a TV special saying, 'Life is what it is and the rest is fantasy'."

"That's a real truism," Sony said. "Maybe it was synchronicity that we crossed paths so you could rescue me," he tightened his grip and I could barely breath.

"First I have to rescue myself. My life's in ruins." I said soulfully.

"I think it's all about the law of attraction." Sonny answered. "Let's fuck our brains out and stay sober together. I'd love to wake up with you in the morning. We'd probably never get out of bed," he said, kissing me softly.

My lips parted, craving more of his mouth, then pushing him away. "I'm an AA baby. I'm not ready for anything heavy. At least not for the first year."

"And I'm fighting depression, dealing with my demons. I'll bet we would have been wild together if we'd met before we got sober," he laughed.

"My ex-lover told me that I was like a character right out of a F. Scott Fitzgerald novel. While the world around me fell apart, I drank French champagne," I said, twirling my hair in my hands, sipping my soda like it was the bubbly, toasting him. There was a joy being genuine with another human being.

"Have you ever been with another woman? You seem so sensual and hedonistic," he said passing me a bag of chocolates.

I propped a dark Hershey square melting into my mouth, my endorphins rising.

"Let's just say that I like to explore my sexual curiosities," I answered coyly picking up my flat coke from the nightstand, taking a quick sip, wrinkling up my nose, falling back on his broad chest.

Suddenly the noise from the TV broke the silence. I looked up, seeing a naked Indian on a wild drunk flash across the screen. The actor was as hung as the stallion he was riding his bare ass bobbing up and down.

"Who's that stud on the screen?" I asked excitedly.

"Yours truly. That's one of the porn flicks I starred in," he answered proudly.

That was when I lost all rationale and control of my senses, then the twitching started between my legs. I was a rebel with a cause and decided to break all the rules at any cost. After all, I had to find out what sober sex was like, didn't I? I flung my arms around Sonny, kissing him as his hand moved slowly up and down my thigh, an electric charge shooting through my body. He tugged at the strap of my cotton sundress, pulling it down between my legs as it dropped to the ground. Erect pink nipples were popping out of my Betsy Johnson black and red satin corset. My shapely long legs clad in ivory lace thigh highs and spiked red heels attached to a garter belt. I always came prepared, didn't I?

"Very provocative pose. I like women that don't wear panties. You live to tease men's cocks," he moaned as his fingers unhooked my corset, caressing my breasts. "You're a knockout, baby. Your skin feels like velvet and your hair smells like wild flowers," he whispered.

"It's my Poison perfume. You like?"

"I'm so hot," he sighed, smelling my hair. "Feel my cock, you make me rock hard," he said positioning my hand on the zipper of his jeans. "You're a volcanic vixen with childlike spirit," he mused as I unzipped his fly, kissing his manhood as he licked my nipples, thrusting himself inside of me.

Well needless to say that night in Sonny's bed I found out how uninhibited I could be in my newly found sobriety. All that hype the AA Nazis preached about needing libations and drugs to partake in great sex was a fallacy. Sonny was the perfect one night stand.

Chapter Forty Three

Group Therapy, Malibu

I loved outpatient rehab. I could get all the hugs, panic grabs and sexual tension from the infamous actors and addicts in my group therapy sessions, and still go home and sleep in my own bed. One day at the clinic, some arrogant celebrity who made local headlines after beating up a notorious Madam, was engaging in a conversation, cellphone in hand, loudly fantasizing about his habit to another guy that was hooked on crystal meth and oxycontin.

"Hey man, you're cool. At least you had the good drugs. April's a lightweight. She only did pot and wine."

"Sorry I wasn't hardcore enough for you, dude," I interrupted.

Obviously he wasn't impressed with my addictions. I was also 'dissed' by an old rock icon. She beat up a cop when she got drunk, ending up incarcerated. Not too slick.

"Would you have a higher opinion of April if she dressed differently and didn't wear all that makeup?" She asked with a hard edge to her voice, the letters F U C K Y O U tattooed on her fingers.

You bitch, I thought. Another member was very impressed with her.

"Why don't you do a concert?" she asked.

"Nobody wants to see a burnt out has-been," the robust, faded looking woman answered angrily.

"Don't feel bad, I just got over the guy I was stalking," another spacey heroine addict said, twisting her hair as she kept touching her ear, revealing the needle marks on her arm. "I have to stay in touch with the energy in the room. My life is a spiritual path, I got thrown in jail for praying on someone's lawn. So after that they brought me into Cedars, then I ended up here." She said with disconnected speech, sniffling, her nose bleeding, her left eye twitching. The counsellor appeared.

"No more cross talking. Group is starting now. Would you please show some respect and put that cell phone away," she said dryly to the movie star idol.

"But I have to call my agent and my girlfriend and see what she picked up at Nordstrom's to wear to the premiere tonight. The brooding rebel sighed with a sharp tongued dismissive scowl.

I felt like I was back in the psych ward in New York at Bellevue when another floosie shared:

"It's not easy being a ho. The game's been good to me, you never know when you go up to a room with a trick if you'll come out alive They take something from me that I can never get back so I'm gonna make them pay for abusing me." she said with a sullen smile. "If you acknowledge your demons you give them power, they're good," she said with tears in her eyes.

I'm glad that I wouldn't let any of those freaks in my car when they tried to hit me up for rides. I thought to myself.

An ethereal, frail looking blonde girl frantically raised her hand.

"I went out again, are you going to dump me off?" she sobbed.

"We've given you enough chances, its up to the administration, but if you'd like to tell us about it we won't judge you."

"One time I had a year without using and my enabler girlfriend brought me a blackout cake spiked with rum and brandy from Greenblatt's. I gulped it down and fell on my face at the podium at an AA meeting. This time I had thirty days and the cravings kicked in again when I went off my meds and got fucked up." she blurted out, her hand covering her nose.

"I'll talk to you in my office after we finish." the counsellor said coldly, passing her the kleenex box. "Haven't you had enough bad experience with opiates?" she scolded.

"April, we haven't heard from you today. What's going on?" the shrink inquired with sincerity.

"The only slip I've had is under my dress," I said candidly.

"I don't see anything under your dress," some smart ass guy said approvingly.

"Let April talk." the leader said sternly.

"I've been taking classes on synchronicity and the Eros of Love at UCLA on Carl Jung. I had a very weird disturbing nightmare last night," I said with an edge in my voice.

"Tell us about it."

"Two goldfish were lying dead at the bottom of a pond. They were blending into the gray rocks. One's eye was eaten away by another carnivorous predator. Then a flock of bright orange koi fish with silver scales swishing their silky textured tails were gulping up air with their pouty little mouths as if they were suffocating."

"That's very profound. What does this mean to you?" she asked.

"I think its symbolic of my life. I've been floating aimlessly just like them. Almost drowning, then swimming upstream for survival."

"Brilliant. You've only been here for such a short time, but I've seen such growth in you. You're very intuitive, brave, and a great asset to the group. Thank you dear. Well, time's up. See you all next week. And remember, nothing from the neck up."

Oh dear God, I thought. *Too late for that after my one-night stand with Sonny.*

Chapter Forty Four

Yolanda
Hollywood Oasis Hotel

The language of the gutter is understood
anywhere that anyone ever fell in it.
Tennessee Williams

Yolanda entered the Mexican drug lord's house high on top of the hill by the Hollywood Sign in Beachwood Canyon. He was a latino about thirty years old, a smooth talker and well put together. He was Antonio's boss.

"Hola, welcome to my humble hacienda. You must be Yolanda, Antonio has told me all about you, but he underestimated your luscious exotic beauty. You're a model and an extra, si? Where's April?" the man asked.

"Yes, I'm jus one of the meat girls. Thank you, you're cool yourself. You look like you could be an actor. April passed on this." she answered defensively.

"Si, si, would you like to try some rock cocaine and crystal methamphetamines so when you sell it you'll know what you're dealing with. It's pure as the driven snow," the man said holding a silver spoon to her nose.

"Ya, this girl's into getting fucked up," she said wearing a sad smile, breathing in the substance.

"Here try some of these Columbian buds, they're primo. You can unwind with me, Cocaine is my drug of choice, I don't waste my time on anything else. Wine has ether in it, it makes me loco."

"Ok, but do you mind if I have some, I'm a little edgy. I ain't sold no drugs before." she blurted out with remorse.

"I just made some iced tea for myself, I don't mind if you drink just as long as it doesn't get in the way of you taking care of business. Have a shot of tequila. Its Cuervo Especial. When you deal drugs you always have to be alert and watch out for the Policia."

After a few shots, Yolanda's eyes dilated as she sat stifly on the couch, sucking on a lemon.

"This shit is smooth, I'm getting buzzed, I don't know if I'll be able to drive. Y'all mind if I hang with you for awhile sugar? I feel a little sick."

"Si, it would be my pleasure, the boys will be dropping by soon, it will be a good opportunity for you to acquaint yourself with them."

"Tell me more about this job." Yolanda inquired anxiously, holding a drink to her lips. Her short skirt hiked up to her thighs.

"The main thing is to enjoy life. We sell enjoyment. When you deal the drugs, you can earn a lot more dinero by pleasuring our customers also." he added slyly.

"I sure could use some extra cash." Yolanda pondered over the question for a moment, then nodded her head.

"The first contact I'll send you to is an established well known male star. He's in his early thirties, suave, wealthy, owns a big casa, and tips three thousand dollars for one night of your time. He might even see you on a regular basis if you know how to work him," the ruthless lowlife bragged, his outcome was manipulation.

"That's more than I can earn at the studios in a few months. When can I see him?" she asked anxiously.

"This man is used to the very best. First I have to test out the merchandise to see if you're really good and then I'll set you up with him."

"Come here, honey. I'm going to give you a blow job before your friends come." She said flatly, sliding down his zipper awkwardly without any passion.

When I arrived home late that Sunday night after attending a 12 step meeting at "The Tar Pits" and clustering with some out of work actors and catwalk queens at The Coffee Bean on Melrose Avenue, the red light was blinking on my answering service. "You have 30 new messages," the robotic voice answered. I hadn't checked it for 2 days.

"Where are you, baby girl? I'm running out of quarters. I've called you ten times. I'm afraid I'm gonna be in big trouble. You gotta get me outta here. Bless you. I'm at *The Hollywood Oasis East.* I think it's on the corner of Hollywood Boulevard and Vermont Avenue. You can't miss it. There's a mini mall with a 7-Eleven right next door."

I was getting tired of the girl's co-dependency and flakiness always getting herself into shaky situations, expecting me to bail her out, ending up at my doorstep at all hours of the night, although I had a deep affection for her, she was a mooch. But if I was on a boring set and she was there I always knew we'd have fun.

Yolanda had a history of violent, abusive men coming from a psychotic, dysfunctional family. She had been a great drinking partner, but if she didn't shape up, her persona would have to be non grata in my world. I had some sobriety under my belt, although I was still on shaky ground. I slipped out of my sexy leopard Prada jumpsuit squeezing on a pair of Lucky jeans, a funky faded blue T and dark glasses praying that I'd be lucky enough not to get murdered. The neighborhood was notorious for being LA's underground, frequented by heavy drug dealers, ex-cons, ho's, pimps, and drive-by shootings. As I approached the sleazy hotel, a homeless man was slumbering wrapped in a shabby blanket next to his pit bull and shopping cart. I walked in the front door into the dingy lobby where Yolanda was slumped down in an over-stuffed chair, her head hanging over her shoulder like a rag doll. Her eyes were half shut, rolling back in her head and the once pretty face was black and blue.

"Who did this to her?" I asked.

"She did it to herself. She almost O.D.ed from narcotics and alcohol," a young paramedic said after giving her mouth-to-mouth resuscitation. "She's breathing but her pulse is weak and her heartbeat irregular."

294 **Too Old to be a Hooker, Too Young to be a Madam**

"She won't die, will she?" I asked, feeling guilty that I didn't come sooner.

He slapped her face several times. "I think she's coming around," he said, without empathy in his voice.

Moments later she came to and the cute Latin man started walking her around the room.

"What happened, Yolanda?" I asked. "I got here as quickly as I could."

"This dealer pimp from the 'hood beat up on me punching away with his fists. He was like a crazy, throwing me around 'cause I sold him a hot Rolex watch for fifty bucks." Her voice was a hollow whisper, the sentences disjointed. "Then I drank some booze and did some crack. Okay. I fucked up, but I'm tryin' to get my thing together," she said. "He brutalized me, calling me a worthless whore, then threw me out."

"What happened to the sober living house? You were doing so well there," I said.

"It wasn't cool, I went out an' you know I get a little crazy sometimes." She started nodding out. "I feel so light headed. It's so peaceful. I ain't got no worries in the world," she moaned slowly as she was coming out of the ether. "I'm so cold."

I threw my faux fur jacket over her shoulders.

"Before I ended up here I went to see my mom and asked if I could stay there for a while. She didn't even let me in the house to take a shower," Tears rolled out of her big, bruised, brown eyes. "I slept in the garage with the dogs," she cried.

"Well, can you blame her? She can't trust you. Last time you stayed with your family, you stole money from them so that you could use."

"I wasn't trying to rip em off or nothing. I just needed to get high," she said, not looking me straight in the eyes.

"If you weren't so busy trying to get dizzy, you could have a life," I said.

"My ex asked me to marry him when Dr. Gland threw me out of rehab. I'm really upset over him so I called Jerome."

"The only foreplay you ever had with the janitor was at the end of a switch blade," I answered. "Where would the wedding be, at the Church of Satan?" I asked with a smirk on my face.

"He brought me a dozen roses. Wasn't that cool?"

"A dozen roses are only $12.00 at Trader Joe's now."

"You're right. I can't be that desperate. He was always trying to get up on my shit," she said. "I asked him why he suddenly wanted to get married, and he said cause he was broke."

"That's romantic," I said.

"My big chocolate warrior an' I had chemical differences anyway. He's not the real deal," she said. "Maybe my therapist will take me back." She said looking frightened.

"Let's go," I demanded, dragging her out of the room.

As we passed the living area filled with rowdy, unsavory characters, the sweet smell of cocaine and pot lingered in the stale air. Drag queens, crack whores, Satanists and psychedelic performance artists in remission were having a mock 12 step meeting. The residents were drinking red Ariel (non-alcoholic) wine, coffee, and smoking joints, cigarettes and pipes. An old hippy speaker with long, stringy hair was standing in front of a big TV screen, drinking an O'Doul's non-alcoholic beer, reciting a passage from the book on the "Fourth Step."

"If we drink, we die," he screamed out bitterly, like he was going to draw blood, followed by a loud clapping. "With dope, there's hope."

I had to escape the smokiness and dank mustiness of the room, and the underbelly of the deranged kick ass chemical lifestyle.

"Come on, Yolanda. We have to bail. This place is filled with toxic energy. We need a connection for life, not a sentence for death. Our obsessions are definitely not going to get lifted in this hellhole. How self destructive you are," I said, dragging her out of the room as she staggered down the hallway.

"I feel so ashamed. You think I'm such a loser. I completely lost it. I could jes' knock on any door and score whatever I wanted," she said, hanging onto me as I led her to the street, propping her up as she almost fell down on the urine-stained pavement in the crisp winter air.

"This mode of sub-culture was a decadent voyage that had no limits," I thought as we approached my silver 280Z.

"I feel dizzy and nauseous. I jes' want to be done with myself. I have nowhere to go. I was sleeping in my car an I got thrown in jail," she cried. "Sometimes I jes' can't bear the burden of being a young, black girl."

"Yo Yo, you know I love you, but you're a recovering addict manipulating anyone on skid row just to get a fix to fill up the dark hole," I said, as I helped her into the car. She smelled and needed a bath and to change out of her grungy sweat pants and soiled shirt, I thought as I drove west, down Hollywood Boulevard, heading for Laurel Canyon.

"You can stay with me for a while, providing you're sober. I'll help you get some jobs at the studios. You'll get on your feet in no time. But I can't hang out with lower companions anymore. If you disappoint me this time, it's all over," I said as her face fell.

"I jes' always felt that I wasn't enough, April, like I'm not who I'm supposed to be," she said. "There ain't no place in L.A. for me except South Central Avenue. I don't have the opportunities like you do April."

"You're exactly where you're supposed to be in life right now, the experience was just another bad lesson. You're safe now with me," I promised, hearing the deafening honking of horns on the bustling boulevard of bright lights, stars, glitter and tourists. "Sometimes my malicious addict, inner child comes out also and I have to nurture it. You're a strong girl," I said.

"It just sucked sitting in that hotel room, getting high. Thank you so much for taking me in and giving me a chance," she said, giving me a hug.

"You don't have an option anymore. You've hit bottom," I said. "The opportunity you have now is the gift of getting your life back and getting over the guilt of your family. Don't you know that alcoholics are the bravest people in the world, although they're not always easy to love," I mustered up a fake laugh.

"But I'm so weak. I need to wake up in the morning and have someone to hang onto and tell me it's gonna be okay," she said. "You is my girl."

"I'm risking my life for you so you can be weak? Cancel that thought," I said.

"I don't even know why you're my friend. Sometimes I feel like I'm just a burden to you," she said, kissing my cheek, hanging all over me. "I love you, April."

"Yolanda, friendship is about revealing your innermost shameful intimate secrets to someone you can trust and relate to when the worst things are happening. A bonding of the souls, not bondage like the obligatory relationship. Leaving messages on someone's service when you know they're not there, then when they return the call, you sit there in dread, not answering the phone," I said.

"I've told you all my sleazy secrets and you still love me?" She held her shaky, clammy hands up to my face. "You're my strength, April, my rock," she sighed.

Yolanda was hyperventilating. She could hardly talk coherently.

"Yes, Yolanda, I've got an emotional invest-ment in you, and although I admit that I can be judgmental, I try not to judge you. When I've told you about my problems, you were always there for me. That was when our once Hollywood friendship reached a new dimension," I said, smiling up at her while driving the car. "Why do you think that of all the people at the studio we always ended up on some of the same sets together, there's an impor-tant message there, don't you think?" I squeezed her hand gently.

"You're really cheering me up, sister. Could we stop at Fatburger before we hit the canyon? I'm having a grease attack. I ain't eaten for days. Them brothers give me drugs and don't feed me nothin'."

"Then they have power over you." I preached.

"I get ya sugar, but I need some meat on these bones, honey. I could really go for a triple cheese-burger, some French fried onion rings, an a order of sweet potato pie," she said, her face lighting up in the dark, shadows. "You got some money on you, April?"

"Yes, you're covered," I said. Seeing Yolanda in that condition and all the freaked out addicts only reinforced my need for sobriety. That scary night I learned one of life's lessons that couldn't be found at AA meetings or reading the "Big Book." This was reality. The surreal riddled pop opiate, low life, exploitations were not my style.

"Yolanda, your gang lifestyle diminishes your spirit. You're a beautiful girl who deserves to live and find some peace. My shrink said that the primate brain fights with the physiological brain and causes cravings."

"I got real suicidal when this chronic masturbator whacked himself off in my room. That made me want to use even more stuff."

"Gross, ew," I said.

"Then one junky shot up in my bathroom sitting on the toilet and he fell off the seat and OD'd. The cops came and put him in a body bag," she cried.

"We'll stay sober together. It will be the biggest challenge of our lives. Think of it as an investment, like money in the bank. I don't want to end up at your memorial. We're still young. We are the sum of our choices," I said, as we pulled into the fast food stand. "It's not about pleasing people, it's about you. You internalize everything. You're expecting a fucking miracle and it's not going to happen unless you have self worth. I surrendered to a power that gets me higher than the poison. I was using to float in and out of reality. We have a very hard commitment ahead of us. We just have to be tough."

"I know," she sighed. "But every time I get with a dude I get fucked over."

"I understand. The male animal always tries to track down and mutilate the youngest and most beautiful of the species." I said with agitation in my voice.

"Ok, I'm in control now." Yolanda said unconvincingly. "I can't hurt any more than I already do or abuse myself more than I already have everyday."

"We're never in control. Get a grip. Last month you were so out of it that your connection brought you to AA because he thought you were going to die. Then awhile after that I got you into an expensive group therapy clinic that didn't cost you a dime. The last day, you called to inform me that you picked up a gallon of Gallo wine. This is your last free pass with me." I said sternly, turning off the key to my car, feeling sad that she'd slid back into a world of drugs and alcohol. It was hard enough to forget when she stayed at my house the last time that the girl drank my cooking sherry I used for gourmet dinners, from under the sink. When I informed her that the bottle was empty she smugly said it must have evaporated.

Chapter Forty Five

Psychotherapy
Epitaph to Heathcliff

"Sit down, April. What was so urgent?"

"Thank you for seeing me today, doctor. I had to put my little dog to sleep yesterday and I'm suicidal again, I feel so guilty." I answered leaning back on the couch, removing my hooded sweat shirt.

"I understand," he said, "but guilt is a useless emotion that darkens our dreams and haunts our days. You're suffering from the fear that you abandoned him. It's done, why relive the incident? You have to let go of the past. If you don't live in the moment and in your feelings you're not living in the real world. Feelings are truth," he answered, as I stared at his drawn, wrinkled face.

"I understand, but sometimes it's so painful. I just don't know if I can deal with life on its own terms. The whole experience took away my thunder. I have problems relating to reality." I sighed.

"Each life experience is the tapestry that weaves together the experiences. Believe in your goodness even if you've done something wrong. You have a habit of internalizing things. You can't be more than you are. Letting go is redeeming your power. Power comes from recognizing your strength, and accepting your weakness. All you are is energy in this incarnation," he answered, picking up his phone. "Sorry, I have to take this, one moment please. I'm booked until next week." he said, briefly putting down the receiver. When he finished the conversation I asked,

"Can I tell you about it? How much time do I have left in this session?"

The therapist quickly looked at his watch. "We have about twenty minutes, please go on."

I began telling the sad story of how I had watched the bulging brown eyes of Heathcliff, my Tibetan soul dog roll permanently and painlessly back in his head after the dashingly handsome Beverly Hills veterinarian to the stars shaved his little paw and injected the red serum of death into it in his brightly fluorescent lit office. I could still smell the anesthesia. It made me sick with grief. He had put a muzzle on Heathcliff's mouth so he wouldn't bite his tongue. I had this horrible feeling, being unsure that I was truly doing the right thing. He reassured me how very weak my dog was, but I never mentioned that I had given him two ten milligram valiums before we left the house. "Heathcliff is fifteen years old. He's had his Camelot. You might have woken up one morning and found him dead in your bed," he said with compassion, giving me a hug. Comforting me, he was my hero.

Heathcliff and I had survived the rain in my life, flash floods and fires in Laurel Canyon. We were inseparable. He looked up at me so lovingly before the life was snuffed out of him. My precious baby was so helpless I lost it in the office, screaming, "Is he still alive, is he still alive?" He told me it was over, and tried to comfort me, telling me that that was one of the hardest things I would ever have to go through. I'll never forget the fun times, our long walks in the woods, ice blue wild flowers tangled in his beard. Now his shaggy smile so full of yesterday. I felt totally devastated and unstable.

Then the shrink looked at his watch again, "I'm sorry April, but it's all just part of life. Animals don't live as long as humans. They're only here to visit for awhile. I hope you won't be alone when you get home tonight."

"My boyfriend deserted me. I'm in emotional flux. The toxic vampires use me, then throw me away."

"April, no response is a response. We have a lot of work to do. If only you could believe that people are coming from the best place they can," he said.

"What about Charles Manson or Jeffrey Dahmer?" I asked.

"That's the worst case scenario. They were victims of child abuse," he answered.

"So that makes it okay." I smugly answered, my body sinking deeper into the plush grey couch.

"The greatest power you have is empowering someone else," he answered, wearing a faint smile.

"I've done that all my life." I answered.

"When you can tolerate being alone that's when you're fit to be with another person. It's the same thing with family. If your family aren't on your team, divorce them and find another family."

"I'm so angry," I screamed, wringing my hands. "I have to learn how to detach myself so I won't hurt as much."

"Don't deny your feelings. Have a mind that is open to everything and attached to nothing. Rewrite your agreement with reality." He said.

"What should I tell my boyfriend? He's so self-righteous."

"You can't solve a problem with the same mind that created it," he answered. "Just say, 'I'm sorry that you didn't turn out to be who I needed you to be. I don't even know who you are anymore. It doesn't work.' Then set him free. Have you been writing lately?" he asked.

"I'm so distressed, I've lost all my inspiration," I answered.

"Stress comes from bottled up feelings that aren't expressed, fear of failing," he said, looking at his watch again impatiently.

"What should I do?" I asked.

"Our time's up, but I'll leave you with a few thoughts. You're just a work in progress. Trust in your passion for writing. Don't die with your dream still inside of you. Visualize who you want to be and believe that you can be that person. Separate the fantasy from reality, but dare to take a risk. Look at your life introspectively, as you will, be an observer. April, you have great insight, that will always get you by in life," he said.

"Then why do I attract the wrong men?" I asked.

"Because you're head-strong and dauntless. You have to start listening to your inner voice. And for the record, just don't go out with anyone that's your type."

"Thank you, doctor. What time next week?"

"Three o'clock Thursday," he answered. " 'Til then just remember, life is the opposite of what it seems to be. It's only the outcome that counts."

Chapter Forty Six

Ovulating Oysters
The Polo Lounge
Part Two

One should never trust a woman who tells her real age. A woman who would tell that would tell one anything.
Oscar Wilde

The Beverly Hills Hotel was a combination of art deco 40's and Hollywood glamour. As I walked through the lobby area, a Venetian glass chandelier threw soft light upon the gold leafed ceiling and grand staircase. This timeless resort has been the favorite watering hole for generations of Silver Screen stars. Chelsea, Yolanda, Brian and I were gossiping over lunch as the sommelier popped the cork pouring glistening bubbles into our glasses.

"Yolanda's having Perrier, thank you." I said. "She's in rehab."

"Whatever," she smirked at me rebelliously. "Look who's talking, you were in there once too, April."

"I hear anybody who's cool has been seen in those rooms," Chelsea said with a smirk.

"I'm on a wine, pot, maintenance program now," I laughed.

"You're no one if you haven't been arrested these days. It's as common in Hollywood as gold cards."

"Chelsea's right," Brian shared.

"My old bloke the plastic surgeon will be very instrumental in my life." Chelsea interrupted. "My greatest talent is to bestow blow jobs on powerful men."

"Did you forget about the hard core sex and shopping?" Brian laughed.

"Bri, how's your treatment 'West Holy Boys', and your love interest?" I asked.

"A UCLA freshman followed me home last week-end. He told me he was impressed because I was a graduate student," Brian bragged. "We were a massive collision of hormones. He thinks I'm an anal warrior. I wouldn't date him though."

Our conversation was interrupted as a waiter popped open another bottle of champagne.

"Enjoy." he smiled pouring it attentively.

My friends lifted their glasses toasting me in glee.

"Here's to Miss Playwright Erotica," and "The Lean Restaurant Queen of Fine Cuisine."

I was wearing a whimsical ethereal Dior black lace up corset glam dress. My electric ringlets framing my cheekbones, a smoky gray pearl necklace strung around my neck. I had that super sultry, light, flirty, fem look.

"Sugar lamb, you're voluminous retro radiance with your vivid shocking pink gloss. Your lips look like cotton candy," Brian said looking at me adoringly.

It was friday afternoon at the Polo Lounge, the global melting pot for the adrenaline pumped, vicodin and blow addicted, indulgent overprivileged and ne'erdowells.

"I'm reflecting on my inner goddess after Botox. I only had a day of downtime. How do I look?" Chelsea asked, fluffing up her hair, fluttering her eyelashes, studying her image, her graceful hand holding a Chanel compact.

"Like a classic beauty with a face as pink as a piglet," Brian said with apprehension.

"Brian, lighten up. You're being really bitchy," I scolded.

"I'm just as sweet as peach pie. I have to call my long haired vegan blond waiter," Brian answered. "He stays hard all night."

"Do you really fancy him? You're a crucial sexaholic," Chelsea laughed. "Naughty boy. I hope he doesn't have a little pinky. That would be a calamity."

"Look at that woman across the room. What a monster of a dress," I laughed disingenuously. "How kitsch."

"And she thinks she can get away with that plunging neckline, flaunting those geriatric breasts."

"Oh stop picking on her. I never wear bras either. I wouldn't know how to," Brian said.

"Check out that Hadassa redhead with those pumped up blood red vampire lips," I chimed in. "She makes me embarrassed to be Jewish."

"When I look at a woman like that I can't figure out why I want to be one," Brian said in disgust.

"I feel very cheeky today, I have a date with my fashion savvy heterosexual mate tonight. He loves to spoil me with multiple injections," Chelsea shared nonchalantly picking up her glass.

Yolanda was getting sloppy spilling her drink all over Chelsea's dress.

"You're garbage can chic, ducky, but this couture dress I'm wearing has on a thirty day return policy at Neiman's. I'm very annoyed with you," Chelsea said, brushing herself off with a napkin.

"Whatever," Yolanda replied defensively.

"I just had silicone shot into my feet so that I can wear my Jimmy Choos all night long."

"That's my Hollywood blonde, she takes care of her feet no matter how many toes she steps on," Brian said pouring her another glass of champagne, squeezing her arm.

The hotel was home for the half starved anesthetized spinsters with menopausal hips, daintily nibbling on bite sized portions after having tummy tucks, washing down their pain killers with celery and carrot sticks and a glass of chardonnay, their sagging skin pinned behind their ears. The table in the corner was filled with wannabe actors and soap stars permanently on hiatus, talking on they're cellphones.

"I know that actor at the table you're looking at, April. I'll bet he's gay," Brian said.

"To you every boy in Hollywood or New York is either gay or borderline homo," I said.

Our waiter approached our booth. Miss Moon, if you're ready to order lunch may I make some suggestions?" he asked. "Our specialty of the day are fresh water oysters on the half shell served with white horseradish and chili sauce. They're excellent!" he said smugly.

"Sounds swell. We'll start with four orders."

"New Zealand Lamb with basil mint sauce is superb also for an entrée."

"I don't eat baby lambs. They're our friends," Brian said in disgust.

"I'm so sorry, sir. I'd be happy to have the chef create special dishes if it would so please you," he said apologetically.

"We'll have some more champagne and then decide. My friends and I enjoy having long leisurely lunches," I said bluntly.

"As you wish, I'll be back with your order shortly," the waiter said in an authoritative haughty manner.

"I heard oysters make you horny," Yolanda perked up.

"I'm so glad that you met a shrink to experiment with," I said patting her head with a ready smile while munching on guacamole and chips.

"I'll never forget the janitor, that horny ass mother fucker with his all slick n' greasy hair when he was gorilla man tapping for gold. Then I tol' him it was just sex an' to get out. An he tol' me I should go back to the swamps of Harlem and my old profession. Then he asked me if there's some kind of pill I can take so I can be with him. Now I'm on Prozac an I'm inta my man, Dr. Gland, no more bad-ass brothers."

"Well a tryst is better than a fist," I said with a little apprehension.

"This hotel is high classed. It sure beats Rock n' Roll Denny's. I got a worm in my salad at dat joint." Yolanda said, frowning.

"Well I'm glad you like it here," I answered arrogantly.

"I used to have to fuck someone to get a free lunch at The Polo Lounge," before you got all them freebies, girl."

"The man at the next table is so not my type," Brian said. "He keeps staring at me. The white look is out. He looks like a tablecloth at an upscale restaurant. He's a hippy hobo."

"I'd like to spill some red wine on him and make him vintage." I laughed.

"So how's your man of the moment, April?" Brian asked. "I'm thrilled that you gave up day labor dating for a cerebral director twit. When are we going to meet him?"

"At opening night," I said. "It's nothing serious babe, he's an egomaniac. My two one acts are playing on Sunset this weekend under the umbrella title of 'Tits and Tombstones'. Its an evening of macabre farce." I said handing everyone flyers and press passes.

"We all fell over ourselves we were laughing so hard at your last production," Chelsea said assuringly.

Brian read the flyer wearing a wicked grin. "Honey buns, sounds like a Sadean orgy with the blood thirsty bourgeois. You're wild bitch. The

Marquis De Sade and Lucrecia Borgia at his chateau in 18th Century France."

"Sounds like a lot of Victorian vaginas taking a good flogging," Chelsea said vicariously.

"Yikes, I need another glass. I drank enough coffee to awaken a xanax addict from a week's sleeping jag." Brian yawned. In a flash the waiter and a busboy rushed over to us pouring more effervescent bubbles.

"Your shellfish over ice, miss."

"Thank you," I replied.

"It's my pleasure." He said as he whisked away.

Brian made a face as he lifted his fork to his mouth tasting the crustaceans.

"Bri, what did you think when you first met April?" Yolanda asked.

"I'll never forget the day I saw her, I'd just moved into Laurel Canyon in the house across the street from hers with my Chihuahua PeeWee. She was walking her Shih Tzu Heathcliff down our long private driveway," Brian answered, pushing his plate away.

"What was I wearing?" I asked.

"A long, black see-though negligée with stiletto heels. Your tits were standing erect in the breeze," he snickered.

"We were working in the movies together. I couldn't have been walking to the set. Maybe one of the neighbor's baby showers," I said.

"You were stoned. You looked like you were going to an orgy. I could tell that you had experienced all the universe's known vices and eternally opposing forces. Then you said that we should be friends and asked me if I had a joint."

"I thought that maybe you'd be my next connection."

"We were like 'The Big Chill' on acid." Brian mused recalling the fun moments of our past. "I thought you were whack. One morning you showed me your resume and it said 'Hooker Number 1', 'Hooker Number 2', 'Barfly', 'Lonely Stripper', etc. You were outrageous, my sweet. That's when I fell in love with your persona."

"This oyster tastes a bit milky," Chelsea remarked, wrinkling up her nose.

"I wonder if that's a hollandaise sauce on top. It tastes rich and creamy, but very tasteless," I said putting my fork back on the plate.

"This slimy thing slid down me screech, it's vulgar. I'd prefer the scampi and crab cakes," Chelsea complained.

"Whatever this thing on my plate is, it's gross," Yolanda added.

I sighed, signaling the waiter over.

"I'm sorry, I think these oysters are spoiled. We'd rather try some other dishes."

Within seconds a handsome Chef and manager surrounded us.

"I bring my expertise and accolades to this grand hotel. My cuisine is perfection, Miss Moon," the eccentric looking man haughtily said with bravado.

"He was named Chef of the Year at 'The Culinary Institute' in Paris," the manager assured us condescendingly.

"The seafood is not very appetizing, love. But I'm sure that you might whet my appetite," Chelsea said flirtatiously in a breathy tone, lifting her champagne glass, smiling, one of her spaghetti straps falling off her shoulder as she raised her permanently lifted eyebrow without wrinkling her forehead.

"This creature looks like a vagina," Brian laughed. "The female oysters are ovulating, sir."

"I'll take them away. The males are fine," the man said as he ordered someone to remove them.

"You're hot," Chelsea said as she took a card out of her purse, handing it to the star Chef.

"You can take the other oysters away also and please send over our server. We'll change our order," I added. "I promise I won't mention this in my column."

After several more bottles and exotic yummy dishes I looked at my rhinestone Guess watch. It was time to leave. I had a rehearsal at six.

"After I see your play I can't wait to get back to my sex slave. It's his perfectly messed up hair and warm blue eyes. You know that trucker trash look that makes me want to roll over and seduce him at six in the morning. Then we both rise with the sunset. He couldn't get any cuter," Brian said. "But he told me he has guilt about being a homo."

"Sounds like the perfect eye candy for a commitophobic like you," I teased.

"I think I just want him because he's a bonafide sex symbol," Brian commented with a happy smile.

The waiter handed me a black leather holder with a bill inside of it marked complimentary. We walked through the lobby towards the porte cochère. Our cars arrived and we said goodbye to yesterday and greeted in tomorrow as palms swayed in the Beverly Hills breezes.

Chapter Forty Seven
Undressed for Success

Chelsea, Yolanda and I were Brian's guests for Sunday Brunch at that priceless romantic hideaway Hotel Bel-Air. He'd just flown in from the Hamptons. I drove my car up the magical wooded canyon, arriving at my destination, anticipating a fun-filled afternoon.

The two-story, pale pink, stucco, 20's mission-style retreat, crowned by a bell tower was reminiscent of a scene from 'The Hunchback of Notre Dame'.

I crossed the quaint old arched bridge, entering the hotel perched on twelve lush acres. My friends were seated in a gazebo, socializing on the bougainvillea winding terrace, studying the brunch menu. After the hostess seated me, I draped myself around the booth as a waiter poured mimosas into long stemmed glasses. We toasted to our forever lasting friendships and the success we'd achieved along the way.

"I hope you like my new hair color," Chelsea inquired nervously.

"When God doesn't give us divas the proper shade, Clairol always does," Brian grinned.

"I'm so thrilled that you're bi-coastal, my darling, now that I'm moments away from becoming the trophy wife of a famous Beverly Hills plastic surgeon.

But I'm devastated that you're not bi," Chelsea said in a flirty purr.

"Chels, you're looking mighty swell in your chiquita banana goddess sundress, with your suave bottle-blonde power ponytail persona," Brian remarked.

My Chloe gilded gold brocade skirt and ivory silk blouse with cascading ruffles down the front was perfect for the old money crowd.

"I'm simply mad for your kinky high-heeled Gaultier open-toed sneakers and ultra chic outfit darling, "Chelsea raved on. "But one over twenty should never wear red lipstick."

The hotel's lush landscaping and flower gardens were a botanical kaleidoscope of splendorous color and bursts of fragrance sweeping across the rambling red-tiled California bungalows and Mediterranean villas.

"Have you decided on your orders yet, sir?" the waiter asked impatiently.

"We'll have the Eggs Florentine, the Crab cakes, and bring us some Poached Eggs with Rare Petite Mignons, please," Brian answered waving him away.

Chelsea looked stunning in her mocha corduroy double-breasted Gucci Capri jacket from Neiman's. Her painted silver toes squeezed into her blue patent leather platforms.

"It's so great to see you babes. I just returned from a press tour in, can you believe, Missoula, Montana. That was where I learned the ancient Japanese art of karaoke at the Veterans Hall. It was so cool. When I belted out "My Way" it was better than Judy Garland. I was as hot as a disco dolly," Brian bragged on. "The place becomes an underground gay bar at night, filled with rednecks, hicks, skinny boys, and fat lesbians dressed like "Sex and the City," getting plastered on cosmopolitans."

"The ambiance sounds dreadful," Chelsea frowned as we drank our champagne.

"These spirits are awesome after the dollar seventy-five cent Red Strike Beer the bartender gave me with a condom next to it. Then I knew I had to go," Brian said turning up his nose.

"Cheers!" I laughed, lifting my glass to the sky.

Brian was wearing a red and black cowboy shirt and Guess jeans.

"I'm so excited about my new outfit. I'm in my western phase. There's a great Barney's Co-op in New York where I bought everything for my trip. I just adore gay cowboys. I get a stiffy over even the hint of hunk-on-hunk simulation. I like to tickle their scrotums with my tongue."

Overlooking Swan Lake in the epitome of luxury, our spirits were lulled by cascading waterfalls.

Brian hailed over the waiter. "More champagne please," he asked handing me a large manila envelope.

"I'm going to open this after everyone has had a few cocktails," I smiled apprehensively, placing it on the starched white linen tablecloth as the server poured more bubbly in our glasses, bringing more plates of delicious cuisine to our table.

"These are some pictures and reviews I down-loaded from www.findallcelebs.com. Babe, I suspect you already knew you had four-star tits, but here's proof. How wonderful it is to have you in my life... and even though sometimes we're separated by three thousand miles, I can always look up naked pictures of you online. I haven't many friends like that."

""Bitch, I need a monogamous gay boyfriend," I said teasing Brian.

"And I can't believe that you're jealous of a flat-chested Asian lesbian who's not even on my speed dial." Brian said, giving me a hug.

"April's got a way hot looking security guard. He has a curvy booty, and he looks hungry for your meat, girl. Sista's still kicking it, Yolanda said, giving me a hug.

"I need a gun-packing man, one under his zipper and one in the holster. A dude that can lock and load," I said.

"She wants the dick." Yolanda teased.

"Where's the dude from?" Brian asked.

"The Middle East. He has a brooding sexuality," I moaned.

"Well you better check him out, over there if a man does something wrong they chop it off." Brian said sarcastically.

"Too much information." I answered, glaring at him.

I picked up the pictures, recalling that tacky film where I'd played James Woods' hooker girlfriend in the 80's. The vision that I portrayed was that of a drenched sultry goddess frolicking in the wilderness being hosed down by her pimp. I was such a frivolous nymph like free spirit in all of my magnificence. Strands of long, fiery red, sun-streaked hair streamed down my shoulders. My tanned sculptured body playfully seducing the camera. It seemed like only yesterday, I thought.

"April, let me see those pictures," Chelsea begged pulling them out of my hand. "Brilliant dolly, you were so daring in those days. Even Raquel always says that you had the best body of any girl in Beverly Hills and she's shamefully jealous of you. You're a mad bird."

"April, you're still smoking hot," Yolanda chimed in.

"She's on fire," Brian beamed.

"We have to read these quotes that the whacks that review websites wrote in," I said.

Yolanda smiled, lipstick smeared on her enameled white teeth. Her green thermal hoodie falling off her bare shoulders, exposing a brown midriff, ever-visible bra straps and ragged hair extensions.

"Check out what this chap says. He gave you a four-star rating. That's the highest one ya can get."

Chelsea grabbed the paper out of Yolanda's hand.

"This chap wrote 'lovely boobs. Nice pointy nipples. Lucky Woods must have had a woody. Forgettable movie. Although I would have preferred to see some graphically portrayed masturbation.' How shockingly demented," she said disgustedly.

"Check this out, Miss Thing. 'Moon's full length frontal nudity, slightly trimmed hairy bush and sweet jiggly ass and boobitties are definitely worth a look and a real joy to behold'," Yolanda read, doubling over with laughter as she sipped her drink.

"That's my girl. Listen to this one, 'Moon's tits are definitely bigger than a C cup. She's very voluptuous. She looks like a cheap high-class bi-polar whore. We could be lovers but no more.' Is that a hoot?" Brian laughed.

"That guy's a fruit loop," Chelsea laughed.

"What a Twinkie," Yolanda added.

"Dorothy Parker was quoted as saying 'You can lead a whore to culture but you can't make her think'," Brian shared.

"You out shined James Woods in the reviews and he's an Academy Award nominated actor," Chelsea chuckled. "I'll see you poolside at the Chateau Marmont for some fashion vulgarity and star wattage at the Victoria Secret trunk show."

"Where bubble-heads reign," Brian quipped.

As we finished our desserts, the fragrant smell of coffee beans filled the air.

"I'll expect you all to tune in to the Shopping Network tonight. I'm launching my own anti-aging skin care line," Chelsea bragged, almost limping towards the valet.

"The pain of high heels and hobnobbing. Now don't Welch out on me, April. It should be jolly," Chelsea said in her low raspy cigarette smoky voice, climbing into Hymie's new Mercedes McLaren with the swinging doors.

"The car's an SLR '06. Doesn't it look like a Lamborghini? They're not making anymore models," she bragged driving away.

"See ya April. That's wild, girl. You never got reviewed for no acting, just nudity," Yolanda said peeling dust in her old battered up Volkswagen.

Chelsea had lost herself in a monetary world and the greatest regret I had was that life gets in the way of art.

Chapter Forty Eight

Grazing at the Ivy
Chelsea Flowers

It was three o'clock in the morning in September. I awoke panic-stricken in a cold sweat. I'd had a chilling nightmare that my black leather watch was missing and that I'd run out of time. I climbed out of bed, walking over to my vanity, opening a silver art deco box. The oval blue face stared up at me. Tick-tock, sounding like the rhythm of my heartbeat. Chelsea and I were supposed to hook up over the weekend, but she'd called me frantically yesterday.

"April, can you meet me tomorrow at The Ivy? I have bad news. I don't know what is going to happen to me. It's bloody awful." she moaned.

"You're freaking me out," I answered. "Tell me."

"We'll talk over lunch," she said. "12:30 and be prepared for a long one. I could use a good chuckle."

I pulled up in front of the trendy LA sidewalk café in my indigo blue BMW, giving my keys to the tired-looking valet. Climbing out of the car, I put a crumbled up five dollar bill in his hand, hoping that my car would arrive in a timely manner when I was ready to leave, and that it would still be in one piece.

Power agents, screen icons and anorexic and androgynous Melrose Avenue model types were squeezed in together scattered around the whimsical white picket fenced patio sipping Evian and white wine. Chelsea was waving at me from one of the tables as I walked up the brick steps, my hips swaying as I sat down.

She greeted me with a kiss. Keanu Reeves was seated on one side of us, and a group of old investor bank account power cocks on the other. My eyes swept the lush sun-drenched latticed restaurant soaking up the last rays of summer.

Our arrogant server arrived reluctantly to his station.

"May I bring you ladies some cocktails?" he asked with a lisp, holding a pad and pen in his hand.

Chelsea was working on her second apple martini, studying the menu.

"Our specials of the day are Soft Shelled Crab with a polenta crust, and Pink Copper River Salmon garnished with Red Pepper Coulis and Aioli."

"I'll have a glass of chardonnay and save time for the flourless chocolate soufflé," I answered.

"I'll have another, sir, and hold the lunch please," Chelsea sighed.

The models were eating Spa Food lifting their forks to their mouths taking dainty pretend bites, wearing blank smiles.

Chelsea was wearing a vintage flowered dress, a floppy felt hat with a black silk flower, and red rhinestone rimmed Dior sunglasses.

"I really appreciate you meeting me on such short notice, I really needed to get plastered and chat it up."

"What's going on?" I asked not having seen her for a few weeks.

"I have a large lump on me left breast," she said swallowing a yellow pill with her drink, her hand shaking as she lifted the glass. "I have to take a dramamine, I feel another wave of nausea, I'm frightened to death." She sobbed.

"How did you find out?" I asked, handing her a napkin as she dried her sad eyes.

"I went for a mammogram, now I must have a biopsy."

"I'm so sorry," I said, trying to act calm.

"What if I have to have me breast removed," she said. "There's a time for living and a time for dying. Maybe it's me time."

"The world is filled with cancer survivors," I said unconvincingly.

"I'm feeling right pissed and helpless," she clutched my hand as the waiter walked by.

"It could be a false scare," I answered.

"Not blimey likely. Another please," she said to the busboy, cradling her perfect breasts in her hands. "How do I look? Now don't lie to me, April," she insisted. Chelsea had an air of cultured sophistication. Emerging crow's feet only enhanced her fading beauty. As she lifted her dark glasses, a touch of sunlight filtered on her face. "You haven't said anything about my appearance," she complained, looking annoyed.

"You look beautiful," I answered.

"What do you think of my color? Does platinum hair age me? It's so hard being twenty-seven," she sighed.

Her twenties had passed her by many years ago but I could fake it couldn't I?

"You look really young," I said.

"I wore this sexy dress so that I could rock the room when I walked in as usual." She bragged, flashing me a wide smile, puffing away on her Marlboro Light trying to hide her pain. We stared at each other awkwardly across the crude wooden table.

"Are you afraid of death, April?"

"No, I'm just afraid of life. It's people like me that have really lived in ecstasy and agony that are ready when the time comes," I said.

"You're so morbid today. Not my cup of tea, ducky," she said.

"Let's face it, honey, we're all going to go. Everyone here dining al fresco is going to die sometime. It's just a flip of the coin who goes first. Maybe in the next five minutes, or next ten decades. At any moment, disaster can cast an evil spell without any preference," I said taking a sip of my drink while studying the menu.

"Do you think God is punishing me because I've been a selfish gold digger and that's why my life has bloody well collapsed?" Chelsea sadly shared as if she'd had a rude awakening of how shallow she really was.

"What if this was all there is? Right now, a trendy restaurant. Could you get into it and live in the moment? If we could be willing to give up our egos and just let go, maybe we could fly instead of crawl," I said in a serious tone.

"Only if I was wearing my Manolos," she answered.

"It's all just a lesson. I've known from the beginning that we're just spirits occupying this body. You had no part in it the minute they cut the umbilical cord, slapped you on the ass and you came out all bloody, frightened and saw your first sunrise." I said. "What did you expect?"

"Well aren't you sassy today. I'm sloshed or I'd tell you to piss off, twit." Chelsea said as she rolled her eyes at me. "You must be listening to Wayne Dyer again." Then moments later, I couldn't get a word in, it was all about her not hearing anything that I had said. "I still get carded. This is so unfair. My breasts are my trophies. This is really happening. I'd rather pop-off." Her graceful hand was clutching her glass, almost dropping it. "My nerves. Here, feel this," she demanded, putting my hand on her breast as one hair plugged movie producer sent us over a bottle of Piper. "I haven't slept a wink since I received the test results, April," she said in a shrilly tragic voice, clenching her hands. Chelsea's anguished face bared a slight resemblance of the once stunning spoiled narcissistic girl I had tried to emulate and had idolized for years. Her persona had reeked of confidence and conceit. She'd never been in a position to be that vulnerable and needy before.

I smiled staring into her lifeless, dull, hollow, dark rimmed eyes. I couldn't bear to cause her more anguish so I told her anything that she wanted to hear.

"April, you're the face of Dorian Grey, ageless," she smiled.

"Age has given me many treasures that youth didn't bear. Wisdom, and insight. I always knew that beauty was a fickle friend." I said with confidence.

"But it has always been the most important facet in my life. I'm not an artist like you are, April," she answered.

"I just keep reinventing myself through nature, theater and creativity. And now I can laugh about the things that used to break my heart," I said sincerely.

"I'm black and blue from the mammogram, what if I really do have cancer and the radiation makes me lose me hair," she said. "Every time I brush it a clump falls out into me hand. I need a fag," she moaned, reaching into her purse, lighting up.

"Don't worry, I'm going to help you. Tomorrow I'll call some prestigious doctors and find you the best specialists at Cedars. We'll get two other opinions. But there's nothing you can do about it today. It's out of your control."

"April, this is our little secret. I haven't even told me mate yet. I'm afraid that he won't want me if I'm less than perfect," she whispered, her hand covering her mouth.

"I'll never repeat this," I answered.

Glamorous regulars were clamoring on the side-walk waiting for a table. The server arrived with our food and as I sipped the wine my stomach was churning. I'd always been so proud and envious of her long lustrous surfer sun-streaked hair, I thought, as I tasted my food. I'd never be the same if anything happened to her.

"How hunky-dory, I'm going to a Cancer Convention at the Hilton, I'll bet all of the women will be wearing phony looking Raquel Welch wigs. I'll go off my trolly if I have to wear one of them. Can you believe this month is National Cancer Month? I'm in with the trend," she laughed nervously in a raspy, whiskey drawl.

"We've had some magical moments together, this will come to pass." I said, giving her hand a squeeze.

"I know we experienced The Summer of Love together with the gang. Remember when we were young," she said. "In your twenties everything seems possible, you don't realize how much you've sublimated. I feel like my future is my past."

"I don't recall ever being innocent again after we became blood sisters," I said. "You turned me out. You're so brave, Chelsea."

"It's easier with cocktails and just knowing you'll come round in case I get really sick," she said.

"You know I will," I promised.

"We were beautiful Beverly Hills brats. All we had to do was pile on our make-up, wear something enticing and we could get anything we wanted out of those bloats," she said.

"I pumped up at the gym and met a lot of dumb-bells," I shared.

"You fucked up with Patrick, getting caught in bed with that burnt out porn star. It was madness, what prompted you?"

"I was crazy," I answered.

"I hope you forgave me for trying to seduce Patrick when I was drunk." She added.

Not answering her question, I held my head up to the sun starting to cry, the strong rays warming my tears. Long ago I had learned that it was of no use feeling the guilt, the universal hang-up.

"I knew that Lust the seed bearer was your executioner, the first time I laid eyes on him," Chelsea said. He was rather protective of you, but somewhat of a menace." She reminded me wrinkling her brow.

"I remember Sunset Plaza Drive, reaching for his big thick hard cock under the comforter, It was loveless passion. Although I'll never regret those decadent days and nights filled with raw untamed sex," I said.

"Was it really worth losing Patrick?" she asked. "And all the drama and intensity. My dilemma in life is that I could never love," she mused. "I'm very fond of Hymie, but he's just a convenient situation. I feel comfortable with him."

"I made choices with the lack of recognition of consequences." I preached.

"People's desires often get them into trouble," She answered with empathy.

The Ivy was buzzing with the hubbub of well-healed upper crust trendsetters and celebrities. The clanging of plates, the popping of corks was great escapism.

"Patrick was supposed to be the straight, normal jock from Orange County that could save me from myself. You said that he wasn't smart enough to hurt me, although I've never recovered from the loss."

"You did that to yourself," she frowned. "And in your own bedroom with me hanging the drapes."

"An insatiable sexual appetite, desperation and boredom makes a person do strange things. I never wanted reality, only fantasy," I said.

"The gin is going to my head," Chelsea smiled. "Remember the gay blade that left his boyfriend for you?"

"Yes, I was the first girl he'd ever slept with," I said. "And the last."

"April, I'll never forget when you stayed at my flat in Chelsea on King's Road and our Brit connection was Jackie Collins. And how about Rome. Remember all the famous gorgeous actors and cowboys that we had ménage a trois with," she looked at me longingly.

"And we'll always have Paris." I answered with a faint smile. "We'll get through this together." I promised her. "Think about that time when we were only twenty years old on acid and we made a crash landing over the apple valley Inn with a whack job Buddhist doctor in his 280 twin Cessna. Now that was a life and death experience. The mysterious man didn't even have a license."

Chelsea looked at me with a blank stare. "I vaguely remember that fellow." She replied.

"He was steering the weaving plane in and out of billowy dark cumulus and nucleus clouds as beads of perspiration dripped down his face. "Try to be calm girls, we've hit a windstorm. The pressure could chew the plane apart." he informed us with quivering lips. "I need a stiff drink," we both called out in unison. He pulled a tudor flask out of his briefcase. We all swigged down straight shots of brandy as we clung to each other fearing that we were doomed. "If we have to die, at least we'll be together and never grow old," I said, hanging on to you. I was having a panic attack feeling a sensation like the fluttering of a birds wings floating inside of my chest. "I'll love you forever in life or death" we promised each other as the plane made a nose dive, streaking through an angry sky crashing into the parking lot. We jumped out kissing the ground giving thanks to our great creator. Relieved that it wasn't our time to die. We were so young and full of mischief."

"It was just another testament to our larger than life friendship," Chelsea mused.

"If we lived through that day we can conquer anything." I said assuringly.

"We've really experienced a lot together," she shared.

"Yes, we lived the high life, but one has to grow up sometime and face reality. All that was alright once long ago. I'm not going to be hypocritical. I still haven't lost my rebellious wild streak, or the temptation of frivolous fun, but I try to protect myself from dangerous situations." I said.

"It was a superb excuse for us to explore our bisexuality darling, and the fact that we were piss poor," Chelsea rationalized.

"I ran in to a girl that you and I used to work with at the studios at Nordstrom and she asked about you," I shared.

"Lovely, did I steal her mate?" Chelsea inquired smugly.

"No, but she remembered when you had your bondage parlor in Venice and I pulled a trick with you."

"That was bizarre, I came into the dungeon and a six foot four football player had you all tied up. I was horrified."

"And then you squinted your eyes at me with a distant smile. "You're supposed to tie them up, not let them have their way with you!", you scolded."

"Do you remember when I brought a trick to your house and he dressed up in a maid's uniform and wore a black mask?" Chelsea asked.

"I'll never forget. You hung him upside down on my chandelier on the terrace and when I was worried about what the neighbors would think you told me that they'd assume that I had a black maid."

"Your most outrageous caper, April darling, was the producer chap that drank warm scotch out of a dog bowl and had an anal carrot fetish."

"I know, he used to prance around in a corset and long red wig flown in from England, his limp grey dick hanging out and rouge smeared on his puffy cheeks. When I was living with Patrick I used my hairdresser's apartment and threw his cock into the aquarium, pouring in fish food. The goldfish nibbled on it and croaked. The next time I ran into the coiffure queen on a set he asked me what happened to his coldblooded pet vertebrate."

"It all sounds so silly now, but I had a mind to call PETA on you then," Chelsea laughed. "That was beastly, darling."

"I just can't even believe some of the escapades in retrospect," I frowned.

"I do the best I can, but I must admit that age is a great detriment and a bad pay-off for knowledge," Chelsea said sadly.

"If you can work out the problem, or dilemma that usually takes a lifetime to deal with you won't become old, bitchy and frustrated," I said.

"If I couldn't reveal myself to you I'd go mad and they'd probably lock me up," she answered.

"It's not too late, I can get you help," I begged.

"When I went to see that cold hearted grumpy cancer surgeon he became pissed when I seemed more concerned about my hair and reconstructive surgery than my life. I felt like a bit of a fool," she moaned.

"One of my plays is premiering in WeHo on Sunset next weekend. I hope you can come. You're one of the main characters. Maybe it will help get your mind off of your problems. My treat," I said as I pulled out money and paid the bill, giving her a big hug goodbye. "The play's a real hoot," I smiled.

We were always so close. Oh my God, how I'd always loved this young girl who'd grown into womanhood that I'd known nearly all of my life. I felt such a dull ache penetrating through my body, praying that I could fix this.

I stood outside the hot spot awaiting the valet to bring my car with the actresses, agents and New York magazine editors in town to take the pulse of the city. This place was the Big Apple's dream of LA. Could I make Chelsea's sad life more bearable?

I couldn't help wondering if the best part of our lives were gone forever, knowing that she was irreplaceable. I tried convincing myself that this was just a bad dream. Was my friend heading the long parade to the graveyard. Running out of time, not my antique watch?

Chapter Forty Nine
Lost Boy / Brian
1989

Friendship is a single soul dwelling in two bodies.
Aristotle

    I walked out of my house into a stormy evening sky. The full moon was hanging low. Barren branches on cypress trees were sprinkled with raindrops. At eight o'clock I rang the doorbell of Brian's fifties retro brick and glass bungalow, surrounded by a lush cactus garden overlooking a sweeping view of the canyon. I was received warmly by the all gay cast of his Indie film. My tight black studded motorcycle jacket and Frye boots were perfect for this occasion. Cabernet colored hair was tucked away neatly in a black tam. A cute huggable boy offered me a glass of merlot, flashing a shy smile.

    "It's the bitch goddess. You look like you just climbed off your Harley." Brian said greeting me with a liplock and a bright smile.

    "Sweetheart, I'm so proud of you that I brought a box of fun for a memorable occasion." I said, handing it to him. "Just promise that you won't open this until everyone leaves." Inside was a pair of my bright red Fredrick's of Hollywood sparkly crotchless panties perfumed with strawberry love potions. They were his favorite lingerie that he always coveted.

In the kitchen I mingled with the boys tasting the rich, cheesy risotto. After the party ended everyone joyfully bid their farewells. Curling up on Brian's over-stuffed couch, taking off my hat, flipping my long tresses I asked,

"Can I help you clean up?"

"No babe, just relax. my cleaning woman is coming tomorrow."

"Cool, can we talk? I have some issues."

"Sure, what's on your mind?" He smiled, pouring us a glass of wine.

" I just feel like I don't really fit in anywhere, but I'm as comfortable here as if I was at my own home."

"We're not going to fit in anywhere. We are observers of life seeing our flaws as human, because we're artists." Brian said with a moody, dark stare.

"I loved your cast, they were so warm and fun."

"They shine. Most of the talent in Hollywood have settled for being generic auteurs," Brian pondered, taking a long sip out of his glass.

"I'm an outsider of life lately and most people are uninvited guests." I said sadly.

"Sometimes its dangerous to let even friends into those secret rooms. Time hardens people especially the world you've lived in." Brian said.

"I love to shock them and I have problems with anxiety and loss of control. As you know I'm often angry and rebellious." I said.

"Thank god you've never turned your wrath on me." Brian answered coldly.

"But I often bond with fellow writer acquaintances." I answered, pulling a joint out of my purse, lighting up. "We share the same joy, hope and pain."

"That's nice, but civilizations mostly let things in that don't challenge themselves or their beliefs." Brian said with a coy glance while throwing the Rock n' Roll Ralph's paper plates and cups in the trash, tasting as he spoke. "Humanity is constructed to reinforce their being. Artists live in the place of re-examining themselves."

"You're quite the philosopher tonight, I must say."

He sat down on a rocking chair as Pee Wee, his co-dependent black and tan apple haired Chihuahua jumped on his lap, licking his face.

"Bri, when I talk to you, it's on a different level. We start looking at what makes people tick."

"April, you demand total loyalty from your friends and put up walls dividing life. Therefore there are a lot of lost opportunities and words never spoken." He said, petting his dog. "Shutting yourself off is a mechanism of self protection so you won't have to deal with the pain, babes."

"I don't want to sound like a victim, but I've been betrayed and abandoned so many times the hurt was so intense that I had to harden up in order to survive those Hollywood lights. I don't believe that most people can satisfy my needs." I pondered, my head propped up against the pillows.

"You won't like this, but your main problem is the fear of intimacy." Brian preached. "It's not about a lack of people in your life, you're just unable to form a deep connection with most of them."

"Great, coming from a controlling commitment-phobe. Be nice, I'm a fragile bitch." I answered in a tone of cordiality.

"You've been a gorgeous woman all of your life. How are you so bright having no formal education?" He asked, wrinkling up his brow.

"I owe it all to the streets, theater and the writer's program at UCLA."

"Its amazing that you've survived with all the debauchery and so many lives crumbling around you."

"I just had to let go of the negativity." I said, taking a long gulp of my drink.

"Your mother and Patrick were always around to bail you out. Therefore you believed that you were helpless until one day they were gone and you realized that you were strong and could stand on your own."

"I stopped having affairs with men who had less to lose than I did." I said between bites of red velvet cake.

"Now don't get me wrong, I love laborers." Brian laughed.

"Ok, I don't want this to be all about me." I said. "How did you get the idea for your screenplay?"

"I've never liked to talk about my background, but I've been through all of your bra wars and times of months and I'll say one thing, bitch, you'll never need a tit job."

"Tell me," I begged.

"Well I was a pretty, young, arian boy and came from a big, mormon polygamist family in Sedona, Arizona. My grandmother was the ninth wife and my grandfather had sixty three children. Some of them were pregnant teen aged girls that he married. When I was fourteen the elders came into my room in the middle of the night grabbing me and another kid, dumping us off in the wilderness like trash. The old geezers threatened to kill us if we ever returned to the community. Their prey were flirting with us and that intimidated the pitiful monsters. Little did they realize that it wouldn't have been a problem. They liked to live far away from civilization, and didn't have any contact with the outside world. No TVs or radios were allowed." He took a long gulp of his drink. His intense hazel eyes and fair skin paled in the flickering candle lit room.

"How horrible." I said trying not to show my distain.

"It was the only way of life that I ever knew." He answered regretfully in a tragic tone. Preachers gave sermons scaring us to death that it was God's law and that if we sinned there would be serious repercussions." He blurted out.

"God, those poor women." I said coldly.

"The best thing you can do if you're a lesbian or a bisexual nymphomaniac is marry a polygamist. You could have sex with all the other wives." Brian teased.

"If I could handle the bloomers and the girls were beautiful," I laughed.

"Maybe you could even take on some of the husbands if you were drunk enough." Brian said mischievously.

"When did you first realize that you were gay?" I inquired.

"After my father threw us out of his truck in the middle of sagebrush territory. We hiked for a few miles through the hills discovering a crystal clear lake. The boy tore his clothes off jumping in. I fell behind him and after swimming ashore, emerging from the icy, brilliant, clover-green water his dick was rock hard, his body trembling. Although he wasn't as well endowed as I was, I craved his flawless, smooth, golden brown flesh in the humid, filtered sunlight. I wasn't sure if his firm, round buttocks were ripe for the plucking, but I was in a frenzy of passion desiring this aesthetic looking creature more than anything I had ever wanted in my life. I had to have him. All I wanted to do was touch it. I couldn't control myself, so I stroked his strong throbbing cock sliding my hand around it, masturbating him until he exploded, sweaty and spent. Then there was that moment when nothing is said but everything is known and without even making eye contact he self consciously ran through a thicket in the trees, disappearing from sight."

"Did you ever see him again?" I asked.

"No, but he remains my fantasy man forever."

"How did you ever end up as my back door boyfriend in Laurel Canyon?"

"I walked for miles to the bus stop, inhaling in the dry desert air, feeling free. But I had no skills. At the complex they toss out the TVs and radios by the side of the road. I picked them up, sold them to a pawn shop and bought a ticket heading for L.A.. Capitalizing on my prize possession, I became a hustler on Santa Monica Boulevard, better known as S&M Blvd. One night at that bar Numbers I met a rich old producer icon, pulled a few tricks with him, eventually moving into his Bel Air digs. I started writing plays and screenplays that he produced, then I had an Indie sweetheart. That's how I got enough money to live up here with the angels in literary luxury. I'll be right back," Brian said, racing through the house. Minutes later he came prancing out of the guest bathroom bare chested wearing my panties, coquettishly flashing me a sly smile. "I just wanted to lighten up the conversation, it was getting a little too heavy," he said, feeding the dog a prozac for his separation anxiety.

"I must say that you're compelling to watch, I'm drawn to people that are complex, full of contradictions and off the wall." I smiled. "And I only have great love for you in spite of the fact that you're impetuous, a little crazy and don't know the difference between adventure and drama. That's why you're so interesting." We embraced as he tousled my hair.

"Well I'm going to have to throw you out now, babes, I'm going on a perilous journey tomorrow."

"Where to?" I asked.

"I got this guy and I free gay passes on The Homo Express at Magic Mountain." He said squeezing me affectionately as I walked out into the dark, starlit night.

Chapter Fifty
Terrance

*We have to distrust each other, it is our only
defense against betrayal.*
Tennessee Williams

After one of our lustful, cock tasting dinners I let
Terrance know that I didn't intend to have a committed relationship while he was living with someone. Unfortunately in retaliation he made sure that
I lost creative control over my production. I wrote
him a card asking for his forgiveness three years
later. A week after I received a corny postcard bar-
ing Ingrid Bergman's classic profile. "Dearest, here's
another woman who loved when she wanted to,
and not by the world's bidding. Love ought to be
reciprocal. The comfort, which you said would last
for an hour, is still with me. Are you sure you're not
'Wonder Woman' in disguise. Let's talk. Much love,
Terrance."

After falling apart with laughter, I remembered
that I needed a director and he had just won a
Tony and several other awards. My ego had gotten in the way of my success so I left him a message, asking if he could meet me at The Coronet
Theatre to discuss directing my play. When Terrance appeared in the lobby, I was going over
script revisions.

"Howdy," he said giving me a tentative hug.

I broke away from him, subtly.

"So you need a director. Cool, we'll see." he said dubiously.

"Why don't we hang out on Melrose Avenue and grab a bite or some drinks?" I said.

"Sounds like a plan," he smiled, taking me by the arm.

We walked down the leafy sidewalk that lazy afternoon, my silk peasant skirt flowing in the summer breeze. He was wearing skinny Bermuda shorts and Boho sandals. The mood on the pierced and tattooed street scene was mellow. There was foot traffic consisting of green and purpled headed, label-obsessed shoppers strutting shoulder to shoulder, down the high-end funky retail haven. A musician was sitting on the sidewalk while strumming a guitar. The valet was perched on a lawn chair in front of a sidewalk café. Designer clad mannequins with painted vacant faces and wine bottles at their feet filled the storefront windows.

Terrance led me into the dank dark bar as all the world faded away in the midst of Happy Hour.

A piano player was banging away on the keyboard. An indifferent looking waitress approached us as we slid into a small banquette.

"You guys want to order some drinks?" she asked.

She had a very '80s Madonna look. The girl was a platinum blonde bimbo with milk white skin, torn black fishnet stockings, bloodshot grey eyes and purple black lips and nails. Her blue mascara was running down her rouged cheeks.

"She doesn't have one natural body part," Terrance said under his breath.

"I'll have an apple martini with a twist of lime. What would you like, April?" he asked.

"I'll have a glass of white wine," I answered as she ran off.

"Your breasts are looking mighty fine tonight," said the Texas born dude. He had a dignified, down to earth quality.

"Your hair's grown, and your abs rip," I laughed.

His thick sandy colored hair spilled over his shoulders onto his khaki thermal t-shirt.

"Perhaps it is an admission of weakness, maybe not, but I've really missed you," he said looking up at me. "I've finally forgiven you for beating me up in the lobby at Theater 40 after I directed your play."

"I've been thinking a lot about you lately," I said squeezing his hand. "I'm sorry."

Then it all came back to me. That night that I lunged at my lover, ripping off his Calvin Klein jacket.

"We have a hit," he said grabbing my rear end, holding me in a deadlock grip, his hands sliding up my dress. I pulled away from him.

"Fuck you, asshole. You're fired!" I shouted, the blood rushing to my head, making me look as if I was wearing too much blush.

"We have a contract. I'll sue you," he threatened. "Egomaniacs like you think that no one else exists, you bitch," he said.

"Dickhead, you ruined my vision," I shouted. "You lied to me. You're still living with your girl," I raged on. "You were abusive to my cast all through the rehearsals," I said kicking him ferociously. I felt the adrenaline rush, I was in a rage, I wanted to kill him. Now I had regret and shame for losing control.

"That's what I get for getting involved with someone as ruthless as you," he said pulling a tape recorder out of his pocket. "You're crazy."

"You cut out my most evocative scenes," I screamed.

"You're going to ruin all of our chances of taking this baby to Broadway," he begged. "You're on tape. I'm going to nail you for assault and battery," he said maliciously, just as he almost tore off my Guess dress.

The producer flew through the lobby. She was a whisperer, thin as a whippet crowned with mousy, brown, stringy hair and unkempt fingernails and toes.

"April, I'm horrified. You're going to give this prestigious theater a bad name. Stop. Come and help me clean up the snow. That scene doesn't work."

"He ruined my play!" I screamed, my hands shaking.

Our drinks arrived and as he took a fast gulp, I sipped on my wine.

"You're a world class woman. You make me bad," he said putting his arm around me.

"I like bad boys, but one of my anonymous theatre critic friends told me that you're still with that famous actress," I said with slight agitation in my voice.

"I'm certainly not trying to convince you nor myself that what we're doing is right. I can only say that for me it is necessary. You're not going to get serious on me are you?"

"I just needed a detour on the freeway of lust for a while," I said firmly.

"April, you're so unpredictable. If only I could tame your mind."

"I can't help it, I keep obsessing on your girl-friend."

"An obsession is a thought that overpowers all other rational thoughts, no matter how important they are," he said sweeping my body with his pale cold blue eyes.

"She knows everybody in my world. It could get very ugly." I answered lifting my glass to my lips, sipping the chilled wine.

"Really darling, I feel awkward, and evil and mischievous, and foolish," he said with a tone of uneasiness in his voice.

"You're being very dramatic," I answered as I leaned over and kissed him on the cheek.

"Dearest, I don't mean to be a kvetch, but not being with you hurts. It is like a medieval test of valor," he said kissing me softly on my mouth.

"If you direct 'Too Old To Be The Hooker, Too Young To Be The Madam', we'd be spending a lot of time together," I coaxed.

"Only under one condition, if you fuck me and fuck me good like you know how I like it. Waitress! We'll have another round. Make mine a double. Please dear," he said signaling over the server.

"Is that all you want of me? Sex, sex, and more sex?" I asked smiling mysteriously.

"I told you the first night we kissed that I was not a hero. I've never attempted to make an arrangement like ours with anyone else," he said hugging me.

"What do you have in mind?" I asked.

"I want you, a few hours of comradeship, and eternity. Is that too much to ask for?"

"Will you read this?" I asked, resting my head on his smooth shoulder, feeling the heat of his body on my cheek, handing him my script.

"Consider it done. The highest happiness I have felt at thirty-eight years old is that enjoyed by your words, your presence, your lips," he said.

"I don't know, we'd have to be careful so that our peers think we're having a professional relationship," I said.

"What else might they think?" he asked.

"You have a reputation for being a womanizer and I think your mate is onto us. One of the letters that you sent me was torn, probably by a jealous woman."

"I admit to having a dozen flaws, but my girlfriend suspects every woman of coming on to her man." he held me tightly, a frown wrinkling his brow.

"Every time I have sex with my girl, I'm being unfaithful to her anyway, because I'm always thinking of you," he said.

"Fantasies don't count," I teased.

"I'm done, I can't live with her insanity anymore now that we've reunited," he sighed.

"What will you do?" I asked.

"Just give me a little time. I don't want to hurt her," he said.

"And I don't have to settle for a shadow lover," I sighed.

"I feel that only if you focus on me, and I on you, we'll have a chance for the future. I'll make it right, I promise you, April."

We kissed unaware of the noise and chatter surrounding us as we swept out of the bar onto the brightly lit street.

Chapter Fifty One

A Fantasy Banquet
Patrick

It was a cool, clear, crisp California day on the sunshine coast. Just divine, picture postcard perfect. Delicate blue raindrops fell softly on snow-capped, carved mountains and there was hail on the hills. Then the raging electric storm broke in all of her fury, lighting up the sky. My shaggy dog, Skylark puppy-love and picturesque calico cat Eclipse and I sat on my sky terrace. Mesmerized by the view, I could see the Hollywood sign clearly surrounded by billowy white marshmallow cloud formations. Then the hues of the faded yellow sunshine on all of nature melting the snow, and fading away. Soon the forest was still except for the sound of a dog's far away bark, and the shrill shriek of a black crow flying by. That twilight moonless night, during a solar eclipse in a dream I was lounging on a burgundy crushed velvet couch in the spacious living room of my house, by the sultry sea. I had just moved into the spiritual, ethereal space. It was a wooded A-frame with a loft. The rich, dark, cypress walls were bare framed by a cathedral ceiling and skylight strewn of muted, multi-colored, leaded, stained glass. Suddenly, the roof disappeared and a flock of colorful, chirping, robust, red sparrows, bluebirds, and plump silver doves flew gracefully over my head. A sand-piper with a beak the color of egg yolk, a starfish in its mouth, dropped a fortune cookie in my lap from the sky. It was wrapped in a velvet white feather. It read, "You full of magnetism, sensuality and sparkle. Soon have good sex with a man who break heart. So sorry. Very truly yours, Psychic Bird." Then he flew away as the crickets sang a haunting melody.

Suddenly a strangely handsome rugged-looking man blew in with the wind. From the loft he looked almost transparent, as if toasting me holding a gob-let of ruby red wine in his weather-beaten hand.

"You look like magic, may I join you in a toast and christen your new house?" The wind howled in my head like a forbidden deserted lost lover. As the man walked slowly down the spiral staircase and sat next to me on the chaise, staring at me atten-tively as our cold hands touched. He held the glass of wine to my lips. I sipped feeling a warm mellow, fuzzy glow. Smiling seductively at him, I asked his name.

"Patrick," he answered.

"How did you find me?" I asked.

"You called out my name in a dream." The deep husky voice answered. "I occupied this space many moons ago and I found my way home once again. You are a goddess of light obsessed with love, but for us there is nothing beyond the moment."

"I understand, my life exists of just the then and now."

"Have another sip, I'll share my spirits with you, April."

The roar of the ocean and foamy white waves crashing on the sand made me feel happy again. I had so missed the sacred sea. Then there was the magical moment when we touched, and an awkward moment before our lips met. I was wearing a clad tight hip-hugger skirt and halter top. My bare torso was tanned, and my hair hung over my shoulders like sun-streaked ringlets. I could tell that he sensed my sensuality the way I crossed my legs. The amber glow and logs crackling in the hearth and the mellow sounds of jazz filled the room as big city lights twinkled like diamonds on the distant horizon.

"I saw the birds fly over your head. That's a symbol of good luck and freedom. You don't deserve to be unfulfilled. I know you feel the passion but you're afraid of intimacy. You don't have to worry about that. I'm a drifter."

I didn't know whether to risk the emotional emptiness of a one night tryst, but I was in a reckless mood from the moment I laid eyes on him I felt the heat and couldn't get the thought of making love out of my head. But there was the fear of feeling something real. I was a collision of spirits. He unlike myself was open to everything and attached to nothing. Patrick slipped his hand inside of my skirt lightly stroking my thighs. I opened my legs as he licked my breasts and erect pink nipples, then pushing his erect manness inside of me as the cinnamon scented candles glowed in the dusky darkness. Two wild hearts, untamed. After we had made love all night long, he sighed, kissing me affectionately, caressing my hair:

"Nothing else matters, but lying here with you. This is so right."

I felt so blessed waking up with this mischievous dreamy man, his blond hair tousled from sleep. I wondered if this fated meeting existed only in my imagination as he thrust his tongue inside my moist mouth.

"We are both so very physical and spiritual. I'm losing myself in you. I love the way you shake your wild curly hair all over my chest."

I laid in his arms feeling complete as our thighs brushed and a flame rose up in my groin. His lips tasted like tart, sweet wine, becoming an aphrodisiac. I was dizzy from his kisses. Then abruptly, he rose from the bed.

"I have to leave you now. I'll come back but like a bird I must stray. We can never be, it would destroy our love. You and I belong to the world and the mind doesn't understand the reason of the heart."

Then with a great gust of wind and a bolt of lightning, he flew out of my life just as quickly as he came into it. We were both transported into an erotic world of sensuality and orgasm, then I was abandoned once again. The participation of the mind and flesh was intoxicating, this celebration of the soul and senses with my ghostly lover. I wake up screaming, clutching my wedding band. The garnet ring is still a constant companion on my finger. But what happened to the marriage?

Chapter Fifty Two
The Canon Theatre, 1989

All the world's a stage
And all the men and women merely players
They have their exits and their entrances
And one man in his time plays many parts
Shakespeare

It was opening night and I was standing in the wings of the Canon Theatre in Beverly Hills. The echoing sounds of laughter and applause coming from the ninety-nine-seat equity theatre was riveting. Standing ovations fulfilled my lifelong dreams. A tall willowy girl with the sunshine smile appeared handing me a large bouquet of bright yellow sunflowers with fuzzy brown faces, holding some newspapers in her other hand.

"Oh my god, wait till you read this review from the L.A. Times. 'Hot blooded, steamy, simmering sexuality,'" she read excitedly, handing them to me. "And this is for you also, from an admirer."

"I wonder who sent these?" I said opening the exquisite gold envelope in anticipation. It was from my director. He had staged the piece turning my work into a dazzling sensation. I glanced at the card, smiling to myself.

"April darling, let's celebrate tonight after the cast party. Adoringly yours, Terrance."

"Was there a review in The Reporter and Variety?" I asked.

"The Reporter said, 'I flew over the moon when April Moon the deliriously Jewish American princess lit up the stage.' Variety said, 'Too Old To Be A Hooker, Too Young To Be A Madam, is over the top Hollywood. Hilarious, evocative and erotic'," she answered.

"This is all I ever wanted from art. I'm really blessed," I smiled.

"You've been there. You have a vast emotional landscape," she said sucking up to me.

"I survived 'The Last Generation of Vipers,' the Hollywood scene so that I could laugh at them and write about all of the drama," I said.

"It's so exciting being the understudy for April. Tell me, is the April character you?" she asked.

"That's for only me to know and you to wonder," I said brushing past her, walking faster trying to escape.

"I have to watch the play." I said running out of breath, I was so excited.

April shone brightly with all her charisma and magnetism in my favorite monologue, 'The Lure of Laurel Canyon'. The actress was a slinky redhead with well-defined breasts and ruby red lips. She was adorned in a see-through dress woven of multi-colored dishrags and peacock feathers were strewn in her crimped hair. It was a very Haight Ashbury vibe.

"69 was my favorite year and my favorite posi-tion. Man landed on the moon and I landed in Rome, throwing my garnet wedding band in the Fontana Di Trevi. That was when my pussy became catnip for all the horny prey."

That line brought the house down. Then came the scene 'Jet-Set Extras.' Gimp The Pimp was being played by a famous dwarf. Seems the little person had gotten drunk at intermission and now had an agenda of his own making up dialogue while grabbing the rear end of a six-foot tall, mar-ried, prudish brunette actress who was playing my mother.

Anna had seen images of herself in many of my works. I had immortalized her. Tonight was a per-fect example of theatre in the raw. No two perfor-mances were ever the same. Even by the actors in my bedroom.

"You have a nice ass," said the drooling, bleary eyed dwarf in a squeaky voice that sounded like he'd sucked on a helium balloon. "I wanna fuck you."

The lights dimmed as the crimson red velvet cur-tain dropped like falling stars on a sea of avid the-atergoers, comprised of network scouts, publishers, jaded critics and friends.

Then after three more standing ovations, I felt the adrenaline rush. As I walked through the brightly lit lobby, my literary agent was smiling while giving me a hug.

"You're the hottest female playwright of the new millennium. The HBO deal is going great," he said. "Call me, we'll talk."

"It's the woman who made a statement. See you at the party," a playwright said. "You're brilliant."

"Thanks." I answered, squeezing through the chic, upscale crowd.

Another woman commented, in awe, "This was a great night in theater."

I looked fabulous in my low cut, long, black halter dress, a massive sweep of auburn tresses flowing over my ruffled lace shrug.

The producer grabbed my arm looking annoyed.

"Do you want to hear what the artistic director said after seeing your play?" she asked condescendingly.

"What?" I begged.

"Thanks for bringing Shakespearean porn to my subscribers," she said smugly.

"I like the Shakespearean part," I laughed.

"That's why we had to cut out the porn star sequence," she frowned. "It wasn't your director's fault."

"But now I have to greet my guests," I replied, starting to walk away.

"And April, you better apologize to the dwarf's sister. She's upset with you for serving Trader Joe's Two Buck Chuck to her brother."

"Why am I responsible for him? He calls me up late at night wanting to rehearse with me and I'm not even in the play."

"Didn't you know that Billy was an alcoholic, and he's diabetic," she asked running off in a huff.

I was enjoying my moment of glory. I'd worry about that little horny dweeb tomorrow. The green room was decorated reflecting on a decadent nostalgic era. Multicolored strobe lights, balloons, flowers and confetti were strewn throughout the space. A large oak table filled with hors d'oeuvres, gourmet cheeses, and pastries were elegantly arranged. Also, a vintage white porcelain bathtub was filled with wine, beer and bottles of designer waters. An artsy eclectic crowd milled around, schmoozing, drinking and tasting.

Chelsea strutted into the spotlight milking her best profile as flashbulbs blared, posing for the paparazzi, draped on the arm of her powerful plastic surgeon husband. She was a diamond encrusted visual in her pricey organza Chanel dress carrying a Louis Vuitton evening bag. The woman was now immersed in five star fund raisers, politics, Yves Saint Laurent pumps, and would never go to a party at anyone's home that only had one bathroom.

"I'm so glad you could come." I said, giving her a hug.

"Hello darling. This is so pleasant. You remember Hymie. We've brought you our vineyard champagne Tushbanger Brut. I don't fancy the rot gut they serve at openings." She complained as Hymie took my hand.

"April, good to see you. You're all Chelsea talks about. You'll have to come over to our mini-mansion soon. Looks like you have a hit play, young lady." he said putting his arm around his wife.

"I'd love to," I said sipping slowly from a flute glass.

"I'd also like to give you a complimentary visit at my clinic." He said, handing me his card.

"Chelsea looks so rested, and thinner." I offered.

"Everyday I give her shots of goat placenta." He bragged on.

"Oh piss off love, you're growing a paunch. You'll have to join me at my spinning class tomorrow. And April, they really do have squirrels in Beverly Hills. If you cut off that mop I might introduce you to the upper crust society and all my philanthropist friends," she said, accompanied by an icy smile as she flipped her ponytail side to side. "And by the way, I'm cancer free." she said with a sigh of relief.

The Hollywood blonde married old denouncing her staunch Catholic background, hosting seders for Hymie's family and friends.

"I'm wildly upset tonight, April. I never dreamed that I'd get chucked out of being chair at the Orangutan Foundation's fundraiser at the Peninsula." She pouted blowing me an air kiss. "Too ta loo, we're going to have a spot of supper and more wine to warm up the night, darling," as she disappeared, blending into the atmosphere.

Chelsea's greatest anxiety occurred in the bedding department at Bloomingdale's wondering how many thread counts were in her Ralph Lauren sheets, 'at least twelve hundred', she demanded.

The trophy wife did well for an ex-bondage queen from the streets of Soho.

Yolanda gave me a big kiss smearing gooey lip gloss on my cheek.

"You rock, girl. See my thirty day chip," she bragged, beaming, waving it in my face. "I've missed you. I've been hanging at the crib. Give it up for my man, Dr. Gland. We made up." A virile looking bruiser hiding behind his porsche glasses wearing a black army surplus jacket, skinny jeans and cycle boots shook my hand.

"Your play was way cool," he smiled, revealing a mouthful of silver hardware. Enough to start his own heavy metal band.

"I just had my jaw wired. One of my patients got a little rowdy." said the tough, hard edged dark soul. His long, brown hair hanging into his face. Yolanda grabbed a glass of wine from the server's tray as her boyfriend politely removed it from her hand.

"You look great, YoYo." I smiled, handing her a ginger ale.

"Ya think?" she asked. "It's my new hot bubble gum, girlie, pink, glam jumpsuit." she said.

And here's to sisterhood, I thought. *Love, loyalty, envy, competition, distance, gossip, betrayal, abandonment and forgiveness.* Yolanda had hooked up with a drug counselor who indulged himself in his own method of therapy. I wondered how long they'd last.

I walked over to the table where Brian was hitting on the gay waiter writing his phone number on his hand.

"Are you married? I'd like a taste." he asked, eating a crab puff. Glancing over at me he held his glass up in the air. Brian was wearing a slim cut black Dolce and Gabbana suit with a blue tie.

"Delectable." He said to his present prey as the boy slipped him his card. "Did you hear about racy Roxie?" Brian laughed.

"No, strange that she didn't show." I answered, unconcerned.

"I heard that when she wouldn't let her gynecologist check out those plastic inserts he cut off her xanax prescriptions and she became so hysterical that she swallowed fifty of her dead dog's tranquilizers and died," he shared.

"No wonder the poor pooch has been gone for five years," I said.

"I called Rodeo Realty and she still has voice mail," Brian smiled mischievously. "The media queen is deceased and she's still doing business." Brian gloated.

"What happened to Antonio?" Brian inquired.

"I just received another postcard from the tragic latin begging me to forgive him."

"I thought the gay caballero had been extradited by the Spanish government." Brian asked.

"An infamous cross-dresser attorney got him out of prison on that drug bust and backed him in a cabaret in Amsterdam." I shared.

"Did you say 'backed'?" Brian teased.

I looked across the room wondering who that dissipated looking man who was approaching me was.

"Congratulations, April. Good show. Remember me, it's Manning, I haven't seen you in years, since New York. Let's grab a drink and catch up on our lives," he coaxed.

"I think it's a little to late for that." I answered, leaving him standing alone in the room, walking over to the bar as the bartender popped open a bottle.

"For you. Bravo, April." I was amazed to see Angel there, pouring the champagne.

"It's you," I whispered to him under my breath.

"Of course! I wouldn't miss big opening for the world." Angel leaned over pouring me a drink. "Don't mean to say 'told you so', but aren't you glad you didn't lose life over that loser?" he motioned toward Manning. "You wouldn't be here to see dream come true, señora," he said squeezing my hand. "Bueno."

I was ecstatic, tomorrow was my book signing party at The Grove at Barnes and Noble, I'd also written my play into novel form. Chelsea was right, once she said,

"I know you have a best-seller. Every single woman all over the globe can relate to your charisma and sexual tragedies. The married ones, wheeling their baby carriages at Nordstrom's won't buy the book, but they'll sneak up to the lounge upstairs and read it over their lattes."

"I wonder what part of the bookstore the marketing PR people will put it at." I asked.

"Certainly not where the romance type novels with Fabio on the cover are. Probably in the section between the trashy, erotic, fantasy novels, James Joyce's 'Ulysses In Nightgown' and Anaïs Nin's 'Fire'.

You're hot, sweetie. You've set a lot of men on fire. I love you, sweets."

I couldn't believe how my life had gotten. After the party was over I was standing on an empty stage reflecting on my success. Now at last, I finally was getting paid for my art. Suddenly I heard the voices of my characters from the stage, my alter egos haunting me....my mother, and many friends had abandoned me for death. Now no man would ever love me like Patrick did again. We were both young and beautiful dreamers. It was sad, the older I got, the more people seemed to float away. I had breathed eternal life into them with my pen. My secret selves were very real, yet I couldn't help wondering had my life been just a lucid dream?

SOPHISTICATED LADY

Her body had flown like a powerful bird through and above the entangling branches of the past few years. But her face now exhibited the record of the flight.
Tennessee Williams

I know I'm not a girl anymore. But at least now I know my own limitations and I've learned to accept my losses and failures as a part of being human, without feeling as much of the guilt. And I still have my dream, a cat sanctuary in Spain. So I pick myself up again and say – Come on, you can do it. Be somebody, no more strange people or places. I can't go back and be used even for the sake of passion.

I can only give what I have to give. So I weave my rice gardens in the rain. No wonder I drank so much champagne. Existing in this strange borrowed gift called life. Planting it, workin' it, growin' it. I haven't been totally corrupted, there's hope, isn't there? And I guess there'll always be those days when the night stretches into disaster.

It's just part of being human. For too long had I tried being what all men wanted me to be. At least now I can stand on my own, destination survival. Perhaps one day I can even fall out of step with one man and into grace with another. It's not fun being alone.

Chapter Fifty Three
Cedars, 1989

When one has given up One's life
The parting with the rest
Feels easy, as when Day lets go
Emily Dickinson

After a long, lonely, dark winter, I awoke from a nightmare. The voice in my dream echoed. You want more than life can give you. It was a gloomy day in LA. Last night the news channels warned the country that a big storm with flash floods was brewing. Scattered showers rained from a cloudy sky. I was having another panic attack, thinking about a visit to Dr. Dread, the She-Wolf with the privileged 90210 zip code. The last time that I had an appointment there the mentally challenged Asian nurse poked the vein in my arm so many times she was unable to draw any more blood from me for additional tests.

"You jest' scared," she grinned nervously like an ape.

"You idiot. I knew I was in trouble when you chased the patient before me down the hall holding a glass slide of blood in your hand, asking if it was hers."

I took the elevator down to the dank, dark, moldy basement, which housed the Hematology/Cancer wing. Suddenly the granite clouds burst and there was a downpour that was visible from a half-open window. As I walked down the long, dingy, chalk-white corridors, yellow signs with skulls on the wall said "Biohazardous Chemicals".

The stench of death filled the air as I passed by the overcrowded waiting room. Terminal ones' heads looked like the skullcaps I used to create when I was a makeup artist on film shoots. Vacant stares of desperation from the faces of victims who'd given up made tears well up in my eyes. The sickly-looking, pallor-faced people were slumped down in chairs, coughing, wheezing and sneezing.

Most of the women were crowned with synthetic-looking wigs or hats with scarves draped around their heads. One elderly man's face turned blue, he was gasping for breath as they whisked him away on a stretcher. The mental pain and angst I was experiencing was inconsolable. I was no longer young, but I still possessed a kind of sensual unfading beauty. Would it be lost forever in these rooms?

My thick wavy strawberry-blonde hair fell around my shoulders in ringlets framing my gaunt face. After slipping into the faded blue gown, there was a knock on the door followed by Dr. D., the unlovely's high-heeled pumps tapping on the hardwood floor.

"How are you today?"

"You're supposed to tell me," I said.

"I'll examine you and you'll know in a minute," she said, glancing at me briefly, and then her cold blue eyes stared into her cell phone as the rain pounded on the roof. She started methodically inspecting me, focusing on my trophies.

"Did you have plastic surgery on your breasts? They're amazing. I could kill myself for asking you that question."

"Is that a promise?" I thought. "They're the only things that are real about me. I didn't pay for them. I enhanced my bank account doing tasteful nudity in the movies," I answered.

"Well, they feel good," she reassured me. "They're firmer than mine and you're older than I am," she answered enviously.

"What is your diagnosis of my condition?" I demanded.

"Thank God. You have ITP," she frowned.

The emotionally shut off, subhuman, less than condescending control freak was a would-be fashion maven and mold for the Chanel suit. Her synthetic ruby red hair looked like it had been coifed by a student attending Marinello Beauty School. I only prayed that she might get a brain tumor from cell phone abuse. The beyond bitch probably went to Radcliffe, Smith or Vassar.

I'll bet she washes down her hormone pill with half a glass of Evian and orders off of the spa menu at Spago or The Ivy at lunch, searching for the highest bidder. Then Ms. Super Chic probably jumps into her Mercedes CLK, Lexus or BMW, never rolling down the sunroof. God forbid one hair should blow out of place or she might get lines from the relentless California sun.

"What is ITP?" I asked.

"It's an auto-immune disease, a rare blood disorder where the body mounts an attack towards one or more seemingly normal organ systems. In your case, platelets are the target," she answered in a monotone voice.

I was frightened and shocked by the diagnosis. "I have no idea what to expect," I said.

"One of the factors of this disease is that you will be subject to spontaneous bleeding, bruising and hospitalization," she said sadistically.

I lay frozen as she continued, looking for bruises, my heart pounding, a pain sharp as a razor blade shot through my churning stomach. I started turning cold and trembling. My throat was tight as a tourniquet.

"Your bone marrow biopsy shows no signs of damage to any of your other organs or the spleen," she said. "Do you drink alcohol? What drugs are you taking?"

"Xanax, Somas and Valium." I answered. "And I smoke a little pot," I said reluctantly. "Do you think those things have anything to do with it? How serious is this?" I asked.

"You are dealing with a difficult and potentially deadly illness. Have you been exposed to chemicals and are you sexually active?"

"With my vibrator," I said going for the shock treatment.

"Have you taken an HIV test in the last six months?" she inquired.

"Can you get AIDS from a vibrator?" I sarcastically quipped. This cunt didn't have a clue. She was linked into the power and materialism that went with the territory of her corrupt career and the wonder drugs that she prescribed to kill.

"Is this an age-related condition?" I asked.

"No. We already went through that," she said impatiently.

I'd never had a life-threatening disease before. I just didn't know if I could live through this ordeal. I was looking at the skeleton of my life. I thought of my animals. Baby Shakespeare wasn't even a year old. Would we ever see the ocean together? What about Sky, my other Shi Tzu, and Eclipse, my picturesque calico. I started examining my life. Had it been all wrong? This was so surreal.

I'd turn it all around, wouldn't I?

"Just avoid substances, toxins and aspirin," she said.

"What are my treatment options?" I mumbled, twisting my hair.

"You don't want to know. You won't like them. We're not at that stage yet."

"I have to know. It's my right to choose," I said raising my voice.

"Well there's Prednisone. It's a steroid. It will make you moon-faced. It causes water retention. You might grow a beard, and it may interfere with your sleep. Sometimes it causes heart palpitations, but there are many other drugs. If they don't work, you might consider having a platelet or blood transfusion."

"Can I get a script for some 10 mg Valium and some Xanax? I'm freaking out."

"Definitely not. Get them from your doctor."

"But I don't have one."

"Valium makes people senile. I can't treat you properly if you want to be your own doctor."

"I care about myself more than anyone else does."

"A lot of this is in your head. I want to put you on an antidepressant and monitor you every month," she said.

"No way," I exclaimed.

"I have to go now. The pharmaceutical company is taking the whole office to lunch," she said glancing at her Gucci watch. "You're not as sick as you think you are, although your platelets are disintegrating rapidly."

"Wait a minute. I'm done, but I won't quit. There has to be something I can do to cure myself."

"You have a chronic case.'

I tried to listen, obsessing on her red alligator shoes, but I was not in denial.

"When will I have to be hospitalized?" I asked.

"When your platelets drop to a dangerous level and you bleed between the eyes," she said without emotion. "It's like having a cerebral hemorrhage."

I tried being calm but to no avail.

"There's no cure," she said running out the door.

As I was leaving the office, by accident I walked into the treatment room. Patients were lined up like ghosts, wearing white smocks, getting blood and platelet transfusions. My heart pounding, I ran down the hallway, trying to escape, collapsing on the cold stone floor. When I came to, the perspiration was dripping down my face. A doctor was standing over me, taking my blood pressure. The nurse's finger was pressing on my pulse.

"I'm a psychotherapist. A lot of patients have panic attacks. Do you ever get them?" he asked. "What's your name, dear?"

"My name's April. I became anxious about this place and my condition. I'm way out of control," I said, wiping the perspiration off of my brow.

"What were your symptoms?" he asked, in a gentle manner.

"My heart started fluttering. I could hardly breath. Then I had a migraine and got dizzy," I answered.

He put a clamp on my finger. "Sounds like a panic attack. The symptoms are more alarming than the actual response. Just try to reframe things in your mind. Your pulse is weak and your pressure is quite elevated. I'm sending you down to the ER for an EKG. I hope you feel better. It's okay. I'm right behind you."

"I've had a lot of anxiety lately."

"I'm sure you have, but quite often that comes from a place earlier in life."

I felt so helpless and hopeless. That morning on my walk with Sky and Shakespeare I'd bent down to pick up a burgundy, burnt orange, star-shaped leaf, finding a copper penny in the dust. Its chiseled face had been run over by a car. I'd always been delighted by finding a coin, believing that it was a lucky omen.

Once I was shiny and new, my world filled with love, laughter and romance. Now it seemed as if I'd also been crushed. I had the heart of a poet surrounded by spiritually and emotionally unavailable depraved people.

The night Patrick and I met, our souls and bodies intertwined. Then my life began. If my days were numbered, I had to find him, if only to see him once again. We never really had closure. Then I could embrace death like a new acquaintance. I wonder if I hadn't abandoned my life for him, even with all of our highs and lows, if we would have lasted for over a decade.

Being an existentialist, I had always believed that life was transitory and that all we have is now, but that day I suddenly felt a longing for my irretrievable past, haunted by wounds that would never heal. That moment I just let go of the picture of what my life was supposed to look like and gave in never giving up my dream, the theater. But God only knows, I might end up being a member of 'The Dead Poets Society'.

Chapter Fifty Four
The Long and Winding Road
April

Nothing that's happened to me since can cancel out the many long nights without sleep when we gave each other pleasure in love as very few people can look back on in their lives.
Tennessee Williams

I wake up screaming, clutching my wedding band. The garnet ring is still a constant companion on my finger. But what happened to the marriage? Last night I had another nightmare of abandonment about Patrick. He was a love that I would never forget.

After a meeting with the cinema sharks at Universal who optioned my play 'Too Old To Be a Hooker, Too Young To Be a Madam', in a bidding war, I headed up the mountain.

It was Black Friday and the underpinnings of the Christmas spirit filled the streets in the cool crisp air. Burgundy wild berries clustered in emerald green trees. That old 70's Beatles song 'The Long and Winding Road' was playing as a tribute to that magical era. I was so emotionally charged by the lyrics, I knew that I could no longer be in denial about Patrick. We'd seen that road so many times throughout the years. With the passage of time my pain was still intense. I always knew that eventually we would fall apart from the danger of each other's lies.

Patrick and I were a volatile mix with reckless lives. I was still a sexually adventurous woman sought after by many exciting men. I had achieved fame and fortune, but there was this deep hole that I never could fill with all of the people that I'd slept with there was something missing in the equation. He was the emotional hook, I was alone. My youth had deserted me and I had a disease of the heart. I wondered if he ever thought about me. The road is the metaphor for life with all its bumps and curves. I'd always fantasized that one day Patrick would come knocking at my door. As I sped over the deserted stretch of Mulholland and the potholes, the stillness drowned out by the faint sound of water splashing on a stone fountain. I couldn't help wondering if he was still alive and if I'd ever see him again in this lifetime. I'd morphed out into womanhood with all the emotional resources that I'd never had as a girl when we were together. Had he evolved also? With the passage of time I was so enraptured by him. I knew that nothing ever remains the same, only in our memories. You go through life, rubbing shoulders with the universe and can't find that connection. Then somewhere in the cosmos he appears seeming so familiar and your whole life begins. Even animals need love or they just crawl into the ground and die. Out of the torment and passion of my existence I have survived and created great works of art that I've unveiled as my legacy.

In the throws of a nightmare, I wake up screaming, clutching my wedding band. The garnet ring is still a constant companion on my finger. But what happened to the marriage?

Chapter Fifty Five
The Long and Winding Road
Patrick

Memory is the diary we all carry about with us.
Oscar Wilde

That 70's Beatle's song "The Long and Winding Road" was blaring out of Patrick's cassette player in his black Mercedes Benz as he sped around the narrow curves of the mountain up Sky Cliffview Drive, a cigarette dangling out of the side of his mouth.

She was Cristal champagne, I was Andre Brut. Lately I've been thinking about why April was so much more exciting and unique than any woman I've ever known. I was just an ordinary young, broke jock from Orange County, born into a large church-going, lower middle class Irish family. April dined on caviar at The Polo Lounge with the elite while I drank beer and ate pizza at diners. We had love, desire and unrepressed erotic passion as our bodies entwined in the throws of orgasm. April was a totally liberated flesh and blood lover.

One night at dinner, her glamorous orthodox Jewish mother warned me,

"Patrick, darling, just remember that the greatest love affairs in history have always been between younger men and older women."

"I'm madly in love with April, and she's the best organic gourmet cook in LA," I said.

"That's because she's Hungarian. They're known for being the finest cooks and having the worst tempers. My daughter is absolutely incorrigible."

She laughed as she squeezed my hand seductively.

"I love it that I'm younger than she is." I said.

"Don't worry dear, after you've lived with her for a while, you'll grow old. But the main fault that I have with April is that she likes a cat better than a mother. I always tell her that she's not stupid, just crazy when she acts like a kook," she said sternly. "I beg her not to sleep with Cokie Calico. I'm afraid that one night she might think her adam's apple is a ball and strangle her." *That was whack*, I thought to myself.

April had so much charisma and street smarts. Probably because she was a runaway at Fourteen. Her offbeat brilliance brought laughter into my life. Her raw sex appeal was such a turn on. I could never keep my hands off of her. April taught me so much about life and the arts, spoiling me with a privileged lifestyle.

It made me sad that she was only considered one of the 'It girls' in Hollywood. April was so much more than that, she was a poet. The first time I ever saw her was late one night when I was working as a bouncer at The Rainbow on the Sunset strip. I was covering the door at the VIP bar. She blew in with Chelsea, chased by an entourage of rockers, looking like Charo on Speed. I fantasized about boning her once then throwing her away. I figured she'd done too many premiers at the Grauman's Chinese and that scared me off.

April was wearing a flesh-colored, suede, feathered low-cut bra trying to walk in her hip-hugging long tight skirt that was split up the front clinging to her curves and silver strappy platform heels. Her slanted green eyes resembled a panther. Crimped flame-red hair spilled over her shoulders as she approached me with a wicked smile like 'The Joker' himself in a Batman movie.

As I dropped the red velvet rope, she wiggled away her shiny gold lip-gloss and bright glass jewelry glowing under tainted neon lights.

I thought to myself, *that chick is the hottest looking talent in the room*, and asked her if I could bum a cigarette.

"That's not the kind that I smoke," she replied flashing me a quick mischievous smile. Then she put a joint in my hand disappearing in a plume of smoke into the dark dingy bar.

About a year later, my buddies dragged me to a bash thrown by Chelsea in The Colony. I'd done some of her girlfriends in the coatroom many times. That was one of the perks of working at a trendy rock 'n' roll haven.

After many chance meetings April and I finally hooked up. It was kinda like that old Bob Seger song 'Hollywood Nights'. I was the young Midwestern boy that was blown away by the big city party girl. That weekend, I took her to Disneyland. When the lights dimmed on young Abe Lincoln, she went down on me. Let's just say that clinched the deal. It was well worth the price of admission.

Then there was another little incident when we went to that snobbish pricey upscale French restaurant L'Orangerie. No sooner than a stiff looking waiter put the sourdough bread on our table, April climbed under, rubbing my cock with a butterball and gave me the best hummer on the planet. Thank God they had long tablecloths. I wondered, *Did this babe really go to finishing school, or was she just fucking with me?*

Two weeks later, on Thanksgiving Day, I moved into the little knotty pine house on top of the hill, up the dirt road. It was known as the Hotel California of Laurel Canyon. You already know about how April was famous for throwing wild, uncivilized parties. All the pretty boys that gravitated to her she "called" friends. On one of her birthdays, we all dropped acid. The party got so loud, a neighbor called the man.

Five LAPD officers raided the house, looking for drugs, and we were holding big time. I couldn't believe that she charmed them and, after checking out the young starlets, they decided to send the shuttle buses back to the precinct and sing Happy Birthday to her. That was a close call. One studio executive threw a rope over the balcony and slid down into the dirt. The Canyon and April were at the peak of their folk rock heyday. We hung out with mega movie stars, Euro-trash Globetrotters, trendsetters and hippies, but April was the original flower child of the beat generation. She'd been there, hiding in the shadows of show business, living a hedonistic lifestyle, battling her darkest demons, and her drug and alcohol addiction long before I came into her life.

After one of her long lunches with the girls at The Polo Lounge, she drove her pink Thunderbird right into the side of the house, knocking me off the throne.

After that little incident, she rationalized that she was on a wine fast. As her behavior had become increasingly erratic and chaos marked our existence, she tried psychotherapy. The diagnosis was that she was a dipsomaniac, druggie and narcissist. I was in her world, but not of her fake existence. It was a culture clash, mingling with the club of the moment prey. They were the small tics of mankind on the planet.

We finally got married and lived together for long over a decade like a song blended with time. Often when our togetherness and my jealousy and insecurity overwhelmed her, she'd kick me out. She loved to challenge me.

"I need to breathe. You've taken all of my soul. I have no more to give," she'd cry. "You're trying to possess me. Let's just have an open marriage."

Then after I could no longer handle her sexual indiscretions and my underlying tension I'd leave, then came her panic calls at all hours of the night and day asking if I was alone. She was never possessive, just obsessive, and I'd come running back, trying to deal with her neurotic bizarre ways.

April had so many different faces that often she'd get confused trying to figure out who she was.

My biggest mistake was being so controlling. Finally there was no turning back, she'd crossed the line of self destruction, moving that porn star degenerate into her house. If I stayed, I knew there would be dire consequences because of her reckless behavior. I made love to her, then barely brushing her cheek, I softly kissed her goodbye.

"We both lose," I said, as I climbed out of bed. "But you'll always be my lady."

All the other women were mere scratches on the surface, but it was all about self-preservation. I could never rescue her from herself. It seems so long ago. I wonder if she's lost herself throughout the years. As I drove through sagebrush territory, coyotes howled in the wind. Sometimes I thought it would be easier remembering her the way she was, but I had to know if she was still alive.

Maybe she'd found someone new. I wondered if she ever thought of me. My heart started racing as I pulled up in front of the bungalow perched on the knoll, hanging over the earth. I was blown away by the sparkling multi-colored lights and a sweeping view of The Hollywood sign. Then I noticed some unfamiliar cars.

The Christmas tree we had planted in her flowerbed before our holiday party had grown taller than the house. It had been untouched by by turbulent winter winds. I felt as though I had been uprooted.

Mustering up of all my nerve I stood at her door where I left the best years of my life behind. Even a love as strong as ours couldn't survive those Hollywood nights. Suddenly I noticed there was a dim light on in the kitchen. I paused, then tapped lightly on the door three times.

Eatonisms

Elissa Eaton

The Hermit
I'd gladly climb the highest steeple
To escape those middle minded people

Jet Set Wedding
I wake up screaming clutching my wedding band
The garnet ring is still a constant companion on my
finger
But what happened to the marriage?

Fruitland Ave
He taught her not to love nor hate
And he my friend was double gate

The Closing
(On Death and Acceptance)
When he died the funeral took place at her bank
And sadly enough she's down to her very last frank

The Misogynist
He sits on his throne a hilltop alone
For women's neurosis cause men's psychosis

Home Sweet Home
The neurotic builds the dreamhouse
The psychotic becomes his spouse

Monogamy
I'd rather be someone's concubine, smell the honeysuckle, taste the wine, Than end up being a clinging vine

The Gour Maid
I like champagne, and french brie, and camembert And men that don't get in my hair

Plays By Elissa Eaton

To be a playwright you have to have the heart of a poet and the skin of a rattlesnake.
Tennessee Williams

"I've drawn upon a lot of my experiences in Hollywood," Eaton explains. "Using a style I would describe as teasing with taste, I explore the decadence and erotic nature of this city and its denizens." Her plays "A Sexual Tragedy - The Silken Silent Sisters of the Silver Screen", "Tits and Tombstones", a 30's drama about fallen star Jean Harlow, and her eight other plays are explosive, revealing the raw core of the rites of passage between men and women as they wade through the seasons of the flesh, the intense and naked people, their amusing entanglements of fiery passion, sexuality, desire and love.

SEASONS OF THE FLESH

"THE SILKEN SILENT SISTERS OF THE SILVER SCREEN - A SEXUAL TRAGEDY"
(A Dramady in Two Acts)
This avant-garde graveyard farce, one act Hollywood fringe fable is about the short, deadly relationship of a porno star and his fallen actress girlfriend.

It shows the insecurities that lie behind bisexuality, drug addiction, and obsessive behavior.
The core of the play is the internal bonding of three women living with wild abandon, the life of jetset extras in Tinseltown.

"LUNCH AT THE RHINELAND VINELAND"
(An Erotic Fantasy)
An Epicurean delight, it's a mouth opener and curtain riser serving edible delectables. This opulent, provocative poem is as light and fluffy as a pastry that keeps rising and rising as Duchess Nicoise, a Royal Duchess; a statuesque French Red Snapper; Apple Charlotte, a crimson Bavarian Apple Cream Torte, meet Prince of Van Witenstein at a French restaurant called "The Rhineland Vineland" and devour each other. The comedy farce should be added to your lunch menu. It's a delicious banquet of sensual delights.

"SCENTS OF TIME"
(Dollars and Cents at Needless Markup)
A bizarre one act hysterical face about the perfume industry (Theater of the Ridiculous), the fragrance wizard and aroma therapists, Trash Eau de Toilette, Seduction, and Infinity hang with Contessa of Camerello and Madame Maybeline at the trendy Beverly Center.

FOUR ONE WOMAN SHOWS

"TITS AND TOMBSTONES"
A two act 30's murder/dramady about blonde bombshell Jean Harlow. This nostalgic piece has all the glam glitz of the golden era.
"TITS AND TOMBSTONES"
A one act rendezvous with Harlow, the Hollywood siren (excerpts from the two act play).

"SMOKE AND MIRRORS"
A dramatic one act slice of life. The angst and agony of the legendary Harlow, a falling star looking back on her doomed wedding night and the fatal drama that caused her death.

"A MELANCHOLY MEDLEY IN MANHATTAN"
A one woman show about Greta Garbo, the infamous Swedish Vamp.

A TRILOGY OF PASSIONS

"TEARS OF BLOOD: THE MARQUIS DE SADE"
A one act, three character macabre farce about the bloodthirsty bourgeoisie. This Gothic tale takes place at Chateau La Coste, The Marquis De Sade's 18th century country estate in France. It spins a tale of corruption and the lusty liaison between the Marquis and Lucrezia Borgia.

"TOMBSTONE TABERNACLE - THE FLESHLESS LOVERS"
A medieval myth about Caligula, the ruthless Roman Emperor, and Emily Dickinson, a spiritual god-gifted poetess from Mount Holyoke female seminary. The curtain riser takes place in Renaissance Rome, the 1800's, and the period from 37 A.D. somewhere between High Heaven and Purgatory, as this play takes you from their minds to their flesh.

"THE INDIAN SUMMER HARVEST OF WHITE FEATHER"
An irreverant and profane portrait of the alleged love affair between Pocahontas, the beautiful Indian Princess, and Captain John Smith. This one act avant-garde fantasy takes place in England, Virginia and Eternity.

Elissa Eaton with Shakespeare, Skylark, and Eclipse

Elissa Eaton with her animals

© Lee Salem Photography

Elissa Eaton with Julia Child
Elissa Eaton with Wolfgang Puck

© Lee Salem Photography

"Too Old To Be A Hooker, Too Young To Be A Madam" is over the top Hollywood High camp, wild, evocative and erotic. Funny, great detail, wild, wild satire."

Eve La Salle Caram
Senior Instructor in Fiction Writing
The Writer's Program - UCLA Extension
Recipient of the UCLA Outstanding Instructor Award In Creative Writing - 2006